THE OTHER WOMAN

Daniel Silva is the award-winning, number one *New York Times* bestselling author of *The Unlikely Spy, The Mark of the Assassin, The Marching Season, The Kill Artist, The English Assassin, The Confessor, A Death in Vienna, Prince of Fire, The Messenger, The Secret Servant, Moscow Rules, The Defector, The Rembrandt Affair, Portrait of a Spy, The Fallen Angel, The English Girl, The Heist, The English Spy, The Black Widow, House of Spies,* and *The Other Woman* (2018). He is best known for his long-running thriller series starring spy and art restorer Gabriel Allon. Silva's books are critically acclaimed bestsellers around the world and have been translated into more than thirty languages. He resides in Florida with his wife, television journalist Jamie Gangel, and their twins, Lily and Nicholas.

For more information visit www.danielsilvabooks.com.

DANIEL SILVA

THE OTHER WOMAN

HarperCollinsPublishers

HarperCollins*Publishers*
1 London Bridge Street
London SE1 9GF

www.harpercollins.co.uk

First published in Great Britain by HarperCollins*Publishers* 2018
1

First published in the United States of America by Harper,
an imprint of HarperCollins*Publishers* 2018

A catalogue record for this book
is available from the British Library

ISBN: 978-0-00-828091-8 (HB)
ISBN: 978-0-00-828093-2 (TPB)

Printed and bound in Great Britain by
CPI Group (UK) Ltd, Croydon CR0 4YY

MIX
Paper from
responsible sources
FSC™ C007454

This book is produced from independently certified FSC™ paper
to ensure responsible forest management.

For more information visit: www.harpercollins.co.uk/green

*Once again, for my wife, Jamie, and
my children, Nicholas and Lily*

He was given a new lease on life when the Centre finally suggested that he take part in the training of a new generation of agents at the KGB spy school, a job he accepted with great enthusiasm. He proved an excellent teacher, imparting what he knew with pleasure, patience and devotion. He loved the work.

—YURI MODIN, *My Five Cambridge Friends*

And what does anyone know about traitors, or why Judas did what he did?

—JEAN RHYS, *Wide Sargasso Sea*

THE
OTHER
WOMAN

PROLOGUE

MOSCOW: 1974

The car was a Zil limousine, long and black, with pleated curtains in the rear windows. It sped from Sheremetyevo Airport into the center of Moscow, along a lane reserved for members of the Politburo and the Central Committee. Night had fallen by the time they reached their destination, a square named for a Russian writer, in an old section of the city known as Patriarch's Ponds. They walked along narrow unlit streets, the child and the two men in gray suits, until they came to an oratory surrounded by Muscovy plane trees. The apartment house was on the opposite side of an alley. They passed through a wooden doorway and squeezed into a lift, which deposited them onto a darkened foyer. A flight of stairs awaited. The child, out of habit, counted the steps. There were fifteen. On the landing was another door. This one was padded leather. A well-dressed man stood there, drink in hand. Something about the ruined face seemed familiar. Smiling, he spoke a single word in Russian. It would be many years before the child understood what the word meant.

PART ONE

NIGHT TRAIN TO VIENNA

BUDAPEST, HUNGARY

None of it would have come to pass—not the desperate quest for the traitor, not the strained alliances nor the needless deaths—were it not for poor Heathcliff. He was their tragic figure, their broken promise. In the end, he would prove to be yet another feather in Gabriel's cap. That said, Gabriel would have preferred that Heathcliff were still on his side of the ledger. Assets like Heathcliff did not come along every day, sometimes only once in a career, rarely twice. Such was the nature of espionage, Gabriel would lament. Such was life itself.

It was not his true name, Heathcliff; it had been generated at random, or so his handlers claimed, by computer. The program deliberately chose a code name that bore no resemblance to the asset's real name, nationality, or line of work. In this regard, it had succeeded. The man to whom Heathcliff's name had been attached was neither a foundling nor a hopeless romantic. Nor was he bitter or vengeful or violent in nature. In truth, he had nothing in common with Brontë's Heathcliff other than his dark complexion, for his mother was from the former Soviet republic of Georgia. The same republic, she was proud to point out, as Comrade Stalin, whose portrait still hung in the sitting room of her Moscow apartment.

Heathcliff spoke and read English fluently, however, and was fond of the Victorian novel. In fact, he had flirted with the idea of studying English literature before coming to his senses and enrolling at the Moscow Institute for Foreign Languages, regarded as the second-most prestigious university in the Soviet Union. His faculty adviser was a talent-spotter for the SVR, the Foreign Intelligence Service, and upon graduation Heathcliff was invited to enter the SVR's academy. His mother, drunk with joy, placed flowers and fresh fruit at the foot of Comrade Stalin's portrait. "He is watching you," she said. "One day you will be a man to be reckoned with. A man to be feared." In his mother's eyes, there was no finer thing for a man to be.

It was the ambition of most cadets to serve abroad in a *rezidentura*, an SVR station, where they would recruit and run enemy spies. It took a certain type of officer to perform such work. He had to be brash, confident, talkative, quick on his feet, a natural seducer. Heathcliff, unfortunately, was blessed with none of these qualities. Nor did he possess the physical attributes required for some of the SVR's more unsavory tasks. What he had was a facility for languages—he spoke fluent German and Dutch as well as English—and a memory that even by the SVR's high standards was deemed to be exceptional. He was given a choice, a rarity in the hierarchical world of the SVR. He could work at Moscow

Center as a translator or serve in the field as a courier. He chose the latter, thus sealing his fate.

It was not glamorous work, but vital. With his four languages and a briefcase full of false passports, he roamed the world in service of the motherland, a clandestine delivery boy, a secret postman. He cleaned out dead drops, stuffed cash into safe-deposit boxes, and on occasion even rubbed shoulders with an actual paid agent of Moscow Center. It was not uncommon for him to spend three hundred nights a year outside Russia, leaving him unsuited for marriage or even a serious relationship. The SVR provided him with female comfort when he was in Moscow— beautiful young girls who under normal circumstances would never look at him twice—but when traveling he was prone to bouts of intense loneliness.

It was during one such episode, in a hotel bar in Hamburg, that he met his Catherine. She was drinking white wine at a table in the corner, an attractive woman in her mid-thirties, light brown hair, suntanned arms and legs. Heathcliff was under orders to avoid such women while traveling. Invariably, they were hostile intelligence officers or prostitutes in their employ. But Catherine did not look the part. And when she glanced at Heathcliff over her mobile phone and smiled, he felt a jolt of electricity that surged from his heart straight to his groin.

"Care to join me?" she asked. "I do hate to drink alone."

Her name was not Catherine, it was Astrid. At least that was the name she had whispered into his ear while running a fingernail lightly along the inside of his thigh. She was Dutch, which meant Heathcliff, who was posing as a Russian businessman, was able to address her in her native language. After several drinks together, she invited herself to Heathcliff's room, where he felt safe. He woke the next morning with a profound hangover, which was unusual for him, and with no memory of engaging in the act of love. By then, Astrid was showered and wrapped in a toweling robe. In the light of day, her remarkable beauty was plain to see.

"Free tonight?" she asked.

"I shouldn't."

"Why not?"

He had no answer.

"You'll take me on a proper date, though. A nice dinner. Maybe a disco afterward."

"And then?"

She opened her robe, revealing a pair of beautifully formed breasts. Try as he might, Heathcliff could not recall caressing them.

They traded phone numbers, another forbidden act, and parted company. Heathcliff had two errands to run in Hamburg that day that required several hours of "dry cleaning" to make certain he was not under surveillance. As he was completing his second task—the routine emptying of a dead-letter box—he received a text message with the name of a trendy restaurant near the port. He arrived at the appointed hour to find a radiant Astrid already seated at their table, behind an open bottle of hideously expensive Montrachet. Heathcliff frowned; he would have to pay for the wine out of his own pocket. Moscow Center monitored his expenses carefully and berated him when he exceeded his allowance.

Astrid seemed to sense his unease. "Don't worry, it's my treat."

"I thought I was supposed to take *you* out on a proper date."

"Did I really say that?"

It was at that instant Heathcliff understood he had made a terrible mistake. His instincts told him to turn and run, but he knew it was no use; his bed was made. And so he stayed at the restaurant and dined with the woman who had betrayed him. Their conversation was stilted and strained—the stuff of a bad television drama—and when the check came it was Astrid who paid. In cash, of course.

Outside, a car was waiting. Heathcliff raised no objections when Astrid quietly instructed him to climb into the backseat. Nor did he protest when the car headed in the opposite direction from his hotel. The driver was quite obviously a professional; he spoke not a word while undertaking several textbook maneuvers designed to shake surveillance. Astrid passed the time sending and receiving text messages. To Heathcliff she said nothing at all.

"Did we ever—"

"Make love?" she asked.

"Yes."

She stared out the window.

"Good," he said. "It's better that way."

When they finally stopped, it was at a small cottage by the sea. Inside, a man was waiting. He addressed Heathcliff in German-accented English. Said his name was Marcus. Said he worked for a Western intelligence service. Didn't specify which one. Then he displayed for Heathcliff several highly sensitive documents Astrid had copied from his locked attaché case the previous evening while he was incapacitated by the drugs she had given him. Heathcliff was going to continue to supply such documents, said Marcus, and much more. Otherwise, Marcus and his colleagues were going to use the material they had in their possession to deceive Moscow Center into believing Heathcliff was a spy.

Unlike his namesake, Heathcliff was neither bitter nor vengeful. He returned to Moscow a half million dollars richer and awaited his next assignment. The SVR delivered a beautiful young girl to his apartment in the Sparrow Hills. He nearly fainted with fear when she introduced herself as Ekaterina. He made her an omelet and sent her away untouched.

The life expectancy for a man in Heathcliff's position was not long. The penalty for betrayal was death. But not a quick death, an unspeakable death. Like all those who worked for the SVR, Heathcliff had heard the stories. The stories of grown men begging for a bullet to end their suffering. Eventually, it would come, the Russian way, in the nape of the neck. The SVR referred to it as *vysshaya mera*: the highest measure of punishment. Heathcliff resolved never to allow himself to fall into their hands. From Marcus he obtained a suicide ampule. One bite was all it would take. Ten seconds, then it would be over.

Marcus also gave Heathcliff a covert communications device that allowed him to transmit reports via satellite with encrypted microbursts. Heathcliff used it rarely, preferring instead to brief Marcus in person during his trips abroad. Whenever possible, he allowed Marcus to photograph the contents of his attaché case, but mainly they talked. Heathcliff was a man of no importance, but he worked for important men, and transported their secrets. Moreover, he knew the locations of Russian dead drops around the world, which he carried around in his prodigious memory. Heathcliff was careful not to divulge too much, too quickly—for his own sake, and for the sake of his rapidly growing bank account. He doled out his secrets piecemeal, so as to increase their value. A half million became a million within a year. Then two. And then three.

Heathcliff's conscience remained untroubled—he was a man without ideology or politics—but fear stalked him day and night. The fear that Moscow Center knew of his treachery and was watching his every move. The fear he had passed along one secret too many, or that one of the Center's spies in the West would eventually betray him. On numerous occasions he pleaded with Marcus to bring him in from the cold. But Marcus, sometimes with a bit of soothing balm, sometimes with a crack of the whip, refused. Heathcliff was to continue his spying until such time as his life was truly in danger. Only then would he be allowed to defect. He was justifiably dubious about Marcus's ability to judge the precise moment the sword was about to fall, but he had no choice but to continue. Marcus had blackmailed him into doing his bidding. And Marcus was going to wring every last secret out of him before releasing him from his bond.

But not all secrets are created equal. Some are mundane, workaday, and can be passed with little or no threat to the messenger. Others, however, are far too dangerous to betray. Heathcliff eventually found such a secret in a dead-letter box, in faraway Montreal. The letter box was actually an empty flat, used by a Russian illegal operating under deep cover in the United States. Hidden in the cabinet beneath the kitchen sink was a memory stick. Heathcliff had been ordered to collect it and carry it back to Moscow Center, thus evading the mighty American National Security Agency. Before leaving the apartment, he inserted the flash drive into his laptop and found it unlocked and its contents unencrypted. Heathcliff read the documents freely. They were from several different American intelligence services, all with the highest possible level of classification.

Heathcliff didn't dare copy the documents. Instead, he committed every detail to his flawless memory and returned to Moscow Center, where he handed over the flash drive to his control officer, along with a sternly worded rebuke of the illegal's failure to secure it properly. The control officer, who was called Volkov, promised to address the matter. Then he offered Heathcliff a low-stress junket to friendly Budapest as recompense. "Consider it an all-expenses-paid holiday, courtesy of Moscow Center. Don't take this the wrong way, Konstantin, but you look as though you could use some time off."

That evening, Heathcliff used the covert communications device to inform Marcus that he had uncovered a secret of such import he had no choice but to defect. Much to his surprise, Marcus did not object. He instructed Heathcliff to dispose of the device in a way it could never be found. Heathcliff smashed it to pieces and dropped the remains down an open sewer. Even the blood-hounds of the SVR's security directorate, he reasoned, wouldn't look there.

A week later, after paying a final visit to his mother in her rabbit's hutch of an apartment, with its brooding portrait of an ever-watchful Comrade Stalin, Heathcliff left Russia for the last time. He arrived in Budapest in late afternoon, as snow fell gently upon the city, and took a taxi to the InterContinental Hotel. His room overlooked the Danube. He double-locked the door and engaged the safety bar. Then he sat down at the desk and waited for his mobile phone to ring. Next to it was Marcus's suicide ampule. One bite was all it would take. Ten seconds. Then it would be over.

2

VIENNA

One hundred and fifty miles to the northwest, a few lazy bends along the river Danube, an exhibition featuring the works of Sir Peter Paul Rubens—painter, scholar, diplomat, spy—limped toward its melancholy conclusion. The imported hordes had come and gone, and by late afternoon only a few regular patrons of the old museum moved hesitantly through its rose-colored rooms. One was a man of late middle age. He surveyed the massive canvases, with their corpulent nudes swirling amid lavish historical settings, from beneath the brim of a flat cap, which was pulled low over his brow.

A younger man stood impatiently at his back, checking the time on his wristwatch. "How much longer, boss?" he asked sotto voce in Hebrew. But the older man responded in German, and loudly enough so the drowsy guard in the corner could hear. "There's just one more I'd like to see before I leave, thank you."

He went into the next room and paused before *Madonna and Child*, oil on canvas, 137 by 111 centimeters. He knew the painting intimately; he had restored it in a cottage by the sea in West Cornwall. Crouching slightly, he examined the surface in raked lighting. His work had held up well. If only he could say the same for himself, he thought, rubbing the fiery patch of pain at the base of his spine. The two recently fractured vertebrae were the least of his physical maladies. During his long and distinguished career as an officer of Israeli intelligence, Gabriel Allon had been shot in the chest twice, attacked by an Alsatian guard dog, and thrown down several flights of stairs in the cellars of Lubyanka in Moscow. Not even Ari Shamron, his legendary mentor, could match his record of bodily injuries.

The young man trailing Gabriel through the rooms of the museum was called Oren. He was the head of Gabriel's security detail, an unwanted fringe benefit of a recent promotion. They had been traveling for the past thirty-six hours, by plane from Tel Aviv to Paris, and then by automobile from Paris to Vienna. Now they walked through the deserted exhibition rooms to the steps of the museum. A snowstorm had commenced, big downy flakes falling straight in the windless night. An ordinary visitor to the city might have found it picturesque, the trams slithering along sugar-dusted streets lined with empty palaces and churches. But not Gabriel. Vienna always depressed him, never more so than when it snowed.

The car waited in the street, the driver behind the wheel. Gabriel pulled the collar of his old Barbour jacket around his ears and informed Oren that he intended to walk to the safe flat.

"Alone," he added.

"I can't let you walk around Vienna unprotected, boss."

"Why not?"

"Because you're the chief now. And if something happens—"

"You'll say you were following orders."

"Just like the Austrians." In the darkness the bodyguard handed Gabriel a Jericho 9mm pistol. "At least take this."

Gabriel slipped the Jericho into the waistband of his trousers. "I'll be at the safe flat in thirty minutes. I'll let King Saul Boulevard know when I've arrived."

King Saul Boulevard was the address of Israel's secret intelligence service. It had a long and deliberately misleading name that had very little to do with the true nature of its work. Even the chief referred to it as the Office and nothing else.

"Thirty minutes," repeated Oren.

"And not a minute more," pledged Gabriel.

"And if you're late?"

"It means I've been assassinated or kidnapped by ISIS, the Russians, Hezbollah, the Iranians, or someone else I've managed to offend. I wouldn't hold out much hope for my survival."

"What about us?"

"You'll be fine, Oren."

"That's not what I meant."

"I don't want you anywhere near the safe flat," said Gabriel. "Keep moving until you hear from me. And remember, don't try to follow me. That's a direct order."

The bodyguard stared at Gabriel in silence, an expression of concern on his face.

"What is it now, Oren?"

"Are you sure you don't want some company, boss?"

Gabriel turned without another word and disappeared into the night.

———————

He crossed the Burgring and set out along the footpaths of the Volksgarten. He was below average in height—five foot eight, perhaps, but no more—and had the spare physique of a cyclist. The face was long and narrow at the chin, with wide cheekbones and a slender nose that looked as though it had been carved from wood. The eyes were an unnatural shade of green; the hair was dark and shot with gray at the temples. It was a face of many possible national origins, and Gabriel had the linguistic gifts to put it to good use. He spoke five languages fluently, including Italian, which he had acquired before traveling to Venice in the mid-1970s to study the craft of art conservation. Afterward, he had lived as a taciturn if gifted restorer named Mario Delvecchio while simultaneously serving as an intelligence officer and assassin for the Office. Some of his finest work had been performed in Vienna. Some of his worst, too.

He skirted the edge of the Burgtheater, the German-speaking world's most prestigious stage, and followed the Bankgasse to the Café Central, one of Vienna's most prominent coffeehouses. There he peered through the frosted windows and in his memory glimpsed Erich Radek, colleague of Adolf Eichmann, tormentor of Gabriel's mother, sipping an Einspänner at a table alone. Radek the murderer was hazy and indistinct, like a figure in a painting in need of restoration.

"Are you sure we've never met before? Your face seems very familiar to me."

"I sincerely doubt it."

"Perhaps we'll see each other again."

"Perhaps."

The image dissolved. Gabriel turned away and walked to the

old Jewish Quarter. Before the Second World War it was home to one of the most vibrant Jewish communities in the world. Now that community was largely a memory. He watched a few old men stepping tremulously from the discreet doorway of the Stadttempel, Vienna's main synagogue, then made his way to a nearby square lined with restaurants. One was the Italian restaurant where he had eaten his last meal with Leah, his first wife, and Daniel, their only child.

In an adjacent street was the spot where their car had been parked. Gabriel slowed involuntarily, paralyzed by memories. He recalled struggling with the straps of his son's car seat and the faint taste of wine on his wife's lips as he gave her one last kiss. And he remembered the sound of the engine hesitating—like a record played at the wrong speed—because the bomb was pulling power from the battery. Too late, he had shouted at Leah not to turn the key a second time. Then, in a flash of brilliant white, she and the child were lost to him forever.

Gabriel's heart was tolling like an iron bell. Not now, he told himself as tears blurred his vision, he had work to do. He tilted his face to the sky.

Isn't it beautiful? The snow falls on Vienna while the missiles rain on Tel Aviv . . .

He checked the time on his wristwatch; he had ten minutes to get to the safe flat. As he hurried along empty streets, he was gripped by an overwhelming sense of impending doom. It was only the weather, he assured himself. Vienna always depressed him. Never more so than when it snowed.

3

VIENNA

The safe flat was located across the Donaukanal, in a fine old Biedermeier apartment building in the Second District. It was a busier quarter, a real neighborhood rather than a museum. There was a little Spar market, a pharmacy, a couple of Asian restaurants, even a Buddhist temple. Cars and motorbikes came and went along the street; pedestrians moved along the pavements. It was the sort of place where no one would notice the chief of the Israeli secret intelligence service. Or a Russian defector, thought Gabriel.

He turned through a passageway, crossed a courtyard, and entered a foyer. The stairs were in darkness, and on the fourth-floor landing a door hung slightly ajar. He slipped inside, closed the door behind him, and padded quietly into the sitting room, where Eli Lavon sat behind an array of open notebook computers. Lavon looked up, saw the snow on Gabriel's cap and shoulders, and frowned.

"Please tell me you didn't walk."

"The car broke down. I had no other choice."

"That's not the way your bodyguard tells it. You'd better let King Saul Boulevard know you're here. Otherwise, the nature of our operation is likely to turn into a search and rescue."

Gabriel leaned over one of the computers, typed a brief message, and shot it securely to Tel Aviv.

"Crisis averted," said Lavon.

He wore a cardigan sweater beneath his crumpled tweed jacket, and an ascot at his throat. His hair was wispy and unkempt; the features of his face were bland and easily forgotten. It was one of his greatest assets. Eli Lavon appeared to be one of life's downtrodden. In truth, he was a natural predator who could follow a highly trained intelligence officer or hardened terrorist down any street in the world without attracting a flicker of interest. He oversaw the Office division known as Neviot. Its operatives included surveillance artists, pickpockets, thieves, and those who specialized in planting hidden cameras and listening devices behind locked doors. His teams had been very busy that evening in Budapest.

He nodded toward one of the computers. It showed a man seated at the desk of an upscale hotel room. An unopened bag lay at the foot of the bed. Before him was a mobile phone and an ampule.

"Is that a photograph?" asked Gabriel.

"Video."

Gabriel tapped the screen of the laptop.

"He can't actually hear you, you know."

"Are you sure he's alive?"

"He's scared to death. He hasn't moved a muscle in five minutes."

"What's he so afraid of?"

"He's Russian," said Lavon, as if that fact alone were explanation enough.

Gabriel studied Heathcliff as though he were a figure in a painting. His real name was Konstantin Kirov, and he was one of the Office's most valuable sources. Only a small portion of Kirov's intelligence had concerned Israel's security directly, but the enormous surplus had paid dividends in London and Langley, where the directors of MI6 and the CIA eagerly feasted on each batch of secrets that spilled from the Russian's attaché case. The Anglo-Americans had not dined for free. Both services had helped to foot the bill for the operation, and the British, after much inter-service arm-twisting, had agreed to grant Kirov sanctuary in the United Kingdom.

The first face the Russian would see after defecting, however, would be the face of Gabriel Allon. Gabriel's history with the Russian intelligence service and the men in the Kremlin was long and blood-soaked. For that reason he wanted to personally conduct Kirov's initial debriefing. Specifically, he wanted to know exactly what Kirov had discovered, and why he suddenly needed to defect. Then Gabriel would place the Russian in the hands of MI6's Head of Station in Vienna. Gabriel was more than happy to let the British have him. Blown agents were invariably a headache, especially blown Russian agents.

At last, Kirov stirred.

"That's a relief," said Gabriel.

The image on the screen deteriorated into digital tile for a few seconds before returning to normal.

"It's been like that all evening," explained Lavon. "The team must have put the transmitter on top of some interference."

"When did they go into the room?"

"About an hour before Heathcliff arrived. When we hacked into the hotel's security system, we took a detour into reservations and grabbed his room number. Getting into the room itself was no problem."

The wizards in the Office's Technology department had developed a magic cardkey capable of opening any electronic hotel room door in the world. The first swipe stole the code. The second opened the lock.

"When did the interference start?"

"As soon as he entered the room."

"Did anyone follow him from the airport to the hotel?"

Lavon shook his head.

"Any suspicious names on the hotel registry?"

"Most of the guests are attending the conference. The Eastern European Society of Civil Engineers," Lavon explained. "It's a real nerds' ball. Lots of guys with pocket protectors."

"You used to be one of those guys, Eli."

"Still am." The shot turned to a mosaic again. "Damn," said Lavon softly.

"Has the team checked out the connection?"

"Twice."

"And?"

"There's no one else on the line. And even if there was, the signal is so encrypted it would take a couple of supercomputers a month to reassemble the pieces." The shot stabilized. "That's more like it."

"Let me see the lobby."

Lavon tapped the keyboard of another computer, and a shot of the lobby appeared. It was a sea of ill-fitting clothing, name tags, and receding hairlines. Gabriel scanned the faces, looking for one that appeared to be out of place. He found four—two male, two female. Using the hotel's cameras, Lavon captured still images of each and forwarded them to Tel Aviv. On the screen of the adjacent laptop, Konstantin Kirov was checking his phone.

"How long do you intend to make him wait?" asked Lavon.

"Long enough for King Saul Boulevard to run those faces through the database."

"If he doesn't leave soon, he'll miss his train."

"Better to miss his train than be assassinated in the lobby of the InterContinental by a Moscow Center hit team." Once again, the shot turned to tile. Annoyed, Gabriel tapped the screen.

"Don't bother," said Lavon. "I've already tried that."

Ten minutes elapsed before the Operations Desk at King Saul Boulevard declared that it could find no matches for the four faces in the Office's digital rogues' gallery of enemy intelligence officers, known or suspected terrorists, or private mercenaries. Only then did Gabriel compose a brief text message on an encrypted BlackBerry and tap the SEND key. A moment later he watched Konstantin Kirov reach for his mobile phone. After reading Gabriel's text, the Russian rose abruptly, pulled on his overcoat, and wrapped a scarf around his neck. He slipped the mobile phone into his pocket but kept the suicide ampule in his hand. The suitcase he left behind.

Eli Lavon tapped a few keys on the laptop as Kirov opened the door of his room and went into the corridor. The hotel's security cameras monitored his short walk to the lifts. There were no other guests or staff present, and the carriage into which the

Russian stepped was empty. The lobby, however, was bedlam. No one seemed to take notice of Kirov as he made his way out of the hotel, including two leather-jacketed toughs from the Hungarian security service who were keeping watch in the street.

It was a few minutes before nine o'clock. There was time enough for Kirov to catch the night train to Vienna, but he had to keep moving. He headed south on Apáczai Csere János Street, followed by two of Eli Lavon's watchers, and then turned onto Kossuth Lajos Street, one of central Budapest's main thoroughfares.

"My boys say he's clean," said Lavon. "No Russians, no Hungarians."

Gabriel dispatched a second message to Konstantin Kirov, instructing him to board the train as planned. He did so with four minutes to spare, accompanied by the watchers. For now, there was nothing more Gabriel and Lavon could do. As they stared at one another in silence, their thoughts were identical. The waiting. Always the waiting.

4

WESTBAHNHOF, VIENNA

But Gabriel and Eli Lavon did not wait alone, for on that evening they had an operational partner in Her Majesty's Secret Intelligence Service, the oldest and grandest such agency in the civilized world. Six officers from its storied Vienna Station—the exact number would soon be a matter of some contention—held a tense vigil in a locked vault at the British Embassy, and a dozen more were hovering over computers and blinking telephones at Vauxhall Cross, MI6's riverfront headquarters in London.

A final MI6 officer, a man called Christopher Keller, waited outside Vienna's Westbahnhof train station, behind the wheel of an unremarkable Volkswagen Passat sedan. He had bright blue eyes, sun-bleached hair, square cheekbones, and a thick chin with a notch in the center. His mouth seemed permanently fixed in an ironic smile.

Having little else to do that evening other than keep watch for any stray Russian hoods, Keller had contemplated the improbable path that had led him to this place. The wasted year at Cambridge, the deep-cover operation in Northern Ireland, the friendly-fire incident during the first Gulf War that cast him into self-imposed exile on the island of Corsica. There he had acquired perfect if Corsican-accented French. He had also performed services for a certain notable Corsican crime figure that might loosely be described as murder for hire. But all that was behind him. Thanks to Gabriel Allon, Christopher Keller was a respectable officer of Her Majesty's Secret Intelligence Service. He was restored.

Keller looked at the Israeli in the passenger seat. He was tall and lanky, with bloodless skin and eyes the color of glacial ice. His expression was one of profound boredom. The anxious drumming of his fingers on the center console, however, betrayed the true state of his mind.

Keller lit a cigarette, his fourth in twenty minutes, and blew a cloud of smoke against the windscreen.

"Must you?" protested the Israeli.

"I'll stop smoking when you stop drumming your damn fingers." Keller spoke with a posh West London drawl, a remnant of a privileged childhood. "You're giving me a headache."

The Israeli's fingers went still. His name was Mikhail Abramov. Like Keller, he was a veteran of an elite military unit. In Mikhail's case, it was the IDF's Sayeret Matkal. They had operated together several times before, most recently in Morocco, where they had tracked Saladin, the leader of ISIS's external operations division, to a remote compound in the Middle Atlas Mountains. Neither man had fired the shot that ended Saladin's reign of terror. Gabriel had beaten them both to the target.

"What are you so nervous about anyway?" asked Keller. "We're in the middle of dull, boring Vienna."

"Yes," said Mikhail distantly. "Nothing ever happens here."

Mikhail had lived in Moscow as a child and spoke English with a faint Russian accent. His linguistic abilities and Slavic looks had allowed him to pose as a Russian in several notable Office operations.

"You've operated in Vienna before?" asked Keller.

"Once or twice." Mikhail checked his weapon, a Jericho .45-caliber pistol. "Do you remember those four Hezbollah suicide bombers who were planning to attack the Stadttempel?"

"I thought EKO Cobra handled that." EKO Cobra was Austria's tactical police unit. "In fact, I'm quite sure I read something about it in the newspapers."

Mikhail stared at Keller without expression.

"That was you?"

"I had help, of course."

"Anyone I know?"

Mikhail said nothing.

"I see."

It was approaching midnight. The street outside the modern glass facade of the station was deserted, only a couple of taxis waiting for the last fares of the night. One would collect a Russian defector and deliver him to the Best Western hotel on the Stubenring. From there he would walk the rest of the way to the safe flat. The decision on whether to admit him would be made by Mikhail, who would be following on foot. The safe flat's location was perhaps the most closely guarded secret of the operation.

If Kirov was clean, Mikhail would search him in the building's foyer and then take him upstairs to see Gabriel. Keller was to remain downstairs in the Passat and provide perimeter security, with what, he did not know. Alistair Hughes, MI6's Vienna Head of Station, had expressly forbidden him to carry a weapon. Keller had a well-deserved reputation for violence; Hughes, for caution. He had a nice life in Vienna—a productive network, long lunches, decent relations with the local service. The last thing he wanted was a problem that would result in him being recalled to a desk at Vauxhall Cross.

Just then, Mikhail's BlackBerry flared with an incoming message. The glow of the screen lit his pale face. "The train is in the station. Kirov is on his way out."

"Heathcliff," said Keller with reproof. "His name is Heathcliff until we get him inside the safe flat."

"Here he comes."

Mikhail returned his BlackBerry to his coat pocket as Kirov emerged from the station, preceded by one of Eli Lavon's watchers and followed by another.

"He looks nervous," said Keller.

"He is nervous." Mikhail was drumming his fingers on the center console again. "He's Russian."

The watchers departed the station on foot; Konstantin Kirov, in one of the taxis. Keller followed at a discreet distance as the car moved eastward across the city along deserted streets. He saw nothing to suggest the Russian courier was being tailed. Mikhail concurred.

At twelve fifteen the taxi stopped outside the Best Western. Kirov climbed out but did not enter the hotel. Instead, he crossed the Donaukanal over the Schwedenbrücke, now trailed by Mikhail on foot. The bridge deposited the two men onto the Taborstrasse, and the Taborstrasse in turn delivered them to a pretty church square called the Karmeliterplatz, where Mikhail closed the distance between himself and his quarry to a few paces.

Together they crossed to an adjacent street and followed it past a parade of darkened shops and cafés, toward the Biedermeier apartment house at the end of the block. Light burned faintly in a fourth-floor window, enough so that Mikhail could make out the silhouetted figure of Gabriel standing with one hand to his chin and his head tilted slightly to one side. Mikhail sent him one final text. Kirov was clean.

It was then he heard the sound of an approaching motorcycle. His first thought was that it was not the sort of night to be piloting a vehicle with only two wheels. This was confirmed a few seconds later when he saw the bike skidding around the corner of the apartment block.

The driver wore black leather and a black helmet, with the dark visor down. He slid to a stop a few yards from Kirov, dropped a foot to the street, and drew a gun from the front of his jacket. It was fitted with a long cylindrical sound suppressor. Mikhail couldn't discern the model of the weapon itself. A Glock, maybe an H&K. Whatever it was, it was pointed directly at Kirov's face.

Mikhail allowed the phone to fall from his grasp and reached for his Jericho, but before he could draw it, the motorcyclist's weapon spat twin tongues of fire. Both shots found their mark. Mikhail heard the sickening crack of the rounds tearing through Kirov's skull, and saw a flash of blood and brain matter as he collapsed to the street.

The man on the motorcycle then swung his arm a few degrees and leveled the gun at Mikhail. Two shots, both errant, drove him to the pavement, and two more sent him crawling toward the shelter of a parked car. His right hand had found the grip of the Jericho. As he drew it, the man on the motorcycle raised his foot and revved the engine.

He was thirty meters from Mikhail, no more, with the ground floor of the apartment block behind him. Mikhail had both hands on the Jericho, with his outstretched arms braced on the boot of the parked car. Still, he held his fire. Office doctrine gave field operatives wide latitude in utilizing deadly force to protect their own lives. It did not, however, allow an operative to fire a .45-caliber weapon toward a fleeing target in a residential quarter of a European city, where a stray round might easily take an innocent life.

The motorcycle was now in motion, the roar of its engine reverberating in the canyon of apartment buildings. Mikhail watched its progress over the barrel of the Jericho until it was gone. Then he clambered over to the spot where Kirov had fallen. The Russian was gone, too. There was almost nothing left of his face.

Mikhail looked up toward the figure in the fourth-floor window. Then, from behind, he heard the rising engine note of a car approaching at high speed. He feared it was the rest of the hit team coming to finish the job, but it was only Keller in the Passat. He snatched up his mobile phone and hurled himself inside. "I told you," he said as the car shot forward. "Nothing ever happens here."

Gabriel remained in the window longer than he should have, watching the shrinking taillight of the motorcycle, pursued by the blacked-out Passat. When the two vehicles were gone, he looked down at the man lying in the street. Snow whitened him. He was as dead as a man could be. He was dead, thought Gabriel, before he arrived in Vienna. Dead before he left Moscow.

Eli Lavon was now standing at Gabriel's side. Another long moment passed, and still Kirov lay there alone, unattended. Finally, a car approached and drew to a stop. The driver climbed out, a young woman. She raised a hand to her mouth and looked away.

Lavon drew the blinds. "Time to leave."

"We can't just—"

"Did you touch anything?"

Gabriel searched his memory. "The computers."

"Nothing else?"

"The door latch."

"We'll get it on the way out."

At once, blue light filled the room. It was a light Gabriel knew well, the light of a Bundespolizei cruiser. He dialed Oren, the chief of his security detail.

"Come to the Hollandstrasse side of the building. Nice and quiet."

Gabriel killed the connection and helped Lavon bag the computers and the phones. On the way out the door, they both gave the latch a thorough scrubbing, Gabriel first, then Lavon for good measure. As they hurried across the courtyard they could hear the first faint sound of sirens, but the Hollandstrasse was quiet, save for the low idle of a car engine. Gabriel and Lavon slid into the backseat. A moment later they were crossing the Donaukanal, leaving the Second District for the First.

"He was clean. Right, Eli?"

"As a whistle."

"So how did the assassin know where he was going?"

"Maybe we should ask him."

Gabriel dug his phone from his pocket and called Mikhail.

5

FLORIDSDORF, VIENNA

The Passat sedan was equipped with Volkswagen's newest version of all-wheel drive. A right turn at one hundred kilometers per hour on fresh snow, however, was far beyond its abilities. The rear tires lost traction, and for an instant Mikhail feared they were about to spin out of control. Then, somehow, the tires regained their grip on the pavement, and the car, with one last spasm of fishtailing, righted itself.

Mikhail lightened his hold on the armrest. "Have much experience driving in winter conditions?"

"A great deal," replied Keller calmly. "You?"

"I grew up in Moscow."

"You left when you were a kid."

"I was sixteen, actually."

"Did your family own a car?"

"In Moscow? Of course not. We rode the Metro like everyone else."

"So you never actually *drove* a car in Russia in winter."

Mikhail did not dispute Keller's observation. They were back on the Taborstrasse, flashing past an industrial park and warehouse complex, about a hundred meters behind the motorcycle. Mikhail was reasonably acquainted with Vienna's geography. He judged, correctly, that they were heading in an easterly direction. There was a border to the east. He reckoned they would need one soon.

The bike's brake light flared red.

"He's turning," said Mikhail.

"I see him."

The bike made a left and briefly disappeared from sight. Keller approached the corner without slowing. An ugly Viennese streetscape flowed sideways across the windscreen for several seconds before he was able to bring the car under control again. The motorcycle was now at least two hundred meters ahead.

"He's good," said Keller.

"You should see the way he handles a gun."

"I did."

"Thanks for the help."

"What was I supposed to do? Distract him?"

Before them rose the Millennial Tower, a fifty-one-floor office-and-residential building standing on the western bank of the Danube. Keller's speed approached a hundred and fifty as they crossed the river, and still the bike was slipping away. Mikhail wondered how long it would take the Bundespolizei to notice them. About as long, he reckoned, as it would take to pull a passport from the pocket of a dead Russian courier.

The bike disappeared around another corner. By the time Keller negotiated the same turn, the taillight was a prick of red in the night.

"We're losing him."

Keller pressed his foot to the floor and kept it there. Just then, Mikhail's mobile pulsed. He took his eyes from the taillight long enough to read the message.

"What is it?" asked Keller.

"Gabriel wants an update." Mikhail typed a brief response and looked up again. "Shit," he said softly.

The taillight was gone.

It was Alois Graf, a pensioner and quiet supporter of an Austrian far-right party—not that that had anything to do with what transpired—who was ultimately to blame. Recently a widower, Graf had been having trouble sleeping of late. In fact, he could not remember the last time he had managed more than two or three hours since the death of his beloved Trudi. The same was true of Shultzie, his nine-year-old dachshund. Actually, the little beast was not really his, it was Trudi's. Shultzie had never much cared for Graf, or Graf for Shultzie. And now they were cellmates, sleepless and depressed, comrades in grief.

The dog was well trained in the etiquette of elimination, and reasonably considerate of others. Lately, however, it had been having urges at the damnedest times. Graf was considerate, too, and he never protested when Shultzie came to him in the small hours with that desperate look in his resentful little eyes.

On that night, the summons occurred at 12:25 a.m., according to the clock on Graf's bedside table. Shultzie's favorite spot was the little patch of grass adjacent to the American fast-food restaurant on the Brünnerstrasse. This pleased Graf. He thought the restaurant, if you could call it that, an eyesore. But then again, Graf had never been fond of Americans. He was old enough to remember Vienna after the war, when it was a divided city of spies and misery. Graf had preferred the British to the Americans. The British, at least, were possessed of a certain low cunning.

To reach Shultzie's little promised land required crossing the Brünnerstrasse itself. Graf, a former schoolmaster, looked right and left before stepping from the curb. It was then he saw the single headlamp of a motorcycle approaching from the direction of the city center. He paused with indecision. The bike was a long way off; there was no sound. Surely, he could reach the opposite side with time to spare. Nevertheless, he gave Shultzie's leash a little jerk, lest the dog loiter in the middle of the street, as he was fond of doing.

Halfway across the road, Graf cast another glance toward the motorcycle. In a matter of three or four seconds, it had covered a great deal of ground. It was traveling at an extremely high rate of speed, a fact evidenced by the high, tight note of the engine, which Graf could now hear quite clearly. Shultzie could hear it, too. The dog stood still as a statue, and no amount of tugging on Graf's part could compel him to move.

"Komm, Shultzie! Mach schnell!"

Nothing. It was as if the creature were frozen to the asphalt.

The bike was approximately a hundred meters away, about the length of the sporting field at Graf's old school. He reached down and snatched the dog, but it was too late; the bike was upon them. It veered suddenly, passing so close to Graf's back it seemed to pluck at the fabric of his overcoat. An instant later he heard the terrible metallic crunch of the collision and saw a figure in black soaring through the air. He might have thought the man capable of flight, he flew so far. But the next sound, the sound of his body smacking the pavement, put that lie to rest.

He somersaulted over and over again for several more meters, horribly, until finally he came to rest. Graf considered going to check on him, if only to confirm the obvious, but another vehicle, a car, was approaching at high speed from the same direction. With Shultzie in his arms, Graf stepped quickly from the road and allowed the car to pass. It slowed to inspect the wreckage of the motorcycle before stopping next to the fallen figure in black lying motionless in the street.

A passenger climbed out. He was tall and thin, and his pale face seemed to glow in the darkness. He looked down at the man in the street—more out of anger than pity, observed Graf—and removed the motorcyclist's shattered helmet. Then he did something quite extraordinary, something Graf would never tell another living soul. He snapped a photograph of the dead man's face with his mobile phone.

The flash startled Shultzie, and the dog erupted in a fit of barking. The man stared coldly at Graf before lowering himself into the car. In a moment, it was gone.

At once, there were sirens in the night. Alois Graf should have remained behind to tell the Bundespolizei what he had witnessed. Instead, he hurried home, with Shultzie squirming in his arms. Graf remembered Vienna after the war. Sometimes, he thought, it was better to see nothing at all.

6

VIENNA—TEL AVIV

Two dead bodies, separated by a distance of some six kilometers. One had been shot twice at close range. The other had died in a high-speed motorcycle accident while in possession of a large-caliber handgun, an HK45 Tactical, fitted with a sound suppressor. There were no witnesses at either scene, and no CCTV cameras. It was no matter; a part of the story was written in the snow, in tire tracks and footprints, with shell casings and blood. The Austrians worked quickly, for there was heavy rain in the forecast, followed by two days of unseasonable warmth. A changing climate was conspiring against them.

The man who had been shot to death had in his possession a mobile phone, a billfold, and a Russian passport identifying him as one Oleg Gurkovsky. Further documentation found inside the billfold suggested he was a resident of Moscow and that he worked for a communications technology company. Reconstructing the final hours of his life proved easy enough. The Aeroflot flight from Moscow to Budapest. The room at the InterContinental, where, curiously, he had left his luggage. The late-night train to Vienna. Security cameras at the Westbahnhof observed him climbing into a taxi, and the driver, who was interviewed by police, recalled dropping him at the Best Western on the Stubenring. From there he had crossed the Donaukanal via the Schwedenbrücke, followed by a man on foot. Police unearthed several clips of video from storefront security systems and traffic cameras in which the pursuer's face was partially visible. He also left a trail of footprints, especially in the Karmeliterplatz, where the snow had largely been undisturbed. The shoes were a European size forty-eight, with no distinctive tread. Crime-scene investigators found several matching prints directly next to the body.

They also found six .45-caliber shell casings and the tracks of a Metzeler Lasertec motorcycle tire. Analysis of the tread pattern would link the tracks conclusively to the mangled BMW on the Brünnerstrasse, and ballistics testing would tie the shell casings to the HK45 Tactical the driver of the bike had been carrying when he crashed into a parked car. The man had nothing else in his possession. No passport or driver's permit, no cash or credit cards. He looked to be about thirty-five but police couldn't be sure; substantial plastic surgery had been performed on the face. He was a professional, they concluded.

But why had an otherwise professional assassin lost control of his motorcycle on the Brünnerstrasse? And who was the man who had followed the murdered Russian from the Best Western hotel to the spot in the Second District where he had been shot twice at close range? And why had the Russian come to Vienna from

Budapest in the first place? Had he been lured? Had he been summoned? If so, by whom? The questions notwithstanding, it bore all the hallmarks of a professional assassination carried out by a highly competent intelligence service.

The Bundespolizei, during the first hours of the investigation, kept such thoughts to themselves, but the media were free to speculate to their hearts' content. By midmorning they had convinced themselves that Oleg Gurkovsky was a dissident, despite the fact no one in the Russian opposition seemed to have heard of him. But there were others in Russia, including a lawyer rumored to be a personal friend of the Tsar himself, who claimed to know him well. But not by the name Oleg Gurkovsky. His real name, they said, was Konstantin Kirov, and he was an undercover officer of the SVR, the Russian intelligence service.

It was at this point, sometime around noon in Vienna, that a steady trickle of stories, tweets, chirps, burps, blog postings, and other forms of modern discourse began to appear on news sites and social media. At first, they appeared spontaneous; in time, anything but. Nearly all the material flowed from Russia or from friendly former Soviet republics or satellites. Not one of the alleged sources had a name—at least not one that could be verified. Each entry was fragmentary, a small piece of a larger puzzle. But when assembled, the conclusion was plain as day: Konstantin Kirov, an officer of the Russian SVR, had been murdered in cold blood by the Israeli secret intelligence service, on the direct order of its chief, the well-known Russophobe Gabriel Allon.

The Kremlin declared as much at three o'clock, and at four the Russian news service Sputnik published what it claimed was a photograph of Allon leaving an apartment building near the scene of the murder, accompanied by an elfin figure whose face was rendered indistinct. The source of the photograph was never reliably established. Sputnik said it obtained the image from the Austrian Bundespolizei, though the Bundespolizei denied it. Nevertheless, the damage was done. The rented television experts in London and New York, including a few who'd had the privilege of meeting Allon personally, admitted that the man in the photo looked a great deal like him. Austria's interior minister agreed.

Publicly, the government of Israel said nothing, in keeping with its long-standing policy of not commenting on intelligence matters. But by early evening, with pressure building, the prime minister took the unusual step of personally denying any Israeli involvement in Kirov's death. His statement was met with skepticism, perhaps deservedly so. What's more, much was made of the fact it was the prime minister who issued the denial and not Allon himself. His silence, said one former American spy, spoke volumes.

Truth was, Gabriel was unavailable for comment at the time; he was locked in a secure room deep inside the Israeli Embassy in Berlin, monitoring the clandestine movements of his operational team. By eight o'clock that evening, all were safely back in Tel Aviv, and Christopher Keller was home and dry in London. Gabriel slipped from the embassy unobserved and boarded an El Al flight for Tel Aviv. Not even the flight crew knew his true identity. For a second consecutive night, he did not sleep. The memory of Konstantin Kirov lying dead in the snow would not let him.

It was still dark when the plane touched down at Ben Gurion. Two bodyguards waited at the foot of the Jetway. They escorted Gabriel through the terminal to an unmarked door to the left of passport control. Behind it was a room reserved for Office personnel returning from missions abroad, thus the permanent odor of cigarettes, burnt coffee, and male tension. The walls were faux Jerusalem limestone, the chairs were modular and covered in black vinyl. In one, bathed in an unforgiving light, sat Uzi Navot. His gray suit looked slept in. The eyes behind his trendy rimless spectacles were red with fatigue.

Rising, Navot glanced at the big silver wristwatch his wife, Bella, had given him on the occasion of his last birthday. There was not an article of clothing or fashion accessory on Navot's large, powerful body that she had not purchased or selected, including a new pair of oxfords that, in Gabriel's opinion, were far too long in the toe for a man of Navot's age and occupation.

"What are you doing here, Uzi? It's three in the morning."

"I needed a break."

"From what?"

Navot smiled sadly and led Gabriel along a corridor with harsh fluorescent lights overhead. The corridor led to a secure door, and the door to a restricted area just off the main traffic circle outside the terminal. A motorcade rumbled in the yellow lamplight. Navot started toward the open rear passenger door of Gabriel's SUV before abruptly stopping and walking around the back of the vehicle to the driver's side. Navot was Gabriel's direct predecessor as chief. In an unprecedented break with Office tradition, he had agreed to stay on as Gabriel's deputy instead of accepting a lucrative job with a defense contractor in California, as Bella had wished. He was doubtless regretting his decision.

"In case you're wondering," said Gabriel as the SUV drew away, "I didn't kill him."

"Don't worry, I believe you."

"It seems you're the only one." Gabriel picked up the copy of *Haaretz* that lay on the seat between them and stared gloomily at the headline. "You know it's bad when your hometown newspaper thinks you're guilty."

"We sent a back-channel message to the press making it clear we had nothing to do with Kirov's death."

"Obviously," said Gabriel as he leafed through the other newspapers, "they didn't believe you."

Every major publication, no matter its political tilt, had declared Vienna a botched Office operation and was calling for an official inquiry. *Haaretz*, which leaned left, went so far as to wonder whether Gabriel Allon, a gifted field operative, was up to the job of chief. How things had changed, he thought. A few months earlier he had been fêted as the man who had eliminated Saladin, ISIS's terror mastermind, and prevented a dirty-bomb attack outside Downing Street in London. And now this.

"I have to admit," said Navot, "it does bear more than a passing resemblance to you." He was scrutinizing Gabriel's photograph on the front page of *Haaretz*. "And that little fellow next to you reminds me of someone else I know."

"There must have been an SVR team in the building on the other side of the street. Judging from the camera angle, I'd say they were on the third floor."

"The analysts say it was probably the fourth."

"Do they?"

"In all likelihood," Navot continued, "the Russians had another static post at the front of the building, a car, maybe another flat."

"Which means they knew where Kirov was going."

Navot nodded slowly. "I suppose you should consider yourself lucky they didn't take the opportunity to kill you, too."

"A pity they didn't. I might have received better press coverage."

They were approaching the end of the airport exit ramp. To the right was Jerusalem and Gabriel's wife and children. To the left was Tel Aviv and King Saul Boulevard. Gabriel instructed the driver to take him to King Saul Boulevard.

"Are you sure?" asked Navot. "You look like you could use a few hours of sleep."

"And what would they write about me then?"

Navot thumbed the combination locks of a stainless-steel attaché case. From it he removed a photograph, which he handed to Gabriel. It was the photograph Mikhail had snapped of Konstantin Kirov's assassin. The eyes were not quite dead; somewhere was a faint trace of light. The rest of the face was a mess, but not from the accident. It had been stretched and pulled and stitched to such a degree it scarcely looked human.

"He looks like a rich woman I once met at an art auction," said Gabriel. "Have you run him through the database?"

"Several times."

"And?"

"Nothing."

Gabriel returned the photograph to Navot. "One wonders why an operative of his obvious skill and training didn't eliminate the one and only threat to his life."

"Mikhail?"

Gabriel nodded slowly.

"He fired four shots at him."

"And all four missed. Even you could have hit him from that distance, Uzi."

"You think he was ordered to miss?"

"Absolutely."

"Why?"

"Maybe they thought a dead Israeli would make their cover story less believable. Or maybe they had another reason," said Gabriel. "They're Russians. They usually do."

"Why kill Kirov in Vienna in the first place? Why didn't they bleed him dry in Moscow and then put a bullet in his neck?"

Gabriel tapped the stack of newspapers. "Maybe they wanted to use the opportunity to fatally wound me."

"There's a simple solution," said Navot. "Tell the world that Konstantin Kirov was working for us."

"At this point, it would smell like a cover story. And it would send a message to every potential asset that we are incapable of protecting those who work for us. It's too high a price to pay."

"So what are we going to do?"

"I'm going to start by finding out who gave the Russians the address of our safe flat in Vienna."

"In case you were wondering," said Navot, "it wasn't me."

"Don't worry, Uzi. I believe you."

7

KING SAUL BOULEVARD, TEL AVIV

It had been Uzi Navot's wish, during the final year of his term as chief, to move the headquarters of the Office from King Saul Boulevard to a flashy new complex just north of Tel Aviv, in Ramat HaSharon. Bella was said to be the driving force behind the relocation. She had never cared for the old building, even when she worked there as a Syria analyst, and found it unbecoming of an intelligence service with a global reach. She wanted an Israeli version of Langley or Vauxhall Cross, a modern monument to Israel's intelligence prowess. She personally approved the architectural designs, lobbied the prime minister and the Knesset for the necessary funding, and even chose the location—an empty plot of land along a high-tech corridor near the Glilot Interchange, adjacent to a shopping center and multiplex called Cinema City. But

Gabriel, in one of his first official acts, had with an elegant stroke of his pen swiftly shelved the plans. In matters of both intelligence and art, he was a traditionalist who believed the old ways were better than the new. And under no circumstances would he countenance moving the Office to a place known colloquially in Israel as Glilot Junction. "What on earth will we call ourselves?" he had asked Eli Lavon. "We'll be a laughingstock."

The old building was not without its charms and, perhaps more important, its sense of history. Yes, it was drab and featureless, but like Eli Lavon it had the advantage of anonymity. No emblem hung over its entrance, no brass lettering proclaimed the identity of its occupant. In fact, there was nothing at all to suggest it was the headquarters of one of the world's most feared and respected intelligence services.

Gabriel's office was on the uppermost floor, overlooking the sea. Its walls were hung with paintings—a few by his own hand, unsigned, and several others by his mother—and in one corner stood an old Italian easel upon which the analysts propped their photographs and diagrams when they came to brief him. Navot had taken his large glass desk to his new office on the other side of the antechamber, but he had left behind his modern video wall, with its collage of global news channels. As Gabriel entered the room, several of the screens flickered with images of Vienna, and in the panel reserved for the BBC World Service he saw his own face. He increased the volume and learned that British prime minister Jonathan Lancaster, a man who owed his career to Gabriel, was said to be "deeply concerned" over the allegations of Israeli involvement in the death of Konstantin Kirov.

Gabriel lowered the volume and went into his private bathroom to shower and shave and change into clean clothing. Returning to his office, he found Yaakov Rossman, the chief of Special Ops, waiting. Yaakov had hair like steel wool and a hard, pitted face. He held a letter-size envelope in his hand and was glaring at the BBC.

"Can you believe Lancaster?"

"He has his reasons."

"Like what?"

"Protecting his intelligence service."

"Duplicitous bastards," murmured Yaakov. "We should never have granted them access to Kirov's material." He dropped the envelope on Gabriel's desk.

"What's that?"

"My letter of resignation."

"Why would you write such a thing?"

"Because we lost Kirov."

"Are you to blame?"

"I don't think so."

Gabriel picked up the envelope and fed it into his shredder. "Is anyone else thinking about tendering their resignation?"

"Rimona."

Rimona Stern was the head of Collections. As such, she was responsible for running Office agents worldwide. Gabriel snatched up the receiver of his internal phone and dialed her office.

"Get down here. And bring Yossi."

Gabriel rang off and a moment later Rimona came rushing through the door. She had sandstone-colored hair, childbearing hips, and a notoriously short temper. She came by it naturally; her uncle was Ari Shamron. Gabriel had known Rimona since she was a child.

"Yaakov says you have something for me," he said.

"What are you talking about?"

"Your letter of resignation. Let me have it."

"I haven't written it yet."

"Don't bother, I won't accept it."

Gabriel looked at Yossi Gavish, who was now leaning in the doorway. He was tall and balding and tweedy and carried himself with a donnish detachment. He had been born in the Golders Green section of London and had earned a first-class degree at Oxford before immigrating to Israel. He still spoke Hebrew with a pronounced English accent and received regular shipments of tea from a shop in Piccadilly.

"What about you, Yossi? Are you thinking about resigning, too?"

"Why should I get the sack? I'm only an analyst."

Gabriel smiled briefly in spite of himself. Yossi was no mere analyst. He was the chief of the entire department, which, in the lexicon of the Office, was known as Research. Oftentimes, he did not know the identities of highly placed assets, only their code names and pseudonyms, but he was among the small circle of officers who had been granted unlimited access to Kirov's file.

"No more talk about resignation. Do you hear me?" asked Gabriel. "Besides, if anyone's going to lose his job, it's me."

"*You?*" asked Yossi.

"Didn't you read the newspapers? Haven't you been watching television?" Gabriel's gaze drifted to the video wall. "They're baying for my blood."

"This too shall pass."

"Maybe," admitted Gabriel, "but I'd like you to increase my chances of survival."

"How?"

"By bringing me the name of the person who signed Kirov's death warrant."

"It wasn't me," quipped Yaakov.

"I'm glad we cleared that up." Gabriel looked at Rimona. "How about you? Did you betray Kirov to the Russians?"

Rimona frowned.

"Or maybe it was you, Yossi. You always struck me as the treacherous type."

"Don't look at me, I'm only an analyst."

"Then go back to your office and start analyzing. And bring me that name."

"It's not something that can be done quickly. It's going to take time."

"Of course." Gabriel sat down at his desk. "You have seventy-two hours."

The rest of the day passed with a torture-chamber slowness; there seemed to be no end to it. There was always one more question for which Gabriel had no answer. He consoled himself by attempting to console others. He did so in small gatherings, for unlike the headquarters of the CIA or MI6, King Saul Boulevard had no formal auditorium. It was Shamron's doing. He believed that spies should never congregate in their place of work, either for purposes of celebration or for mourning. Nor did he approve of American-style motivational speeches. The threats facing Israel, he said, were incentive enough.

In late afternoon, as vermilion light flooded Gabriel's room, he received a summons from the prime minister. He cleared his desk of several routine matters, checked in on a pair of ongoing operations, and at half past eight climbed, exhausted, into his motorcade for the drive to Kaplan Street in Jerusalem. Like all visitors to the prime minister's office, he was forced to surrender his mobile phone before entering. The anti-eavesdropping box into which he placed the device was known as the "beehive," and the secure area beyond was the "fishbowl." The prime minister greeted Gabriel cordially but with a distinct coolness. An inquiry involving his personal finances was threatening to unravel his premiership, the longest since David Ben-Gurion's. The last thing he needed now was a scandal involving his intelligence service.

Ordinarily, Gabriel and the prime minister adjourned to the comfortable seating area for briefings or private discussions, but on that evening the prime minister chose to remain at his desk beneath the portrait of Theodor Herzl, founder of the nineteenth-century Zionist movement that led to the reconstitution of Jewish rule over a portion of historic Palestine. Under Herzl's unremitting gaze, Gabriel relayed the facts as he knew them to be. The prime minister listened impassively, as motionless as the man in the photograph over his shoulder.

"Do you know how I spent my day?" he asked when Gabriel had finished.

"I can only imagine."

"Eighteen of my foreign counterparts took it upon themselves to phone me directly. Eighteen! That's the most in a single day since our last war in Gaza. And all of them asked the same question. How could I be so reckless as to permit my celebrated intelligence chief to gun down a Russian intelligence officer in the heart of Vienna?"

"You did no such thing. Nor did I."

"I tried to explain that, and not a single one believed me."

"I'm not sure I would have believed you, either," admitted Gabriel.

"Even my friend in the White House was skeptical. Some nerve," murmured the prime minister. "He's in more trouble than I am. And that's saying something."

"I don't suppose Jonathan Lancaster called."

The prime minister shook his head. "But the chancellor of Austria kept me on the phone for almost an hour. He told me he had incontrovertible proof we were behind the Russian's murder. He also asked me whether we wanted the body of our assassin back."

"Did he elaborate on the evidence?"

"No. But it didn't sound like he was bluffing. He made it clear that diplomatic sanctions are on the table."

"How serious?"

"Expulsions. Maybe a full break in diplomatic relations. Who knows? They might issue an arrest warrant or two." The prime minister regarded Gabriel for a moment. "I don't want to lose a Western European embassy over this. Or the chief of my intelligence service."

"On that," said Gabriel, "we are in complete agreement."

The prime minister glanced at the television, where a newscast played silently. "You've managed to dislodge me from the lead position. That's quite an accomplishment."

"Trust me, it wasn't my intention."

"There are serious voices calling for an independent review."

"There's nothing to review. We didn't kill Konstantin Kirov."

"It certainly looks like you did. A review might be necessary for appearances' sake."

"We can handle it ourselves."

"Can you?" The prime minister's tone was dubious.

"We'll find out what went wrong," said Gabriel. "And if we bear any blame, appropriate measures will be taken."

"You're starting to sound like a politician."

"Is that supposed to be a compliment?"

The prime minister smiled coldly. "Not at all."

8

NARKISS STREET, JERUSALEM

C hiara rarely watched television in the evening. Raised in the cloistered world of Venice's Jewish ghetto, educated at the University of Padua, she regarded herself as an ancient woman and was disdainful of modern distractions such as smartphones, social media, and fiber-optic television systems that delivered one thousand high-definition channels of largely unwatchable fare. Usually, Gabriel arrived home to find her engrossed in some weighty historical tract—she was commencing work on a PhD in the history of the Roman Empire when she was recruited by the Office—or in one of the serious literary novels she received by post from a bookseller on the Via Condotti in Rome. Lately, she had started reading pulp spy novels as well. They provided her with a connection, however tenuous and improbable, to the life she had gladly given up to become a mother.

On that evening, however, Gabriel arrived at his heavily guarded apartment in the Nachlaot neighborhood of Jerusalem to find his wife glaring at one of the American cable news networks. A reporter was recounting, with obvious skepticism, Israel's stated contention that it had had nothing to do with the events in Vienna. The chief of Israel's secret intelligence service, he intoned, had just departed Kaplan Street. According to one of the prime minister's national security aides, who wished to remain anonymous, the meeting had gone as well as could be expected.

"Is any of it true?" asked Chiara.

"I had a meeting with the prime minister. That's about the extent of it."

"It didn't go well?"

"He didn't offer me Chinese food. I took it as a bad sign."

Chiara aimed the remote at the screen and pressed the power button. She wore a pair of stretch jeans that flattered her long slender legs, and a sweater the color of clotted cream, upon which her dark hair, with its shimmering auburn and chestnut highlights, tumbled riotously. Her eyes were the color of caramel and flecked with gold. At present, they were appraising Gabriel with thinly veiled pity. He could only imagine how he looked to her. The stress of the field had always been unkind to his appearance. His first operation, Wrath of God, had left him with gray hair at the age of twenty-five. He had gone swiftly downhill after that.

"Where are the children?" he asked.

"Out with friends. They told us not to wait up." She raised an eyebrow provocatively. "We have the place all to ourselves. Perhaps you'd like to drag me to bed and have your way with me."

Gabriel was sorely tempted; it had been a long time since Gabriel had made love with his beautiful young wife. There was no time for it. Chiara had two children to raise, and Gabriel a country to protect. They saw one another for a few minutes each morning and, if they were lucky, for an hour or so in the evening when Gabriel returned from work. He had use of an Office safe flat in Tel Aviv for those nights when events didn't permit him to make the long drive to Jerusalem. He hated it, the flat. It reminded him of what his life had been like before Chiara. The Office had brought them together. And now it was conspiring to keep them apart.

"Do you think it's possible," he asked, "that the children slipped back into the apartment without your knowing it?"

"Anything's possible. Why don't you check?"

Gabriel moved silently to the door of the children's room and entered. Before departing for Vienna, he had traded out their cribs for a pair of junior beds, which meant they were free to move nocturnally about the apartment at will. For now, though, they were sleeping soundly beneath a mural of Titianesque clouds that Gabriel had painted after a blood-soaked confrontation with the Russian secret service.

He leaned down and kissed Raphael's forehead. The child's face, lit by a shaft of light from the half-open door, looked shockingly like Gabriel's. He had even been cursed with Gabriel's green eyes. Irene, however, looked more like Gabriel's mother, for whom she was named. Chiara was the forgotten ingredient of the children's genetic recipe. Time would change that, thought Gabriel. A beauty like Chiara's could not be suppressed forever.

"Is that you, Abba?"

It was Irene. Raphael could sleep through a bomb blast, but

Irene, like Gabriel, was easily woken. He thought she had the makings of a perfect spy.

"Yes, sweetheart," he whispered. "It's me."

"Stay for a while."

Gabriel sat down at the edge of her bed.

"Pat my back," she commanded, and he laid his hand gently on the warm fabric of her pajamas. "Did you have a good trip?"

"No," he answered honestly.

"I saw you on television."

"Did you?"

"You looked very serious."

"Where did you learn a word like that?"

"Like what?"

"Serious."

"From Mama."

Such was the language of the Allon household. The children referred to Gabriel as "Abba," the Hebrew world for father, but Chiara they called only "Mama." They were learning Hebrew and Italian simultaneously, along with German. As a result, they spoke a language only their parents could possibly comprehend.

"Where did you go, Abba?"

"Nowhere interesting."

"You always say that."

"Do I?"

"Yes."

The children had only the vaguest sense of what their father did for a living. They knew that his picture sometimes appeared on television, that he was recognized in public places, and that he was surrounded constantly by men with guns. So were they.

"Did you take good care of your mother while I was gone?"

"I tried, but she was sad."

"Was she? Why?"

"Something she saw on television."

"Be a good girl and go back to sleep."

"Can I sleep with you and Mama?"

"Absolutely not."

His tone was stern. Even so, Irene giggled. This was the one place where no one followed his orders. He patted the child's back for another minute more, until her breathing grew deep and regular. Then he lifted himself cautiously from the edge of the bed and moved toward the door.

"Abba?"

"Yes, my love?"

"Can I have one last kiss?"

He kissed her more times than he could possibly count. He kissed her until, happily, she begged him to leave.

Entering the kitchen, Gabriel found a stockpot of water bubbling on the stovetop and Chiara working a lump of Parmigiano-Reggiano cheese over the surface of a grater. She did so deftly and seemingly without effort, the way she did most things, including caring for the children. When she had produced the allotted amount, she traded the lump of Parmigiano-Reggiano for Pecorino and grated that, too. Gabriel quickly surveyed the other ingredients arrayed on the counter. Butter, olive oil, a tall pepper grinder: the makings of *cacio e pepe*. The simple Roman pasta dish was one of his favorites, especially the way Chiara prepared it.

"You know," he said, watching her work, "there's a very nice man in the Mahane Yehuda Market who will do that for you."

"Or maybe I should just buy it in a jar at the supermarket." She shook her head reproachfully. "The cheese has to be grated to the proper consistency. Otherwise, the results will be disastrous."

He frowned at the small television at the end of the counter. "Just like Vienna."

Chiara plucked a strand of spaghetti from the pot and after testing it poured the rest through a colander. Next she tossed it with melted butter, olive oil, the grated cheeses, and a few ounces of pasta water, and seasoned the dish with enough pepper to give it a bit of bite. They ate together at the little café table in the kitchen, the baby monitor between them, the television playing silently. Gabriel declined Chiara's offer of Tuscan red wine; only heaven knew what the night might bring. She poured a small glass for herself and listened intently to his description of the events in Vienna.

"What happens now?" she asked.

"We undertake a rapid but unsparing review to determine where the leak occurred."

"Who knew the address of the safe flat?"

"Eli, Mikhail, the Neviot officers, the deskman from House-keeping who rented it, and six field security men, including my bodyguards. And Uzi, of course."

"You didn't mention the British."

"Didn't I?"

"Surely, you have a suspect."

"I wouldn't want to prejudice the investigation in any way."

"You've been spending too much time with the prime minister."

"It's one of the hazards of my new job."

Chiara's gaze wandered to the television. "Forgive me for what I'm about to say, but Uzi must be secretly enjoying this. Kirov was recruited on his watch. And now he's dead."

"Uzi has been nothing but supportive."

"He has no choice. But try to imagine how this looks from his point of view. He ran the Office competently for six years. Not brilliantly," she added, "but competently. And for his reward, he was pushed out in favor of you."

A silence fell between them. There was only the rhythmic breathing of the children on the monitor.

"You were adorable with Irene," said Chiara at last. "She was so excited you were coming home that she refused to go to sleep. I must say, Raphael deals with your absences rather well. He's a stoic young boy, just like his father must have been. But Irene misses you terribly when you're away." She paused, then added, "Almost as much as I do."

"If this affair turns into a full-fledged scandal, you might be seeing much more of me."

"Nothing would make us happier. But the prime minister would never dare fire the great Gabriel Allon. You're the most popular figure in the country."

"Second," said Gabriel. "That actress is much more popular than I am."

"Don't believe those polls, they're never right." Chiara smiled. "You know, Gabriel, there are worse things than being fired."

"Like what?"

"Having your brains blown out by a Russian assassin." She raised her wineglass to her lips. "Are you sure you won't have a little? It's really quite good."

9

KING SAUL BOULEVARD, TEL AVIV

The concerns of the prime minister notwithstanding, Gabriel left the inquiry in the hands of Yossi Gavish and Rimona Stern, two of his most trusted senior officers and closest friends. His reasons were personal. The Office's last independent inquiry, conducted after a string of botched operations in the late 1990s, had hastened the recall of Ari Shamron from his restless retirement. Among his first official acts was to make his way to West Cornwall, where Gabriel had locked himself away in an isolated cottage with only his paintings and his grief for company. Shamron, as usual, had not arrived empty-handed; he had come bearing an operation. It would prove to be the first step of Gabriel's long journey from self-imposed exile to the executive suite of King Saul Boulevard. The moral of the story, at least from Gabriel's perspective, was that spies admitted outsiders into their midst at their peril.

The first order of business for Yossi and Rimona was to clear themselves of any suspicion over the leak. They did so by submitting to a pair of wholly unnecessary polygraph tests, which they passed with flying colors. Next they requested the assistance of an additional analyst. Reluctantly, Gabriel lent them Dina Sarid, a terrorism expert with a pile of active cases on her cluttered desk, including three involving ISIS that fell into the category of ticking time bombs. Dina knew almost nothing about the Kirov case or the Russian's pending defection. Even so, Gabriel had her strapped to the poly. Not surprisingly, she passed. So did Eli Lavon, Mikhail Abramov, Yaakov Rossman, the Neviot team, the members of the field security unit, and the desk officer from Housekeeping.

The primary phase of the investigation, which was concluded at noon the following day, was predictable in its findings. The three analysts uncovered no evidence to suggest a leak by any Office personnel. Nor could they find fault with the execution of the operation itself. All had participated in undertakings far more complex than a garden-variety defection and exfiltration. It was, as Yossi wrote in his memorandum, "child's play, by our standards." Still, he acknowledged there were "knowns and unknowns." Chief among them was the possibility the leak had come from none other than Konstantin Kirov himself.

"How?" asked Gabriel.

"You sent a total of four text messages to him that night—is that correct?"

"You have them all, Yossi. You know it's correct."

"The first message instructed Kirov to leave the InterContinental and walk to the train station. The second instructed him to board the last train to Vienna. Upon arrival, you told him to take a taxi to the Best Western. But a minute before he arrived there, you sent him the address of the safe flat."

"Guilty as charged."

"He was still in the taxi, which meant Mikhail and Keller couldn't see him clearly."

"Your point?"

"He could have forwarded the message."

"To whom?"

"Moscow Center."

"He had himself killed?"

"Maybe he was under the impression the evening would turn out differently."

"In what way?"

"A different target, for example."

"Who?"

Yossi shrugged. "You."

Which heralded the second phase of the inquiry: a full review of Konstantin Kirov's recruitment, handling, and enormous output of intelligence. With the benefit of hindsight, the three analysts weighed each of Kirov's reports. They found no evidence of deception. Kirov, they concluded, was that rarest of birds. Despite the circumstances of his coerced recruitment, he remained as good as gold.

But the Office had not kept Kirov's precious intelligence to itself; it had shared the bounty with the Americans and the British. Each instance of sharing was logged in Kirov's voluminous case file: the type of material, the date, the all-important distribution list. No one in Washington or London, however, knew the true identity of the agent code-named Heathcliff, and only a handful of senior officers were aware of his intention to defect. One MI6 officer had been given the address of the Vienna safe flat in advance. He had insisted on it, claiming it was necessary to ensure the defector's safe transfer to Vienna International Airport, where a Falcon executive jet had been waiting to fly him to London.

"We would have demanded the same thing," said Uzi Navot. "Besides, having access to a piece of information isn't the same as having proof he gave it to the Russians."

"That's true," agreed Gabriel. "But it's a good place to start."

Navot raised a dainty china teacup to his lips. It contained hot water with a slice of lemon. Next to the saucer was a plate of celery sticks. They were carefully arranged so as to enhance their appeal. Clearly, Bella was unhappy with Navot's current weight, which fluctuated like a Latin American stock exchange. Poor Uzi had spent the better part of the last decade on a diet. Food was his only weakness, especially the heavy, calorie-laden cuisine of Central and Eastern Europe.

"It's your call," he went on, "but if I were in your position, I'd want more than a pile of supposition before making an accusation against an officer from a friendly intelligence service. I've actually met him. He doesn't strike me as the sort to betray his country."

"I'm sure Angleton said the same thing about Kim Philby."

Navot, with a sage nod of his head, conceded the point. "So how do you intend to play it?"

"I'm going to fly to London and have a word with our partners."

"Care for a prediction?"

"Why not?"

"Your partners are going to reject your findings categorically. And then they'll blame us for what happened in Vienna. That's the way it works when there's a disaster in our business. Everyone runs for the nearest foxhole."

"So I should let it drop? Is that what you're saying?"

"What I'm saying," answered Navot, "is that pursuing the issue based on a flimsy estimate is liable to do serious damage to a valuable relationship."

"There is no relationship between us and the British. It is suspended until further notice."

"And I was afraid you were going to do something rash." Lowering his voice, Navot added, "Don't cut off your nose to spite your face, Gabriel."

"My mother always told me that. I still don't know what it means."

"It means you should drop that report into your shredder."

"Not a chance."

"In that case," said Navot with a sigh, "you should send someone back to Vienna to see if he can add a few more details. Someone who speaks the language like a native. Someone with a contact or two inside the local security service. Who knows? If he plays his cards right, he might be able to disabuse the Austrians of the notion we killed our own defector."

"Know anyone who fits the bill?"

"I might."

Gabriel smiled. "You can have a nice Wiener schnitzel while you're in town, Uzi. I know how much you love the way they make it in Vienna."

"And the Rindsgulasch." Navot ran a hand absently over his ample midsection. "Just what I need. Bella's liable to put me on punishment rations."

"You sure you don't mind going?"

"Someone has to do it." Navot stared morosely at the plate of celery sticks. "It might as well be me."

10

VIENNA WOODS, AUSTRIA

Uzi Navot passed an uneventful evening with Bella at their comfortable home in the Tel Aviv suburb of Petah Tikva, and in the morning, having risen at the hateful hour of three, he boarded the five-ten El Al flight to Warsaw, known affectionately inside the Office as the Polish Express. His overnight bag contained two changes of clothing and three changes of identity. His seatmate, a woman of thirty-three from a town in the Upper Galilee, did not recognize him. Navot was both relieved and, when he analyzed his feelings honestly, deeply resentful. For six years he had led the Office without blemish, and yet already he was forgotten. He had long ago resigned himself to the fact he would be remembered merely as a placeholder chief, the one who had kept a chair warm for the chosen one. He was an asterisk.

But he was also, at his core, a fine spy. Admittedly, he was no action figure like Gabriel. Navot was a true spy, a recruiter and runner of agents, a collector of other men's secrets. Before his bureaucratic ascent at King Saul Boulevard, Western Europe had been his primary field of battle. Armed with an array of languages, a fatalistic charm, and a small fortune in financing, he had recruited a far-flung network of agents inside terrorist organizations, embassies, foreign ministries, and security services. One was Werner Schwarz. Navot rang him that evening from a hotel room in Prague. Werner sounded as though he'd had one or two more than was good for him. Werner was rather too fond of his drink. He was unhappily married. The alcohol was anesthesia.

"I've been expecting your call."

"I really hate to be predictable."

"A drawback in your line of work," said Werner Schwarz. "I suppose Vienna is in your travel plans."

"Tomorrow, actually."

"The day after would be better."

"I have time considerations, Werner."

"We can't meet in Vienna. My service is on edge."

"Mine, too."

"I can only imagine. How about that little wine garden in the Woods? You remember it, don't you?"

"With considerable fondness."

"And who will I be dining with?"

"A Monsieur Laffont." Vincent Laffont was one of Navot's old cover identities. He was a freelance travel writer of Breton descent who lived out of a suitcase.

"I look forward to seeing him again. Vincent was always one of my favorites," said Werner Schwarz, and rang off.

Navot, as was his habit, arrived at the restaurant thirty minutes early, bearing a decorative box from Demel, the famous Viennese chocolatier. He had eaten most of the treats during the drive and in their place tucked five thousand euros in cash. The owner of the restaurant, a small man shaped like a Russian nesting doll, remembered him. And Navot, playing the role of Monsieur Laffont, regaled him with stories of his latest travels before settling in a quiet corner of the timbered dining room. He ordered a bottle of Grüner Veltliner, confident it would not be the last. Only three other tables were occupied, and all three parties were in the last throes of their luncheon. Soon the place would be deserted. Navot always liked a bit of ambient noise when he was doing his spying, but Werner preferred to betray his country unobserved.

He arrived at the stroke of three, dressed for the office in a dark suit and overcoat. His appearance had changed since Navot had seen him last, and not necessarily for the better. A bit thicker and grayer, a few more broken blood vessels across his cheeks. His eyes brightened as Navot filled two glasses with wine. Then the usual disappointment returned. Werner Schwarz wore it like a loud necktie. Navot had spotted it during one of his fishing trips to Vienna, and with a bit of money and pillow talk he had reeled Werner into his net. From his post inside the BVT, Austria's capable internal security service, he had kept Navot well informed about matters of interest to the State of Israel. Navot had been forced to relinquish control of Werner during his tenure as chief. For several years they had had no contact other than the odd clandestine Christmas card and the regular cash deposits in Werner's Zurich bank account.

"A little something for Lotte," said Navot as he handed Werner the box.

"You shouldn't have."

"It was the least I could do. I know you're a busy man."

"Me? I have access but no real responsibility. I sit in meetings and bide my time."

"How much longer?"

"Maybe two years."

"We won't forget you, Werner. You've been good to us."

The Austrian waved his hand dismissively. "I'm not some girl you picked up in a bar. Once I retire, you'll struggle to remember my name."

Navot didn't bother with a denial.

"And what about you, Monsieur Laffont? Still in the game, I see."

"For a few more rounds, at least."

"Your service treated you shabbily. You deserved better."

"I had a good run."

"Only to be cast aside for Allon." In a confessional murmur, Werner Schwarz asked, "Did he really think he could get away with killing an SVR officer in the middle of Vienna?"

"We had nothing to do with it."

"Uzi, please."

"You have to believe me, Werner. It wasn't us."

"We have evidence."

"Like what?"

"One of the members of your hit team. The tall one," Werner Schwarz persisted. "The one who looks like a cadaver. He helped Allon with that little problem at the Stadttempel a few years ago, and Allon was foolish enough to send him back to Vienna to take care of the Russian. You would have never made a mistake like that, Uzi. You were always very cautious."

Navot ignored Werner's flattery. "Our officers were present that night," he admitted, "but not for the reason you think. The

Russian was working for us. He was in the process of defecting when he was killed."

Werner Schwarz smiled. "How long did it take you and Allon to come up with that one?"

"You didn't actually see the assassination, did you, Werner?"

"There were no cameras at that end of the street, which is why you chose it. The ballistics evidence proves conclusively the operative on the motorcycle was the one who pulled the trigger." Werner Schwarz paused, then added, "My condolences, by the way."

"None necessary. He wasn't ours."

"He's sitting on a slab in the central morgue. Do you really intend to leave him there?"

"He's of no concern to us. Do with him what you please."

"Oh, we are."

The proprietor appeared and took their order as the last of the three luncheon parties made their way noisily toward the door. Beyond the windows of the dining room the Vienna Woods were beginning to darken. It was the quiet time, the time Werner Schwarz liked best. Navot filled his wineglass. Then, with no warning or explanation, he spoke a name.

Werner Schwarz raised an eyebrow. "What about him?"

"Know him?"

"Only by reputation."

"And what's that?"

"A fine officer who serves his country's interests here in Vienna professionally and in accordance with our wishes."

"Which means he makes no attempt to target the Austrian government."

"Or our citizenry. Therefore, we let him go about his work unmolested. For the most part," Werner Schwarz added.

"You keep an eye on him?"

"When resources permit. We're a small service."

"And?"

"He's very good at his job. But in my experience, they usually are. Deception seems to come naturally to them."

"No crimes or misdemeanors? No personal vices?"

"The occasional affair," said Werner Schwarz.

"Anyone in particular?"

"He got himself involved with the wife of an American consular officer a couple of years ago. It caused quite a row."

"How was it handled?"

"The American consular officer was transferred to Copenhagen, and the wife went back to Virginia."

"Anything else?"

"He's been taking a lot of flights to Bern, which is interesting because Bern isn't part of his territory."

"You think he's got a new girl there?"

"Or maybe something else. As you know, our authority stops at the Swiss border." The first course arrived, a chicken liver terrine for Navot and for Werner Schwarz the smoked duck breast. "Am I allowed to ask why you're so interested in this man?"

"It's a housekeeping matter. Nothing more."

"Is it connected to the Russian?"

"Why would you ask such a thing?"

"The timing, that's all."

"Two birds with one stone," explained Navot airily.

"It's not so easily done." Werner Schwarz dabbed his lips with a starched napkin. "Which brings us back to the man lying in the central morgue. How long do you intend to carry on this pretense he isn't yours?"

"Do you really think," said Navot evenly, "that Gabriel Allon would allow you to bury a Jew in an unmarked grave in Vienna?"

"I'll grant you that's not Allon's style. Not after what he's been through in this city. But the man in the morgue isn't Jewish. At least not ethnically Jewish."

"How do you know?"

"When the Bundespolizei couldn't identify him, they ordered a test of his DNA."

"And?"

"Not a trace of the Ashkenazi gene. Nor does he have the DNA markers of a Sephardic Jew. No Arabian, North African, or Spanish blood. Not a single drop."

"So what is he?"

"He's Russian. One hundred percent."

"Imagine that," said Navot.

11

ANDALUSIA, SPAIN

The villa clung to the edge of a great crag in the hills of Andalusia. The precariousness of its perch appealed to the woman; it seemed it might lose its grip on the rock at any moment and fall away. There were nights, awake in bed, when she imagined herself tumbling into the abyss, with her keepsakes and her books and her cats swirling about her in a ragged tornado of memory. She wondered how long she might lie dead on the valley floor, entombed in the debris of her solitary existence, before anyone noticed. Would the authorities give her a decent burial? Would they notify her child? She had left a few carefully concealed clues concerning the child's identity in her personal effects, and in the beginnings of a memoir. Thus far, she had managed only eleven pages, handwritten in pencil, each page marked by the brown ring of her coffee mug. She had a title, though, which she regarded as a notable achievement, as titles were always so difficult. She called it *The Other Woman*.

The scant eleven pages, the sum total of her labors, she regarded less charitably, for her days were nothing if not a vast empty quarter of time. What's more, she was a journalist, at least she had masqueraded as one in her youth. Perhaps it was the topic that blocked her path forward. Writing about the lives of others— the dictator, the freedom fighter, the man who sells olives and spice in the souk—had for her been a relatively straightforward process. The subject spoke, his words were weighed against the available facts—yes, *his* words, because in those days women were of no consequence—and a few hundred words would spill onto the page, hopefully with enough flair and insight as to warrant a small payment from a faraway editor in London or Paris or New York. But writing about oneself, well, that was an altogether different matter. It was like attempting to recall the details of an auto accident on a darkened road. She'd had one once, with *him*, in the mountains near Beirut. He'd been drunk, as usual, and abusive, which was not like him. She supposed he had a right to be angry; she had finally worked up the nerve to tell him about the baby. Even now, she wondered whether he had been trying to kill her. He'd killed a good many others. Hundreds, in fact. She knew that now. But not then.

She worked, or pretended to work, in the mornings, in the shadowed alcove beneath the stairs. She had been sleeping less and rising earlier. She supposed it was yet another unwelcome consequence of growing old. On that morning she was more prolific than usual, an entire page of polished prose with scarcely a correction or revision. Still, she had yet to complete the first chapter. Or would she call it a prologue? She'd always been dubious about prologues; she regarded them as cheap devices wielded by lesser writers. In her case, however, a prologue was justified, for she was starting her story not at the beginning but in the middle, a stifling afternoon in August 1974 when a certain Comrade Lavrov—it was a pseudonym—brought her a letter from Moscow. It bore neither the name of the sender nor the date it was composed. Even so, she knew it was from *him*, the English journalist she had known in Beirut. The prose betrayed him.

It was half past eleven in the morning when she set down her pencil. She knew this because the tinny alarm on her Seiko wristwatch reminded her to take her next pill. It was her heart that ailed her. She swallowed the bitter little tablet with the cold dregs of her coffee and locked the manuscript—it was a pretentious word, admittedly, but she could think of no other—in the antique Victorian strongbox beneath her writing table. The next item on her busy daily schedule, her ritual bath, consumed all of forty minutes, followed by another half hour of careful grooming and dressing, after which she left the villa and set out through the fierce early-afternoon glare toward the center of the village.

The town was white as dried bone, famously white, and balanced atop the highest point of the incisor-like crag. One hundred and fourteen normal paces along the paseo brought her to the new hotel, and another two hundred and twenty-eight steps carried her across a patch of olive and scrub oak to the edge of the *centre ville*, which was how, privately, she referred to it, even now, even after all her years of splendid exile. It was a game she had played with her child long ago in Paris, the counting of steps. How many steps to cross the courtyard to the street? How many steps to span the Pont de la Concorde? How many steps until a child of ten disappeared from her mother's sight? The answer was twenty-nine.

A graffiti artist had defiled the first sugar-cube dwelling with a Spanish-language obscenity. She thought his work rather decent, a hint of color, like a throw pillow, to break the monotony of white. She wound her way higher through the town to the Calle San Juan. The shopkeepers watched her disdainfully as she passed. They had many names for her, none flattering. They called her *la loca*, the crazy one, or *la roja*, a reference to the color of her politics, which she'd made no attempt to hide, contrary to the instructions of Comrade Lavrov. In fact, there were few shops in the village where she had not had an altercation of some sort, always over money. She regarded the shopkeepers as vulture capitalists, and they thought her, justifiably, a communist and a troublemaker, and an imported one at that.

The café where she preferred to take her midday meal was in a square near the town's summit. There was a hexagonal islet with a handsome lamp at its center and on the eastern flank a church, ocher instead of white, another respite from the sameness. The café itself was a no-nonsense affair—plastic tables and chairs, plastic tablecloths of a peculiarly Scottish pattern—but three lovely orange trees, heavy with fruit, shaded the terrace. The waiter was a friendly young Moroccan from some godforsaken hamlet in the Rif Mountains. For all she knew, he was an ISIS fanatic who was plotting to slit her throat at the earliest opportunity, but he was one of the few people in the town who treated her kindly. They addressed one another in Arabic, she in the stilted classical Arabic she had learned in Beirut, he in the Maghrebi dialect of North Africa. He was generous with the ham and the sherry, despite the fact he disapproved of both.

"Did you see the news from Palestine today?" He placed a *tortilla española* before her. "The Zionists have closed the Temple Mount."

"Outrageous. If the fools don't open it soon, it will be the ruin of them."

"Inshallah."

"Yes," she agreed as she sipped a pale Manzanilla. "Inshallah, indeed."

Over coffee she scratched a few lines into her Moleskine notebook, memories of that August afternoon so long ago in Paris, impressions. Diligently, she tried to segregate what she knew then from what she knew now, to place herself, and the reader, in the moment, without the bias of time. When the bill appeared, she left twice the requested amount and went into the square. For some reason the church beckoned. She climbed its steps—there were four—and heaved on the studded wooden door. Cool air rushed out at her like an exhalation of breath. Instinctively, she stretched a hand toward the font and dipped the tips of her fingers into the holy water, but stopped before performing the ritual self-blessing. Surely, she thought, the earth would tremble and the curtain in the temple would tear itself in two.

The nave was in semidarkness and deserted. She took a few hesitant steps up the center aisle and inhaled the familiar scents of incense and candle smoke and beeswax. She'd always loved the smell of churches but thought the rest of it was for the birds. As usual, God on his Roman instrument of execution did not speak to her or stir her to rapture, but a statue of the Madonna and Child, hovering above a stand of votive candles, moved her quite unexpectedly to tears.

She shoved a few coins through the slot of the box and stumbled into the sunlight. It had turned cold without warning, the way it did in the mountains of Andalusia in winter. She hurried toward the base of the town, counting her steps, wondering why at her age it was harder to walk downhill than up. The little El Castillo supermarket had awakened from its siesta. From the orderly shelves she plucked a few items for her supper and carried them in a plastic sack across the wasteland of oak and olive, past the new hotel, and finally into the prison of her villa.

The cold followed her inside like a stray animal. She lit a fire in the grate and poured herself a whisky to take the chill out of her bones. The savor of smoke and charred wood made her think, involuntarily, of *him*. His kisses always tasted of whisky.

She carried the glass to her alcove beneath the stairs. Above the writing desk, books lined a single shelf. Her eyes moved left to right across the cracked and faded spines. Knightley, Seale, Boyle, Wright, Brown, Modin, Macintyre, Beeston . . . There was also a paperback edition of his dishonest memoir. Her name appeared in none of the volumes. She was his best-kept secret. No, she thought suddenly, his second best.

She opened the Victorian strongbox and removed a leather-bound scrapbook, so old it smelled only of dust. Inside, carefully pasted to its pages, was the meager ration of photographs, clippings, and letters Comrade Lavrov had allowed her to take from her old apartment in Paris—and a few more she had managed to keep without his knowledge. She had only eight yellowed snapshots of her child, the last one taken, clandestinely, on Jesus Lane in Cambridge. There were many more of *him*. The long boozy lunches at the St. Georges and the Normandie, the picnics in the hills, the drunken afternoons in the bathing hut at Khalde Beach. And then there were the photos she had taken in the privacy of her apartment when his defenses were down. They had never met in his large flat on the rue Kantari, only in hers. Somehow, Eleanor had never found them out. She supposed deception came naturally to them both. And to their offspring.

She returned the scrapbook to the Victorian strongbox and in the sitting room switched on her outmoded television. The evening news had just begun on La 1. After several minutes of the usual fare—a labor strike, a football riot, more unrest in neighboring Catalonia—there was a story about the assassination of a Russian agent in Vienna, and about the Israeli spymaster alleged to be responsible. She hated the Israeli, if for no other reason than the fact he existed, but at that moment she actually felt a bit sorry for him. The poor fool, she thought. He had no idea what he was up against.

12

BELGRAVIA, LONDON

Official protocol dictated that Gabriel inform "C," the director-general of Britain's Secret Intelligence Service, of his intention to visit London. He would be met by a reception committee at Heathrow Airport, shepherded around passport control, and whisked to Vauxhall Cross in a motorcade worthy of a prime minister, a president, or a potentate from some corner of an empire lost. Nearly everyone who mattered in official and secret London would know of his presence. In short, it would be a disaster.

Which explained why Gabriel flew to Paris on a false passport instead and then stole quietly into London on a midday Eurostar train. For his accommodations he chose the Grand Hotel Berkshire on the West Cromwell Road. He paid for a two-night stay in cash—it was that sort of place—and climbed the stairs to his room because the lift was out of order. It was that sort of place, too.

He hung the DO NOT DISTURB sign on the latch and engaged the safety bar before lifting the receiver of the room phone. It smelled of the last occupant's aftershave. He started to dial but stopped himself. The call would be monitored by GCHQ, Britain's signals intelligence service, and almost certainly by the American NSA, both of which knew the sound of his voice in multiple languages.

He replaced the receiver and opened a text-to-speech application on his mobile phone. After typing the message and selecting the language in which he wanted it read, he lifted the foul-smelling receiver a second time and dialed the number to completion.

A male voice answered, cool and distant, as though annoyed by an unwanted interruption. Gabriel held the speaker of the mobile to the mouthpiece of the room phone and pressed the PLAY icon. The software's automated voice stressed all the wrong words and syllables but managed to convey his wishes. He wanted a word with "C" in private, far from Vauxhall Cross and without the knowledge of anyone else inside MI6. He could be reached at the Grand Hotel Berkshire, room 304. He did not have long to wait.

When the playback of the message was complete, Gabriel rang off and watched the rush-hour traffic hurtling along the road. Twenty minutes elapsed before the room phone finally rattled with an incoming call. The voice that spoke to Gabriel was human. "Fifty-six Eaton Square, seven o'clock. Business casual." Then there was a click, and the call went dead.

Gabriel had expected to be sent to a dreary MI6 safe house in a place like Stockwell or Stepney or Maida Vale, and so the address in tony Belgravia came as something of a surprise. It corresponded to a large Georgian dwelling overlooking the square's southwestern quadrant. The house, like its neighbors along the terrace, had a snow-white stucco exterior on the ground floor, with tan brick on the upper four. A light burned brightly between the pillars of the portico, and the bell push, when thumbed by Gabriel, produced a sonorous tolling within. While awaiting a response, he surveyed the other houses along the square. Most were darkened, evidence that one of London's most sought-after addresses was the preserve of wealthy absentee owners from Arabia and China and, of course, Russia.

At last, there were footfalls, the crack of high heels on a marble floor. Then the door withdrew, revealing a tall woman of perhaps sixty-five, in fashionable black pants and a jacket with a pattern that looked like Gabriel's palette after a long day's work. She had resisted the siren's song of plastic surgery or collagen implants and thus had retained an elegant, dignified beauty. Her right hand was holding the latch, her left a glass of white wine. Gabriel smiled. It promised to be an interesting evening.

She returned his smile. "My God, it's really you."

"I'm afraid so."

"Hurry inside before someone takes a shot at you or tries to blow you up. I'm Helen, by the way. Helen Seymour," she added as the door closed with a solid thump. "Surely, Graham's mentioned me."

"He never stops talking about you."

She made a face. "Graham warned me about your dark sense of humor."

"I'll do my best to keep it in check."

"Please don't. All our other friends are so bloody dull." She led him along a checkerboard hall, to a vast kitchen that smelled wonderfully of chicken and rice and saffron. "I'm making paella. Graham said you wouldn't mind."

"I beg your pardon?"

"The chorizo and the shellfish," she explained. "He assured me you weren't kosher."

"I'm not, though I generally avoid the forbidden meats."

"You can eat around them. That's what the Arabs do when I make it for them."

"They come often?" probed Gabriel.

Helen Seymour rolled her eyes.

"Anyone in particular?"

"That Jordanian chap was just here. The one who wears Savile Row suits and speaks like one of us."

"Fareed Barakat."

"He's quite fond of himself. And you, too," she added.

"We're on the same side, Fareed and I."

"And what side is that?"

"Stability."

"There's no such thing, my dear. Not anymore."

Gabriel gave Helen Seymour the room-temperature bottle of Sancerre he had purchased from Sainsbury's in Berkeley Street. She placed it directly in the freezer.

"I saw your picture in the *Times* the other day," she said, closing the door. "Or was it the *Telegraph*?"

"Both, I'm afraid."

"It wasn't one of your better ones. Perhaps this will help." She poured a large glass of Albariño. "Graham's waiting for you upstairs. He says you two have something to discuss before dinner. I suppose it has to do with Vienna. I'm not allowed to know."

"Consider yourself fortunate."

Gabriel climbed the wide staircase to the second floor. Light spilled from the open doorway of the stately book-lined study where Graham Seymour, the successor of Cumming, Menzies, White, and Oldfield, waited in splendid isolation. He wore a gray chalk-stripe suit and pewter necktie that matched the color of his plentiful locks. His right hand cradled a cut-glass tumbler filled with a clear distilled beverage. His eyes were fixed on the television screen, where his prime minister was responding to a reporter's question about Brexit. For his part, Gabriel was glad for the change of subject.

"Please tell Lancaster how much his unwavering support meant to me in the days after Vienna. Let him know he can call anytime he needs a favor."

"Don't blame Lancaster," replied Seymour. "It wasn't his idea."

"Whose was it?"

"Mine."

"Why not keep your mouth shut? Why hang me out to dry?"

"Because you and your team ran a bad operation, and I didn't want it to rub off on my service or prime minister." Seymour glanced disapprovingly at Gabriel's wine and then wandered over to the trolley and refreshed his drink. "Can I interest you in something a bit stronger?"

"An acetone on the rocks, please."

"Olives or a twist?" With a careful smile, Seymour declared a temporary cessation of hostilities. "You should have let me know you were coming. You're lucky you didn't miss me. I'm flying to Washington in the morning."

"The cherry blossoms aren't in bloom for at least another three months."

"Thank God."

"What's on the agenda?"

"A routine meeting at Langley to review current joint operations and set future priorities."

"My invitation must have been lost in the mail."

"There are some things we do without your knowledge. We're family, after all."

"Distant family," said Gabriel.

"And getting more distant by the day."

"The alliance has been under strain before."

"Strain, yes, but this is different. We are facing the very real prospect of the collapse of the international order. The same order, I might add, that gave birth to your country."

"We can look after ourselves."

"Can you really?" asked Seymour seriously. "For how long? Against how many enemies at once?"

"Let's talk about something pleasant." Gabriel paused, then added, "Like Vienna."

"It was a simple operation," said Seymour after a moment. "Bring the agent in from the cold, have a word with him in private, put him on a plane to a new life. We do it all the time."

"So do we," replied Gabriel. "But this operation was made more complicated by the fact my agent was blown long before he left Moscow."

"*Our* agent," said Seymour pointedly. "We were the ones who agreed to take him in."

"Which is why," said Gabriel, "he's now dead."

Seymour was squeezing the tumbler so tightly his fingertips had gone white.

"Careful, Graham. You're liable to break that."

He placed the glass on the trolley. "Let us stipulate," he said calmly, "that the available evidence suggests Kirov was blown."

"Yes, let's."

"But let us also stipulate it was your responsibility to bring him in, regardless of the circumstances. You should have spotted the SVR surveillance teams in Vienna and waved him off."

"We couldn't spot them, Graham, because there weren't any. They weren't necessary. They knew where Kirov was going and that I would be waiting there. That's how they got the photograph of me leaving the building. That's how they used their bots, trolls, message boards, and news services to create the impression we were the ones behind Kirov's killing."

"Where was the leak?"

"It didn't come from our service. Which means," said Gabriel, "it came from yours."

"I've got a Russian spy on my payroll?" asked Seymour. "Is that what you're saying?"

Gabriel went to the window and gazed at the darkened houses on the opposite side of the square. "Any chance you could put a Harry James record on the gramophone and turn the volume up very loud?"

"I've got a better idea," said Seymour, rising. "Come with me."

13

EATON SQUARE, LONDON

The door, while outwardly normal in appearance, was mounted within an invisible high-strength steel frame. Graham Seymour opened it by entering the correct eight numerical digits into the keypad on the wall. The chamber beyond was small and cramped, and raised several inches from the floor. There were two chairs, a telephone, and a screen for secure videoconferences.

"An in-home safe-speech room," said Gabriel. "What will they think of next?"

Seymour lowered himself into one of the chairs and gestured Gabriel into the second. Their knees were touching, like passengers sharing a compartment on a train. The overhead lighting played havoc with Seymour's handsome features. He looked suddenly like a man Gabriel had never met.

"It's all rather convenient, isn't it? And entirely predictable."

"What's that?" asked Gabriel.

"You're looking for a scapegoat to explain your failure."

"I'd be careful about tossing around the word *scapegoat*. It makes people like me uneasy."

Somehow, Seymour managed to maintain a mask of British reserve. "Don't you dare play that card with me. We go back too far for that."

"We do indeed. Which is why I thought you might be interested to know that your Head of Station in Vienna is a Russian spy."

"Alistair Hughes? He's a fine officer."

"I'm sure his controllers at Moscow Center feel the same way." The chamber's ventilation system roared like an open freezer. "Will you at least give me a hearing?"

"No."

"In that case, I have no choice but to suspend our relationship."

Seymour only smiled. "You're not much of a poker player, are you?"

"I've never had much time for trivial pursuits."

"There's that card again."

"Our relationship is like a marriage, Graham. It's based on trust."

"In my opinion, most marriages are based either on money or the fear of being alone. And if you divorce me, you won't have a friend in the world."

"I can't operate with you or share intelligence if your Vienna Head is on the Russian payroll. And I'm quite sure the Americans will feel the same way."

"You wouldn't dare."

"Watch me. In fact, I think I'll tell my good friend Morris Payne about all this in time for your little meeting tomorrow." Payne was the director of the CIA. "That should liven things up considerably."

Seymour made no response.

Gabriel glanced at the camera lens above the video screen. "That thing isn't on, is it?"

Seymour shook his head.

"And no one knows we're in here?"

"No one but Helen. She adores him, by the way."

"Who?"

"Alistair Hughes. She thinks he's dishy."

"So did the wife of an American diplomat who used to work in Vienna."

Seymour's eyes narrowed. "How do you know about that?"

"A little bird told me. The same little bird that told me about Alistair Hughes demanding to know the address of the safe flat where I was planning to debrief Kirov."

"London Control wanted the address, not Alistair."

"Why?"

"Because it was our responsibility to get Kirov out of Vienna and onto a plane safely. It's not like ordering a car from Uber. You can't press a button at the last minute. We had to plan the primary route and put in place a backup in case the Russians intervened. And for that, we needed the address."

"How many people knew it?"

"In London?" Seymour glanced at the ceiling. "Eight or nine. And another six or seven in Vienna."

"What about the Vienna Boys' Choir?" Greeted by silence, Gabriel asked, "How much did the Americans know?"

"Our Head of Station in Washington informed them that Heathcliff was coming out and that we had agreed to grant him defector status. She didn't tell them any of the operational details."

"Not the location?"

"City only."

"Did they know I would be there?"

"They might have." Seymour made a show of thought. "I'm sorry, but I'm getting a bit confused. Are you accusing the Americans of leaking the information to the Russians, or us?"

"I'm accusing dishy Alistair Hughes."

"What about the fourteen other MI6 officers who knew the address of your safe flat? How do you know it wasn't one of them?"

"Because we're sitting in this room. You brought me here," said Gabriel, "because you're afraid I might be right."

14

EATON SQUARE, LONDON

G raham Seymour sat for a long moment in a contemplative silence, his gaze averted, as though watching the countryside marching past the window of Gabriel's imaginary train carriage. At last, he quietly spoke a name, a Russian name, that Gabriel struggled to make out over the howling of the ventilation system.

"Gribkov," Seymour repeated. "Vladimir Vladimirovich Gribkov. We called him VeeVee for short. He masqueraded as a press attaché at the Russian diplomatic mission in New York. Rather badly, I might add. In reality, he was an SVR officer who trolled for spies at the United Nations. Moscow Center has a massive *rezidentura* in New York. Our station is much smaller, and yours is smaller still. One man, actually. We know his identity, as do the Americans."

But that, added Seymour, was neither here nor there. What mattered was that Vladimir Vladimirovich Gribkov, during an otherwise tedious diplomatic cocktail party at a posh Manhattan hotel, approached MI6's man in New York and intimated he wished to discuss something of a highly sensitive nature. The MI6 officer, whom Seymour did not identify, duly reported the contact to London Control. "Because, as any MI6 field officer knows, the surest route to the career ash heap is to conduct an unauthorized heart-to-heart with an SVR hood." London Control formally blessed the encounter, and three weeks after the initial contact—enough time, said Seymour, to allow Gribkov to come to his senses—the two officers agreed to meet at a remote location east of New York, on Long Island.

"Actually, it was on a smaller island off the coast, a place called Shelter Island. There's no bridge, only car ferries. Much of the island is a nature preserve, with miles of walking trails where it's possible to never bump into another living soul. In short, it was the perfect place for an officer of Her Majesty's Secret Intelligence Service to meet with a Russian who was thinking about betraying his country."

Gribkov wasted little time on preliminaries or professional niceties. He said he had become disillusioned with the SVR and with Russia under the rule of the Tsar. It was his wish to defect to England along with his wife and two children, who were living with him in New-York at the Russian diplomatic compound in the Bronx. He said he could provide MI6 with a treasure trove of intelligence, including one piece of information that would make him the most valuable defector in history. Therefore, he wanted to be well compensated in return.

"How much?" asked Gabriel.

"Ten million pounds in cash and a house in the English countryside."

"One of those," said Gabriel contemptuously.

"Yes," agreed Seymour.

"And the piece of information that made him worthy of such riches?"

"The name of a Russian mole working at the pinnacle of the Anglo-American intelligence establishment."

"Did he specify which service or which side of the divide?"

Seymour shook his head.

"What was your reaction?"

"Caution bordering on skepticism, which is our default opening position. We assumed he was telling us a tall tale, or that he was an agent provocateur sent by Moscow Center to mislead us into carrying out a self-destructive witch hunt for a traitor in our midst."

"So you told him you weren't interested?"

"The opposite, actually. We told him we were very interested but that we needed a few weeks to make the necessary arrangements. In the meantime, we checked his references. Gribkov was no probationer. He was a veteran SVR officer who'd served in several *rezidenturas* in the West, most recently in Vienna, where he'd had numerous contacts with my Head of Station."

"Dishy Alistair Hughes."

Seymour said nothing.

"What was the nature of the contacts?"

"The usual," said Seymour. "What's important is that Alistair reported each and every one of them, as he's required to do. They were all logged in his file, with cross-references in Gribkov's."

"So you brought Hughes to Vauxhall Cross to get his impressions of Gribkov and what he was selling."

"Exactly."

"And?"

"Alistair was even more skeptical than London Control."

"Was he really? I'm shocked to hear that."

Seymour frowned. "By this point," he said, "six weeks had passed since Gribkov's initial offer of defection, and he was starting to get nervous. He made two highly inadvisable phone calls to my man in New York. And then he did something truly reckless."

"What's that?"

"He reached out to the Americans. As you might expect, Langley was furious at the way we'd handled the case. They put pressure on us to take Gribkov as quickly as possible. They even offered to pay a portion of the ten million. When we resisted, it turned into a full-blown family feud."

"Who won?"

"Moscow Center," said Seymour. "While we were bickering with our American cousins, we failed to notice when Gribkov was ordered home for urgent consultations. His wife and children returned to Russia a few days later, and the following month the Permanent Mission of the Russian Federation to the United Nations announced the appointment of a new press attaché. Needless to say, Vladimir Vladimirovich Gribkov has never been seen or heard from since."

"Why wasn't I told about any of this?"

"It didn't concern you."

"It *concerned* me," said Gabriel evenly, "the minute you let Alistair Hughes within a mile of my operation in Vienna."

"It didn't cross our mind not to let him work on the operation."

"Why not?"

"Because our internal inquiry cleared him of any role in Gribkov's demise."

"I'm relieved to hear that. But how exactly did the Russians learn Gribkov was trying to defect?"

"We concluded he must have tipped them off with his behavior. The Americans agreed with our assessment."

"Thus ending a potentially destabilizing fight among friends. But now you have another dead Russian defector on your hands. And the one common denominator is your Head of Station in Vienna, a man who carried on an extramarital affair with the wife of an American consular officer."

"Her husband wasn't a consular officer, he was Agency. And if marital infidelity were an accurate indicator of treason, we wouldn't have a service. Neither would you."

"He's been spending a lot of time across the border in Switzerland."

"Did your little bird tell you that, too, or have you been watching him?"

"I would never watch one of your officers without telling you, Graham. Friends don't do that to one another. They don't keep each other in the dark. Not when lives are at stake."

Seymour offered no response. He looked suddenly exhausted and weary of the quarrel. Gabriel did not envy his friend's predicament. A spymaster never won in a situation like this. It was only a question of how badly he lost.

"At the risk of putting my nose somewhere it doesn't belong," said Gabriel, "it seems to me you have two choices."

"Do I?"

"The most logical course of action would be to open an internal investigation into whether Alistair Hughes is flogging your secrets to the Russians. You'll be obligated to tell the Americans about the inquiry, which will send your relationship into the deep freeze. What's more, you'll have to bring your rivals at MI5 into the picture, which is the last thing you want."

"And the second option?" asked Seymour.

"Let us watch Hughes for you."

"Surely, you jest."

"Sometimes. But not now."

"It's without precedent."

"Not entirely," replied Gabriel. "And it's not without its advantages."

"Such as?"

"Hughes knows your surveillance techniques and, perhaps more important, your personnel. If you try to watch him, there's a good chance he'll spot you. But if we do it—"

"You'll have license to rummage into the private affairs of one of my officers."

With a shrug of his shoulders, Gabriel made it clear that such license was his already, with or without Seymour's acquiescence. "He won't be able to hide it from us, Graham, not if he's under round-the-clock surveillance. If he's in contact with the Russians, we'll see it."

"And then what?"

"We'll hand the evidence over to you, and you can do with it as you see fit."

"Or as *you* see fit."

Gabriel did not rise to the bait; the contest was nearly over. Seymour lifted his eyes irritably toward the grate in the ceiling. The air was Siberian cold.

"I can't let you watch my Vienna Head without someone from our side looking over your shoulder," he said at last. "I want one of my officers on the surveillance team."

"That's how we got into this mess in the first place, Graham." Greeted by silence, Gabriel said, "Given the current circumstances, there's only one MI6 officer I'd accept."

"Have you forgotten that he and Alistair know each other?"

"No," replied Gabriel, "that important fact has not suddenly slipped my mind. But don't worry, we won't let them within a mile of each other."

"Not a word to the Americans," demanded Seymour.

Gabriel raised his right hand, as though swearing a solemn oath.

"And no access whatsoever to any MI6 files or the inner workings of Vienna station," Seymour insisted. "Your operation will be limited to physical surveillance only."

"But his apartment is fair game," countered Gabriel. "Eyes and ears."

Seymour made a show of deliberation. "Agreed," he said finally. "But do try to show a little discretion with your cameras and microphones. A man is entitled to a zone of immunity."

"Unless he's spying for the Russians. Then he's entitled to *vysshaya mera*."

"Is that Hebrew?"

"Russian, actually."

"What does it mean?"

Gabriel punched the eight-digit numerical code into the internal keypad, and the locks opened with a snap.

Seymour frowned. "I'll have that changed first thing in the morning."

"Do," said Gabriel.

Seymour was distracted during dinner, and so it fell to Helen, the perfect service wife, to guide the conversation. She did so with admirable discretion. Gabriel was no stranger to the London press, yet never once did she raise the unpleasant topic of his past exploits on British soil. Only later, as he was preparing to take his leave, did he realize they had spoken of nothing at all.

He had hoped to walk back to his hotel, but a Jaguar limousine waited curbside. Christopher Keller was sitting in the backseat, reading something on his MI6 BlackBerry. "I'd get in if I were you," he said. "A good friend of the Tsar lives on the other side of the square."

Gabriel ducked into the car and closed the door. The limousine moved away from the curb with a lurch and a moment later was speeding along the King's Road through Chelsea.

"How was dinner?" asked Keller warily.

"Almost as bad as Vienna."

"I hear we're going back."

"Not me."

"Too bad." Keller stared out the window. "I know how much you love the place."

15

BRITISH EMBASSY, WASHINGTON

The director-general of Her Majesty's Secret Intelligence Service had no private aircraft of his own—only the prime minister had such a perquisite—and so Graham Seymour crossed the Atlantic the next morning aboard a chartered Falcon executive jet. He was met on the tarmac at Dulles International Airport by a CIA reception team and driven at high speed through the sprawl of suburban Northern Virginia, to the British Embassy compound on Massachusetts Avenue. Upon arrival, he was shown upstairs for the obligatory meeting with the ambassador, a man he had known nearly all his life. Their fathers had served together in Beirut in the early 1960s. The ambassador's father had worked for the Foreign Office, Seymour's for MI6.

"Dinner tonight?" asked the ambassador as he showed Seymour to the door.

"Back to London, I'm afraid."

"Pity."

"Quite."

Seymour's next stop was the MI6 station, which lay behind a bank vault of a door, a secret kingdom, separate and apart from the rest of the embassy. It was MI6's largest station by far, and without question its most important. By standing agreement, its officers made no attempt to collect intelligence on American soil. They served merely as liaisons to the sprawling U.S. intelligence community, where they were regarded as valued customers. MI6 had helped to build America's espionage capability during World War II, and now, decades later, it was still reaping the rewards. The close familial relationship allowed the United Kingdom, a hollowed-out former imperial power with a small military, to play an outsize role on the world stage, and thus maintain the illusion it was a global power to be reckoned with.

Rebecca Manning, the Washington Head of Station, was waiting for Seymour on the other side of the security barrier. She had been beautiful once—far too beautiful to be an intelligence officer, in the opinion of one long-forgotten service recruiter—but now, in the prime of her professional life, she was merely formidably attractive. A stray lock of dark hair fell over a cobalt-blue eye. She moved it aside with one hand and extended the other toward Seymour. "Welcome to Washington," she intoned, as though the city and all it represented were hers exclusively. "I trust the flight wasn't too terrible."

"It gave me a chance to read your briefing materials."

"There are one or two more points I'd like to review before we leave for Langley. There's coffee in the conference room."

She released her grip on Seymour's hand and led him along the station's central corridor. Her stylish jacket and skirt smelled faintly of tobacco; she had no doubt stepped into the garden for a quick L&B before Seymour's arrival. Rebecca Manning was an unrepentant and wholly unapologetic smoker. She had acquired the habit at Cambridge, and it had worsened considerably during a posting in Baghdad. She had also served in Brussels, Paris, Cairo, Riyadh, and Amman, where she had been the Head of Station. It was Seymour, early in his tenure as chief, who had given her the job as H/Washington, as it was known in the lexicon of the service. In doing so, he had virtually anointed her as his successor. Washington would be Rebecca's final overseas station; there was nowhere else for her to go. Nowhere but a final lap at Vauxhall Cross so that she might be formally introduced to the barons of Whitehall. Her appointment would be historic, and long overdue. MI5 had already had two female chiefs—including Amanda Wallace, the current director-general—but Six had never entrusted the reins of power to a woman. It was a legacy Seymour would be proud to leave.

Family ties aside, Washington Station observed the same security procedures as any other post in the world, especially when it came to sensitive conversations between senior officers. The conference room was impervious to electronic eavesdropping. A leather-bound briefing book had been left at Seymour's place at the table. Inside was the agenda for the meeting with CIA director Morris Payne, along with summaries of current policies, future goals, and ongoing operations. It was one of the most valuable documents in the world of global intelligence. Moscow Center would surely have killed for it.

"Cream?" asked Rebecca Manning.

"Black."

"That's not like you."

"Doctor's orders."

"Nothing serious, I trust."

"My cholesterol is a bit too high. So is my blood pressure. It's one of the fringe benefits of the job."

"I gave up worrying about my health a long time ago. If I can survive Baghdad, I can survive anything." She handed Seymour his coffee. Then she prepared one for herself and frowned. "Coffee without a fag. What's the point?"

"You really should quit, you know. If I can do it, anyone can."

"Morris tells me the same thing."

"I didn't realize you were on a Christian-name basis."

"He's not so bad, Graham."

"He's ideological, which makes me nervous. A spy should believe in nothing." He paused, then added, "Like you, Rebecca."

"Morris Payne isn't a spy, he's the director of the Central Intelligence Agency. There's an enormous difference." She opened her copy of the briefing book. "Shall we begin?"

Seymour had never doubted the wisdom of Rebecca Manning's appointment to Washington, never less so than in the forty-five minutes of her briefing. She moved through the agenda swiftly and sure-footedly—North Korea, China, Iran, Iraq, Afghanistan, Syria, the global effort against ISIS and al-Qaeda. Her command of the policy issues was complete, as was her exposure to American covert operations. As MI6's Head of Station in Washington, Rebecca Manning knew far more about the secret workings of the American intelligence community than most members of the Senate. Her thinking was subtle and sophisticated, and not given to hyperbole or rashness. For Rebecca, the world was not a dangerous place spinning rapidly out of control; it was a problem to be managed by men and women of competence and training.

The last item on the agenda was Russia. It was inherently treacherous ground. The new American president had made no secret of his admiration for Russia's authoritarian leader and expressed a desire for better relations with Moscow. Now he was embroiled in an investigation into whether the Kremlin had provided covert assistance that helped him prevail in a close election against his Democratic opponent. Seymour and MI6 had concluded it was so, as had Morris Payne's predecessor at the Central Intelligence Agency.

"For obvious reasons," said Rebecca, "Morris has no desire to discuss American domestic politics. He's interested in one topic and one topic only."

"Heathcliff?"

Rebecca nodded.

"If that's the case, he should invite Gabriel Allon to Washington for a chat."

"It was Allon's fault—is that your position?" There was a brief silence. "May I speak frankly?"

"That's why we're here."

"The Americans won't buy it. They've worked closely with Allon for many years, as have you. And they know he's more than capable of taking in a defecting Russian agent."

"You seem to have your fingers firmly on the American pulse."

"That's part of my job, Graham."

"What should I expect from them?"

"Grave concern," answered Rebecca. She said nothing more, for nothing more needed to be said. If the CIA shared Gabriel's belief that MI6 had been penetrated by the Russians, it was a disaster.

"Is Morris going to make the accusation explicitly?" asked Seymour.

"I'm afraid I don't know. That said, he's not one to mince words. I'm already detecting a change in temperature in my dealings with them. The air is getting a bit chilly. Lots of long silences and blank stares. We have to address their concerns head-on. Otherwise, they'll begin withholding the crown jewels."

"And if I tell them I share their concerns?"

"Do you?" asked Rebecca Manning.

Seymour sipped his coffee.

"You need to be aware of the fact that Heathcliff's assassination has led the Americans to take another look at what went wrong with the Gribkov case. A very hard look," Rebecca added.

"They would be fools not to." After a pause, Seymour said, "And so would we."

"Have you opened a formal investigation?"

"Rebecca, you know I can't possibly—"

"And I can't possibly carry out my duties as your Washington Head of Station unless I know the answer to that question. I'll be left in an untenable situation, and any residual trust the Americans have in me will evaporate."

Her point was valid. "No formal investigation," said Seymour evenly, "has been opened at this time."

The response was a masterpiece of passive, bureaucratic murk. It did not escape Rebecca's notice. "What about an *informal* one?" she asked.

Seymour allowed a moment to pass before answering. "Suffice it to say, certain inquiries are being made."

"Inquiries?"

He nodded.

"Have you identified a suspect?"

"Rebecca, really." Seymour's tone was chastising.

"I'm not some low-level desk officer, Graham. I'm your H/ Washington. And I'm entitled to know whether Vauxhall Cross thinks I've got a traitor working in my station."

Seymour hesitated, then shook his head slowly. Rebecca appeared relieved.

"What are we going to say to the Americans?" she asked.

"Nothing at all. It's too dangerous."

"And when Morris Payne informs you of his suspicion that we're harboring a Russian spy in our midst?"

"I'll remind him about Aldrich Ames and Robert Hanssen. And then I'll tell him he's mistaken."

"He won't accept it."

"He'll have no other choice."

"Unless your unofficial inquiry uncovers a Russian mole."

"What inquiry?" asked Seymour. "What mole?"

16

BELVEDERE QUARTER, VIENNA

The British Embassy in Vienna was located at Jauresgasse 12, not far from the Belvedere gardens, in the city's gilded Third District. The Jordanians were across the street, the Chinese were next door, and the Iranians were just down the block. So, too, were the Russians. Consequently, Alistair Hughes, MI6's Vienna Head of Station, had occasion to innocently pass the SVR's large *rezidentura* several times daily, either in his chauffeured car or on foot.

He lived on a quiet street called the Barichgasse, in a flat large enough to accommodate his wife and two sons, who visited from London at least once a month. Housekeeping snared a short-term lease on a furnished apartment in the building directly opposite. Eli Lavon moved in the morning of Graham Seymour's visit to Washington; Christopher Keller, the day after that. He had worked with Lavon on several operations, most recently in Morocco. Even so, Keller scarcely recognized the man who unchained the door and pulled him hastily inside.

"What exactly," asked Keller, "is the nature of our relationship?"

"Isn't it obvious?" answered Lavon.

Keller glimpsed Alistair Hughes for the first time at half past eight that evening when he emerged from the back of an embassy sedan. And then he saw Hughes again two minutes later, on the screen of a laptop computer, when he let himself into his flat. A Neviot team had broken into the apartment that afternoon and concealed cameras and microphones in every room. They had also placed a tap on the apartment's landline phone and its Wi-Fi network, which would allow Lavon and Keller to monitor Hughes's activity in cyberspace, including keystrokes. MI6 regulations forbade him from conducting official business on any computer outside the station, or on any phone other than his secure BlackBerry. He was free, however, to conduct personal business on an insecure network, using a personal device. Like most declared MI6 officers, he carried a second phone. Hughes's was an iPhone.

He passed that first evening as he would pass the subsequent nine, in the manner of a middle-aged man living alone. His arrival time varied slightly each night, which Lavon, who logged his comings and goings, put down to proper tradecraft and personal security. His meals were of the frozen microwavable variety and were generally taken while watching the news on the BBC. He drank no wine with his dinner—indeed, they observed no consumption of alcoholic beverages at all—and usually phoned his wife and sons around ten. They lived in the Shepherd's Bush section of West London. The wife, who was called Melinda, worked for Barclays at its headquarters in Canary Wharf. The boys were fourteen and sixteen and attended St. Paul's, one of London's costliest schools. Money appeared not to be an issue.

Insomnia, however, was. His first recourse was a dense biography of Clement Attlee, Britain's postwar Labour prime minister, and when that didn't work he would reach for the bottle of tablets that remained always on his bedside table. There were two more bottles in the medicine chest of the bathroom. Hughes took those with his morning coffee. He was careful in his grooming and his dress, but not unduly so. He never failed to send a "good morning" text message to the boys and Melinda, and none of the texts or e-mails he sent or received while in the apartment were outwardly romantic or sexual in nature. Eli Lavon forwarded all the outgoing or incoming phone numbers and addresses to King Saul Boulevard, which in turn handed them over to Unit 8200, Israel's highly capable signals and cyberintelligence service. None appeared suspicious. For good measure, Unit 8200 trolled through the names, phone numbers, and e-mail addresses in his contacts. All those were clean, too.

A car collected Hughes each morning around nine o'clock, sometimes a few minutes earlier, sometimes later, and took him to the embassy, at which point he disappeared from sight for several hours. The strict security measures along the Jauresgasse made it impossible for Lavon's watchers to maintain a fixed presence there. Nor were there any parks or squares or public spaces where a surveillance artist might loiter for any length of time. It was no matter; the location services of the iPhone, which Hughes kept in his briefcase, alerted them when he left the grounds.

As the declared Head of Station in a small and reasonably friendly country, Alistair Hughes was something of a diplomat-spy, which required him to maintain a busy schedule of meetings and appointments outside the embassy. He was a frequent visitor to various Austrian ministries and to the headquarters of the BVT, and he lunched daily in Vienna's finest restaurants with spies and diplomats and even the odd journalist—including a beautiful reporter from German television who pressed him for information on Israel's role in the murder of Konstantin Kirov. Eli Lavon knew this because he was lunching at the next table with one of his female watchers. Lavon was also present at a diplomatic reception at the Kunsthistorisches Museum when Hughes briefly rubbed shoulders with a man from the Russian Embassy. Lavon covertly snapped a photo of the encounter and shot it to King Saul Boulevard. The Office could not attach a name to the Russian's face, and neither could the Israeli Ministry of Foreign Affairs. Graham Seymour, however, had no problem identifying him. "Vitaly Borodin," he told Gabriel over the dedicated secure link between their offices. "He's a deputy second secretary with no connection whatsoever with the SVR."

"How do you know?"

"Because Alistair reported the contact the minute he returned to the station."

That evening, the tenth of the surveillance operation, Hughes managed only two pages of the Attlee biography before reaching for the tablets on his bedside table. And in the morning, after dispatching text messages to his wife and children, he clawed a tablet from each of the two bottles in his medicine chest and washed them down with his coffee. The embassy car arrived at twelve minutes past nine o'clock, and at nine thirty Keller entered Hughes's flat with the help of one of Lavon's break-in artists. He made straight for the bottle on the bedside table. It had no label or markings of any kind. Neither did the bottles in the medicine cabinet. Keller took a sample from each and laid them on the bathroom counter and photographed them, top and bottom. Across the street in the observation post, he entered the prescription numbers in an Internet pill-identifier database.

"Now we know why he's the only MI6 officer who doesn't drink," said Eli Lavon. "The side effects would kill him."

Lavon flashed an update to King Saul Boulevard, and Gabriel broke the news to Graham Seymour in a secure phone call late that afternoon. MI6's Vienna Head of Station was a manic-depressive who was struggling with anxiety and having trouble sleeping at night. There was a silver lining, however. Thus far, there was no evidence to suggest he was a Russian spy as well.

For three more days and nights they watched him. Or, as Eli Lavon would later describe it, and Keller would concur, they watched over him. Such was the impact of the three unmarked bottles, one for Ambien, one for Xanax, and one for Lithobid, a powerful mood stabilizer. Even Lavon, a professional voyeur who had spent a lifetime chronicling the secret lives of others—their weaknesses and vanities, their private indiscretions and infidelities—could no longer think of Alistair Hughes as only a target and a potential Russian spy. He was theirs to care for and to protect from harm. He was their patient.

He was not the first professional intelligence officer to suffer from mental illness, and he would not be the last. Some came to the game with their disorders in place; others found it was the game itself that made them sick. Hughes, however, concealed his ailments better than most. Indeed, Keller and Lavon struggled to reconcile the Ambien-addled figure who rose unsteadily from his bed each morning with the polished professional spy who emerged a few minutes later from the doorway of the apartment building, the very archetype of British sophistication and competence. Still, the watchers tightened their orbit as they followed Hughes to his daily appointments. And when he nearly stepped in front of a tram on the Kärntner Ring—he was distracted at the time by something on his BlackBerry—it was Eli Lavon who seized his elbow and in German quietly warned him to watch his step.

"And you're sure he didn't see you?" asked Gabriel over the secure link.

"I turned away before he looked up from the phone. He never had a clear view of my face."

"You broke the fourth wall between watcher and quarry." Gabriel's tone was admonitory. "You shouldn't have done it."

"What *should* I have done? *Watch* while he gets run down by a streetcar?"

The next day was a Wednesday, gray and despondent, but warm enough so that the low clouds dispensed rain rather than snow. Hughes's mood matched the weather. He was slow in rising from his bed, and when he swallowed the tablets from the medicine chest, the Xanax and the Lithobid, he did so as though they had been forced down his throat. Outside in the street he paused before climbing into the back of his embassy car and lifted his eyes toward the windows of the observation flat, but otherwise the day proceeded in the same manner as the previous twelve. He spent his morning inside the embassy, he lunched well with an official from the International Atomic Energy Agency, he had coffee at Café Sperl with a reporter from the *Telegraph*. He left no chalk marks, took no long walks in a Viennese park or isolated woodland, and engaged in no visible acts of impersonal communication. In short, he did nothing to suggest he was in contact with an adversarial intelligence service.

He remained at the embassy later than was typical and returned to his flat at nine fifteen. There was barely time enough for a microwave chicken curry and quick phone call to Shepherd's Bush before climbing into his bed. There he reached not for his book but for his laptop computer, which he used to book a flight and reserve a hotel room for two nights. The flight was SkyWork 605, departing Vienna at two in the afternoon on Friday, with a scheduled arrival in Bern at half past three. The hotel was the Schweizerhof, one of Bern's finest. He did not tell his wife of his travel plans. Nor, admitted Graham Seymour in a secure phone call with Gabriel, did he inform Vienna Station or Vauxhall Cross.

"Why not?" asked Gabriel.

"It's not required as long as the trip is personal in nature."

"Maybe it should be."

"Do you know where your station chiefs are every minute of every day?"

"No," said Gabriel. "But none of mine are spying for the Russians."

Alistair Hughes slept soundly that night with the help of ten milligrams of Ambien, but at King Saul Boulevard the lights burned late. In the morning Mikhail Abramov flew to Zürich; Yossi Gavish and Rimona Stern, to Geneva. All three eventually made their way to Bern, where they were met by Christopher Keller and several Neviot officers from the Vienna watch.

Which left only Gabriel. Early on Friday morning he rose in

darkness and dressed in the clothing of a German businessman called Johannes Klemp, quietly, so as not to wake Chiara. In the next room, Raphael slept through his gentle kiss, but Irene woke with a start and fixed him with an accusatory glare.

"You look different."

"Sometimes I have to pretend to be someone else."

"Are you leaving again?"

"Yes," he admitted.

"How long will you be gone?"

"Not long," he answered faithlessly.

"Where are you going this time?"

Operational security did not permit him to answer. He gave Irene one last kiss and went downstairs, where his motorcade disturbed the quiet of Narkiss Street. *Where are you going this time?* Switzerland, he thought. Why did it have to be Switzerland?

17

THE PALISADES, WASHINGTON

As Gabriel's flight rose over the eastern Mediterranean, Eva Fernandes was wiping down the small bar at Brussels Midi, a popular Belgian bistro located on MacArthur Boulevard in Northwest Washington. The last of the evening's guests had finally departed, and the narrow dining room was deserted, save for Ramon, who was running the vacuum rhythmically over the carpet, and Claudia, who was setting the tables for tomorrow's lunch service. Both were recent arrivals from Honduras—Claudia was legal, Ramon was not—and neither spoke much in the way of English. The same was true of most of the kitchen staff. Fortunately, Henri, the Belgian-born owner and head chef, had enough Spanish to make his wishes known, as did Yvette, his ruthlessly efficient business partner and wife.

Yvette managed the restaurant's day-to-day operations and jealously guarded the reservations book, but it was Eva Fernandes, trim, blond, strikingly attractive, who served as the restaurant's public face. Its well-heeled clientele were members in good standing of Washington's ruling elite—lawyers, lobbyists, journalists, diplomats, and intellectuals from the city's most prominent policy shops and think tanks. Most were Democrats and leftward leaning. They were globalists, environmentalists, and supporters of reproductive rights, unrestricted immigration, universal health care, robust gun control, and a guaranteed basic income for those at the bottom of the economic ladder. Eva they adored. She greeted them when they entered the restaurant and relieved them of their overcoats and their cares. And when their tables weren't available because Yvette had taken too many reservations, Eva soothed their anger with a dazzling smile and a complimentary glass of wine and a few soft words in her untraceable accent. "Where are you from?" they would ask, and she would tell them she was from Brazil, which was true to a point. And if they asked about the origin of her European looks, she would explain that her grandparents were from Germany, which was not true at all.

She had arrived in America seven years earlier, living first in Miami, then hopscotching her way northward, through a series of dead-end jobs and relationships, before finding herself in Washington, which had been her destination all along. She had found the job at Brussels Midi quite by accident after bumping into Yvette at the Starbucks across the street. She was overqualified for the work—she had earned a degree in molecular biology from a prestigious university—and the pay was dreadful. She supplemented her wages by teaching three classes a week at a yoga studio in Georgetown and received additional financial support from a friend who taught history at Hunter College in Manhattan.

Combined, the three sources of income gave her the appearance of self-sufficiency. She lived alone in a small apartment on Reservoir Road, owned a Kia Optima sedan, and traveled frequently, mainly to Canada.

It was eleven fifteen when Ramon and Claudia departed. Eva collected her handbag from the cloakroom, engaged the restaurant's alarm system, and went out. Her car was parked along the curb. Her apartment was less than a mile away, but Eva never walked home alone at night. There had been a string of muggings along MacArthur Boulevard that winter, and a week earlier a young woman had been dragged into the woods of Battery Kemble Park at knifepoint and raped. Eva was quite confident she could look after herself in the event of a robbery or sexual assault, but such prowess didn't necessarily fit the profile of a hostess and part-time yoga instructor. Nor did she want to take the risk of becoming involved with the police.

She unlocked the doors of the Kia using the remote and slipped quickly inside. The handbag she placed carefully on the passenger seat. It was heavier than usual, for it contained a polished chrome object, electronic, about the size of an average paperback novel. Eva had been ordered to turn on the device that evening—for fifteen minutes only, beginning at 9:00 p.m.—to allow an agent of Moscow Center to electronically hand over documents. The device had a range of about one hundred feet in all directions. It was possible the agent had transmitted the documents from the sidewalk or from a passing car, but Eva doubted it. In all likelihood, the exchange had taken place inside Brussels Midi. For reasons of security, Eva did not know the identity of the agent, but she had a suspect. She noticed things most people did not, little things. Her survival depended on it.

MacArthur Boulevard was deserted and wet with night rain. Eva drove east, minding her speed because of the cameras. Her small redbrick apartment building overlooked the reservoir. She parked the Kia about a hundred yards away and checked the parked cars as she walked along the damp pavement. Most she recognized, but one, an SUV with Virginia plates, she had never seen before. She committed the license number to memory—she did so not in English or Portuguese, the language of her cover identity, but in Russian—and went inside.

In the foyer she found her mailbox stuffed to capacity. She dropped the catalogues and the other junk into the recycle bin and carried a couple of bills upstairs to her apartment. There, at the kitchen table, with the lights dimmed and the shades drawn, she connected the chrome device to her laptop computer and entered the correct 27-character password in the dialogue box that appeared on the screen.

She inserted an unused memory stick and when prompted tapped the mousepad. The files on the device moved automatically to the memory stick, but it was Eva's responsibility to lock the stick and encrypt its contents. Now, as always, she performed this step slowly and meticulously. To make certain of her work, she ejected the memory stick and reinserted it into the USB port, then clicked on the icon that appeared. She was refused entry without the proper 27-character password. The memory stick was locked tight.

Eva disconnected the chrome device and hid it in its usual place, beneath the loose carpet and floorboard in her bedroom closet. The memory stick she zipped into a compartment in her handbag. The first act was complete; she had successfully taken possession of the intelligence from the agent. Now she had to deliver it to Moscow Center in a way that the American NSA would not detect. That meant handing it off to a courier, the next link in the chain that stretched from Washington to Yasenevo. In the past, Eva had left her memory sticks beneath the kitchen sink of an empty apartment in Montreal. But Moscow Center, for reasons it had not bothered to share with Eva, had shut down the site and created a new one.

To account for her regular travel to Canada, the Center had created a legend, or cover story. It seemed she had a maternal aunt living in the Quartier Latin of Montreal—renal failure, dialysis, not good. Monday and Tuesday were Eva's next days off, but the agent's reports were always of the highest priority. Friday or Saturday were out of the question—Yvette would fly into a rage if Eva asked for either night off on such short notice—but Sundays were slow, especially in winter. Yvette could easily handle the door and the phone. All Eva had to do was find someone to take her nine o'clock class Sunday morning at the studio. That would be no problem. Emily, the new girl, was desperate for extra work. Such was life in the gig economy of modern America.

Eva sat before her laptop and dispatched three brief e-mails, one to Yvette, one to the manager of the yoga studio, and a third to her nonexistent maternal aunt. Then she booked an economy-class seat on the Sunday-morning United Airlines flight to Montreal and reserved a room for the night at the downtown Marriott. She earned valuable mileage and points for both. Her controller at Moscow Center encouraged Eva to apply for membership in frequent-flier and rewards programs, for it helped to defray the high price of keeping her in place in the West.

Finally, at half past one, she switched off the computer and fell exhausted into her bed. Her hair smelled of Brussels Midi, of escargot and grilled salmon with saffron sauce, and of Flemish beef stew simmered in dark beer. As always, the mundane events of the evening played out in her thoughts. It was involuntary, this private screening, an unwanted side effect of the tedious nature of her cover employment. She relived every conversation and saw every face at each of Midi's twenty-two tables. One party she remembered more clearly than the rest—Crawford, party of four, eight o'clock. Eva had seated them at table seven. At 9:08 p.m., they were waiting for their main entrees to arrive. Three were in animated conversation. One was staring at a phone.

18

VIENNA—BERN

It did not take long for Eli Lavon to notice that Alistair Hughes was hiding something. There was, for example, the small matter of his overnight bag. He left it behind at the apartment, despite the fact he was leaving for Bern on an early-afternoon flight. And then there was the car that took Hughes from the embassy to Café Central at half past ten. Ordinarily, the driver waited nearby during one of Hughes's appointments, but this time he departed as soon as Hughes passed through the coffeehouse's famous doorway. Inside, Hughes was met by a man who looked as though he purchased his clothing from a tailor that catered exclusively to European Union diplomats. Eli Lavon, from his outpost on the other side of the crowded dining room, was unable to definitively determine the man's nationality, but had the distinct impression he was French.

Hughes left the café a few minutes after eleven and walked to the Burgring, where he caught a taxi, the first he had taken while under Office surveillance. It drove him to his apartment and waited curbside while he fetched the overnight bag. Lavon knew this because he was watching from the passenger seat of a dark-blue Opel Astra, piloted by the last member of his team still in Vienna. They made the eleven-mile run to the airport in record time, passing Hughes's taxi along the way, which allowed Lavon to check in for the flight to Bern before Hughes entered the terminal. The Englishman did so with his MI6 BlackBerry pressed to his ear.

The young Austrian woman at the SkyWork counter appeared to recognize Hughes, and Hughes her. He flowed through passport control and security without delay and took a seat in a quiet corner of the departure lounge, where he sent and received several text messages on his personal iPhone. Or so it appeared to Lavon, who was huddled among the midday boozers at the bar on the other side of the concourse, picking at the sweating label of Austrian Stiegl.

At twelve forty the overhead speakers blared; boarding for the Bern flight was about to commence. Lavon drank enough of the beer to satisfy the curiosity of any watching SVR countersurveillance officer and then wandered over to the gate, followed a moment later by Alistair Hughes. The plane was a Saab 2000, a fifty-seat turboprop. Lavon boarded first and was dutifully tucking his carry-on beneath the seat in front of him when Alistair Hughes came through the cabin door.

Hughes's seatmate appeared a moment later, a brightly made-up woman of perhaps forty-five, attractive, professionally attired, who was speaking Swiss German into a mobile phone. Out of an abundance of caution, Lavon surreptitiously took her photograph and then watched while she and Hughes fell into easy conversation. Lavon's own seatmate was not the talkative sort. He was a Balkan-looking man, a Serb, a Bulgarian perhaps, who had downed three bottles of lager at the bar before the flight. As the aircraft shuddered into a low-hanging cloud, Lavon wondered whether the man's face, with its five days' worth of stubble, would be the last he ever saw.

The clouds thinned over Salzburg, providing the passengers with a stunning view of the snowbound Alps. Lavon, however, had eyes only for Alistair Hughes and the attractive German-speaking woman seated next to him. She was drinking white wine. Hughes, as usual, was nipping at a glass of sparkling mineral water. The drone of the turboprop engines made it impossible for Lavon to hear their conversation, but it was obvious the woman was intrigued by whatever the handsome, urbane Englishman was saying. It was hardly surprising; as an MI6 officer, Alistair Hughes was a trained seducer. It was possible, however, that Lavon was watching something other than a chance encounter between a man and a woman on an airplane. Perhaps Hughes and the woman were already lovers. Or perhaps she was Hughes's SVR control officer.

Forty-five minutes into the flight, Hughes removed a copy of the *Economist* from his briefcase and read it until the Saab 2000 plopped onto the runway of Bern's small airport. He exchanged a few last words with the woman while the plane taxied toward the terminal, but as he crossed the windswept tarmac he was speaking on his personal iPhone. The woman was walking a few steps behind him, and Lavon was a few steps behind the woman. He, too, was on his phone. It was connected to Gabriel.

"Seat 4B," said Lavon quietly. "Female, Swiss German, maybe forty. Find her name on the manifest and run it through the databases so I can sleep tonight."

The terminal building was the size of a typical municipal airport, low and gray, with a control tower at one end. A handful of Lavon's fellow passengers convened around the baggage-claim carousel, but most hurried toward the exit, including Alistair Hughes and the woman. Outside, she climbed into the passenger seat of a mud-spattered Volvo estate car and kissed the man behind the wheel. Then she kissed the two young children in back.

A line of taxis waited on the opposite side of the road. Hughes climbed into the first; Lavon, the third. Bern was a few kilometers to the northeast. The noble Schweizerhof Hotel overlooked the Bahnhofplatz. As Lavon's taxi passed the entrance, he glimpsed Alistair Hughes trying to fend off the advances of an overeager bellman.

As requested, Lavon's driver dropped him on the opposite side of the busy square. His real destination, however, was the Hotel Savoy, which was located around an elegant corner, on a pedestrian lane called the Neuengasse. Mikhail Abramov was drinking coffee in the lobby. Gabriel and Christopher Keller were in a room upstairs.

Several laptops lay on the writing desk. On one was an overhead shot of the Schweizerhof's check-in counter, courtesy of the hotel's internal network of security cameras. Alistair Hughes was in the process of handing over his passport, a requirement at all Swiss hotels. A needless one in the case of Hughes, thought Lavon, for he and the clerk seemed well acquainted.

Room key in hand, Hughes made for the lifts, leaving the

screen of one computer and walking onto the next. Two more hotel cameras monitored his journey along the fourth-floor corridor, to the door of his junior suite overlooking the spires of the Old City. Inside the room, however, the cameras were of the concealed variety, with heavily encrypted signals that easily made the short hop between the Schweizerhof and the Savoy. There were four cameras in all—two in the main room, one in the bedroom, and one in the bathroom—and microphones as well, including on the room phones. As long as Alistair Hughes was in Bern, a city beyond the boundaries of his territory, a city where he was not supposed to be, he would be granted no zone of immunity. For the time being, at least, the Office owned him.

Entering the room, Hughes placed his overcoat and suitcase on the bed, and his briefcase on the writing desk. His personal iPhone was now compromised in every way possible: voice calls, Internet browser, text messages and e-mails, the camera and microphone. Hughes used it to send greetings to his wife and sons in London. Then he placed a call on his MI6 BlackBerry.

True to Gabriel's agreement with Graham Seymour, the Office had made no attempt to attack the device. Therefore, only Hughes's end of the conversation was audible. His tone was that of superior to subordinate. He said his luncheon meeting—in truth, he had skipped lunch—had run longer than expected and that he intended to get an early start on the weekend. He said he had no plans other than to catch up on a bit of reading and would be reachable by phone and e-mail in the event of a crisis, which was unlikely, given the fact his territory was Vienna. There was a silence of several seconds, presumably while the subordinate spoke. Then Hughes said, "Sounds like something that can wait until Monday," and rang off.

Hughes checked the time; it was 3:47 p.m. He locked his Black-Berry, iPhone, and passport in the room safe, and inserted his billfold into the breast pocket of his jacket. Then he washed down two tablets of pain reliever with a complimentary bottle of Swiss mineral water and went out.

19

SCHWEIZERHOF HOTEL, BERN

The stately Schweizerhof Hotel has long been beloved by British travelers and spies, in part for its afternoon tea service, which takes place daily in the lounge bar. Alistair Hughes was clearly a regular. The hostess greeted him warmly before offering him a table beneath a reproduction portrait of some long-dead Swiss nobleman. Hughes chose the spy's seat, the one facing the hotel's front entrance, and for protection wielded a copy of the *Financial Times*, compliments of Herr Müller, the joyless concierge.

Six hotel security cameras peered down upon the lounge, but because Alistair Hughes had left his iPhone in his room, there was no audio coverage. Gabriel quickly messaged Yossi and Rimona, who were booked at the hotel under false identities, and ordered them downstairs. They arrived in less than ninety seconds and, feigning marital disharmony, settled into the table behind Hughes's. There was no chance of the MI6 man recognizing them as agents of the Office. Yossi and Rimona had played no role in the failed defection of Konstantin Kirov—other than to identify Alistair Hughes as a potential source of the fatal leak—and at no point in their illustrious careers had they worked with Hughes on a joint Office-MI6 operation.

The next guests came not from inside the hotel but from the street, a man and a woman, late thirties or early forties, Central European or Scandinavian in appearance. Both were attractive and expensively dressed—the man in a dark suit and neon-blue shirt, the woman in a sleek pantsuit—and both were quite obviously in robust physical condition, the woman especially. The hostess escorted them to a table near the bar, but the man objected and pointed toward one that offered him line-of-sight coverage of both the hotel's entrance and the table where MI6's Vienna Head of Station was reading the *Financial Times*. They ordered drinks rather than tea and never once looked at their phones. The man sat with his right hand on his knee and his left forearm braced on the tabletop. The woman spent several minutes tending to her flawless face.

"Who do you suppose they are?" asked Gabriel.

"Boris and Natasha," murmured Eli Lavon.

"Moscow Center?"

"No question."

"Mind if we get a second opinion?"

"If you insist."

With Camera 7, Lavon captured a close-up of the man's face. Camera 12 gave him the best look at the woman's. He copied both images into a file and fired it securely to Tel Aviv.

"Now let me see the exterior of the hotel."

Lavon called up the shot from Camera 2. It was mounted above the hotel's entrance and pointed outward, toward the arches of the arcade. At present, two bellmen were hauling a cache of costly luggage from the boot of an S-Class Mercedes. Behind them, late-afternoon traffic hurtled across the Bahnhofplatz.

"Rewind it," said Gabriel. "I want to see their arrival."

Lavon moved the time-code bar backward five minutes, to the point where Boris and Natasha entered the lounge bar. Then he backed it up two more minutes and clicked the PLAY icon. A few seconds later Boris and Natasha strode into the shot.

Lavon clicked PAUSE. "The happy couple," he said acidly. "They arrived at the hotel on foot so we wouldn't be able to grab the registration of the car."

Lavon quickly switched to Camera 9, the widest-angled shot of the lounge bar. A new patron had arrived, a large, well-dressed man with a glistening marble jaw and pale hair combed closely to his scalp. He requested a table at the front of the lounge and settled into the chair facing Alistair Hughes. The MI6 officer scrutinized him briefly over the top of the *Financial Times*, without expression, and then resumed reading.

"Who's that one?" asked Gabriel.

"Igor," answered Lavon. "And Boris has him covered, front and back."

"Let's have a closer look."

Once again, Camera 12 provided the best shot. His features were decidedly Slavic. Lavon magnified the image and produced several stills, which he sent to King Saul Boulevard on a flash priority basis.

"How did he get here?" asked Gabriel.

Lavon switched to Camera 2, the exterior shot, and wound it

backward long enough to see the man they called Igor climbing out of an Audi A8 sedan. The car was still outside the hotel, one man behind the wheel, another in the backseat.

"Looks like Igor doesn't enjoy walking," said Lavon. "Even for the sake of his cover."

"Maybe he should," said Keller. "He looks like he could lose a few pounds."

Just then, the secure link flashed with an incoming message from Tel Aviv.

"Well?" asked Gabriel.

"I was wrong," answered Lavon. "His name isn't Igor, it's Dmitri."

"Better than Igor. What's his family name?"

"Sokolov."

"Patronymic?"

"Antonovich. Dmitri Antonovich Sokolov."

"And what does Dmitri do for a living?"

"He's a nobody at the Russian Federation's permanent mission in Geneva."

"Interesting. What does he really do?"

"He's a Moscow Center hood."

Gabriel stared at the screen. "What's a Moscow Center hood doing in the lounge bar of the Schweizerhof Hotel, twenty feet from MI6's Vienna Head of Station?"

Lavon switched the shot to Camera 9, the widest in his arsenal.

"I don't know. But we're about to find out."

20

SCHWEIZERHOF HOTEL, BERN

T here are numerous methods for a paid or coerced asset of an intelligence service to communicate with his controllers. He can leave coded messages or film at a drop site or in a dead-letter box. He can surreptitiously hand over intelligence in choreographed encounters known as "brush contacts," send messages over the Internet using encrypted e-mail, via satellite using a miniature transmitter, or by ordinary post using tried-and-true methods of secret writing. He can even leave them in ordinary-looking false objects like rocks, logs, or coins. All of the methods have drawbacks and none is foolproof. And when something goes wrong, as it did in Vienna on the night of Konstantin Kirov's attempted defection, it is the asset rather than the controller who almost always pays the ultimate price.

But when asset and controller are both known or declared officers of their respective services, and when both are holders of diplomatic passports, there is a far less perilous option of communication known as the casual contact. It can occur at a cocktail party, or a reception, or the opera, or a restaurant, or in the lobby of a luxury hotel in sleepy Bern. A certain amount of impersonal communication might be involved in the foreplay—a newspaper, for example, or the color of a necktie. And if the controller were so inclined, he might bring along a pair of bodyguards for protection. For even the lobby bar of a Swiss hotel can be a dangerous place when the secrets of nations are changing hands.

For the better part of the next five minutes, no one seemed to move. They were like figures in a painting—or actors on a darkened stage, thought Gabriel, waiting for the first burst of light to animate them. Only Eli Lavon's watchers stirred, but they were in the wings. Two were sitting in a parked Škoda in the Bahnhofplatz, and two more, a man and a woman, were sheltering beneath the arcades. The two in the car would follow Dmitri Sokolov. The ones beneath the arcades would see to Boris and Natasha.

Which left only Alistair Hughes, who was supposed to be in Vienna getting an early start on his weekend. But he was not in Vienna; he was in Bern, twenty feet from an undeclared SVR officer. It was possible the two were already in contact via a short-range agent communication device—a SRAC, in the jargon of the trade. It acted as a sort of private Wi-Fi network. The agent carried a transmitter; the controller, a receiver. All the agent had to do was pass within range, and his message moved securely from one device to the other. The system could even be arranged so that no action, no incriminating press of a button, was required on the agent's part. But the agent could not carry the device forever. Eventually, he would have to remove it from his pocket or his briefcase and plug it into a charger or his personal computer. And if he performed this act within range of a camera, or a watcher, he would be exposed as a spy.

Gabriel, however, doubted that Alistair Hughes was carrying a SRAC device. Keller and Eli Lavon had seen no evidence of one in Vienna, where Hughes had been under near-constant physical and electronic surveillance. What's more, the very point of the system was to avoid face-to-face encounters between an agent and his controller. No, thought Gabriel, something else was taking place in the lobby of the Schweizerhof Hotel.

Finally, at 4:24, Alistair Hughes signaled for the check. A moment later Dmitri Sokolov did the same. Then the Russian hauled his considerable bulk out of his chair and, buttoning his blazer, traveled the twenty feet separating his table from the one where Alistair Hughes was affixing his signature to a room-charge bill.

The shadow of the SVR officer fell over Hughes. He looked up and, frowning, listened while Sokolov, in the manner of a headwaiter explaining the specialties of the house, delivered a short tableside homily. A brief exchange followed. Hughes spoke, Sokolov responded, Hughes spoke again. Then Sokolov smiled and shrugged his heavy shoulders and sat down. Hughes slowly folded his newspaper and placed it on the table between them.

"Bastard," whispered Christopher Keller. "Looks like you were right about him. Looks like he's spying for the Russians."

Yes, thought Gabriel, watching the screen, that was exactly what it looked like.

"Excuse me, but I believe I am addressing Mr. Alistair Hughes of the British Embassy in Vienna. We met at a reception there last year. It was at one of the palaces, I can't remember which. They have so many in Vienna. Almost as many as in St. Petersburg."

These were the words Dmitri Antonovich Sokolov spoke while standing at Alistair Hughes's table, as faithfully recalled by Yossi Gavish and Rimona Stern. Neither could make out what was said next—not the brief exchange that occurred while Sokolov was still standing, and not the longer one that took place after he sat down—for both were conducted at a volume better suited for betrayal.

The second exchange lasted two minutes and twelve seconds. For much of that time, Sokolov was holding Hughes's left wrist. The Russian did most of the talking, all of it through a counterfeit smile. Hughes listened impassively and made no attempt to reclaim his hand.

When Sokolov finally released his grip, he reached inside the lapel of his blazer and removed an envelope, which he slid beneath the copy of the *Financial Times*. Then he rose abruptly and with a curt bow took his leave. With Camera 2 they watched him climbing into the back of the Audi. Gabriel ordered Lavon's watchers not to follow.

Inside the hotel, Boris and Natasha remained at their table. Natasha was speaking in an animated manner, but Boris wasn't listening; he was watching Alistair Hughes, who was staring at the newspaper. At length, the Englishman gave his wristwatch a theatrical glance and rose hastily to his feet, as though he had stayed in the lounge too long. He left a banknote atop the bill. The newspaper—and the envelope tucked inside it—he took almost as an afterthought.

Leaving the lounge, he bade farewell to the hostess and made his way to the lifts. A door opened the instant he pressed the call button. Alone in the carriage, he removed Dmitri Sokolov's envelope and, lifting the flap, peered inside. Once again, his face remained impassive, the professional spy's blank mask.

He returned the envelope to the newspaper for the short walk down the corridor, but inside his room he opened the envelope a second time and removed its contents. He scrutinized them while standing in the window overlooking the Old City, unintentionally shielding the material from both concealed cameras.

Next he went into the bathroom and closed the door. It was no matter; there was a camera there, too. It peered judgmentally down on Hughes as he wet a bath towel and laid it along the base of the door. Then he crouched next to the commode and began burning the contents of Dmitri Sokolov's envelope. Once again, the camera angle was such that Gabriel could not clearly see the material. He looked at Keller, who was glaring angrily at the screen.

"There's a British Airways flight leaving Geneva tonight at nine forty," said Gabriel. "It arrives at Heathrow at ten fifteen. With a bit of luck, you can be at Graham's place in Eaton Square by eleven. Who knows? Maybe Helen will have some leftovers for you."

"Lucky me. And what do you want me tell him?"

"That's entirely up to you." Gabriel watched as Alistair Hughes, MI6's Vienna Head of Station, burned one last item— the envelope with his fingerprints and the fingerprints of Dmitri Antonovich Sokolov. "He's your problem now."

21

SCHWEIZERHOF HOTEL, BERN

He had always known it would come to this, that one day they would find him out. A secret like his could not be kept forever. Truth be told, he was surprised he had managed to hide it so long. For years, no one had suspected him, even in Baghdad, where he spent ten deplorable months trying to find the nonexistent weapons of mass destruction that had been used as a pretext to take his country into a disastrous war. He might have gone mad in Baghdad were it not for Rebecca. He'd had many affairs—too many, it was true—but Rebecca he had loved. She had prevailed over him in a hard-fought contest to become H/Washington. Now she was on a glide path toward becoming Six's first female director-general. Perhaps she might use her rising influence to help him. No, he thought, not even Rebecca could save him now. He had no choice but to confess everything and hope that Graham might sweep his perfidy under the rug.

He removed the wet towel from the base of the door and flung it into the tub. It landed like a dead animal. A fog of smoke from his bonfire of lies hung reprovingly in the air. Leaving, he closed the door quickly behind him so the smoke did not escape and set off the fire alarm. What a comic masterpiece that would be, he thought. What tradecraft!

He supposed the room was wired. His apartment, too. He'd had a nagging sense for a couple of weeks he was being followed. He glanced at his watch; he was running late for his appointment. Despite his present circumstances, he felt a stab of profound guilt. They had agreed to stay late to accommodate him, but now he had no choice but to leave them in the lurch and flee Bern as quickly as possible.

There were no more flights to Vienna that day, but there was an overnight train that arrived at half past six. He could spend the rest of Saturday in his office, the very model of dedication and hard work. Like Rebecca, he thought suddenly. Rebecca never took a day off. It was why she would soon be chief. Imagine if she had agreed to marry him. He would have dragged her down, too. Now he was but a blotch on an otherwise perfect record, a regrettable indiscretion.

He punched the code into the room safe—it was Melinda's birthdate, backward, twice—and tossed his BlackBerry and iPhone into his briefcase. The phones were no doubt compromised. In fact, they were probably staring at him now, recording his every word and misdeed. He was only glad he had left them in the room. He always did when he had tea at the Schweizerhof. The last thing he wanted during his half hour of private time was an interruption from home or, worse yet, Vauxhall Cross.

He slammed the lid on the briefcase and snapped the latches into place. The corridor smelled of Rebecca's perfume, the stuff she used to hose herself down with to cover the odor of her wretched L&Bs. He thumbed the call button for the lift and when the carriage arrived sank gratefully to the lobby. Herr Müller the concierge spotted the bag over his shoulder and with a worried expression asked whether there was a problem with Herr Hughes's room. There *was* a problem, but it was not the room. It was the pair of SVR hoods watching Herr Hughes from the lounge bar.

He passed them without a glance and went into the arcade. Night had fallen and with it had come a sudden snow. It was dropping heavily on the traffic rushing across the Bahnhofplatz. He looked over his shoulder and saw the two SVR hoods advancing toward him. And if that wasn't enough, his phone was howling in his briefcase. The ringtone told him it was the iPhone, which meant it was probably Melinda checking up on him. Another lie to tell . . .

He had to hurry if he was going to make his train. He passed beneath one of the archways of the arcade and stepped into the square. He was nearly to the other side when he heard the car. He never saw the headlamps, for they were doused. Nor would he remember the pain of the initial impact or his broken-backed collision with the street. The last thing he saw was a face peering down at him. It was the face of Herr Müller the concierge. Or was it Rebecca? Rebecca whom he had loved. *Tell me everything*, she whispered as he lay dying. *Your secrets are safe with me.*

PART TWO

PINK GIN AT
THE NORMANDIE

22

BERN

The story appeared shortly after midnight on the Web site of *Berner Zeitung*, the Swiss capital's largest daily newspaper. Frugal in detail, it stated only that a British diplomat named Alistair Hughes had been struck by a motorcar and killed while attempting to make an illegal crossing of the Bahnhofplatz during the evening rush. The car had fled the scene; all subsequent attempts to locate it had failed. The incident was being investigated, said a spokesman for the Kantonspolizei Bern, as a hit-and-run accident.

The British Foreign Office waited until morning before issuing a brief statement declaring that Alistair Hughes was an officer of the British Embassy in Vienna. The savvier reporters—the ones who knew how to read between the lines of official Whitehall drivel—detected a telltale vagueness of tone that suggested the involvement of the secretive organization based in the hideous riverfront complex known as Vauxhall Cross. Those who tried to confirm their suspicions by contacting MI6's underworked press officer were met with a thunderous silence. As far as Her Majesty's Government was concerned, Alistair Hughes was a diplomat of minor consequence who had died while tending to a private matter.

Elsewhere, however, reporters were not constrained by tradition and draconian laws regarding the activities of the secret services. One was the Vienna correspondent for the German television network ZDF. She claimed to have lunched with Alistair Hughes ten days prior to his death, with the full understanding that he was the Head of Station for MI6. Other reporters followed suit, including one from the *Washington Post* who said she used Hughes as a source for a story regarding the missing weapons of mass destruction in Iraq. In London the Foreign Office begged to differ. Alistair Hughes was a diplomat, insisted a spokesman, and no amount of wishful thinking would change that fact.

The one place where no one seemed to care what Alistair Hughes did for a living was the place where he died. As far as the Swiss press was concerned, Hughes was "di cheibe Usländer"—a damned foreigner—who would still be alive if he had had the sense to obey traffic laws. The Kantonspolizei took its cues from the British Embassy, which did not look favorably on a detailed probe. The police searched for the offending vehicle—thankfully, it was of German registry rather than Swiss—but Alistair Hughes they left largely in peace.

There was at least one man in Bern, however, who was not prepared to accept the official version of the story. His inquiry was private and largely invisible, even to those who witnessed it. It was conducted primarily in his room at the Hotel Savoy, where he had remained, much to the dismay of his prime minister and his wife, after ordering his underlings to engage in a hasty evacuation from the country. The management of the Savoy believed him to be Herr Johannes Klemp, a German citizen from the city of Munich. His real name, however, was Gabriel Allon.

By rights, it should have been a time for at least a quiet celebration, though, truth be told, it had never really been his style. Still, he was entitled to a certain amount of private revelry. After all, he was the one who had insisted there was a Russian mole inside MI6. And he was the one who had convinced the director-general of MI6 that Alistair Hughes, the Vienna Head of Station, was the likely culprit. He had placed Alistair Hughes under surveillance and followed him to Bern, where Hughes had met with Dmitri Sokolov of the SVR in the lounge bar of the Schweizerhof Hotel. Gabriel had witnessed the meeting in real time, as had several of his most trusted officers. It had happened, there was no denying it. Dmitri Sokolov had given Hughes an envelope, Hughes had accepted it. Upstairs in his room, he had burned the contents, along with the envelope itself. Four minutes and thirteen seconds later, he was lying dead in the Bahnhofplatz.

A part of Gabriel did not mourn Hughes's passing, for it appeared he had met with the end he richly deserved. But why had Alistair Hughes died? It was possible it was an accident, that Hughes had simply rushed into the street, into the path of an oncoming car. *Possible*, thought Gabriel, but unlikely. Gabriel did not believe in accidents; he made accidents happen. So did the Russians.

But if Alistair Hughes's death was not an accident, if it was an act of intentional murder, why had it been ordered? To answer that question, Gabriel first had to determine the true nature of the encounter he had witnessed and recorded in the lounge bar of the famed Schweizerhof Hotel in Bern.

To that end, he spent the better part of the next three days hunched over a laptop computer, watching the same thirty minutes of video over and over again. Alistair Hughes arriving at the Schweizerhof Hotel after an uneventful flight from Vienna. Alistair Hughes, in his compromised room, misleading his station about his whereabouts and plans for the weekend. Alistair Hughes locking his phones in his room safe before going downstairs, presumably so they could not be used to monitor his meeting with Dmitri Sokolov of the SVR. For better or worse, Gabriel had no video of Alistair Hughes's death in the Bahnhofplatz. The view from Camera 2 of the Schweizerhof's security system was blocked by the arches of the arcade.

The maids at the Savoy thought Gabriel a novelist and were quiet in the corridor. He allowed them to enter the room each afternoon when he left the hotel to walk in the Old City, always with the laptop in a smart-looking shoulder bag. Had anyone tried to follow him, they might have noticed that twice he slipped into the Israeli Embassy on the Alpenstrasse. They might also have noticed that for three consecutive afternoons, he took tea and savories in the lobby lounge of the Savoy's main competitor, the Schweizerhof.

On the first day, he sat at Herr Hughes's table. The day after that it was Herr Sokolov's. And, finally, on the third, he requested the table where Boris and Natasha had been sitting. He chose Boris's seat, the gunner's view of the room, and took careful note of the angles and the placement of the various security cameras. None of it, he thought, had happened by accident. Everything had been chosen with care.

Returning to his room at the Savoy, he took up a sheet of hotel stationery and, with a backing of glass from the coffee table to conceal his impressions, wrote out two possible scenarios to explain why Alistair Hughes had died in Bern.

The first was that the meeting in the lounge bar, while casual in tradecraft, was of the crash variety. Sokolov had warned Hughes he was under suspicion, and under surveillance, and that his arrest was imminent. He had offered Hughes a lifeline in the form of the envelope. It contained instructions for his exfiltration to Moscow. Hughes disposed of the instructions after reading them and hurried from the hotel to begin the first leg of his journey into permanent exile. Presumably, he had been told a car was waiting somewhere near the Bahnhofplatz, a car that would take him to a friendly airport somewhere behind the old Iron Curtain where he could use a Russian passport to board an airplane. In his haste, and in the grips of a full-blown panic, he had tried to cross the square illegally and had been killed, thus depriving Moscow Center of its prize.

It was, thought Gabriel, entirely plausible, with one glaring hole. Alistair Hughes worked for MI6, a service renowned for the quality of its tradecraft and its officers. What's more, if Hughes was also a spy for Moscow Center, he had been walking a tightrope for many years. He would not have panicked when told he had been exposed; he would have faded quietly into the shadows and disappeared. For that reason, Gabriel rejected the first scenario outright.

The second explanation was that Dmitri Sokolov came to the Schweizerhof Hotel with another intention, to kill the mole before the mole could be arrested and interrogated by his service, thus denying MI6 the opportunity to estimate the extent of the mole's treachery. Under that scenario, Hughes was dead long before he arrived in Bern, just as Konstantin Kirov had been dead before he arrived in Vienna. Hughes, however, recognized his fate, which explained his panicked dash from the hotel. The murder weapon was waiting outside in the square, and the driver had taken the opportunity presented to him. Case closed. No more mole.

Gabriel preferred the second scenario to the first, but again he was dubious. Hughes could have provided valuable help to the SVR for many years to come from the safety of a Moscow apartment. He could also have been used as a valuable propaganda tool, like Edward Snowden and the Cambridge spies of the Cold War—Burgess, Maclean, and Kim Philby. The Tsar loved nothing more than showing off the prowess of his spies. No, thought Gabriel, the Russians would not have let their prize slip so easily through their fingers.

Which led Gabriel, late that same night, as the Hotel Savoy dozed around him and cats prowled the cobbled street beneath his window, to consider one more possibility, that he himself was to blame for the death of Alistair Hughes. It was for that reason he reluctantly picked up the phone on his bedside table and called Christoph Bittel.

Bittel agreed to meet Gabriel at nine the following morning at a café near the headquarters of the NDB, Switzerland's foreign intelligence and domestic security service. Gabriel arrived twenty minutes early, Bittel ten minutes late, which wasn't like him. Tall and bald, he had the stern demeanor of a Calvinist minister and the pallor of a man with no time for outdoor pursuits. Gabriel had once spent several unpleasant hours seated across an interrogation table from Bittel. Now they were something like allies. The NDB employed fewer than three hundred people and had an annual budget of only $60 million, less than the intelligence community of the United States spent in a typical afternoon. The Office was a valuable force multiplier.

"Nice place," said Gabriel. He looked slowly around the interior of the sad little café, with its cracked linoleum floor and wobbly Formica tables and faded posters of Alpine vistas. The neighborhood outside was a hodgepodge of office blocks, small industrial concerns, and recycling yards. "Do you come here often, or only for special occasions?"

"You said you wanted something off the beaten path."

"What path?"

Bittel frowned. "How long have you been in the country?"

Gabriel made an authentic show of thought. "I believe I arrived Thursday."

"By plane?"

Gabriel nodded.

"Zurich?"

"Geneva, actually."

"We routinely review the passenger manifests of all incoming flights." Bittel was the chief of the NDB's counterterrorism division. Keeping unwanted foreigners out of the country was part of his job description. "I'm quite certain I never saw your name on any of the lists."

"With good reason." Gabriel's gaze wandered to the folded copy of *Berner Zeitung* that lay on the tabletop between them. The lead story concerned the arrest of a recent immigrant from Morocco who was plotting to carry out a truck-and-knife attack in the name of the Islamic State. "Mazel tov, Bittel. Sounds as though you dodged a bullet."

"Not really. We had him under round-the-clock surveillance. We waited until he rented the truck to make our move."

"What was his intended target?"

"The Limmatquai in Zurich."

"And the original tip that led you to the suspect?" wondered Gabriel. "Where did that come from?"

"His name was found on one of the computers taken from that compound in Morocco where Saladin was killed. One of our partners gave it to us a couple of days after the attempted dirty bomb attack in London."

"You don't say."

Bittel smiled. "I can't thank you enough. It would have been a bloodbath."

"I'm glad we were able to be of help."

They were speaking quietly in Hochdeutsch, or High German. Had Bittel been speaking the dialect of Swiss German particular to the valley where he was raised in Nidwalden, Gabriel would have required an interpreter.

A waitress came over and took their order. When they were alone again, Bittel asked, "Were you the one who killed the bomber in London?"

"Don't be silly, Bittel. I'm the chief of Israeli intelligence, for God's sake."

"And Saladin?"

"He's dead. That's all that matters."

"But ISIS's ideology endures, and it's finally managed to seep into Switzerland." Bittel fixed Gabriel with a reproachful stare. "And so I will overlook the fact you entered the country without bothering to inform the NDB, and on a false passport at that. I assume you're not here for the skiing. It's been terrible this year."

Gabriel turned over the copy of *Berner Zeitung* and tapped the story about the death of a British diplomat in the Bahnhofplatz.

Bittel raised an eyebrow. "A nasty piece of work, that."

"They say it was an accident."

"Since when do you believe what you read in the newspapers?" Lowering his voice, Bittel added, "Please tell me you weren't the one who killed him."

"Why would I kill a mid-level British diplomat?"

"He was no diplomat. He was MI6's Head of Station in Vienna."

"And a frequent visitor to your country."

"Like you," remarked Bittel.

"Do you happen to know why he was so fond of Bern?"

"There were rumors he was seeing a woman here."

"Was he?"

"We're not sure."

"The NDB never looked into it?"

"That's not our style. This is Switzerland. Privacy is our religion." The waitress delivered their coffees. "You were about to tell me," said Bittel quietly, "why the chief of Israeli intelligence is looking into the death of an MI6 officer. I can only assume it has something to do with that Russian you killed in Vienna a couple of weeks ago."

"I didn't kill him, either, Bittel."

"The Austrians don't see it that way. In fact, they asked us to arrest you if you happened to set foot in Switzerland, which means you're in a rather precarious situation at the moment."

"I'll take my chances."

"Why change now?" Bittel added sugar to his coffee and stirred it slowly. "You were saying?"

"We've had our eye on Hughes for some time," confessed Gabriel.

"The Office?"

"And our British partners. We followed him here from Vienna on Friday afternoon."

"Thanks for letting us know you were coming."

"We didn't want to be a bother."

"How many officers did you bring into the country?"

Gabriel lifted his gaze to the ceiling and began counting on his fingers.

"Never mind," muttered Bittel. "That would explain all the microphones and cameras we dug out of Hughes's hotel room. It's quality stuff, by the way. Much better than ours. My technicians are reverse-engineering them as we speak." Bittel laid his spoon thoughtfully on the table. "I suppose you noticed Hughes meeting with that Russian in the lobby."

"Rather hard to miss."

"His name is—"

"Dmitri Sokolov," interjected Gabriel. "Moscow Center's man in Geneva."

"You're acquainted?"

"Not personally."

"Dmitri doesn't exactly play by the rules."

"There are no rules, Bittel. Not where Russians are concerned."

"In Geneva there are, but Dmitri breaks them on a regular basis."

"How so?"

"Aggressive recruiting, lots of dirty tricks. He specializes in *kompromat*." It was the Russian term for damaging material used to silence political opponents or to blackmail assets into doing the Kremlin's bidding. "He's back in Moscow, by the way. He left two nights ago."

"Do you know why?"

"We've never managed to crack the Russians' ciphers, but Onyx picked up a burst of traffic between the Geneva *rezidentura* and Moscow Center last Friday night after Hughes was killed." Onyx was Switzerland's signals intelligence system. "Heaven knows what they were talking about."

"Congratulations on a job well done."

"You think the Russians killed Hughes?"

"Let's just say they're at the top of my list."

"Was Hughes on their payroll?"

"Have you seen the hotel security video?"

"Have *you*?"

Gabriel didn't answer.

"Why would the Russians kill their own agent?" asked Bittel.

"I've been asking myself the same question."

"And?"

"If I knew the answer, I wouldn't be sitting in this dump confessing my sins to you."

"You should know," said Bittel after a moment, "the British aren't terribly interested in a thorough inquiry. The ambassador and the Bern Head of Station are putting pressure on us to shut it down."

"Allow me to second that motion."

"That's it? That's *all* you want from me?"

"I want my cameras and microphones." Gabriel paused, then added, "And I want you to find out why Alistair Hughes was spending so much time in your fair city."

Bittel swallowed his coffee in a single gulp. "Where are you staying?"

Gabriel answered truthfully.

"What about the rest of your team?"

"Long gone."

"Bodyguards?"

Gabriel shook his head.

"How do you want me to contact you if I find anything?"

Gabriel slid a business card across the tabletop. "The number is on the back. Call it on your most secure line. And be discreet, Bittel. The Russians have an eavesdropping service, too."

"Which is why you shouldn't be in Bern without a security detail. I'll put a couple of my men on you, just to be sure."

"Thanks, Bittel, but I can look after myself."

"I'm sure Alistair Hughes thought the same thing. Do me a favor, Allon. Don't get yourself killed on my turf."

Gabriel rose. "I'll do my best."

Gabriel spotted the two bodyguards in the cobbled street beneath his window at midday. They were as inconspicuous as a couple of burning cars. He referred to them as Frick and Frack, but only inwardly. They were Helvetian lads, built like oxen, and not to be trifled with.

They followed him through the galleries of the Kunstmuseum, and to the café in the Kramgasse where he took his lunch, and to the Israeli Embassy on the Alpenstrasse, where he learned his service was humming along satisfactorily without his hand on the tiller. His family, too. Secretly, this pleased him. He had never wished to be indispensable.

That night, as he labored over his laptop in his room at the Savoy, Frick and Frack were replaced by a car containing two uniformed officers from the Kantonspolizei Bern. They remained there until morning, when Frick and Frack returned. Gabriel led them on a merry chase for much of that afternoon, and once, if only to see whether he still had it in him, he dropped them like rocks while crossing the Nydeggbrücke, which connected the Old City of Bern to the new.

Free of surveillance, he took afternoon tea at the Schweizerhof, in the same chair where Alistair Hughes had sat during the final minutes of his life. Gabriel imagined Dmitri Sokolov seated across from him. Dmitri who did not play by Geneva rules. Dmitri who specialized in *kompromat*. Gabriel remembered the way Sokolov had been clutching Alistair Hughes's wrist—right hand Dmitri, left wrist Alistair. He supposed something could have passed between them, a flash drive or a message in code, but he doubted it. He had watched the video a hundred times at least. The transaction had been one way, Dmitri Sokolov to Alistair Hughes. It was the envelope Sokolov had slid beneath the copy of the *Financial Times*. Hughes had burned the contents of the envelope upstairs in his room. Perhaps they were instructions for his exfiltration to Moscow, perhaps they were something else. Four minutes and thirteen seconds later he was dead.

When Gabriel returned to the Savoy, Frick and Frack were licking their wounds in the street. They all three had drinks together that night in the hotel's bar. Frick's real name was Kurt. He was from Wassen, a village of four hundred souls in Canton Uri. Frack was called Matthias. He was a Catholic kid from Fribourg and a former member of the Vatican Swiss Guards. Gabriel realized that they had met once before, when Gabriel was restoring Caravaggio's *Deposition of Christ* in the lab of the Vatican Museum.

"Bittel's getting close," he informed Gabriel. "He says he might have something for you."

"When?"

"Tomorrow afternoon, maybe sooner."

"Sooner would be better."

"If you wanted a miracle, you should have gone to your friend the Holy Father."

Gabriel smiled. "Did Bittel say what it was?"

"A woman," said Matthias into his glass of beer.

"In Bern?"

"Münchenbuchsee. It's—"

"A little town just north of here."

"How do you know Münchenbuchsee?"

"Paul Klee was born there."

Gabriel did not sleep that night, and in the morning he headed straight to the Israeli Embassy, followed by two uniformed officers from the Kantonspolizei Bern. And there he passed one of the longest days of his life, nibbling at a container of stale Viennese butter cookies left over from the days when Uzi Navot was chief and the stations used to keep snacks on hand in case he dropped in unannounced.

By six that evening, there was still no word. Gabriel considered calling Bittel but decided forbearance was the better course of action. He was rewarded at half past eight, when Bittel finally rang. He did so from a secure line at NDB headquarters.

"It turns out the rumors were true. He *did* have a woman here."

"What's her name?"

"Klara Brünner."

"What does she do?"

"She's a psychiatrist," said Bittel, "at the Privatklinik Schloss in Münchenbuchsee."

Privatklinik Schloss . . .

Yes, thought Gabriel, that would explain everything.

25

HAMPSHIRE, ENGLAND

Destruction of Alistair Hughes's mortal remains took place at a crematorium in south London; interment, at an ancient cemetery in the rolling chalk hills of Hampshire. The graveside ceremony was a private affair and dampened by rain. "I am the resurrection and the life," recited the papery vicar as umbrellas sprouted like mushrooms against a sudden downpour. "And whosoever liveth and believeth in me shall never die." It was an epitaph, thought Graham Seymour, for a spy.

Despite the invitation-only nature of the service, it was an impressive turnout. Much of Vauxhall Cross was present, along with a better part of Vienna Station. The Americans sent a delegation from Nine Elms, and Rebecca Manning had flown in from Washington, bearing a personal note from CIA director Morris Payne.

At the conclusion of the service, Seymour approached Melinda Hughes to offer his condolences. "A word in private?" she asked. "I think we have a few things to discuss."

They walked among the headstones, Seymour holding the umbrella, Melinda Hughes holding his arm. The composure she had shown at the graveside while clutching her two boys had abandoned her, and she was weeping softly. Seymour wished he could summon the words to comfort her. Truth was, he had never been much good at it. He blamed his father, the great Arthur Seymour, an MI6 legend, for his inability to show even a trace of genuine empathy. He could recall only one period of affection between them. It had occurred during an extended visit to Beirut, when Seymour was a boy. But even then, his father was distracted. It was because of Philby, the greatest traitor of them all.

Philby . . .

But why, wondered Seymour, was he thinking about his father and Kim Philby at a time like this? Perhaps it was because he was walking through a graveyard with the wife of a Russian spy on his arm. *Suspected* spy, he reminded himself. Nothing had been proven yet.

Melinda Hughes blew her nose loudly. "How very American of me. Alistair would be mortified if he could see me now."

The tears had left tracks in her makeup. Even so, she was very beautiful. And successful, too, thought Seymour—in monetary terms, at least, much more successful than her government-salaried husband. Seymour could only wonder why Alistair had betrayed her time and time again. Perhaps betrayal came easily to him. Or perhaps he thought it was a perquisite of the job, like the ability to skip the long lines at passport control when arriving at Heathrow Airport.

"Do you think he can?" Melinda Hughes asked suddenly.

"I'm sorry?"

"See us. Do you think Alistair is up there"—she lifted her eyes to the slate-gray sky—"with Christ and the apostles and the angels and saints? Or is he a few ounces of pulverized bone in the cold ground of Hampshire?"

"Which answer would you prefer?"

"The truth."

"I'm afraid I can't tell you what's on the mind of the Russian president, let alone answer the question of eternal life."

"Are you a believer?"

"I am not," admitted Seymour.

"Nor am I," replied Melinda Hughes. "But at this moment, I wish I were. Is this how it ends? Is there really nothing more?"

"You have Alistair's children. Perhaps we live on through them." And again, involuntarily, Seymour thought of his father— and of Philby, reading his mail in the bar of the Hotel Normandie.

"I'm Kim. Who are you?"

"Graham."

"Graham what?"

"Seymour. My father is—"

"I know who your father is. Everyone does. Pink gin?"

"I'm twelve."

"Don't worry, it will be our little secret."

A tug at Seymour's arm hauled him back to the present; Melinda Hughes had stepped in a shallow depression and nearly fallen. She was talking about Barclays, how she was looking forward to going back to work now that Alistair was finally home and buried.

"Is there anything more you need from us?"

"Personnel has been very helpful, and surprisingly kind. Alistair always loathed them, by the way."

"We all do, but I'm afraid they're part of the job."

"They're offering me a rather large sum of money."

"You're entitled to it."

"I don't want your money. What I want," she said with a sudden vehemence, "is the truth."

They had reached the farthest end of the cemetery. The mourners had largely dispersed, but a few remained graveside, smiling awkwardly and shaking hands, using the occasion of a colleague's burial to form useful alliances. One of Rebecca Manning's Americans was lighting the cigarette that had found its way to her lips. She was feigning intense interest in whatever it was he was saying, but her gaze was fixed on Seymour and Alistair Hughes's grieving widow.

"Do you really expect me to believe," Melinda Hughes was saying, "that a highly trained MI6 officer was killed while crossing the street?"

"It wasn't a street, it was the busiest square in Bern."

"The Bahnhofplatz?" she said dismissively. "It's not exactly Trafalgar Square or Piccadilly. And what was he doing in Bern in the first place? He told me he was planning to spend the weekend in Vienna with a good book. Clement Attlee. Can you imagine? The last book my husband read was a biography of Clement Attlee."

"It's not uncommon for a Head of Station to operate beyond the boundaries of his country."

"I'm sure the Bern Head might have a different opinion on that. In fact, why don't we ask him?" Melinda Hughes glanced toward the knot of mourners near her husband's open grave. "He's standing right over there."

Seymour made no reply.

"I'm not some neophyte, Graham. I've been a service wife for nearly thirty years."

"Then surely you realize there are certain matters I cannot discuss. Perhaps someday, but not now."

Her gaze was reproving. "You disappoint me, Graham. How terribly predictable. Hiding behind your veil of secrecy, the way Alistair always did. Every time I asked him about something he didn't want to talk about, the answer was always the same. 'Sorry, my love, but you know the rules.'"

"They're real, I'm afraid. Without them, we wouldn't be able to function."

But Melinda Hughes was no longer listening, she was staring at Rebecca Manning. "They were lovers once, in Baghdad. Did you know that? For some reason, Alistair was quite fond of her. Now she's going to be the next 'C,' and Alistair is dead."

"I can assure you, the next director-general hasn't been chosen."

"You know, for a spy, you're a terrible liar. Alistair was much better." Melinda Hughes stopped suddenly and turned to face Seymour beneath the umbrella. "Tell me something, Graham. What was my husband really doing in Bern? Was he involved with another woman? Or was he spying for the Russians?"

They had reached the edge of the car park. The Americans were clambering noisily into a hired motor coach, as if at the conclusion of a company picnic. Seymour returned Melinda Hughes to the care of her family and, lowering his umbrella, made for his limousine. Rebecca Manning had positioned herself next to the rear door. She was lighting a fresh L&B.

"What was that all about?" she asked quietly.

"She had a few questions regarding her husband's death."

"So do the Americans."

"It was an accident."

"Was it really?"

Seymour made no reply.

"And that other matter?" asked Rebecca. "The one we discussed in Washington?"

"The inquiry has concluded."

"And?"

"There was nothing to it." Seymour glanced at Alistair Hughes's grave. "It's dead and buried. Go back to Washington and tell anyone who'll listen. Get the spigot open again."

She dropped her cigarette to the wet earth and started toward a waiting car.

"Rebecca?" Seymour called after her.

She stopped and turned. In the half-light, with the rain falling weakly, he saw her face as if for the first time. She looked like someone he had met a long time ago, in another life.

"Is it true about you and Alistair?" he asked.

"What did Melinda tell you?"

"That you were lovers in Baghdad."

She laughed. "Alistair and me? Don't be ridiculous."

Seymour lowered himself into the back of his car and through the rain-spattered window watched her walk away. Even by the lofty standards of MI6, he thought, she was a damn good liar.

26

HAMPSHIRE, ENGLAND

The text message arrived on Graham Seymour's Black-Berry as he was nearing Crawley. It was from Nigel Whit-combe, his personal aide and runner of off-the-record errands. "Change in plan," Seymour told his driver, and a few minutes later they were racing south on the A23 toward Brighton. From there, they moved westward along the seacoast, through Shoreham and Worthing and Chichester and Portsmouth, until finally they arrived in tiny Gosport.

The ancient fortress, with its empty moat and walls of gray stone, was reached by a narrow track that bisected the first fair-way of the Gosport & Stokes Bay Golf Club. Seymour's car passed through the outer checkpoint, then a gate that led to an internal courtyard. Long ago, it had been converted into a car park for the

Directing Staff. Its longest-serving member was George Halliday, the bursar. He was standing straight as a ramrod in his nook in the west wing.

"Morning, sir. What a pleasant surprise. I wish the Cross had given us at least a modicum of warning that you were coming."

"We're a little out of sorts at the moment, George. Today was the burial."

"Ah, yes, of course. A terrible business, that. I remember when he came down for the IONEC. A good lad. And smart as a whip, wasn't he? How's the wife?"

"As well as can be expected."

"Shall I open your rooms, sir?"

"I shouldn't think so. I won't be staying long."

"I assume you're here to see our guest. The Cross didn't give us any warning about him, either. Mr. Whitcombe left him in a basket on our doorstep and made a run for it."

"I'll have a word with him," promised Seymour.

"Please do."

"And our guest? Where is he?"

"I locked him away in Mr. Marlowe's old room."

Seymour climbed a flight of stone steps to the residential quarters of the west wing. The room at the end of the central corridor contained a single bed, a writing desk, and a simple armoire. Gabriel was standing at the arrow slit of a window, staring across the granite sea.

"We missed you at the service," said Seymour. "Half the CIA was there. You should have come."

"It wouldn't have been right."

"Why not?"

Gabriel turned and looked at Seymour for the first time. "Because I'm the reason Alistair Hughes is dead. And for that," he added, "I am eternally sorry."

Seymour frowned thoughtfully. "A couple of hours ago in a cemetery not far from here, Melinda Hughes asked me whether her husband was a Russian spy."

"And what did you tell her?"

"Nothing."

"That's good. Because Alistair Hughes wasn't a spy. He was a patient," said Gabriel. "At Privatklinik Schloss."

27

FORT MONCKTON, HAMPSHIRE

The fort was called Monckton. Officially, it was run by the Ministry of Defense and known vaguely as the No. 1 Military Training Establishment. Unofficially, it was MI6's primary school for fledgling spies. Most of the instruction took place in the lecture halls and laboratories of the main wing, but beyond the ancient walls were a shooting range, a helipad, tennis courts, a squash facility, and a croquet pitch. Guards from the Ministry of Defense patrolled the grounds. None followed Gabriel and Graham Seymour as they set out along the beach, Gabriel in denim and leather, Seymour in his funereal gray suit and overcoat and a pair of Wellington boots that George Halliday had dug from the stores.

"Privatklinik Schloss?"

"It's very exclusive. And very private," added Gabriel, "as the name would suggest. Hughes was seeing a doctor there. Dr. Klara Brünner. She was treating him for bipolar disorder and severe depression, which explains the medication we found in his apartment. She supplied it to him off the books so no one would know. She saw him the last Friday of every month, after hours. He used an alias when he visited. Called himself Richard Baker. It's not unusual. Privatklinik Schloss is that sort of place."

"Says who?"

"Christoph Bittel of the NDB."

"Can he be trusted?"

"Think of him as our Swiss banker."

"Who else knows?"

"The Russians, of course." On the golf course a brave foursome paused from their labors on a windswept putting green to watch Gabriel and Graham Seymour pass. "They also knew that Alistair had neglected to inform his superiors in London about his illness, lest it derail his career. Moscow Center doubtless considered using the information to coerce him into working for them, which is exactly what you or I would have done in their position. But that's not what happened."

"What *did* happen?"

"They sat on it until Dmitri Sokolov, a known Moscow Center hood with a taste for *kompromat*, handed Hughes an envelope in the lobby of the Schweizerhof Hotel in Bern. If I had to guess, the envelope contained photos of Hughes entering and leaving the clinic. That's why he accepted it instead of throwing it back in Dmitri's face. And that's why he tried to leave Bern in a panic. By the way, Dmitri is back in Moscow. The Center yanked him a couple of days after Alistair was killed."

They had reached the Gosport Lifeboat Station. Seymour

slowed to a stop. "It was all an elaborate subterfuge designed to make us think Alistair was a spy?"

Gabriel nodded.

"Why?" asked Seymour.

"Vladimir Vladimirovich Gribkov. You remember VeeVee, don't you, Graham? VeeVee wanted a cottage in the Cotswolds and ten million pounds in a London bank. In exchange, he was going to give you the name of a Russian mole at the pinnacle of the Anglo-American intelligence establishment."

"It rings a distant bell."

"The Russians got to VeeVee before he could defect," Gabriel continued. "But from their point of view, it was too late. Gribkov had already told MI6 about the mole. The damage was already done. Moscow Center had two choices. They could sit on their hands and hope for the best, or they could take active measures to protect their investment. They chose active measures. Russians," said Gabriel, "don't believe in hope."

They left the beach and followed a single-lane road that cut through a green field like a scar. Gabriel walked along the pavement. Seymour, in his Wellington boots, tramped through the grassy verge.

"And Konstantin Kirov?" he asked. "How does he fit in?"

"That involves a certain amount of supposition on my part."

"So has the rest of it. What's stopping you now?"

"Kirov," said Gabriel, ignoring Seymour's skepticism, "was good as gold."

"And the secret of all secrets he claimed to have discovered? The one that required him to defect?"

"It was chickenfeed. Very convincing chickenfeed," added Gabriel, "but chickenfeed nonetheless."

"Spread by Moscow Center?"

"Of course. It's possible they also whispered something into his ear to make him jumpy, but it probably wasn't necessary. Heathcliff was jumpy enough already. All they had to do was send him on an errand, and he would make the leap on his own."

"They *wanted* him to defect?"

"No. They wanted him to *try* to defect. There's an enormous difference."

"Why let him leave Russia at all? Why not hang him by his heels and let the secrets fall out of his pockets? Why not put a bullet in the nape of his neck and be done with it?"

"Because they wanted to get a little mileage out of him first. All they needed was the address of the safe flat where I would be waiting, but that was the easy part. The distribution list was a mile long, and the mole's name was certainly on it. When Heathcliff arrived in Vienna, they had an assassin in place and a surveillance team with a long-lens camera in the building next door."

"I'm still listening," said Seymour grudgingly.

"Killing Heathcliff beneath my window and splashing my photo across the Internet had one obvious benefit. It made it seem as though I was the one who had ordered the murder of an SVR agent in the middle of Vienna, thus weakening the Office. But that's not the main reason they did it. They wanted me to launch an investigation and identify Alistair Hughes as the likely source of the leak, and I stepped into their trap."

"But why did they kill him?"

"Because keeping him around was too dangerous to the overall operation, the goal of which was to throw us off the scent of the real mole. After all, there's no need to hunt for a mole if the mole is dead."

An unmarked van waited at the end of the lane, two men in front. "Don't worry," said Seymour, "they're mine."

"You sure about that?"

Seymour turned without answering and started back toward the lifeboat station. "The night you came to my house in Belgravia, I asked for the name of the person who told you that Alistair was traveling frequently to Switzerland. You pointedly refused to tell me."

"It was Werner Schwarz," said Gabriel.

"The same Werner Schwarz who works for the Austrian BVT?"

Gabriel nodded.

"What's the nature of your relationship?"

"We pay him money, and he gives us information. That's how it works in our business." A bicycle squeaked toward them along the lane, ridden by a man with a crimson face. "You're not carrying a gun, are you?"

"He's one of mine, too." The bicycle rattled past. "Where do you suppose he is, this mole of yours? Is he in my service?"

"Not necessarily."

"Langley?"

"Why not? Or maybe it's someone in the White House. Someone close to the president."

"Or maybe it's the president himself."

"Let's not get carried away, Graham."

"But that's the danger, isn't it? The danger that we chase our tails and tie ourselves in knots. You're in the wilderness of mirrors. It's a place where you can arrange the so-called facts to come to any conclusion you desire. You've put forward a compelling circumstantial case, I'll grant you that, but if one element crumbles, all of it does."

"Alistair Hughes wasn't a Russian spy, he was a patient at the

Privatklinik Schloss in the Swiss village of Münchenbuchsee. And someone told the Russians."

"Who?"

"If I had to guess," said Gabriel, "it was the mole. The *real* mole."

They had returned to the beach. In both directions it was deserted. Seymour walked down to the water's edge. Wavelets lapped at his Wellington boots.

"I suppose this is the part where you tell me you're suspending our relationship until the real mole is discovered."

"I can't work with you if there's a direct pipeline running between Langley, Vauxhall Cross, and Moscow Center. We're reassessing several operations now under way in Syria and Iran. Our assumption," said Gabriel, "is that they're blown to high heaven."

"That's your assumption to make," Seymour replied pointedly. "But it is the official position of the Secret Intelligence Service that we are not now, nor have we ever been, harboring a Russian mole in our midst." He paused, then asked, "Do you understand what I'm saying?"

"Yes," said Gabriel, "I believe I do. You'd like me to find the mole in your service that doesn't exist."

The van had moved from the end of the lane to the small car park at the lifeboat station. Seymour didn't notice; he was staring across the sea toward the Isle of Wight.

"I could give you a list of names," he said after a moment, "but it would be long and of no use. Not without the power to strap someone to a chair and ruin his career."

"I already have a list," said Gabriel.

"Do you?" asked Seymour, surprised. "And how many names are on it?"

"Only one."

28

VIENNA WOODS, AUSTRIA

The annals of the ensuing operation—it had no code name, then or ever—would record that the first blow in the quest for the mole would be struck not by Gabriel but by his luckless predecessor, Uzi Navot. The time was half past two that same afternoon, the place was the same timbered lodge at the edge of the Vienna Woods where Navot had dined some three weeks previously. The seeming carelessness of his tradecraft was not without forethought. Navot wanted Werner Schwarz to think there was nothing out of the ordinary. For the sake of his security, he wanted the Russians to think the same.

Prior to his arrival in Vienna, however, Navot had left nothing to chance. He had come not from the East and the nations of the long-dead Warsaw Pact but from the West—from France and northern Italy and, eventually, into Austria itself. He had not made the journey alone; Mikhail Abramov had acted as his traveling companion and bodyguard. Inside the restaurant they sat apart, Navot at his usual table, the one he had reserved under the name Laffont, Mikhail near a window. His jacket was unbuttoned for easy access to his gun, which he wore on his left hip. Navot had a gun of his own, a Barak SP-21. It had been a long time since he had carried one, and he was dubious about his ability to deploy the weapon in an emergency without killing himself or Mikhail in the process. Gabriel was right; Navot had never been all that dangerous with a firearm. But the gentle pressure of the holster against his lower spine felt comforting nonetheless.

"A bottle of Grüner Veltliner?" asked the corpulent proprietor, and Navot, in the accent and manner of Monsieur Laffont, the French travel writer of Breton descent, replied, "In a minute, please. I'll wait for my friend."

Ten more minutes passed with no sign of him. Navot, however, was not concerned; he was receiving regular updates from the watchers. Werner had caught a bit of traffic leaving the city. There was no evidence to suggest he was being followed by elements of the service that employed him, or by anyone who answered to Moscow Center.

Finally, a car pulled up outside Mikhail's window, and a single figure, Werner Schwarz, emerged. When he entered the restaurant, the proprietor pumped his hand vigorously, as though trying to draw water from a well, and led him to the table where Navot sat. Werner was clearly disappointed by the absence of wine. There was only a small decorative box from Demel, the Viennese chocolatier.

"Open it," said Navot.

"Here?"

"Why not?"

Werner Schwarz lifted the lid and looked inside. There was no money, only a brief note that Navot had composed in German. Werner Schwarz's hand trembled as he read it.

"Maybe we should take a walk in the woods before lunch," said Navot as he rose. "It will be good for our appetite."

29

VIENNA WOODS, AUSTRIA

It's not true, Uzi! Where ever did you get an idea like that?"

"Don't call me by my real name. I'm Monsieur Laffont, remember? Or are you having trouble keeping the names of your controllers straight in your head?"

They were walking along a footpath of trampled snow. On their right, the trees climbed a gentle hill; on their left, they sank into the cleft of a small valley. The orange sun was low in the sky and shining directly into their faces. Mikhail was walking about thirty yards behind them. His overcoat was tightly buttoned, which meant he had moved his gun from his hip to his pocket.

"How long, Werner? How long have you been working for them?"

"Uzi, really, you have to come to your senses."

Navot stopped suddenly and seized Schwarz's elbow. Schwarz grimaced in pain. He was sweating in spite of the bitter cold.

"What are you going to do, Uzi? Get rough with me?"

"I'll leave that to him." Navot glanced at Mikhail, who was standing motionless on the footpath, his long shadow stretched behind him.

"The cadaver," sneered Schwarz. "One phone call and he spends several years in an Austrian prison for murder. You, too."

"Go for it, Werner." Navot squeezed harder. "Make the call."

Werner Schwarz made no movement for his phone. Navot, with a flick of his thick wrist, flung him down the footpath, deeper into the woods.

"How long, Werner?" asked Navot again.

"What difference does it make?"

"It might make a great deal of difference. In fact, it might determine whether you live to see Lotte tonight or whether I have my friend put a bullet in your head."

"A year. Maybe a year and a half."

"Try again, Werner."

"Four years."

"Five, perhaps? Or six?"

"Let's say five."

"Who made the first move?"

"You know how it goes with these things. It's a bit like a love affair. In the end, it's hard to remember who pursued whom."

"Try, Werner."

"We flirted for a while and then I sent them a bouquet of flowers."

"Daisies?"

"Orchids," said Werner Schwarz with a defenseless smile. "The best stuff I could lay my hands on."

"You wanted to make a good first impression?"

"They really do matter."

"How much did you get for it?"

"Enough to buy something nice for Lotte."

"Who handles you?"

"At first, it was a local boy from the Vienna *rezidentura*."

"Risky."

"Not really. I was working counterintelligence then. I was allowed the occasional contact."

"And now?"

"An out-of-towner."

"Neighboring country?"

"Germany."

"Berlin *rezidentura*?"

"Nonofficial cover, actually. Private practice."

"What's the fellow's name?"

"He calls himself Sergei Morosov. Works for a consulting firm in Frankfurt. His clients are German firms wishing to do business in Russia, of which there are many, I can assure you. Sergei introduces them to the right people in Moscow and makes sure they put money in the right pockets, including Sergei's. The company is a real cash cow. And the cash flows directly into the coffers of Moscow Center."

"He's SVR? You're sure of it?"

"He's a Moscow Center hood, one hundred percent."

They walked on, the snow icy and slick beneath their feet. "Does Sergei give you your marching orders?" asked Navot. "Or are you a self-starter?"

"A little of both."

"What's the tradecraft?"

"Old school. If I have something, I draw the shades in an upstairs window on a Friday. The following Tuesday, I get a wrong-number phone call. They always ask to speak to a woman. The name they use corresponds to the place Sergei wants to meet."

"For example?"

"Trudi."

"Where's Trudi?"

"Linz."

"Who else?"

"Sophie and Anna. They're both in Germany."

"Is that all?"

"No. There's Sabine. Sabine is a flat in Strasbourg."

"How do you account for all the travel?"

"I do a lot of liaison work."

"I'll say." Somewhere a dog was barking, deep and low. "And me?" asked Navot. "When did you tell the Russians about your relationship with me?"

"I never did, Uzi. I swear on Lotte's life, I never told them."

"Don't swear, Werner. It insults my intelligence. Just tell me where it happened. Was it Trudi? Sophie? Anna?"

Werner Schwarz shook his head. "It happened before Sergei came on the scene, when I was still under the control of the Vienna *rezidentura*."

"How much did you get for me?"

"Not much."

"Story of my life," said Navot. "I assume the Russians exploited the situation?"

"Exploited?"

"They used you as a means of spying on *me*. They also used you as a conduit to whisper false or misleading information into my ear. In fact, I'm well within my rights to assume that everything you've told me for the past five years was written by Moscow Center."

"That not's true."

"Then why didn't you tell me the Russians had approached you? Why didn't you give me the opportunity to whisper a little filth into *their* ear?" Greeted by silence, Navot answered his own question. "Because Sergei Morosov said he would kill you if you did." After a pause, Navot asked, "No denial, Werner?"

Werner Schwarz shook his head. "They play rough, the Russians."

"Not as rough as we do." Navot slowed to a stop and seized Werner Schwarz's arm in an iron grip. "But tell me something else. Where did the Russians tell you they were planning to kill an SVR defector in Vienna? Was it Trudi? Anna?"

"It was Sophie," admitted Werner Schwarz. "The meeting happened at Sophie."

"Too bad," said Navot. "I've always liked the name Sophie."

30

VIENNA WOODS, AUSTRIA

Sophie was a safe flat in East Berlin near Unter den Linden. The building was an old Soviet-style monstrosity with several courtyards and lots of ways in and out. A girl lived there; she went by the name Marguerite. She was about thirty, skinny as a waif, pale as milk. The flat itself was quite large. Apparently, it had belonged to some Stasi colonel before the Wall came down. There were two entrances, the main door off the landing and a second one in the kitchen that led to a little-used flight of service stairs. It was classic old-school tradecraft, thought Uzi Navot, as he listened to Werner Schwarz's description. A Moscow Center–trained hood never set foot in an apartment that didn't have an escape hatch. Neither, for that matter, did an Office-trained hood.

"Which door did you use?" asked Navot.

"The front."

"And Sergei? I suppose he's a backdoor man."

"Always."

"And the girl? Did she stay or go?"

"Usually, she served us something to eat and drink and then beat it. But not that day."

"What did she do?"

"She wasn't there."

"At whose request did the meeting take place?"

"Sergei's."

"Routine?"

"Crash."

"How was it arranged?"

"Thursday-night phone call, wrong number. 'Is Fraulein Sophie there?' I made up an excuse to consult our German partners on a pressing security matter and flew to Berlin the next day. I spent the morning at BfV headquarters and popped over to the safe flat on my way to the airport. Sergei was already there."

"What was so urgent?"

"Konstantin Kirov."

"He mentioned Kirov by name?"

"Of course not."

"What exactly did he say?"

"He said there was going to be a considerable amount of intelligence activity in Vienna in the coming days. Israeli, British, Russian. He wanted my service to take no steps to interfere. He suggested it involved a defector."

"An SVR defector?"

"Come on, Uzi. What else would it be?"

"Did he mention that a Russian assassin was going to blow the defector's brains out?"

"Not specifically, but he did say Allon would be dropping into town for the festivities. He said he would be staying at a safe flat."

"Did he have the address?"

"Second District, near the Karmeliterplatz. He said there was going to be some unpleasantness. He wanted us to follow Moscow's lead and place the blame squarely on the Israelis."

"And it never occurred to you to tell me?"

"I would have ended up like that Kirov fellow."

"You might still." The sun was hovering a few degrees above the horizon, blazing through the trees. Navot reckoned they had about twenty minutes of daylight at most. "What if Sergei Morosov had been lying to you, Werner? What if they'd been planning to kill my chief?"

"Official Austria would not have shed a tear."

Navot clenched and unclenched his fist several times and counted slowly to ten, but it was no good. The blow landed in Werner Schwarz's fattened abdomen where it would leave no mark. It went deep. Deep enough so that Navot, at least for a moment, wondered whether his old asset would ever get up again.

"But that's not all Sergei told you, is it?" Navot asked of the figure writhing and choking at his feet. "He was fairly confident I would come calling on you after Kirov was killed."

Werner Schwarz gave no answer; he wasn't capable of it.

"Shall I go on, Werner, or would you like to pick up the story? The part about Sergei telling you to leave me with the impression that MI6's Head of Station in Vienna had a girlfriend in Switzerland. They killed her, too, by the way," lied Navot. "I suppose you're next. Frankly, I'm surprised you're still alive."

Navot reached down and effortlessly hauled the fat Austrian to his feet.

"So it was true?" gasped Werner Schwarz. "There really was a girl?"

Navot placed his hand in the center of Werner Schwarz's back and sent him stumbling along the footpath. What remained of the sun was now at their backs. Mikhail led the way through the fading light.

"What are they up to?" asked Schwarz. "What are they playing at?"

"We haven't a clue," answered Navot untruthfully. "But you're going to help us find out. Otherwise, we're going to tell your chief and your minister that you've been working for Moscow Center. By the time we're finished, the world will believe *you* were the one driving the car that killed Alistair Hughes in Bern."

"This is the way you treat me, Uzi? After everything I've done for you?"

"If I were in your position, I'd watch my step. You have one chance to save yourself. You're working for me again. Exclusively," added Navot. "No more double and triple games."

Their shadows were gone, the trees were all but invisible. Mikhail was a faint black line.

"I know it won't change anything," said Werner Schwarz, "but I want you to know—"

"You're right," said Navot, cutting him off. "It won't change anything."

"I'll need a bit of money to tide me over."

"Careful, Werner. The snow is slippery, and it's dark now."

31

ANDALUSIA, SPAIN

That same afternoon, in the bone-white town in the mountains of Andalusia, the old woman known derisively as *la loca* and *la roja* sat at her desk in the alcove beneath her stairs, writing about the moment she first set eyes on the man who would forever alter the course of her life. Her first draft, which she had tossed onto the grate in disgust, had been a purple passage full of violins and beating hearts and swelling breasts. Now she adopted the spare prose of a journalist, with an emphasis on time, date, and place—half past one o'clock on a chill winter's afternoon in early 1962, the bar of the seaside St. Georges Hotel in Beirut. He was drinking vodka and V8 juice and reading his post, a handsome if somewhat battered man, recently turned fifty, with blue eyes set within a deeply lined face and an excruciating stammer she found irresistible. She was twenty-four at the time, a committed communist, and very beautiful. She told him her name, and he told her his, which she already knew. He was perhaps the most famous, or infamous, correspondent in Beirut.

"Which paper do you write for?" he asked.

"Whichever one will print my stories."

"Are you any good?"

"I think so, but the editors in Paris aren't so sure."

"Perhaps I can be of help. I know a good many important people in the Middle East."

"So I've heard."

He smiled warmly. "Sit down. Have a d-d-drink with me."

"It's a bit early in the day, isn't it?"

"Nonsense. They make a fierce martini. I taught them how."

And that, she wrote, was how it all began, a drink at the bar of the St. Georges, then another, and then, inadvisably, a third, after which she could scarcely stand, let alone walk. Gallantly, he insisted on seeing her back to her flat, where they made love for the first time. In describing the act, she once again resorted to the unadorned prose of a reporter, for her memories of the event were fogged by alcohol. She recalled only that he had been exceedingly tender and rather skillful. They made love again the following afternoon, and the afternoon after that. It was then, with a cold Mediterranean wind rattling the windows, that she screwed up the nerve to ask whether any of the things they had said about him in England in the 1950s were true.

"Do I look like the kind of man who could d-d-do that?"

"You don't, actually."

"It was an American witch hunt. They're the worst people in the world, the Americans, with the Israelis a close second."

But her thoughts were running ahead of her pencil, and her

hand was growing weary. She glanced at her plastic wristwatch and was surprised to see it was nearly six; she had written all afternoon. Having skipped lunch, she was famished, and there was nothing edible in the pantry, for she had skipped her daily visit to the supermarket, too. She decided an evening in town might do her good. A quartet from Madrid was performing a program of Vivaldi in one of the churches, hardly daring material but it would be a welcome break from the television. The village was a destination for tourists but something of a cultural wasteland. There were other places in Andalusia where she would have preferred to settle after the divorce—Seville, for one—but Comrade Lavrov had chosen the bone-white village in the mountains. "No one will ever find you there," he had said. And by "no one," he meant her child.

It was cold outside and a wind was getting up. Eighty-seven steps along the paseo a van was parked along the rocky verge, haphazardly, as though it had been abandoned. The winding streets of the town smelled of cooking; lights burned warmly in the windows of the little houses. She entered the one restaurant in the Calle San Juan were she was still treated respectfully and was shown to a lesser table. She ordered a glass of sherry and an assortment of tapas and then opened the paperback novel she had brought along for protection. *And what does anyone know about traitors, or why Judas did what he did* . . . What indeed? she thought. He had fooled everyone, even her, the woman with whom he had shared the most intimate of human acts. He had lied to her with his body and with his lips, and yet when he asked for the thing she loved most, she had given it to him. And this was her punishment, to be an old woman, pitied and reviled, sitting alone in a café in a land not her own. If only they had not met that afternoon in the bar of the St. Georges Hotel in Beirut. If only she had declined his offer of a drink, and then another, and then, inadvisably, a third. *If only* . . .

The sherry arrived, a pale Manzanilla, and a moment later the first of the food. As she laid down her book she noticed the man watching her unreservedly from the end of the bar. Then she noticed the couple at the nearby table, and instantly she realized why a van had been parked along the paseo eighty-seven steps from her villa. How little their tradecraft had changed.

She ate her meal slowly, if only to punish them, and leaving the restaurant hurried to the church for the recital. It was poorly attended and uninspired. The couple from the restaurant sat four pews behind her; the man, on the opposite side of the nave. He approached her after the performance, as she walked among the orange trees in the square.

"Did you enjoy it?" he asked in labored Spanish.

"Bourgeois drivel."

His smile was the one he reserved for young children and foolish old women. "Still fighting the same old war? Still waving the same old banner? I'm Señor Karpov, by the way. I was sent by our friend. Allow me to walk you home."

"That's how I got into this mess."

"I beg your pardon?"

"Never mind."

She set out along the darkened street. The Russian walked beside her. He had attempted to dress down for the village but had not quite succeeded. His loafers were too polished, his overcoat too stylish. She thought of the old days when it was possible to spot a Russian intelligence officer by the poor quality of his suit and by his dreadful shoes. Like Comrade Lavrov, she remembered, on the day he brought her the letter from the famous

English journalist she had known in Beirut. But not this one, she thought. Karpov was definitely a new Russian.

"Your Spanish is dreadful," she declared. "Where are you from?"

"The Madrid *rezidentura.*"

"In that case, Spain has nothing to fear from the SVR."

"They warned me about your sharp tongue."

"What else did they warn you about?"

He didn't answer.

"It's been a long time," she said. "I was beginning to think I would never hear from the Center again."

"Surely, you've noticed the money in your bank account."

"The first of every month, never a day late."

"Others are not so fortunate."

"Few," she countered, "have given so much." Their footfalls echoed in the dead silence of the narrow street, as did those of the two support officers, who followed several paces behind. "I was hoping you might have something for me other than money."

"As a matter of fact, I do." He drew an envelope from his stylish coat and held it aloft between two fingers.

"Let me see it."

"Not here." He returned the letter to his pocket. "Our mutual friends would like to make you a generous offer."

"Would they?"

"A holiday in Russia. All expenses paid."

"Russia in the dead of winter? How could I possibly resist?"

"St. Petersburg is lovely this time of year."

"I still call it Leningrad."

"Like my grandparents," he said. "We've arranged an apartment overlooking the Neva and the Winter Palace. I can assure you, you will be very comfortable."

"I prefer Moscow to Leningrad. Leningrad is an imported city. Moscow is the real Russia."

"Then we'll find something for you near the Kremlin."

"Sorry, not interested. It's not my Russia any longer. It's your Russia now."

"It's the same Russia."

"You've become everything we fought against!" she snapped. "Everything we despised. My God, he's probably turning somersaults in that grave of his."

"Who?"

Apparently, Karpov did not know the reason she received the rather substantial sum of ten thousand euros in her bank account the first of each month, never a day late.

"Why now?" she asked. "Why do they want me to come to Moscow after all these years?"

"My brief is limited."

"Like your Spanish." He absorbed her insult in silence. "I'm surprised you bothered to ask. Once upon a time, you would have bundled me onto a freighter and taken me to Moscow against my will."

"Our methods have changed."

"I doubt that very much." They had reached the base of the town. She could just make out her little villa at the edge of the crag. She had left the lights on so she could find her way home in the dark. "How's Comrade Lavrov?" she asked suddenly. "Still with us?"

"It is not in my purview to say."

"And Modin?" she asked. "He's dead now, isn't he?"

"I wouldn't know."

"I don't suppose you would. He was a great man, a true professional." Contemptuously, she looked him up and down, Comrade

Karpov, the new Russian. "I believe you have something that belongs to me."

"Actually, it belongs to Moscow Center." He fished the envelope from his pocket again and handed it over. "You may read it, but you cannot keep it."

She carried the envelope a few paces along the street and opened it in the glow of an iron lamp. Inside was a single sheet of paper, typewritten, in stilted French. She stopped reading after a few lines; the words were counterfeit. She returned the letter coolly and set out alone through the darkness, counting her steps, thinking of him. One way or another, voluntarily or by force, she would be leaving for Russia soon, she was sure of it. Perhaps it would not be so horrid after all. Leningrad was really quite lovely, and in Moscow she could visit his grave. *Have a d-d-drink with me* . . . If only she had said no. *If only* . . .

32

FRANKFURT—TEL AVIV—PARIS

Globaltek Consulting occupied two floors of a glassy modern office tower on the Mainzer Landstrasse in Frankfurt. Its shimmering Web site offered all manner of services, most of which were of no interest to its clients. Companies hired Globaltek for one reason, to gain access to the Kremlin and by extension the lucrative Russian market. All of Globaltek's senior advisers were Russian nationals, as were most of the support and administrative staff. Sergei Morosov's advertised area of expertise was the Russian banking sector. His curriculum vitae spoke of an elite Russian education and business career but made no mention of the fact he was a full colonel in the SVR.

Planning for his defection to the State of Israel commenced within minutes of Uzi Navot's return to King Saul Boulevard from Vienna. It would not be a typical defection, with its mating rituals and offers of safe harbor and a new identity. It would be of the crash variety, and highly coerced. Furthermore, it would have to be conducted in such a way that Moscow Center would not suspect Sergei Morosov was in the hands of the opposition. All undercover intelligence officers, regardless of their country or service, maintained regular contact with their controllers at headquarters; it was a basic operating principle of the trade. If Sergei Morosov missed more than one check-in, Moscow Center would automatically make one of three assumptions—that he had defected, that he had been kidnapped, or that he had been killed. Only under the third scenario, Sergei Morosov's death, would the SVR believe its secrets to be safe.

"So you're going to kill *another* Russian?" asked the prime minister. "Is that what you're telling me?"

"Only temporarily," answered Gabriel. "And only in the minds of his controllers at Moscow Center."

It was late, a few minutes after ten in the evening, and the prime minister's office was in semidarkness. "They're not fools," he said. "Eventually, they're going to figure out he's alive and well and in your hands."

"Eventually," agreed Gabriel.

"How long will it take?"

"Three or four days, a week at the outside."

"What happens then?"

"That depends on how many secrets he has rattling around in his head."

The prime minister regarded Gabriel in silence for a moment. On the wall behind his desk, the portrait of Theodor Herzl did the same. "The Russians aren't likely to take this lying down. They're liable to retaliate."

"How much worse can it get?"

"A lot worse. Especially if it's directed at you."

"They've tried to kill me before. Several times, actually."

"One of these days, they might succeed." The prime minister picked up the single-page document Gabriel had brought from King Saul Boulevard. "This represents a lot of valuable resources. I'm not prepared to let this run indefinitely."

"It won't. In fact, once I get my hands around Sergei Morosov's neck, I suspect it will be over very quickly."

"How quickly?"

"Three or four days." Gabriel shrugged. "A week at the outside."

The prime minister signed the authorization and slid it across the desk. "Remember Shamron's Eleventh Commandment," he said. "Don't get caught."

The next day was a Thursday—an ordinary Thursday throughout much of the world, with a typical allotment of murder, mayhem, and human misery—but inside King Saul Boulevard, no one would ever speak of it again without first uttering the word *black*. For it was on Black Thursday that the Office went on war footing. The prime minister had made it clear Gabriel was playing on borrowed time, and he resolved not to waste a minute of it. A week from Friday, he decreed, the shade would be drawn in the window of a Vienna apartment. And the following Tuesday evening, a phone would ring in the same apartment, and a caller would ask for one of four women: Trudi, Anna, Sophie, or Sabine. Trudi was Linz, Anna was Munich, Sophie was Berlin, and Sabine was Strasbourg, capital of the Alsace region of France. The Office would have no say in choosing the venue; it was Sergei Morosov's party. Or, as Gabriel put it coldly, it was Sergei's going-away party.

Trudi, Anna, Sophie, Sabine: four safe flats, four cities. Gabriel ordered Yaakov Rossman, his chief of Special Operations, to plan for Sergei Morosov's abduction from all four sites. "Out of the question. Not possible, Gabriel, really. We're stretched to the breaking point already chasing Sergei around Frankfurt and keeping an eye on Werner Schwarz in Vienna. The watchers are doubled over. They're folding like deck chairs." Yaakov then did precisely as Gabriel asked, though for operational reasons he stated a clear preference for Sabine. "She's lovely, she's the girl of our dreams. Friendly country, lots of bolt-holes. Get me Sabine, and I'll get you Sergei Morosov, gift-wrapped with a bow on top."

"I'd rather have him bruised and a little bloody."

"I can do that, too. But get me Sabine. And don't forget the body," said Yaakov over his shoulder as he sulked out Gabriel's door. "We need the body. Otherwise, the Russians won't believe a word of it."

Black Thursday was followed by Black Friday, and Black Friday by a black weekend. And by the time the sun rose on Black Monday, King Saul Boulevard was at war with itself. Banking and Identity were in open rebellion, Travel and Housekeeping were secretly plotting a coup, and Yaakov and Eli Lavon were barely speaking. It fell to Uzi Navot to play the role of in-house referee and peacemaker because more often than not Gabriel was one of the combatants.

There was little mystery as to the source of his dark mood. It was Ivan who drove him. Ivan Borisovich Kharkov, international arms dealer, friend of the Russian president, and Gabriel's personal bête noire. Ivan had taken a child from Chiara's womb, and in a frozen birch forest outside Moscow he had placed a gun to the side of her head. *Enjoy watching your wife die, Allon . . .* One never forgot a sight like that, and surely one never forgave. Ivan was the warning shot the rest of the world missed. Ivan was proof that Russia was once more reverting to type.

On the Wednesday of that terrible week, Gabriel slipped from King Saul Boulevard and rode in his motorcade across the West Bank to Amman, where he met with Fareed Barakat, the Anglophile chief of Jordanian intelligence. After an hour of small talk, Gabriel politely requested use of one of the king's many Gulfstream jets for an operation involving a certain gentleman of Russian persuasion. And Barakat readily agreed, for he loathed the Russians almost as much as Gabriel did. The Butcher of Damascus and his Russian backers had driven several hundred thousand Syrian refugees across the border into Jordan. Fareed Barakat was anxious to return the favor.

"But you won't make a mess in the cabin, will you? I'll never hear the end of it. His Majesty is very particular about his planes and his motorcycles."

Gabriel used the aircraft to fly to London, where he briefed Graham Seymour on the current state of the operation. Then he popped into Paris to have a quiet word with Paul Rousseau, the professorial chief of the Alpha Group, an elite counterterrorism unit of the DGSI. Its officers were skilled practitioners in the art of deception, and Paul Rousseau was their undisputed leader and lodestar. Gabriel met him in a safe flat in the twentieth arrondissement. He spent most of the time batting away the smoke of Rousseau's pipe.

"I wasn't able to find an exact fit," the Frenchman said as he handed Gabriel a photograph, "but this one should do."

"Nationality?"

"The police were never able to determine that."

"How long has he been—"

"Four months," said Rousseau. "He's a bit ripe but not offensive."

"The fire will take care of that. And remember," Gabriel added, "take your time with the investigation. It's never good to rush in a situation like this."

That was midmorning of the Friday, the same morning a shade was drawn in the window of an apartment in Vienna. The following Tuesday evening, a telephone rang in the same apartment, and a caller asked to speak to a woman who did not reside there. The next morning the members of Gabriel's team boarded flights for five different European cities. All, however, would eventually make their way to the same destination. It was Sabine, the girl of their dreams.

33

TENLEYTOWN, WASHINGTON

Rebecca Manning awoke the next morning with a start. She had been dreaming, unpleasantly, but as always she had no memory of the subject matter. Outside her bedroom window the sky was dishwater gray. She checked the time on her personal iPhone. It was six fifteen, eleven fifteen at Vauxhall Cross. The time difference meant her day typically started early. In fact, it was rare she was permitted to sleep so late.

Rising, she pulled on a robe against the chill and padded downstairs to the kitchen, where she smoked her first L&B of the day while waiting for the coffee to brew. The house she rented was on Warren Street, in the section of Northwest Washington known as Tenleytown. She had inherited it from a consular officer who had lived there with his wife and two young children. It was quite small, about the size of a typical English cottage, with a peculiar Tudor facade above the portico. At the end of the flagstone walkway stood an iron lamp, and across the street was a communal green garden. The lamp burned weakly, almost invisibly, in the flat light of morning. Rebecca had switched it on the previous evening and had neglected to switch it off again before going to bed.

She drank her coffee from a bowl, with frothy steamed milk, and skimmed the headlines on her iPhone. There were no more stories about Alistair's death. The news from America was the usual fare—a looming government shutdown, another school shooting, moral outrage over a presidential tryst with an adult film star. Like most MI6 officers who served in Washington, Rebecca had come to respect the professionalism and immense technical capabilities of America's intelligence community, even if she didn't always agree with the underlying policy priorities. She found less to admire, however, in America's culture and politics. It was a crude and unsophisticated country, she thought, always lurching from crisis to crisis, seemingly unaware of the fact its power was fading. The postwar global security and economic institutions America had so painstakingly built were crumbling. Soon they would be swept away, and with them would go the Pax Americana. MI6 was already planning for the post-American world. So, too, was Rebecca.

She carried the bowl of coffee upstairs to her room and pulled on a cold-weather tracksuit and a pair of Nike trainers. Despite her pack-a-day habit, she was an avid runner. She saw no contradiction in the two activities; she only hoped that one might counteract the effects of the other. Downstairs, she zipped her iPhone, a house key, and a ten-dollar bill into the pocket of her trousers. On her way out the door, she switched off the lamp at the end of the walk.

Sunlight was starting to seep through the clouds. She performed a few halfhearted stretching exercises beneath the shelter of the portico while scanning the quiet street. Under the rules of the Anglo-American intelligence accord, the FBI was not supposed to follow her or keep watch on her home. Still, she always checked to make certain the Americans were living up to their word. It wasn't difficult; the street offered little protection for watchers. Commuters used it occasionally, but only residents and their guests and housekeepers ever parked there. Rebecca kept a detailed mental catalogue of the vehicles and their license plates. She had always been good at memory games, especially games involving numbers.

She set out at an easy pace along Warren Street and then turned onto Forty-Second and followed it to Nebraska Avenue. As always, her pace slowed as she passed the house on the corner, a large three-story colonial with tan brick, white trim, black shutters, and a stubby addition on the southern-facing flank.

The addition had not been there in 1949 when a deeply respected MI6 officer, a man who had helped to build America's intelligence capability during World War II, moved into the house with his long-suffering wife and young children. It was soon a popular gathering spot for Washington's intelligence elite, a place where secrets flowed as easily as the martinis and the wine, secrets that eventually found their way to Moscow Center. On a warm late-spring evening in 1951, the deeply respected MI6 officer removed a hand trowel from the potting shed in the rear garden. Then, from a hiding place in the basement, he retrieved his miniature KGB camera and supply of Russian film. He concealed the items in a metal canister and drove into the Maryland countryside, where he buried the evidence of his treachery in a shallow grave.

Down by the river near Swainson Island, at the base of an enormous sycamore tree. The stuff is probably still there if you look . . .

Rebecca continued along Nebraska Avenue, past the Department of Homeland Security, around Ward Circle, and through the campus of American University. The rear entrance of the sprawling Russian Embassy compound, with its enormous SVR *rezidentura* and permanent FBI surveillance presence, was on Tunlaw Road in Glover Park. From there, she headed south to Georgetown. The streets of the West Village were still quiet, but rush-hour traffic was pouring across Key Bridge onto M Street.

The sun was now shining brightly. Rebecca entered Dean & DeLuca and ordered a café latte and carried it outside to a cobbled alleyway stretching between M Street and the C&O Canal. She sat down next to three young women dressed, as she was, in athletic wear. There was a yoga studio on the opposite side of M Street, thirty-one paces from the table where Rebecca now sat, ninety-three feet exactly. The class the three young women would be attending commenced at 7:45. It would be taught by a Brazilian citizen named Eva Fernandes, a trim, blond, strikingly attractive woman who was at that moment walking along the sunlit pavement, an athletic bag over her shoulder.

Rebecca took out her iPhone and checked the time. It was 7:23. For the next several minutes she drank her coffee and saw to a few personal e-mails and texts while trying to block out the conversation of the three women at the next table. They really were insufferable, she thought, these pampered millennial snowflakes with their yoga mats and their designer leggings and their contempt for concepts such as hard work and competition. She only wished she'd brought along a packet of L&Bs. One whiff of smoke would have sent them scurrying.

It was now 7:36. Rebecca sent one final text before returning the phone to her pocket. It rang a few seconds later, giving her a terrible start. It was Andrew Crawford, a junior officer from the station.

"Something wrong?" he asked.

"Not at all. Just out for a run."

"I'm afraid you'll have to cut it short. Our friend from Virginia would like a word."

"Can you give me a hint?"

"NSA is picking up rumblings from AQAP." Al-Qaeda on the Arabian Peninsula. "Apparently, they're rather interested in getting back in the game. It seems London is in their sights."

"What time does he want to see me?"

"Ten minutes ago."

She swore softly.

"Where are you?"

"Georgetown."

"Don't move, I'll send a car for you."

Rebecca killed the connection and watched the three young snowflakes floating across the street. The spigot was open again, the cloud had lifted. She thought about the house on Nebraska Avenue and the man, the deeply respected MI6 officer, burying his camera in the Maryland countryside. *The stuff is probably still there if you look* . . . Perhaps one day she would do just that.

34

STRASBOURG, FRANCE

The Germans had left their indelible mark on the architecture of Strasbourg, the much-conquered city on the western bank of the river Rhine, but Sabine was defiantly French in appearance. She stood on the corner of the rue de Berne and rue de Soleure, tan and vaguely Mediterranean, with wide balconies and white aluminum shutters. Two businesses occupied the ground floor, a Turkish kebab stand and a forlorn hair studio for men whose owner spent many hours each day peering idly into the street. Between the two enterprises was the tenant entrance. The call buttons were located on the right side. The tiny nameplate for apartment 5B read BERGIER.

The building directly opposite wore its Germanness without apology. Gabriel arrived there unaccompanied by bodyguards at four fifteen. He found apartment 3A in a state of permanent night, with the shades tightly drawn and the lights dimmed. Eli Lavon was hunched over an open laptop, as he had been that night in Vienna, but now Yaakov Rossman was hovering over him, pointing at something on the screen like a sommelier offering advice to a dithering customer. Mikhail and Keller, pistols in their outstretched hands, were pivoting with the silence of ballet dancers through the doorway to the kitchen.

"Can you please make them stop?" begged Yaakov. "They're driving us to distraction. Besides, it's not as if they've never cleared a room before."

Gabriel watched Mikhail and Keller repeat the exercise. Then he looked down at the computer screen and saw a blinking blue light moving southward between Heidelberg and Karlsruhe, on the German side of the border.

"Is that Sergei?"

"Two of my boys," explained Lavon. "Sergei's several hundred meters ahead of them. He left Frankfurt about forty minutes ago. No SVR gorillas, no Germans. He's clean."

"So was Konstantin Kirov," said Gabriel gloomily. "What about Werner?"

"He caught the Vienna-to-Paris sunrise express and was inside the Interior Ministry by ten. He and his French colleagues, including a certain Paul Rousseau from the Alpha Group, had a working lunch. Then Werner complained of a migraine and said he was going to his hotel to rest. He went to the Gare de l'Est instead and caught the two fifty-five to Strasbourg. He's due in at four forty. It's a ten-minute walk at most from the train station."

Gabriel tapped the blinking blue light, which was passing through the small German town of Ettlingen. "And Sergei?"

"If he makes a beeline to the flat, he'll arrive at four twenty. If he takes a trip to the dry cleaners first . . ."

On a second computer was an exterior shot of the apartment building code-named Sabine. Gabriel pointed toward the figure standing in the doorway of the men's hair salon. "What about him?"

"Yaakov thinks we should kill him," said Lavon. "I was hoping to find a more just solution."

"The solution," said Gabriel, "is a customer."

"He's only had two all day," said Yaakov.

"So we'll find him a third."

"Who?"

Gabriel tousled Lavon's unruly head of hair.

"I'm a little busy at the moment."

"What about Doron?"

"He's one of my best pavement artists. And he's very particular about his hair."

Gabriel leaned down and tapped a few keys on the laptop. Then he watched Mikhail and Keller pirouetting soundlessly through the doorway.

"Don't even think about it," said Eli Lavon.

"Me? I'm the chief of Israeli intelligence, for God's sake."

"Yes," said Lavon as he watched the approaching blue light. "Tell that to Saladin."

The blinking blue light entered Strasbourg at four fifteen, and on Gabriel's orders the watchers broke off their pursuit. It was one thing to follow an SVR hood at a hundred miles an hour along the Autobahn, quite another to tail him through the quiet streets of an ancient Franco-German city on the banks of the river Rhine.

Besides, Gabriel knew where the SVR hood was going. It was the building code-named Sabine on the opposite side of the rue de Berne. The building with two businesses on the ground floor—a Turkish kebab café where two former elite soldiers, one Israeli, the other British, were now partaking of a late lunch, and a men's hair salon that had just received its third customer of the day.

The SVR hood made a first motorized pass at 4:25 and a second at 4:31. Finally, at 4:35, he parked his BMW sedan directly beneath the window of the command post and crossed the street. When they saw him next it was at 4:39, and he was standing on the balcony of apartment 5B. In the corner of his mouth was an unlit cigarette, and in his right hand was something that might have been a book of matches. The cigarette was the signal. Lighted cigarette meant the coast was clear. Unlit cigarette meant abort. Old school all the way, thought Gabriel. *Moscow Rules* . . .

At 4:40 a train arrived at the Gare de Strasbourg, and ten minutes later an Austrian secret policeman who was supposed to be recovering from a migraine in a Paris hotel room strolled past the window of the Turkish café. He glanced toward the balcony five floors above, where the SVR hood's cigarette glowed like the running light of a ship. Then he went to the door of the building and pressed the call button for apartment 5B. Five floors above, the SVR hood flicked his cigarette carelessly into the street and disappeared through the French doors.

"Move!" said Yaakov Rossman into the microphone of his miniature radio, and in the Turkish café the two former elite soldiers rose simultaneously to their feet. Outside on the pavement, they walked with no visible haste toward the tenant entrance, where the Austrian was now holding the door for them. Then the door closed and the three men vanished from view.

It was at this point, for reasons known only to himself, that

Eli Lavon began recording the feed from the exterior surveillance camera. The final unedited file was five minutes and eighteen seconds in length, and like the security video from the Schweizerhof Hotel, it would become required viewing inside King Saul Boulevard, at least for those of sufficient seniority and clearance.

The action commences with the arrival of a Ford panel van, from which two men alight and casually enter the building. They reappear four minutes later, each carrying one end of a long and quite obviously heavy duffel bag containing a Russian intelligence officer. The bag is placed in the cargo hold of the van, and the van pulls from the curb, just as the two former elite soldiers, one Israeli, the other British, exit the apartment building. They cross the street to a BMW sedan and climb inside. The engine starts, lights flicker to life. Then the car turns onto the rue de Soleure and slides from the shot.

There is no recording of what happened next, for Gabriel would not allow it. In fact, he insisted the camera be entirely disconnected before he stepped once more into the somber quiet of the rue de Berne. There he dropped into the passenger seat of a Citroën that never quite came to a full stop. The man behind the wheel was Christian Bouchard, Paul Rousseau's chamberlain and strong right hand. He looked like one of those characters in French films who always had affairs with women who smoked cigarettes after making love.

"Any problems?" asked Bouchard.

"My back is killing me," answered Gabriel. "Otherwise, everything is fine."

The airport was southwest of the city and bordered by farmland. By the time Gabriel and Christian Bouchard arrived, the Ford transit van was parked at the tail of a Gulfstream jet owned by the Jordanian monarch. Gabriel climbed the airstair and ducked into the cabin. The long duffel bag lay vertically on the floor. He tugged the zipper, exposing a red and swollen face, heavily bound with silver duct tape. The eyes were closed. They would remain closed for the duration of the flight. Or perhaps a bit longer, thought Gabriel, depending on the Russian's metabolism. Generally speaking, Russians handled their sedatives about as well as they handled their vodka.

Gabriel closed the zipper and settled into one of the swivel seats for takeoff. The Russians weren't fools, he thought. Eventually, they would piece together what had happened. He reckoned he had three or four days to find the mole at the pinnacle of the Anglo-American intelligence establishment. A week at the outside.

35

UPPER GALILEE, ISRAEL

There are interrogation centers scattered throughout Israel. Some are in restricted areas of the Negev Desert, others are tucked away, unnoticed, in the middle of cities. And one lies just off a road with no name that runs between Rosh Pina, one of the oldest Jewish settlements in Israel, and the mountain hamlet of Amuka. The track that leads to it is dusty and rocky and fit for only Jeeps and SUVs. There is a fence topped with concertina wire and a guard shack staffed by tough-looking youths in khaki vests. Behind the fence is a small colony of bungalows and a single building of corrugated metal where the prisoners are kept. The guards are forbidden to disclose their place of work, even to their wives and parents. The site is as black as black can be. It is the absence of color and light.

Sergei Morosov knew none of this. In fact, he knew little if anything at all. Not his location or the time of day, and not the identity of his captors. He knew only that he was very cold, that he was hooded and secured to a metal chair in a state of semi-undress, and that he was being subjected to dangerously loud music. It was "Angel of Death" by the thrash metal band Slayer. Even the guards, who were a hard-bitten lot, felt a little sorry for him.

On the advice of Yaakov Rossman, an experienced interrogator, Gabriel allowed the stress-and-isolation phase of the proceedings to last thirty-six hours, which was longer than he preferred. The clock was already working against them. There were reports in the French media regarding a road accident near Strasbourg. The known facts were sparse—a BMW, a fiery crash, a single badly burned body, as yet unidentified, or so said the French authorities. It seemed Moscow Center knew full well the identity of the dead man, at least it thought it did, because a pair of hoods from the Berlin *rezidentura* paid a visit to Sergei Morosov's apartment in Frankfurt the evening after his disappearance. Gabriel knew this because the apartment was under Office surveillance. He feared the SVR's next stop would be Sergei Morosov's last known contact, a senior official from the Austrian security service named Werner Schwarz. For that reason, Werner Schwarz was under Office surveillance, too.

It was 12:17 p.m.—the time was carefully noted in the facility's logbook—when the thrash metal music in the isolation chamber finally fell silent. The guards removed the bindings from Sergei Morosov's hands and ankles and led him to a shower where, blindfolded and hooded, he was allowed to wash. Next they dressed him in a blue-and-white tracksuit and frog-marched him, still blindfolded, to the interrogation hut, where he was secured to another chair. Five more minutes elapsed before the hood and blindfold were removed. The Russian blinked several times while his eyes grew accustomed to the sudden light. Then he recoiled in fear and began to flail wildly against the restraints.

"Take care, Sergei," said Gabriel calmly. "Otherwise, you're liable to dislocate something. Besides, there's no need to be afraid. Welcome to Israel. And, yes, we accept your offer to defect. We'd like to begin your debriefing as quickly as possible. The sooner we get started, the sooner you can begin your new life. We have a nice little place picked out for you in the Negev, somewhere your friends at Moscow Center will never find you."

Gabriel said all this in German, and Sergei Morosov, when he ceased his thrashing, responded in the same language. "You'll never get away with this, Allon."

"Accepting a defecting SVR officer? It happens all the time. It's how the game is played."

"I made no offer to defect. You kidnapped me." The Russian looked at the four windowless walls of the interrogation room, and at the two guards standing to his left, and at Mikhail, who was reclining to his right. Lastly, he looked at Gabriel and asked, "Am I really in Israel?"

"Where else would you be?"

"I rather thought I was in the hands of the British."

"No such luck. That said, MI6 is anxious to have a word with you. Can't blame them, really. After all, you murdered their Vienna Head of Station."

"Alistair Hughes? The newspapers said it was an accident."

"I would advise you," cautioned Gabriel, "to choose another path."

"And what path is that?"

"Cooperation. Tell us what we want to know, and you'll be treated better than you deserve."

"And if I refuse?"

Gabriel looked at Mikhail. "Recognize him, Sergei?"

"No," lied Morosov badly. "We've never met."

"That's not what I asked. What I asked," said Gabriel, "is whether you recognize him. He was in Vienna that night. Your assassin took four shots at him, but somehow all four missed. His marksmanship was a little better when it came to Kirov. Konstantin took two in the face, hollow point, so there could be no open casket at his funeral. Unless you start talking, my associate and I are going to return the favor. Oh, we won't do the deed ourselves. We're going to make a gift of you to some friends of ours across the border in Syria. They've suffered greatly at the hands of the Butcher of Damascus and his Russian benefactors, and they'd love nothing more than to get their hands on a real live SVR officer."

The silence in the room was heavy. At last, Sergei Morosov said, "I had nothing to do with Kirov."

"Of course you did, Sergei. You warned Werner Schwarz a few days before the assassination that there was going to be some unpleasantness in Vienna involving an SVR defector. You then instructed Werner to follow the Kremlin's lead and point the finger of suspicion toward our service."

"He's a dead man. And so are you, Allon."

Gabriel sailed on as though he hadn't heard the remark. "You also instructed Werner to whisper a bit of gossip into my deputy's ear regarding the private life of Alistair Hughes. Something about frequent trips across the border to Switzerland. You did this," said Gabriel, "because you wanted to leave us with the impression Alistair was on your payroll. The goal of this operation was to protect the *real* spy, a mole at the pinnacle of the Anglo-American intelligence establishment."

"Mole?" asked Morosov. "You've been reading too many spy novels, Allon. There is no mole. Alistair was our asset. I should know, I was his control officer. I've been running him for years."

Gabriel only smiled. "Well played, Sergei. I admire your loyalty, but it's of no value here. Truth is the only currency we accept. And only the truth will prevent us from handing you over to our friends in Syria."

"I'm telling you the truth!"

"Try again."

Morosov feigned impassivity. "If you know so much," he said after a moment, "why do you need me?"

"You're going to help us fill in the blanks. In exchange, you will be well compensated and allowed to live out the rest of your life in our beautiful country."

"In a nice little place in the Negev?"

"I chose it myself."

"I'd rather take my chances across the border in Syria."

"I would advise you," said Gabriel, "to choose another path."

"Sorry, Allon," replied the Russian. "No such luck."

The Black Hawk flew east over the Golan Heights and crossed into Syrian airspace above the village of Kwdana. Its eventual destination was Jassim, a smallish city in the Daraa Governorate of southern Syria held by elements of the rebel Free Syrian Army. Under Gabriel's leadership, the Office had forged close ties with the non-jihadist Syrian opposition, and several thousand Syrians had been brought to Israel for medical treatment. In portions of the Daraa Governorate, if nowhere else in the Arab world, Gabriel Allon was a revered figure.

The helicopter never touched down on Syrian soil, that much is beyond dispute. The two guards on board claimed that Mikhail fixed a line to Sergei Morosov's handcuffs and dangled him above a seething encampment of rebel fighters. Mikhail, however, took issue with this account. Yes, he had *threatened* to lower Sergei into the mob, but it had never come to that. After one look at the fate that awaited him, the Russian had begged—yes, *begged*—to be taken back to Israel.

Whatever the case, Colonel Sergei Morosov was a changed man when he returned to the interrogation room. After first apologizing for his earlier intransigence, the Russian said he would be more than willing to offer any and all assistance to the Office in exchange for sanctuary and a reasonable financial settlement. He acknowledged, however, that Israel was not his first choice as a permanent home. He was no anti-Semite, mind you, but he had strong personal views about the Middle East and the plight of the Palestinians and had no desire to live among people whom he regarded as colonizers and oppressors.

"Give us a few months," said Gabriel. "If you still feel the same way, I'll reach out to one of our friends."

"I didn't know you had any."

"One or two," said Gabriel.

With that, they took him to one of the bungalows and allowed him to sleep. It was nearly 10:00 p.m. when finally he awoke. They gave him a change of clothing—proper clothing, not another tracksuit—and served him a dinner of warm borscht and chicken Kiev. At midnight, rested and fed, he was brought back to the interrogation room, where Gabriel waited, an open notebook before him.

"What is your name?" he asked.

"Sergei Morosov."

"Not your work name," said Gabriel. "Your real name."

"It's been so long, I'm not sure I remember it."

"Try," said Gabriel. "We have plenty of time."

Which wasn't at all the case; the clock was working against them. They had three or four days to find the mole, thought Gabriel. A week at the outside.

36

UPPER GALILEE, ISRAEL

His real name was Aleksander Yurchenko, but he had
shed it many years ago after his first posting abroad,
and no one, not even his sainted mother, called him
anything but Sergei. She had served as a typist at Lubyanka, and
later as personal secretary to KGB chairman Yuri Andropov, who
would eventually succeed Leonid Brezhnev as leader of the dying
Soviet Union. Sergei's father was also a servant of the old order. A
brilliant economist and Marxist theoretician, he had worked for
Gosplan, which produced the blueprint for the Soviet Union's cen-
trally planned economy known as the Five-Year Plan. They were
Orwellian documents, full of wishful thinking, that frequently set
output targets in terms of weight rather than actual units produced. Sergei's father, who lost faith in communism near the end

of his career, kept a framed Western cartoon above his desk in the family's Moscow apartment. It depicted a group of glum factory workers standing around a single nail the size of a Soviet ballistic missile. "Congratulations, Comrades!" declares the proud factory director. "We have met our quota for the current Five-Year Plan!"

Sergei's parents were by no means Party elites—the members of the *nomenklatura* who zipped through Moscow's traffic in special lanes, in the backs of Zil limousines—but they were Party members nonetheless, and as such they lived a life far beyond the reach of ordinary Russians. Their apartment was larger than most, and they had it entirely to themselves. Sergei attended a school reserved for the children of Party members and at eighteen entered the Moscow State Institute of International Relations, the Soviet Union's most prestigious university. There he studied political science and German. Many of his classmates entered the Soviet Union's diplomatic corps, but not Sergei. His mother, the personal secretary of a KGB legend, had other ideas.

The Red Banner Institute was the KGB's academy. It maintained four secluded sites scattered around Moscow, with the main campus at Chelobityevo, north of the Ring Road. Sergei arrived there in 1985. One of his classmates was the son of a KGB general. But not just any KGB general; he was the head of the First Chief Directorate, the KGB's foreign espionage division, a very powerful man indeed.

"The son had been spoiled rotten as a child. He'd been raised abroad and exposed to Western culture. He had blue jeans and Rolling Stones records, and thought he was much cooler than the rest of us. As it turned out, he wasn't terribly bright. After graduation they sent him to the Fifth Chief Directorate, which handled internal security. Thanks to his father, he did quite well for himself after the fall. He founded a bank and then diversified into a number of different fields, including international arms dealing. Perhaps you've heard of him. His name is—"

"Ivan Kharkov."

Sergei Morosov smiled. "Your old friend."

Because he came to the Red Banner Institute directly from university, Sergei Morosov's training period was three years in length. Upon graduation he was assigned to the First Chief Directorate and placed on the German operations desk at Moscow Center, the directorate's wooded headquarters in Yasenevo. A year later he was assigned to the *rezidentura* in East Berlin, where he witnessed the fall of the Berlin Wall, knowing full well the Soviet Union would crumble next. The end came in December 1991. "I was inside Yasenevo when they lowered the hammer and sickle at the Kremlin. We all got drunk, and we stayed drunk for the better part of the next decade."

In the post-Soviet era, the KGB was disbanded, renamed, reorganized, and renamed again. Eventually, the basic elements of the old organization were split into two new services: the FSB and the SVR. The FSB handled domestic security and counterintelligence, and took over the KGB's old central headquarters in Lubyanka Square. The SVR became Russia's new foreign intelligence service. Headquartered in Yasenevo, it was essentially the old First Chief Directorate of the KGB with a new name. The United States, ostensibly a Russian ally, remained the SVR's primary obsession, though officially the SVR referred to America as the "main target" instead of the "main enemy." NATO and Great Britain were also primary targets for collection.

"And Israel?" asked Gabriel.

"We never gave you more than a passing thought. That is, until you got into your feud with Ivan."

"What about you?" asked Gabriel. "How did Sergei Morosov fare in the new world order?"

He hung around Berlin, where he constructed a stay-behind network of agents that would spy the daylights out of the re-unified Germany for years to come. Then it was off to Helsinki where, under a new name, he served as deputy *rezident*. He became a *rezident* for the first time in 2004 in The Hague and then, in 2009, he reprised the role in Ottawa, an important post, given its proximity to the United States. Unfortunately, he got into a bit of trouble—"A girl and the Canadian minister of defense, water under the bridge"—and the Canadians told him to take a hike, quietly, so as not to start a tit-for-tat scandal. He cooled his heels at Moscow Center for a couple of years, changed his name and his face, and then returned to Germany as Sergei Morosov, a Russian banking specialist employed by Globaltek Consulting.

"The German services were so clueless, no one remembered me from my days in East Berlin."

"Does Globaltek do any actual consulting?"

"Quite a bit. And we're rather good, I must say. But mainly we function as a *rezidentura* in the heart of the German business community, and I'm the *rezident*."

"Not anymore," said Gabriel. "You're a defector now, but please continue."

Globaltek, said Sergei Morosov, served two functions. Its main task was to identify potential assets and steal German industrial technology, which Russia needed desperately. To that end, Globaltek ran numerous *kompromat* operations against prominent German businessmen. Most of the operations involved illicit payments of money, or sex.

"Women, boys, animals . . ." Sergei Morosov shrugged. "The Germans, Allon, are a freewheeling lot."

"And the second function?"

"We service sensitive assets."

"Assets who require special care because their exposure would create problems for the Kremlin." Gabriel paused, then added, "Assets like Werner Schwarz."

"Correct."

By any objective measure, Sergei Morosov continued, the Globaltek operation was a smashing success. Which was why he was surprised by the message that arrived in his encrypted mailbox on an unusually warm October afternoon.

"What was it?"

"A summons from Moscow Center."

"Surely," said Gabriel, "you returned home for consultations frequently."

"Of course. But this one was different."

"What did you do?"

Sergei Morosov did what any SVR officer would have done under similar circumstances. He put his affairs in order and penned a letter of farewell to his sainted mother. And in the morning, certain in the knowledge he would soon be dead, he boarded an Aeroflot flight to Moscow.

37

UPPER GALILEE, ISRAEL

Y ou've been to Moscow, yes?"

"Several times," admitted Gabriel.

"You like Moscow?"

"No."

"And Lubyanka?" wondered Sergei Morosov.

Again, Gabriel acknowledged what was already well known among Russian intelligence officers of a certain age and rank, that some years ago he had been arrested in Moscow and interrogated, violently, in the cellars of Lubyanka.

"But you've never been to Yasenevo, have you?" asked Sergei Morosov.

"No, never."

"Too bad. You might have liked it."

"I doubt it."

"Oh, they'll let almost anyone into Lubyanka these days," Sergei Morosov went on. "It's something of a tourist attraction. But Yasenevo is special. Yasenevo is—"

"Moscow Center."

Sergei Morosov smiled. "Would it be possible to have a sheet of paper and something to write with?"

"Why?"

"I'd like to draw a map of the grounds to help you better visualize what came next."

"I have a very good imagination."

"So I hear."

Yasenevo, Sergei Morosov resumed, is a world unto itself, a world of privilege and power, surrounded by miles of razor wire and patrolled at all hours by guards with vicious attack dogs. The main building is shaped like a giant cruciform. About a mile to the west, hidden in a dense forest, is a colony of twenty dachas reserved for senior officers. One dacha stands slightly alone and bears a small sign that reads INNER-BALTIC RESEARCH COMMITTEE, a nonsensical title, even by SVR standards. It was to this dacha that Sergei Morosov was taken under armed escort. Inside, surrounded by thousands of books and piles of dusty old files— including several that bore the stamp of the NKVD, the precursor of the KGB—a man was waiting to see him.

"Describe him, please."

"Winner of the Vladimir Lenin look-alike contest."

"Age?"

"Old enough to remember Stalin and to have feared him."

"Name?"

"Let's call him Sasha."

"Sasha what?"

"Sasha It Doesn't Matter. Sasha is a ghost of a man. Sasha is a state of mind."

"Had you ever met this state of mind before?"

No, said Sergei Morosov, he had never had the honor of being introduced to the great Sasha, but he had heard whispers about him for years.

"Whispers?"

"Loose talk. You know how spies are, Allon. They love to gossip."

"What did they say about Sasha?"

"That he ran a single asset. That this asset had been his entire life's work. That he had been assisted in this endeavor by a legendary figure in our business."

"Who was this legendary figure?"

"The whispers never addressed this."

Gabriel was tempted to press Morosov on this point, but didn't. He had learned long ago that, when it came to debriefing a source, it was sometimes better to sit quietly and bide one's time. And so he allowed the identity of the legendary figure to fall temporarily by the wayside and asked for the date.

"I told you, Allon, it was October."

"Last October?"

"The October before."

"Did he offer you tea?"

"No."

"Black bread and vodka?"

"Sasha regards vodka as a Russian illness."

"How long did the meeting last?"

"Meetings with Sasha are never short."

"And the topic?"

"The topic," said Sergei Morosov, "was a traitor named Konstantin Kirov."

Gabriel turned to a fresh page in his notebook, indifferently, as though he were not surprised to learn that the Office's prized SVR source had been blown for well over a year. "Why would a man like Sasha be interested in Kirov?" he asked, his pen hovering above the page. "Kirov was a nothing man."

"Not in Sasha's mind. Kirov's treachery was for Sasha a great opportunity."

"For what?"

"To protect his asset."

"And the reason for the ominous summons?"

"Sasha wanted me to work with him."

"You must have been honored."

"Greatly."

"Why do you suppose he chose you?"

"He knew my mother had worked for Andropov. As far as Sasha was concerned, I was someone who could be trusted."

"With what?"

"Alistair Hughes."

Moscow Center's primary file on MI6's Vienna Head of Station made for dull reading. It stated that Alistair Hughes was loyal to his service and his country, that he harbored no personal or sexual vices, and that he had rejected several offers of recruitment, including one made when he was still an undergraduate at Oxford and assumed—by Moscow Center at least—to be bound for a career in British intelligence.

To this meager offering, Sasha added a file of his own. It contained intimate portraits of Hughes's wife and his two sons. There were also details of his sexual preferences, which were rather specific, and his mental health, which was not good. Hughes suffered from bipolar disorder and acute anxiety. His condition had worsened during a tour of Baghdad, and he hoped his posting to Vienna, while dull in comparison, would help restore his equilibrium. He was seeing a prominent specialist from the Privatklinik Schloss in neighboring Switzerland, a fact he was concealing from his superiors at Vauxhall Cross.

"And his wife as well," added Sergei Morosov.

"Who was the source of the material?"

"The file didn't say, and neither did Sasha."

"When was it opened?"

"Sasha never dated his private files."

Gabriel instructed Sergei Morosov to hazard a guess.

"I'd say it was some time in the mid-nineties. Hughes had been an MI6 officer for about ten years. By then, he was working in the Berlin station. I was one of the officers who made a pass at him."

"So you and Alistair were already acquainted."

"We were on a first-name basis."

"When did you start watching him in Vienna?"

"I had the surveillance operation up and running by mid-November. Sasha reviewed every aspect, down to the makes of the cars and the clothing worn by the pavement artists."

"How pervasive was it?"

It was total, said Sergei Morosov, with the exception of the station itself. The SVR had been trying for years to bug the place but without success.

"Specifics, please," said Gabriel.

"We had two flats on the Barichgasse, one on each side of the street. The inside of his flat was wired to the hilt, and we owned his Wi-Fi network. On any given day we had twenty or thirty pavement specialists at our disposal. We brought them in on the Danube river ferry from Budapest disguised as day-trippers. When Alistair had lunch with a diplomat or a fellow intelligence officer, we were at the next table. And when he stopped for a coffee or a drink, we had a coffee or a drink, too. And then there were the girls he brought home to his apartment."

"Any of them yours?"

"A couple," admitted Sergei Morosov.

"What about the trips to Bern?"

"Same story, different town. We flew with Hughes on the plane, stayed with Hughes at the Schweizerhof, and went with him to his appointments at the clinic up in Münchenbuchsee. It was a ten-minute ride by taxi. Alistair never took a car from the hotel, always from a taxi stand and never the same stand twice in a row. And when he returned to Bern after his appointment, he had the car drop him somewhere other than the entrance of the hotel."

"He didn't want the staff to know where he was going?"

"He didn't want *any*one to know."

"What about when he wasn't at the clinic?"

"That's where he made his mistake," replied Sergei Morosov. "Our friend Alistair was a bit predictable."

"How so?"

"There's only one flight a day from Vienna to Bern, the two o'clock SkyWork. Unless the flight was delayed, which was rare, Alistair was always at the hotel by four at the latest."

"Leaving him with more than an hour and a half before his appointment."

"Exactly. And he always spent it the same way."

"Afternoon tea in the lobby lounge."

"Same table, same time, last Friday of every month."

With the exception of December, said Sergei Morosov. Alistair spent the holidays with his family in Britain and the Bahamas. He returned to duty three days after the New Year, and a week later, on a Wednesday evening, he was called to the station late at night to take delivery of an urgent eyes-only telegram from Vauxhall Cross. Which returned them once more to the subject of the traitor Kirov and his murder on a snowy night in Vienna.

38

UPPER GALILEE, ISRAEL

Under normal circumstances, he would have been arrested and interrogated for days, weeks, perhaps even months, until they had wrung every last secret out of him, until he was too exhausted, too crazed with pain, to offer a coherent answer to even the simplest question. Then he might well have been given one last beating before being taken to a windowless room in the basement of Lefortovo Prison with walls of concrete and a drain in the floor for ease of cleaning. There he would have been forced to kneel, and a large-caliber handgun would have been placed, in the Russian way, to the nape of his neck. One shot would have been fired. It would have exited through his face, leaving his body unsuitable for proper burial. Not that he would have received one. He would have been hurled into an unmarked hole in the Russian earth and hastily buried. No one, not even his mother, would have been told of his grave's whereabouts.

But these were not normal circumstances, continued Sergei Morosov. These were Sasha circumstances, and Sasha handled the traitor Kirov with extraordinary care. He sent the traitor Kirov on numerous errands, unwatched, knowing full well that on some of those errands he was meeting with his Israeli handlers, which was precisely what Sasha wanted. To that end, he made certain the material to which Kirov was exposed was of sufficient quality that his Israeli handlers and their Anglo-American partners would not be suspicious. In the jargon, it was fool's gold. It shone and glittered but was without strategic or operational value.

Finally, Sasha dispatched the traitor Kirov on the errand that would result in his decision to defect. By all appearances, it was a routine assignment. The traitor Kirov was instructed to clean out a dead-letter box in Montreal and return the contents to Moscow Center. The dead-letter box was actually an apartment, used by a Brazilian citizen, a woman, living permanently in the promised land of the United States. But the woman was not Brazilian at all. She was a Russian illegal operating under deep cover in Washington.

"Doing what?"

"Sasha never divulged her assignment to me."

"And if you were to hazard a guess?"

"I'd say the Russian illegal was servicing a mole."

"Because officers from the local *rezidentura* are under constant FBI surveillance, making it impossible for them to run a high-level asset."

"Difficult," suggested Sergei Morosov, "but not impossible."

"Did Sasha ever tell you the name of this Russian illegal operating in Washington?"

"Sasha? Don't be silly."

"Her cover occupation?"

"No."

Gabriel asked what had been left in the apartment.

"A memory stick," replied Sergei Morosov. "It was hidden beneath the kitchen sink. I placed it there myself."

"What did it contain?"

"Forgeries."

"Of what?"

"Documents of the highest possible classification."

"American?"

"Yes."

"CIA?"

"NSA as well," said Sergei Morosov, nodding. "Sasha instructed me to leave the memory stick unlocked so Kirov would see the contents."

"How did you know he would look at them?"

"No SVR fieldman would ever transport an unlocked, unencrypted flash drive across international borders. They always check to make certain."

"What if he hadn't returned to Moscow?" asked Gabriel. "What if he had walked straight into our arms?"

"It was the one errand where he was watched. If he had made a break for the other side, he would have been shipped back to Moscow in a box."

But that wasn't necessary, Sergei Morosov continued, because the traitor Kirov returned to Moscow on his own. At which point he faced a painful dilemma. The documents he had seen were too dangerous to share with his Israeli handlers. If Moscow Center ever learned they had gone astray, Kirov would instantly fall under suspicion. Defection, therefore, was his only option.

The rest of Sasha's conspiracy unfolded precisely as planned. The traitor Kirov traveled to Budapest and then to Vienna, where Gabriel Allon, the chief of Israeli intelligence and an implacable enemy of the Russian Federation, waited in a safe flat. An assassin waited, too, one of Moscow Center's very best. His death on the Brünnerstrasse was the evening's only false note. Otherwise, the performance was pitch perfect. The traitor Kirov had been granted the undignified death he so richly deserved. And the enemy Allon would soon embark on an investigation, guided at every step by the hidden hand of Sasha, that would identify Alistair Hughes as Moscow Center's mole inside British intelligence.

"How did you know we'd targeted him?" asked Gabriel.

"We saw Eli Lavon and your friend Christopher Keller move into an observation flat on the Barichgasse. And our watchers saw your watchers following Alistair around Vienna. On Sasha's orders, we pared our teams to the bone to minimize the risk of detection."

"But not in Bern," said Gabriel. "That boy-girl team you sent into the Schweizerhof were rather hard to miss. So was Dmitri Sokolov."

"A protégé of Sasha's."

"I suppose Sasha deliberately chose Dmitri so there would be no confusion."

"He does cut quite a dashing figure on the Geneva party circuit."

"What was in the envelope?"

"You tell me."

Photographs, said Gabriel, of Alistair Hughes entering and leaving Privatklinik Schloss.

"*Kompromat.*"

"I don't suppose there was a chance Alistair was going to leave Bern alive."

"None whatsoever. But even we were surprised when he came running helter-skelter out of the hotel."

"Who was driving the car?"

Sergei Morosov hesitated, then said, "I was."

"And what if Alistair hadn't presented you with such an easy opportunity to kill him?"

"We had the plane."

"Plane?"

"The return flight to Vienna. While we were watching Alistair, we figured out how to get a bomb on board. Bern Airport isn't exactly Heathrow or Ben Gurion."

"You would have killed all those innocent people in order to kill one man?"

"When making an omelet . . ."

"I doubt the civilized world would see it that way," said Gabriel. "Especially when they heard it directly from the mouth of a senior KGB officer."

"We're called the SVR now, Allon. And we had a deal."

"Indeed, we did. You were supposed to tell me everything in exchange for your life. Unfortunately, you haven't lived up to your end of the bargain."

Sergei Morosov managed a smile. "The name of the mole? Is that what you want?"

Gabriel smiled in return.

"Do you really think," asked Sergei Morosov, his tone belittling, "that the great Sasha would tell me such a thing? Only a tiny cadre of officers at Moscow Center know the mole's identity."

"What about the woman?" asked Gabriel. "The illegal who poses as a Brazilian national?"

"You can be sure she and the mole never meet face-to-face."

Gabriel asked for the address of the dead drop in Montreal. Sergei Morosov replied that the information was obsolete. Sasha had shut it down and set up a new drop.

"Where?"

Sergei Morosov was silent.

"Would you like me to have the technicians play back the part of your interrogation where you admit to killing MI6's Vienna Head of Station?"

The dead drop, said Sergei Morosov, was located at 6822 rue Saint-Denis.

"Apartment or house?"

"Neither. The dead drop is a Ford Explorer. Dark gray. The illegal leaves the memory stick in the glove box, and one of Sasha's couriers brings it back to Moscow Center."

"Old school," said Gabriel.

"Sasha prefers the old ways to the new."

Gabriel smiled. "We have that in common, Sasha and I."

39

UPPER GALILEE, ISRAEL

There was one final piece of business to attend to. It was the question that Gabriel, many hours earlier, had allowed to fall by the wayside. It was nothing serious, he told himself, a housekeeping matter, a bit of dust that had to be swept into the pan before Sergei Morosov could be allowed to get a few hours of sleep. This was the lie Gabriel told himself. This was his internal cover story.

In truth, he had thought of almost nothing else all through the long night. That was the gift of a master interrogator, the ability to hold a single unanswered question in reserve while probing elsewhere. In the process, Gabriel had unearthed a mountain of valuable intelligence, not least of which was the location of a dead drop in Montreal used by a Russian illegal operating in

Washington. A Russian illegal whose primary task was to service a long-term agent of penetration operating at the pinnacle of the Anglo-American intelligence establishment. Sasha's one and only asset. Sasha's life's work. Sasha's endeavor. In the jargon of the trade, a mole.

The dead drop alone was worth the cost and risk of Sergei Morosov's abduction. But who was the legendary figure who had assisted Sasha in creating the mole in the first place? Gabriel posed the question again now, as an afterthought, while preparing to take his leave.

"I told you, Allon, the rumors never addressed this."

"I heard you the first time, Sergei. But who was it? Was he one man or two? Was he a team of officers? Was he a woman?" Then, after a long pause, "Was he even a Russian?"

And this time, perhaps because he was too exhausted to lie, or perhaps because he knew it would be pointless, Sergei Morosov answered truthfully.

"No, Allon, he wasn't a Russian. Russian in his sympathies, yes. Russian in his historical outlook, surely. But he remained English to the core, even after he came to us. He ate English mustard and marmalade, drank scotch whisky by the barrel, and followed the cricket scores religiously in the *Times*."

Because these words were spoken in German, the two guards standing at Gabriel's back did not react. Neither did Mikhail, who was sprawled drowsily to Sergei Morosov's right, looking as though he were the one who had spent the night under interrogation. Gabriel made no reaction, either, other than to slow the pace with which he was gathering up his notes.

"Sasha told you this?" he asked quietly, so as not to break the spell.

"Not Sasha." Sergei Morosov shook his head vigorously. "It was in one of his files."

"Which file?"

"An old one."

"From the days when the KGB was known as the NKVD?"

"You were listening, after all."

"To every word."

"Sasha left it on his desk one evening."

"And you had a look?"

"It was against Sasha's rules, but, yes, I had a look when he ran up to the main building to have a word with the boss."

"What would have happened if he'd seen you?"

"He would have assumed I was a spy."

"And had you shot," said Gabriel.

"Sasha? He would have shot me himself."

"Why did you take the risk?"

"I couldn't resist. Files like that are the sacred texts of our service. The Torah," he added for Gabriel's benefit. "Even a man like me, a man whose mother worked for Andropov, is rarely allowed to see such documents."

"And when you opened the file? What did you see?"

"A name."

"*His* name?"

"No," answered Sergei Morosov. "The name was Otto. It was the code name of an NKVD operative. The file concerned a meeting Otto conducted in Regent's Park in London."

"When?"

"In June," said Sergei Morosov. "June 1934."

Otto, Regent's Park, June 1934 . . . It was perhaps the most famous and fateful meeting in the history of espionage.

"You saw the *actual* file?" asked Gabriel.

"It was like reading the original copy of the Ten Commandments. I could barely see the page, I was so blinded by excitement."

"Were there other files?"

Yes, said Sergei Morosov, there were many others, including several written in laborious Russian by Sasha's legendary helper, the man who was Russian in his sympathies but English to his core. One concerned a woman he had known in Beirut, where he had worked for several years as a journalist beginning in 1956.

"Who was she?"

"A journalist, too. More important, she was a committed communist."

"What was the nature of their relationship?"

"It wasn't professional, if that's what you're asking."

"She was his lover?"

"One of many," said Sergei Morosov. "But she was different."

"How so?"

"There was a child."

The rapid pace of Gabriel's questions stirred Mikhail from his reverie.

"What was the woman's name?" asked Gabriel.

"The file didn't say."

"Nationality?"

"No."

"What about the child? Was it a boy or a girl?"

"Please, Allon, I've had enough for one night. Let me get some sleep, and we'll start over in the morning."

But it was morning already, late morning in fact, and there was no time for sleep. Gabriel squeezed harder, and Sergei Morosov, drunk with fatigue, described the contents of the last file he had dared to open that night before the great Sasha returned to the dacha.

"It was a private assessment written by the Englishman in the early 1970s predicting the collapse of communism."

"Heretical stuff," interjected Gabriel.

"No Soviet citizen, not even my father, would have dared to write such a thing."

"The Englishman was free to say what others could not?"

"Not publicly, but internally he could speak his mind."

"Why would he write such a document?"

"He was afraid that if communism collapsed, the Soviet Union would no longer serve as a beacon for those in the West who believed capitalism to be unjust."

"The useful idiots."

"Admittedly, one of the few times Comrade Lenin should have chosen his words more carefully."

The Englishman, Sergei Morosov went on, certainly didn't consider himself to be a useful idiot or even a traitor. He regarded himself first and foremost as an officer of the KGB. And he was afraid that if communism failed in the one country where it was applied, few Westerners from the upper reaches of their societies would imitate his path of secret allegiance to Moscow, leaving the KGB no choice but to rely on paid and coerced assets. But if the KGB wanted a true agent of penetration in the heart of Western intelligence—a mole who burrowed into a position of influence and spied for reasons of conscience rather than money—it would have to create one out of whole cloth.

This, said Sergei Morosov, was the true nature of Sasha's endeavor—to create the perfect spy, with the help of the greatest traitor of them all. This was why Konstantin Kirov had been given the highest measure of punishment in Vienna. And it was why Alistair Hughes, whose only crime was mental illness, had been murdered in the Bahnhofplatz in Bern.

There was a child . . .

Yes, thought Gabriel, that would explain everything.

40

WORMWOOD COTTAGE, DARTMOOR

Wormwood Cottage was set upon a swell in the moorland and fashioned of Devon stone that had darkened with time. Behind it, across a broken courtyard, was a converted barn with offices and living quarters for the staff. When the facility was unoccupied, a single caretaker called Parish kept a lonely watch over it. But when guests were present—in the lexicon of the cottage, they were referred to as "company"—the staff could number as many as ten, including a security detail. Much depended on the nature of the guest and the men from whom he was hiding. A "friendly" might be given the run of the place. But for a man with many enemies, a hunted man, Wormwood Cottage could be turned into the most secure MI6 safe house in all of Britain.

The man who appeared at the cottage early the following after-noon fell into the second category, though Parish received only a few minutes' warning of his pending arrival. It came not through the usual channels at Vauxhall Cross but from Nigel Whitcombe, the chief's boyish personal assistant and general factotum. Whit-combe had cut his teeth at Five, a sin for which Parish, who was old service, had granted him no absolution.

"And how long will he be staying with us this time?" Parish asked dryly.

"To be determined," answered Whitcombe down the encrypted line.

"How many in his party?"

"He'll be alone."

"Bodyguards?"

"No."

"And what do we do if he wants to take one of his forced marches across the moor? He does love to walk, you know. Last time he was here, he trekked halfway to Penzance without telling anyone."

"Leave a gun with the Wellies. He can look after himself."

"And will he be having guests?"

"Just one."

"Name?"

"Third letter of the alphabet."

"What time should I expect him?"

"Unclear."

"And our company?"

"Look out your window."

Parish did as he was told and glimpsed an unmarked van bumping along the rutted drive. It stopped in the cottage's gravel forecourt, and a single figure alighted from the back. Five-foot-nothing, bright green eyes, short dark hair, gray at the temples. The last time Parish had seen him was the night the esteemed *Telegraph* newspaper reported that he was dead. In fact, Parish was the one who had brought him the printout of the story from the *Telegraph*'s Web site. Company were not permitted the use of phones or computers. Cottage rules.

"Parish!" called out the green-eyed man with surprising cheer. "I was hoping you'd be here."

"Things change slowly down here on the moor."

"And thank heaven for that." He surrendered his mobile without Parish having to ask. "You'll take good care of it, won't you? I wouldn't want anyone to get their hands on it."

With that, the green-eyed man smiled unexpectedly and entered the cottage as though he were returning home from a long absence. When Parish saw him next he was striking out into the moorland, with the collar of his Barbour coat around his ears and the weight of the world on his shoulders. What was it this time? Given his track record, it could be almost anything. Something about his grim expression told Parish that Wormwood Cottage would once again be the setting of a great undertaking. And though Parish did not know it, he was entirely and absolutely correct.

He followed a hedgerowed track down to the hamlet of Postbridge, a collection of farm buildings at the intersection of two roads. There he headed west toward the faint warmth of the sun, which was already hovering just above the empty horizon. He wondered, only half in jest, whether he was following the course

Sasha had plotted for him. Or was it Sasha's legendary accomplice? The Englishman who followed the cricket scores religiously in the *Times*, even after he had committed the final act of betrayal. The Englishman who helped Sasha prepare and then insert a mole into the heart of Western intelligence, an agent motivated by a personal devotion to him. The Englishman had lived for a time in the Beirut of old, the Beirut where one heard French while strolling the Corniche. He had known a young woman there, there was a child. Find the woman, thought Gabriel, and he might very well find the child.

But how? The woman had no name or country—at least not in the files Sergei Morosov had seen that night in Sasha's private dacha—but surely someone must have known of the affair. Perhaps someone attached to MI6's Beirut station, which was a vital Middle East listening post at the time. Someone who was acquainted with the Englishman. Someone whose career had suffered as a result of the Englishman's treachery. Someone whose son was now the director-general of MI6 and could access old files without raising any dust. It was possible—*possible*, Gabriel cautioned himself—he was at long last one step ahead of the great Sasha.

At Two Bridges, Gabriel turned to the north. He followed the road for a time, then swung his leg over a stone fence and hiked across the moorland, up the slope of a tor. In the distance he could see a single car, a limousine, speeding across the barren landscape. He descended the opposite slope and in the dying twilight found a groove in the earth that led him to the door of Wormwood Cottage. The latch yielded to his touch. Inside, he found Miss Coventry, the cook and housekeeper, hovering over several bubbling pots at the stove, an apron around her ample waist.

Graham Seymour was listening to the news on the old Bakelite radio in the sitting room. Entering, Gabriel raised the volume nearly to full. Then he told Seymour about Sasha's lifelong endeavor. Sasha, he explained, had not worked alone. He had been assisted by an Englishman. There was a woman, and the woman had given birth to a child. The child of treason. The child of Kim Philby . . .

41

WORMWOOD COTTAGE, DARTMOOR

He was born on the first day of 1912, in the Punjab Province of British India. His full name was Harold Adrian Russell Philby, but his father—the irascible diplomat, explorer, Orientalist, and convert to Islam, St. John Philby—called him Kim after Kimball O'Hara, the hero of Rudyard Kipling's novel of Anglo-Russo rivalry and intrigue set in the subcontinent. Kipling's fictitious character and the young Kim Philby shared more than a nickname. Philby, too, could masquerade as an Indian.

He returned to England at the age of twelve to attend the prestigious Westminster School and in the autumn of 1929, on the eve of the Great Depression, went up to Trinity College, Cambridge.

There, like many privileged young Englishmen of his generation, he promptly fell under communism's spell. He earned an upper second-class degree in economics and a Trinity College prize of fourteen pounds. He used the money to purchase a copy of the collected works of Karl Marx.

Before leaving Cambridge in 1933, he confessed to Maurice Dobb, the Marxist economist and leader of a Cambridge communist cell, that he wanted to devote his life to the Party. Dobb sent him to see an agent of the Comintern in Paris who went by the name Gibarti, and Gibarti placed him in contact with the communist underground in Vienna, which in the autumn of 1933 was a city under siege. Philby took part in the bloody street clashes between Austrian leftists and the fascist regime of Chancellor Engelbert Dollfuss. He also fell in love with Alice "Litzi" Kohlmann, a young Jewish divorcee and committed communist with connections to Soviet intelligence. Philby married her at the Vienna Town Hall in February 1934 and took her back to London, the next stop on his journey into treachery.

For it was in London, on a warm day in June, on a bench in Regent's Park, that Kim Philby met a charming, curly-haired academic from Eastern Europe who called himself Otto. His real name was Arnold Deutsch, and he was a talent-spotter and recruiter working in Britain on behalf of the NKVD. In time, Philby would tell Otto about two like-minded friends from Cambridge, Guy Burgess and Donald Maclean; and Burgess would later give Otto the name of a noted art historian, Anthony Blunt. John Cairncross, a brilliant mathematician, would be the fifth. Philby, Burgess, Maclean, Blunt, Cairncross: the Cambridge Five. To better protect their origins, Moscow Center referred to them as the Magnificent Five.

At Otto's suggestion, Philby publicly adopted the politics of a Nazi sympathizer and pursued a career in journalism, first in London, then in Spain, where civil war erupted in 1936, pitting Franco's Nationalists against the Moscow-leaning Republicans. Philby covered the war from the Nationalist side, sending thoughtful dispatches to several London papers, including the *Times*, while simultaneously collecting valuable battlefield intelligence for his masters in Moscow. On New Year's Eve 1937, during the bloody Battle of Teruel, a shell landed near the car in which Philby was eating chocolates and drinking brandy. The three other occupants were killed instantly, but Philby received only a minor head wound. Franco personally awarded Philby the Red Cross of Military Merit for his support of the Nationalist cause. Despite his loathing of fascism, Philby kept the medal always.

His marriage to Litzi Kohlmann did not survive his outward conversion to right-wing politics. The couple separated but did not divorce, and Litzi moved to Paris. Philby took a staff job with the *Times* and in 1940 was one of a handful of journalists selected to accompany the ill-fated British Expeditionary Force to France. Traveling back to London after the French collapse, he shared a train compartment with Hester Harriet Marsden-Smedley, a veteran war correspondent from the *Sunday Express* who had many friends and contacts in the British secret services. The two spoke at length about Philby's future. With Britain facing the prospect of German invasion, Philby believed he had no choice but to enlist. "You're capable of doing a lot more to defeat Hitler," said Marsden-Smedley. "We'll figure something out."

It was not long—a few days, in fact—before MI6 came calling. Philby was interviewed twice, and MI5 made quiet inquiries into his background. The Security Service stamped Philby's file "Nothing Recorded Against," despite the fact he had been a brazen communist at Cambridge and working as a spy for Moscow for six years. He was in.

Philby's new career began inauspiciously. For two weeks he sat in a small empty room at MI6 headquarters at 54 Broadway and did nothing at all, except partake in drunken lunches with Guy Burgess, his fellow Cambridge spy. But by the summer of 1941, Philby was the head of the all-important Iberian division of Section V, MI6's counterintelligence department. From the safety of a desk, he adroitly attacked Germany's large intelligence network in neutral Spain and Portugal. He also stole every secret he could lay his hands on and passed them in bulging briefcases to his controllers at the Soviet Embassy in London. The other members of the Cambridge spy ring—Burgess, Maclean, Blunt, and Cairncross, all entrenched in positions of wartime influence—did the same.

But Philby's star shone brightest. Section V was headquartered not in Broadway but in a large Victorian house called Glenalmond, in the village of St. Albans. Philby lived in a cottage nearby with Aileen Furse, a former store detective from Marks & Spencer who suffered severe bouts of depression. She swiftly bore him three children between 1941 and 1944. The trusted colleagues from Section V who gathered each Sunday at the Philby cottage would have been shocked to learn the couple were not actually husband and wife. For Philby, marriage to Aileen was out of the question; he was still wed to Litzi Kohlmann. Even in his personal life, he was prone to deception.

By war's end it was obvious to everyone inside MI6 that Philby was destined for greatness. But there was one gaping hole in his otherwise impressive résumé: he had fought the war from behind a desk, never once venturing into the field. MI6 chief Stewart Menzies sought to rectify that deficiency by appointing Philby

Head of Station in Istanbul. Before leaving for Turkey, he put his domestic affairs in order by quietly divorcing Litzi and marrying Aileen. They were wed on September 25, 1946, in a civil ceremony in Chelsea attended by a handful of close friends. The mentally unstable bride was seven months pregnant with her fourth child.

In Turkey, Philby settled his family into a villa on the Bosporus and began recruiting networks of anticommunist émigrés that could be inserted into the Soviet Union. He then betrayed his own networks to Moscow Center, using his old friend Guy Burgess as the intermediary. In the meantime, Philby's domestic situation deteriorated. Aileen became convinced her husband was having an affair with his secretary. Distraught, she injected herself with her own urine and became violently ill. Philby sent her to a private clinic in Switzerland for treatment.

His chaotic home life had no impact on his meteoric rise at MI6, and in the autumn of 1949 Philby was sent to Washington as Head of Station. Inside America's rapidly expanding intelligence community, Philby was respected and admired for his intellect and deadly charm. His closest confidant was James Jesus Angleton, the CIA's legendary counterintelligence chief, whom he had befriended in London during the war. The two lunched regularly at Harvey's Restaurant on Connecticut Avenue, soaking up massive quantities of alcohol and swapping secrets, which Philby promptly passed along to Moscow. His spacious home on Nebraska Avenue was a popular watering hole for American spies such as Allen Dulles, Frank Wisner, and Walter Bedell Smith. Philby's parties were legendary for their alcoholic debauchery, a situation that only worsened when Guy Burgess, a spectacular drunk, was transferred to the British Embassy in Washington and took up residence in Philby's basement.

Philby's star turn in Washington, however, was about to come to an end. Venona was the code name for one of the most classified American programs of the Cold War. Unbeknownst to Moscow, American cryptanalysts had broken a supposedly unbreakable Soviet code and were slowly unbuttoning thousands of cables intercepted between 1940 and 1948. The cables revealed the presence of some two hundred Soviet spies inside the U.S. government. They had also revealed the existence of a network of influential spies in Britain. One was code-named Homer. Another was known as Stanley. Philby knew what the American code-breakers did not. Homer was Donald Maclean. Stanley was the code name of a spy who was now serving as MI6's Head of Station in Washington. Stanley was Philby himself.

In April 1951 the Venona team undeniably linked Homer to Donald Maclean. Philby knew it was only a matter of time before they discovered the real identity of the agent known as Stanley. With the noose tightening, he dispatched Guy Burgess to London to instruct Maclean to flee to the Soviet Union. Despite Philby's warnings to the contrary, Burgess fled, too, with the help of a London-based Soviet intelligence officer named Yuri Modin. When word of their defection reached Washington, Philby reacted with outward calm, though privately he was terrified his past was about to catch up with him. That evening he buried his Soviet-supplied miniature camera and film in a shallow grave in the Maryland countryside. Then he returned home to await the inevitable summons from London.

It came a few days later, a handwritten note, followed by a telegram, inviting Philby to return to London to discuss the disappearance of his two friends from Cambridge. His first interrogation took place at Leconfield House, the headquarters of MI5. Many more would follow. In none did Philby admit to being the one who warned Maclean of his pending arrest, or to being the

"Third Man" in the Cambridge spy ring, though MI5 clearly believed he was guilty. MI6 was not convinced. But under pressure from the Americans, MI6 chief Menzies had no choice but to part company with his brightest star. Despite a generous severance, Philby's finances quickly deteriorated. He took a job at a small import-export firm, and Aileen went to work in the kitchen of a house in Eaton Square. Their marriage became so strained Philby often slept in a tent in the garden.

Gradually, however, the cloud of suspicion began to lift, and after a convivial final interview in October 1955, MI6 cleared Kim Philby of being a Soviet spy. MI5 reacted with fury, as did J. Edgar Hoover, the virulently anticommunist director of the FBI, who engineered a sensational story in the *New York Sunday News* accusing Philby of being the Third Man. A public scandal ensued. Accusations were hurled in Parliament; reporters followed Philby everywhere. It was Foreign Secretary Harold Macmillan who put an end to it. On November 7, 1955, he rose in Parliament and declared: "I have no reason to conclude that Mr. Philby has at any time betrayed the interests of his country." The next day, Philby himself convened a press conference in the drawing room of his mother's flat in Draycott Gardens and, in a stunning display of charm and deception, declared his innocence as well. The storm had passed. Kim Philby was formally in the clear.

Which meant he was free to resume his career. An official return to duty was not yet possible, but Nicholas Elliott, Philby's closest friend inside MI6, arranged for him to be sent to Beirut as a freelance stringer for the *Observer* and the *Economist*, a post that would allow him to do a little spying on the side. Unencumbered by his five children and his ailing wife, whom he happily left behind in the dreary London suburb of Crowborough, Kim Philby arrived in the Paris of the Middle East on September 6, 1956, and headed for the bar at the St. Georges Hotel. The following day he met with an officer from MI6's Beirut station. The officer's name was Arthur Seymour.

42

WORMWOOD COTTAGE, DARTMOOR

Y ou knew him?"

"Kim Philby?" asked Graham Seymour. "I'm not sure anyone really did. But we were acquainted. He gave me my first drink. My father nearly killed me. Him, too."

"Your father disapproved of alcohol?"

"Of course not. But he loathed Kim."

They were seated at the small table in the corner of the kitchen, next to a leaded window overlooking the moorland. The window was black with night and lashed with rain. Between them lay the remnants of Miss Coventry's thoroughly English supper. At Seymour's request, she had departed early, leaving the two spy chiefs to tidy up for themselves. They were alone in the cottage. Not entirely alone, thought Gabriel. Philby was with them.

"What did he give you to drink?"

"A pink gin," said Seymour with a trace of a smile, "at the bar of the Normandie. He used it as his office. He used to arrive there around noon to read his post and have a drink or two for the sake of his hangover. That's where the Russians reestablished contact. A KGB officer named Petukhov walked over and handed Philby a card. They met the following afternoon at Philby's apartment and put in place their tradecraft. If Philby had something he wanted to share with Moscow, he would stand on the balcony of his flat on a Wednesday evening with a newspaper in his hand. He and Petukhov used to meet in an out-of-the way restaurant in the Armenian quarter called Vrej."

"If I remember correctly, there was another wife. A third wife," Gabriel added. "An American, for a change of pace."

"Her name was Eleanor Brewer. Philby stole her from Sam Pope Brewer, the *New York Times* correspondent. She drank almost as much as Philby. They were married not long after Aileen was found dead in the house in Crowborough. Philby was positively overjoyed when he received the news. My father never forgave him."

"Your father worked with Philby?"

"My father refused to have anything to do with him," said Seymour, shaking his head. "He'd known Kim during the war and was never seduced by the famous Philby charm. Nor was he convinced of Philby's innocence in the Third Man affair. Quite the opposite, actually. He thought Philby guilty as sin, and he was furious when he learned Philby had been given a service retainer and posted to Beirut. He was not alone. There were several senior officers in London who were of a similar mind. They prevailed upon my father to keep an eye on him."

"Did he?"

"To the best of his ability. He was as shocked as everyone else when Philby disappeared."

"It was 1963," said Gabriel.

"January," elaborated Seymour.

"Remind me of the circumstances. Titian and Caravaggio, I can do in my sleep," said Gabriel. "But Kim Philby is rather outside my area of expertise."

Seymour carefully refilled his glass with claret. "Don't play the fool with me. Your bloodshot eyes tell me you brushed up on Philby on the flight from Tel Aviv. You know as well as I do what happened."

"George Blake was arrested for spying for the Soviets."

"And promptly sentenced to forty-two years in prison."

"Then there was a Russian defector who told British intelligence about a so-called Ring of Five agents who had met when they were students."

"The defector's name," said Seymour, "was Anatoliy Golitsyn."

"And let's not forget Philby's old friend from Cambridge," said Gabriel. "The one who suddenly remembered he had tried to recruit her as a Soviet spy in the thirties."

"Who could possibly forget Flora Solomon?"

"Philby started to spiral dangerously out of control. On the Beirut party circuit, it was not unusual to find him passed out on the floor of the host's apartment. His decline did not go unnoticed by Moscow Center. Nor was the KGB unaware of the rising threat against him. Yuri Modin, the controller of the Cambridge Five, traveled to Beirut to warn Philby he would be arrested if he ever returned to Britain. As it turned out, trouble came to Philby instead, in the form of his closest friend, Nicholas Elliott."

Seymour picked up the thread of the story. "They met in an apartment in the Christian quarter, at four o'clock in the afternoon on the twelfth of January. The room had been thoroughly bugged. My father was sitting over the recorders in the next room. Philby arrived wearing a turban of bandages and two black eyes. He'd taken a couple of drunken falls on New Year's Eve and was lucky to be alive. Elliott foolishly opened the windows to let some fresh air into the room, and let in street noise as well. Much of the conversation is unintelligible."

"You've heard the recording?"

Seymour nodded slowly. "I used the privilege of my office to listen to the tapes not long after I became chief. Philby denied everything. But when he returned to the apartment the next afternoon, he offered a partial confession in exchange for a grant of immunity. Elliott and Philby met a few more times, including once over dinner at Chez Temporel, one of Beirut's most expensive restaurants. Then Elliott left Beirut without making any provision for Philby's security. Philby made his escape on the night of January twenty-third, with the help of Petukhov, his KGB contact. Within a few days, he was in Moscow."

"What was your father's reaction?"

"Outrage, of course, most of it directed at Nicholas Elliott. He thought Elliott had blundered by not placing Philby under lock and key. He later came to the conclusion it was no blunder, that Elliott and his friends in London actually *wanted* Philby to escape."

"Thus avoiding another public spectacle."

Seymour abruptly changed the subject. "Know much about Philby's time in Moscow?"

"The Russians set him up in a comfortable apartment in the Patriarch's Pond section of the city. He read old editions of the *Times* that were sent to him by post, listened to the news on the BBC World Service, and drank a great deal of Johnnie Walker

Red Label, almost always to the point of unconsciousness. The former Eleanor Brewster lived with him for a while, but the marriage collapsed when she found out he was having an affair with Donald Maclean's wife. Later, Philby took a fourth wife, a Russian named Rufina, and was generally quite miserable."

"And his relationship with the KGB?"

"For a time, they kept him at arm's length. They thought he escaped from Beirut rather too easily and were convinced he might be a triple agent. Gradually, they started giving him little projects to keep him busy, including helping to train new recruits at the KGB's Red Banner Institute." Gabriel paused, then added, "Which is where Sasha entered the picture."

"Yes," said Seymour, "the phantom Sasha."

"Ever heard the name?"

"No. And with good reason," added Seymour. "Sasha exists only in the imagination of Sergei Morosov. He spun you a tale of treachery and deceit, and you bought it hook, line, and sinker."

"Why would he lie?"

"To prevent you from killing him, of course."

"I never threatened to kill him. I only threatened to hand him over to the Syrian opposition."

"That," said Seymour, "is a distinction without a difference."

"And the woman?" asked Gabriel. "The communist Philby met in Beirut? The woman who bore him a child? Did Sergei Morosov invent her, too?"

Seymour made a show of thought. "And what shall I tell the prime minister and the esteemed members of the Joint Intelligence Committee? Shall I tell them Kim Philby has risen from his grave to create one last scandal? That he turned his illegitimate child into a Russian agent?"

"For the moment," answered Gabriel, "you tell them nothing at all."

"Don't worry, I won't."

A silence fell between them. There was only the rain rattling against the window.

"But what if I were able to find her?" asked Gabriel at last. "Would you believe it then?"

"Philby's lover from Beirut? You're assuming there was only one. Kim Philby was the most faithless man in history. Trust me, I know."

"Your father knew it, too," said Gabriel quietly.

"My father's been dead for nearly twenty years now. We can't very well ask him."

"Maybe we can."

"How?"

"Old spies never die, Graham. They have eternal life."

"Where?"

Gabriel smiled. "In their files."

43

SLOUGH, BERKSHIRE

For an intelligence service, the management of files is a deadly serious business. Access to information must be restricted to those who truly need to see it, and a careful log must be kept of those who read a specific file and when they read it. At MI6, this is the job of Central Registry. Current files are kept within easy reach at Vauxhall Cross, but the bulk of MI6's institutional memory is stored in a warehouse in Slough, not far from Heathrow Airport. The warehouse is guarded at all hours and monitored by cameras, but late on a wet Tuesday evening only a single registrar called Robinson was on duty. Robinson, like Parish the caretaker at Wormwood Cottage, was old service. He had a long face and a thin mustache and wore brilliantine cream in his hair that fouled the air in his vestibule. He regarded Nigel Whitcombe and his written request with a cold eye.

"*All* of them?" he asked at last.

Whitcombe offered only a benevolent smile in reply. He had the mind of a professional criminal and the face of a country parson. It was a dangerous combination.

"The entire output of a single officer over a seven-year period? It's unprecedented."

"Look at the name of the officer." Whitcombe tapped it with the tip of his forefinger in case Robinson, who was blind as a bat, hadn't seen it.

SEYMOUR, ARTHUR . . .

"Yes, I saw it, but it can't be done. Not without a countersignature from the Registry Head."

"Chief's prerogative. Chief's birthright, too."

"Then perhaps the chief should be the one making the request."

This time, Whitcombe's smile was not so benevolent. "He *is* the one, Robinson. Think of me as his personal emissary."

Robinson was squinting at the name on the chit. "One of the greats, Arthur. A pro's pro. I knew him, you know. Oh, we weren't friends, mind you. I wasn't in Arthur's category. But we were acquainted."

Whitcombe wasn't surprised. The old fossil had probably known Philby, too. During the war, Central Registry had been at St. Albans, next door to Philby's Section V. The chief registrar was a world-class boozer named William Woodfield. Philby used to fill him up with pink gin at the King Harry so he could get his files for free. At night he would copy the contents by hand at the kitchen table for delivery to his Soviet controller.

Philby . . .

Whitcombe felt his face flush with anger at the very thought of the traitorous bastard. Or maybe it was Robinson's hair cream. The smell of it was making him light-headed.

Robinson looked up at the wall clock, which read 10:53. "It's going to take a while."

"How long?"

"Two days, maybe three."

"Sorry, old boy, but I need them tonight."

"You can't be serious! They're scattered all over the facility. I have to find the relevant cross-references. Otherwise, I'm liable to miss something."

"Don't do that," cautioned Whitcombe. "The chief specifically requested all of his father's files from that period. All means *all*."

"It would be helpful if you gave me the name of a specific operation or target."

It would indeed, thought Whitcombe. In fact, all he had to do was add *Philby, H.A.R.* to the chit, and Robinson would be able to locate the relevant files in a matter of minutes. But the chief wanted the search to be as broad and innocuous-sounding as possible, lest word of it reach the wrong pair of ears at Vauxhall Cross.

"Maybe I can be of help," suggested Whitcombe.

"Don't even think about it," scolded Robinson. "There's a staff room down the hall. You can wait there."

With that, he shuffled, chit in hand, into the shadows of the vast warehouse. Watching him, Whitcombe's spirits sank. The place reminded him of the IKEA in Wembley where he'd hastily furnished his flat. He went down the hall to the staff room and fixed himself a cup of Darjeeling. It was horrible. Worse than horrible, thought Whitcombe, as he settled in for a long night. It tasted like nothing.

———

Shift change at the annex was at six. The early-morning registrar was a battleax named Mrs. Applewhite who was impervious to Whitcombe's charms, such as they were, and fearless in the face of his veiled threats. As a consequence, he was relieved when Robinson poked his head into the staff room at half past four and announced the order was complete.

The files were contained in eight boxes, each marked with the usual warning regarding disclosure and proper handling, which forbade their removal from the facility. Whitcombe immediately violated that particular regulation by loading the files into the back of a Ford hatchback. Robinson was predictably appalled and threatened to wake the Registry Head, but here again Whitcombe prevailed. The files in question, he argued, had *zero* national security value. Furthermore, they were for the chief's private use. And the chief, he added with a lofty tone, could not be expected to read them in a drafty warehouse in Slough. Never mind that the chief was holed up in a cottage at the edge of Dartmoor. That was none of Robinson's affair.

Whitcombe had a reputation, well deserved, of being a lead-footed driver. He was in Andover by five thirty and had crossed the chalk plateau of Cranborne Chase before the sun came up. He stopped for a coffee and a bacon sandwich at the Esso in Sparkford, survived a biblical cloudburst in Taunton, and was careening up the drive of Wormwood Cottage by eight. From his office window, Parish watched him unloading the boxes, assisted by none other than "C" himself and the infamous chief of the Israeli secret intelligence service, who seemed to be struggling with a nagging pain at the small of his back. The great undertaking had commenced. Of that, Parish was certain.

44

WORMWOOD COTTAGE, DARTMOOR

Taken together, the files were a secret tour of the Middle East from 1956 to 1963, a time when Britain was fading, America was rising, the Russians were encroaching, the youthful State of Israel was flexing its newfound muscle, and the Arabs were flirting with all the failed *isms*—Pan-Arabism, Arab Nationalism, Arab Socialism—that would eventually lead to the rise of Islamism and jihadism and the mess of the present.

Arthur Seymour, as MI6's chief spy in the region, had a front-row seat for all of it. Officially, he was attached to Beirut station, but in practice it was only the place where he hung his hat. His brief was the region, and his masters were in London. He was in near constant motion, breakfast in Beirut, dinner in Damascus, Baghdad the next morning. Egypt's Nasser entertained him frequently, as did the House of Saud. He was even welcome in Tel Aviv, though the Office regarded him, with some justification, as unsympathetic to the Israeli predicament. Seymour's grudge against the Jewish state was personal. He had been inside the King David Hotel on July 22, 1946, when a bomb planted by the extremist Irgun killed ninety-one people, including twenty-eight British subjects.

Given the demands of Seymour's assignment, Kim Philby was something of a hobby. His reports to London were irregular at best. He sent them directly to Dick White, Philby's main nemesis from MI5 who was appointed chief of MI6 on the eve of Philby's arrival in Beirut. In his telegrams, Seymour referred to Philby by the code name Romeo, which lent their correspondence a faintly comic air.

"I bumped into Romeo on the Corniche on Wednesday last," he wrote in September 1956. "He was in fine form and good humor. We talked, about what, I cannot recall, as Romeo somehow managed to say nothing at all." It would be three weeks before the next update. "I attended a picnic with Romeo in the mountains outside Beirut. He became unspeakably drunk." Then, the next month: "Romeo became insultingly drunk during a party at the home of the American Miles Copeland. I don't know how he manages to function in his work as a correspondent. I fear for his health if present trends continue."

Gabriel and Graham Seymour had divided the eight boxes of files equally between them. Gabriel worked at a folding table in the sitting room, Seymour in the kitchen. They could see one another through the open communicating door, but their eyes rarely met; they were both reading as quickly as possible. Seymour might have doubted the woman's existence, but he was determined to find her first.

It was Gabriel, however, who discovered the first reference to Philby's complicated love life. "Romeo has been spotted at a café called the Shaky Floor with the wife of an important American newspaper correspondent. An affair might prove harmful to British interests." The important American correspondent was Sam Pope Brewer of the *New York Times*. More reports followed. "I have it on reliable authority the relationship between Romeo and the American woman is intimate. Her husband is unaware of the situation, as he is away on a long reporting trip. Perhaps someone should intervene before it is too late." But it was already too late, as Seymour soon discovered. "I have it on good authority Romeo has informed the American correspondent of his intention to marry his wife. Apparently, the American took the news quite well, telling Philby, 'That sounds like the best possible solution. What do you make of the situation in Iraq?'"

The internal politics of MI6's outpost in Beirut changed dramatically in early 1960 when Nicholas Elliott, Philby's closest friend, was appointed Head of Station. Philby's fortunes rose overnight, while Arthur Seymour, a known Philby doubter, was suddenly out of favor. It was no matter; he had his own back channel to Dick White in London, which he used to undermine Philby at every turn. "I've had occasion to review some of the intelligence Romeo is producing for H/Beirut. It is as dubious as Romeo's newspaper reporting. I fear H/Beirut is blinded to this fact by his friendship with Romeo. They are inseparable."

But Elliott left Beirut in October 1962 and returned to London to become controller for North Africa. Philby's drinking, already extreme, grew worse. "Romeo had to be carried out of a party last night," wrote Arthur Seymour on October 14. "Truly appalling." Three days later: "Romeo is so saturated with alcohol he becomes drunk after a single whisky." Then, on October 27: "Romeo hurled an object of some sort at his wife. It was most embarrassing for all of us who were forced to watch. I fear the marriage is unraveling before our eyes. I am told reliably that Romeo's wife is convinced he is having an affair."

Gabriel felt a tingling in his fingertips. *I am told reliably that Romeo's wife is convinced he is having an affair . . .* Rising, he carried the telegram into the kitchen and placed it solicitously before Graham Seymour. "She exists," he whispered and then withdrew once more to the sitting room. The great undertaking had entered the homestretch.

Gabriel had a single box of files remaining, Seymour a box and a half. Unfortunately, the files were in no particular order. Gabriel lurched from year to year, place to place, crisis to crisis, with no rhyme or reason. What's more, Arthur Seymour's habit of adding brief postscripts to his telegrams meant that each one had to be reviewed in its entirety. At times, it made for compelling reading. In one telegram, Gabriel found a reference to Operation Damocles, a clandestine campaign by the Office to assassinate former Nazi scientists who were helping Nasser develop rockets at a secret site known as Factory 333. There was even an oblique reference to Ari Shamron. "One of the Israeli operatives," wrote Seymour, "is a thoroughly unpleasant figure who fought for the Palmach during the war of independence. He is rumored to have taken part in the Eichmann operation in Argentina. One can almost hear chains clanking when he walks."

But it was Graham Seymour who found the next reference to Kim Philby's mistress in the long-forgotten files of his father. It was contained in a telegram dated November 3, 1962. Seymour dropped it triumphantly beneath Gabriel's nose, like an undergraduate who had just proven the unprovable. The relevant material was contained in a postscript. Gabriel read it slowly, twice. Then he read it again.

I have been told by a source I consider reliable that the affair has been going on for some time, perhaps as long as a year . . .

Gabriel placed the telegram atop the first one that referenced an affair and burrowed on, but once again it was Graham Seymour who unearthed the next clue.

"It's a message from Dick White to my father," he called through the doorway. "White sent it on November fourth, the very next day."

"What does it say?"

"He's concerned the other woman might actually be Philby's KGB controller. He instructed my father to find out who she is."

"Your father took his damn sweet time about it," replied Gabriel a moment later.

"What are you talking about?"

"He didn't send a response until November twenty-second."

"What was it?"

"He was reliably informed that the woman is quite young and a journalist."

"A freelance journalist," added Seymour a moment later.

"What have you got?"

"A telegram dated the sixth of December."

"Was he *reliably* informed?"

"By Richard Beeston," answered Seymour. "The British reporter."

"Is there a name?"

From the kitchen there was silence. They were getting closer, but they were both running low on files. And Arthur Seymour, though he didn't know it, was running out of time. By the end of the first week of December 1962, he had not yet learned the identity of Philby's lover. In a little more than a month, Philby would be gone.

"I've got another one," said Seymour. "She's French, our girl."

"Says who?"

"Says a source whose been reliable in the past. The source also says they see each other in the woman's apartment rather than Philby's."

"What's the date?"

"The nineteenth."

"December or January?"

"December."

Gabriel had about an inch of documents remaining. He discovered another trace of her in a telegram dated December 28. "They were spotted together in the bar of the St. Georges. Romeo was pretending to edit something she had written. It was obviously a ruse for a romantic assignation." And another two days after that: "She was overheard at the Normandie spouting Marxist drivel. It's no wonder Romeo finds her attractive."

And then, quite suddenly, December turned to January and she was forgotten. Nicholas Elliott had returned to Beirut to interrogate Philby and extract his confession and a pledge of cooperation. And Arthur Seymour was deeply worried Philby might make a run for it. His worst fears came true on the night of the twenty-third: "Romeo is nowhere to be found. I fear he has flown the coop."

It was the last telegram in Gabriel's stack, but in the kitchen Graham Seymour had several more to review. Gabriel sat down at the opposite side of the table and watched the rainwater running over the windows and the wind making patterns in the dormant grass of the moor. There was no sound other than the gentle rustle of paper. Seymour was reading with maddening slowness, running the tip of his forefinger down the length of each page before moving on to the next.

"Graham, *please . . .*"

"Quiet."

And then, a moment later, Seymour slid a single sheet of paper across the table. Gabriel didn't dare look at it. He was watching Kim Philby walking across the moor, holding the hand of a child.

"What is it?" he asked at last.

"A sort of after-action report, written in mid-February, after Philby was in Moscow."

"Is there a name?"

"See for yourself."

Gabriel looked down at the document before him.

The other woman's name is Charlotte Bettencourt. While it is true she is a bit of a leftist, she is certainly no agent of Moscow. Recommend no further action . . .

Gabriel looked up sharply. "My God! We found her!"

"That's not all we found. Read the postscript."

Gabriel looked down again.

I am reliably informed Mademoiselle Bettencourt is now several months pregnant. Has Philby no conscience at all?

No, thought Gabriel, he did not.

45

DARTMOOR—LONDON

The only computer at Wormwood Cottage with a connection to the outside world was the one on Parish's desk. Gabriel used it to conduct a perfunctory search of the name Charlotte Bettencourt. He found several dozen, young professionals mainly, including nine in France. None were journalists, and none were of the appropriate age. And when, on a lark, he added the name Kim Philby to the white rectangular box, he received fourteen thousand meaningless results, the Internet equivalent of an invitation to look elsewhere.

Which is precisely what Gabriel did. Not from Wormwood Cottage, but from the secure-communications room at the Israeli Embassy in London. He arrived there in the early evening after a white-knuckle ride from Devon in Nigel Whitcombe's Ford hatchback and placed a call to Paul Rousseau, chief of the Alpha Group, in Paris. Rousseau, as it turned out, was still at his desk. France was on high alert, with a stream of intelligence indicating an attack by ISIS was imminent. Contritely, Gabriel made his request.

"Bettencourt, Charlotte."

"Birthdate?" asked Rousseau with a heavy sigh.

"Sometime around 1940."

"And she was a journalist, you say?"

"Apparently."

"Apparently *yes*, or apparently *no*?" asked Rousseau impatiently.

Gabriel explained she had worked in Beirut as a freelancer in the early sixties, and that by all accounts she subscribed to left-wing politics.

"So did everyone else in the early sixties."

"Is it possible the old DST might have opened a file on her?"

"It's possible," admitted Rousseau. "They opened a file on anyone with pro-Moscow sympathies. I'll run her name through the database."

"Quietly," cautioned Gabriel, and hung up the phone. And for the next three hours, alone in a soundproof box in the embassy's basement, he considered all the reasons why Rousseau's search might prove fruitless. Perhaps Arthur Seymour had been mistaken and Charlotte Bettencourt was not her real name. Perhaps after giving birth to Philby's child, she had changed her name and gone into hiding. Perhaps she had fled to Moscow and was living there still. Perhaps the great Sasha had killed her, as he had killed Konstantin Kirov and Alistair Hughes.

Whatever had happened to the woman, it was a very long time ago. It had been a long time, too, since Gabriel had slept.

At some point, he laid his head on the table and drifted into unconsciousness. The phone woke him with a start. It was half past eleven. Eleven in the morning or eleven at night, he did not know; the soundproof box was a world without sunrise or sunset. He snatched up the receiver and raised it swiftly to his ear.

"She left Beirut in 1965 and returned to Paris," said Paul Rousseau. "She was a somewhat minor figure in the demonstrations in sixty-eight. After that, the DST lost interest in her."

"Is she still alive?"

"Apparently so."

Gabriel's heart gave a sideways lurch. "Apparently *yes*, or apparently *no*?"

"She still receives her state pension. The checks are sent to an address in Spain."

"You don't happen to have it, do you?"

As a matter of fact, he did. Charlotte Bettencourt, the mother of Kim Philby's illegitimate child, lived on the Paseo de la Fuente in Zahara, Spain.

46

ZAHARA, SPAIN

It was shortly after two o'clock the following afternoon when Charlotte Bettencourt concluded she was being watched by a pair of men, one tall and lanky, the other a few inches shorter and more powerfully built. Kim would have been proud of her for spotting them, but truth be told they made little effort to conceal themselves. It was almost as if they wanted her to see them. A pair of Russians sent to kidnap or kill her would not have behaved so. Therefore, she did not fear the men. In fact, she was looking forward to the moment they finally put all pretense aside and introduced themselves. Until then, she would think of them as Rosencrantz and Guildenstern, two indifferent creatures of the earth who functioned as one.

She had noticed them for the first time earlier that morning strolling along the paseo. The second sighting occurred on the Calle San Juan, where they were sitting beneath an umbrella at one of the cafés, each staring at a mobile phone, seemingly oblivious to her presence. And now here they were again. Charlotte was lunching among the orange trees at Bar Mirador, and the two men were crossing the paving stones of the plaza toward the church of Santa María de la Mesa. They did not strike her as believers, especially the taller of the two, the one with pale skin. Perhaps they were in search of absolution. They looked as though they could use it.

The two men climbed the steps of the church—*one, two, three, four*—and disappeared inside. Charlotte picked up her pen and tried to resume her work, but it was no good; the sight of the two men had dammed the flow of words. She had been writing about an afternoon in September 1962 when Kim, rather than make love to her, became drunk instead. He was inconsolable with grief. Jackie, his beloved pet fox, had recently fallen to its death from the terrace of his apartment. But Charlotte was convinced something else was troubling him and had pleaded with him to take her into his confidence. "You couldn't p-p-possibly understand," he had stammered into his drink, his eyes hidden beneath the mantle of his unruly forelock. "Everything I did, I did as a matter of c-c-conscience." She should have known at that instant it was all true, that Kim was a Soviet spy, the Third Man, a traitor. She would not have despised him. Quite the opposite, actually. She would have loved him all the more.

She returned her pen and Moleskine notebook to her straw bag and finished the last of her wine. There was only one other patron in the café, an elfin man with wispy hair and a face that defied description. The weather was ideal, warm in the sun, chill in the shade of the orange trees. Charlotte wore a fleece pullover and a pair of denim trousers with a dreaded elastic waist. It was perhaps the worst thing about growing old, the pouch she was forced to lug around all day, like her memories of Kim. She could scarcely recall the lithe, supple body he had devoured each afternoon before running home to Eleanor for the evening quarrel. He had loved her body, even when the bump appeared in her abdomen. "Do you suppose it will be a b-b-boy or a girl?" he had asked, stroking her skin softly. Not that it mattered. Two weeks later he was gone.

The man with wispy hair was studying a newspaper. Poor lamb, thought Charlotte. He was alone in the world, like her. She was tempted to strike up a conversation, but the two men were stepping from the church, into the glare of the plaza. They passed her table in silence and headed down the steep slope of the Calle Machenga.

After paying her check, Charlotte did the same. She was not attempting to follow the two men; it was merely the shortest route to the little El Castillo supermarket. Inside, she saw one of the men yet again. It was the one she thought of as Rosencrantz, the taller one. He was contemplating a container of milk, as though searching for the expiration date. For the first time, Charlotte felt a stab of fear. Perhaps she had been mistaken. Perhaps they were an SVR snatch team after all. She thought Rosencrantz looked a little Russian, now that she had a chance to see him up close.

She hastily tossed a few items into her basket and then surrendered her money to a busty girl with a bare belly and too much makeup. "La loca," hissed the girl contemptuously as Charlotte carried her plastic bags into the street. And there stood Guildenstern. He was leaning against an orange tree, smiling.

"Bonjour, Madame Bettencourt." His tone was agreeable. He

took a cautious step toward her. "Sorry to bother you, but I was wondering whether we might have a word in private."

His eyes were very blue, like Kim's.

"A word about what?" she asked.

"The matter I wish to discuss with you," said the man, "is quite sensitive in nature."

Charlotte smiled bitterly. "The last time someone said that to me . . ." She watched the wispy-haired man walking toward them down the slope of the hill. She hadn't suspected him. She supposed he was of a higher caliber.

She directed her gaze toward the one she thought of as Guildenstern, the one with Kim's blue eyes. "Are you from the French government?" she asked.

"Heavens, no."

"Where, then?"

"I work for the British Foreign Office."

"So you're a spy." She glanced toward the wispy-haired man. "And him?"

"He's an associate."

"He doesn't look British to me."

"He isn't."

"What about Rosencrantz?"

"Who?"

"Oh, never mind." She heard resignation in her own voice. It was finally over. "How on earth did you find me?"

Her question seemed to take the Englishman by surprise. "It's a long story, Madame Bettencourt."

"I'm sure it is." The bags were growing heavy. "Am I in some sort of trouble?"

"I shouldn't think so."

"Everything I did, I did as a matter of conscience." She was confused. Was it Kim talking, or her? "And what about my—" Abruptly, Charlotte stopped herself.

"Who, Madame Bettencourt?"

Not yet, she thought. Better to keep something in reserve in case she needed to purchase her freedom. She didn't trust the man, nor should she. The British were the greatest liars God ever created. This she knew for a fact.

The tall, pale one was now standing next to her. Gently, he pried the plastic sacks from her grasp and placed them in the trunk of a Renault sedan before sliding agilely behind the wheel. The wispy-haired man sat in front; Charlotte and the one with blue eyes, in back. As the car drew away, she thought of the books lining the shelf in her alcove, and the antique Victorian strongbox beneath her desk. Inside was a leather-bound scrapbook, so old it smelled only of dust. The long boozy lunches at the St. Georges and the Normandie, the picnics in the hills, the afternoons in the privacy of her apartment, when his defenses were down. There were also eight yellowed snapshots of a child, the last one taken in the autumn of 1984, on Jesus Lane in Cambridge.

47

ZAHARA—SEVILLE

The car shot past Charlotte's villa without slowing. The tiny forecourt was empty, but she thought she glimpsed movement in one of the windows. Jackals, she thought, picking over the bones. It had finally happened. Her life had teetered over the edge of the crag and crashed to the floor of the valley. She had been a willing participant, it was true, but it was Kim at long last who had dragged her down. Charlotte was not the first; Kim had left much human wreckage in his wake. She thought again of the Victorian strongbox beneath her desk. They knew, she thought. Perhaps not all of it, but they knew.

"Where are we going?" she asked.

"Not far," replied the blue-eyed Englishman.

Just then, her Seiko wristwatch shrieked. "My pills!" Charlotte exclaimed. "I can't leave without my pills. Please go back."

"Don't worry, Madame Bettencourt." He fished an amber prescription bottle from his jacket pocket. "These?"

"The other, please."

He handed her the second bottle. She shook a tablet into her palm and swallowed it without water, which seemed to impress him. The villa was gone from view. Charlotte wondered whether she would ever see it again. It had been a long time since she had ventured more than walking distance from it. When she was younger she had traveled the length and breadth of Spain by motorcar—such was the life Comrade Lavrov's money had afforded her. But now that she was old and could no longer drive, her world had shrunk. Oh, she supposed she could have traveled by coach, but it held no appeal, all those sweaty proletarians with their garlic sandwiches and howling children. Charlotte was a socialist—a communist, even—but her commitment to the revolution did not extend to public transport.

The valley was green with the winter rains. Rosencrantz had only his left hand on the steering wheel. With his right he was tapping a nervous rhythm on the center console. It was driving Charlotte to distraction.

"Does he always do that?" she asked the Englishman, but he only smiled in response.

They were approaching the turnoff for the A375. The signpost that flashed past Charlotte's window read SEVILLA. Rosencrantz lurched into the exit lane without slowing or bothering to signal. So did the car in front of them, observed Charlotte, and the one following.

"How much longer?" she asked.

"An hour and a half," answered the Englishman.

"Maybe a little less"—Charlotte raised an eyebrow disapprovingly toward Rosencrantz—"the way he's driving."

The Englishman took a long look over his shoulder.

"Are they still behind us?" asked Charlotte.

"Who?"

Charlotte knew better than to ask again. Her pill was making her drowsy, as was the gentle rise and fall of the speeding car over the rolling terrain, and the warm sun on the side of her face. She leaned her head against the rest and closed her eyes. A part of her was actually looking forward to it. It had been a long time since she had been to Seville.

She awoke to the sight of La Giralda, the minaret turned bell tower of the Seville Cathedral, rising above the Barrio de Santa Cruz, the city's ancient Jewish quarter. They had stopped on a narrow side street, outside an American coffeehouse. Charlotte frowned at the ubiquitous green-and-white sign.

"They're everywhere," said the Englishman, noting her reaction.

"Not in Zahara. We have a hill town's mentality."

The Englishman smiled, as if he were familiar with such thinking. "I'm afraid this is as far as we can drive. Are you capable of walking a short distance?"

"Capable?" Charlotte was tempted to tell him that she walked more than a mile each day. In fact, she could have told him the precise number of her daily steps, but she didn't want him to think her a madwoman. "Yes, I'm fine," she said. "I've always liked walking in Seville."

The little man with unkempt hair was now standing at her door with the attentiveness of a bellman. Charlotte accepted his hand. It was firm and dry, as though he spent a great deal of time digging in parched earth.

"What about my groceries?" she asked. "They'll spoil if you leave them in the trunk."

The little man stared at her silently. He was a watcher, she thought, not a talker. The Englishman raised a hand toward La Giralda and said, "This way, please."

His solicitous manners were beginning to grate on her almost as much as his friend's tapping. All the smiles and charm in the world couldn't conceal the fact they were taking her into custody. If he said "please" one more time, she thought, she would show him a flash of her legendary temper. It had frightened even Kim.

They followed a succession of narrow alleyways deeper into the quarter until at last they came to a Moorish passageway. It gave onto an arcaded courtyard, shadowed and fragranced by the scent of Seville oranges. A man waited there alone, contemplating the water splashing in the fountain. He looked up with a start, as though surprised by her arrival, and stared at her with unconcealed curiosity. Charlotte did the same, for she recognized him at once. His eyes betrayed him. He was the Israeli who had been blamed for the murder of that Russian intelligence officer in Vienna.

"I thought it would be you," she said after a moment.

He smiled broadly.

"Did I say something funny?"

"Those were the same words Kim Philby spoke when Nicholas Elliott came to Beirut to accuse him of being a spy."

"Yes, I know," said Charlotte. "Kim told me all about it."

48

SEVILLE

T he room into which Gabriel led Charlotte Bettencourt was somber and paneled and hung with many paintings of questionable provenance that were darkened by time and neglect. Leather-bound editions of great books lined the heavy wooden shelves, and on the seventeenth-century credenza was an ormolu clock set to the wrong time. One object looked slightly out of place, an antique Victorian strongbox, wooden, its varnish faded and cracked, resting on the low center table.

Charlotte Bettencourt had yet to notice it; she was surveying her surroundings with evident disapproval. Or perhaps, thought Gabriel, it was familiarity. Her name suggested an aristocratic lineage. So, too, did her posture. Even in old age, it was very erect, like a dancer's. Mentally, he retouched her lined and sun-spotted face, restoring her to the age of approximately twenty-four, when she had traveled to Beirut to take up the craft of journalism. There, for reasons Gabriel could not yet fathom, she had given herself to the likes of Kim Philby. Love was one possible explanation for the attraction. The other was politics. Or perhaps it was a combination of the two, which would make her a very formidable opponent indeed.

"Is it yours?" she asked.

"I'm sorry?"

"This house."

"I'm afraid," said Gabriel, "I am oftentimes forced to rely on the kindness of strangers."

"We have that in common."

Gabriel smiled in spite of himself.

"Who owns it?" she asked.

"A friend of a friend."

"Jewish?"

Gabriel shrugged indifferently.

"He's obviously wealthy, this friend of yours."

"Not as wealthy as he once was."

"What a pity." She said this to the ormolu clock. Turning, she scrutinized Gabriel carefully. "You're smaller than I imagined."

"So are you."

"I'm old."

"We have that in common, too."

This time, it was Charlotte Bettencourt who smiled. It faded quickly when at last she noticed the antique box. "You had no right to break into my house and take my things. Then again, I suppose my offenses are of a far greater magnitude. And now it seems someone else is going to pay the price."

Gabriel didn't respond, he didn't dare. Charlotte Bettencourt was staring at Christopher Keller, who was comparing the time on his wristwatch to the time on the clock.

"Your friend told me he was British," she said. "Is that true?"

"I'm afraid so."

"And what is your interest in this affair?" she demanded to know. "On whose authority are you here?"

"In this matter," said Gabriel, his tone judicial, "the British and Israeli intelligence services are working together."

"Kim would be turning in his grave."

Again Gabriel chose silence as his response. It was far more useful than telling Charlotte Bettencourt how he felt about Kim Philby's opinions regarding the State of Israel. She was still watching Keller, with a mildly bemused expression on her face.

"Your friend also refused to tell me how you managed to find me. Perhaps you would."

Gabriel decided there was no harm in it, it was so long ago. "We found your name in an old MI6 file."

"From Beirut?"

"Yes."

"Kim assured me no one knew about us."

"He was wrong about that, too," said Gabriel coolly.

"Who was it? Who found us out?"

"His name was Arthur Seymour."

She gave a mischievous smile. "Kim loathed him."

"The feeling was mutual." Gabriel felt as though he were conversing with a figure in a historical diorama. "Arthur Seymour suspected Philby was a Soviet spy from the beginning. His superiors in London thought you might be a spy, too."

"I wasn't. I was merely an impressionable young woman with strong beliefs." Her gaze fell upon the wooden box. "But you know that, don't you? You know everything."

"Not everything," admitted Gabriel.

"Am I in legal jeopardy?" she asked.

"You are a French citizen of advanced age living in Spain."

"Money has changed hands."

"It almost always does."

"Not in Kim's case. Oh, he took a little money, just enough to survive when he needed it. But his actions were motivated by his faith in communism. I shared that faith. So did a great many of your coreligionists, Mr. Allon."

"I was raised on that faith."

"Do you have it still?" she pried.

"Another matter for another time."

She was staring at the box again. "And what about my . . ."

"I'm afraid I can't offer you any guarantees," said Gabriel.

"Will there be an arrest? A prosecution? Another scandal?"

"That's a decision for the chief of MI6, not me."

"He's the son of Arthur Seymour, is he not?"

"Yes," said Gabriel, surprised. "He is."

"Imagine that. I met him once, you know."

"Arthur Seymour?"

"No. His son. It was at the bar of the Normandie. Kim was being naughty and trying to buy him a pink gin. I'm sure he doesn't remember. He was only a boy, and it was so long ago." She smiled wistfully. "But we're getting ahead of ourselves. Perhaps we should start at the beginning, Monsieur Allon. It will help you to better understand why it happened."

"Yes," agreed Gabriel. "Perhaps we should."

49

SEVILLE

The beginning, she said, was a small village near Nantes, in the Loire Valley of western France. The Bettencourts were an ancient family, rich in land and possessions. Charlotte was old enough to recall the sight of German soldiers on the streets of her village, and the well-mannered Wehrmacht captain who was billeted in the family's château. Charlotte's father treated the German occupiers respectfully—too respectfully, in the opinion of some in the village—and after the war there were whispers of collaboration. The communists were very powerful in the *département*. The children of the working class taunted young Charlotte mercilessly and on one occasion attempted to cut off her hair. They might well have succeeded were it not for Monsignor Jean-Marc, who intervened on her behalf. Many years later, a historical commission would accuse the monsignor, a family friend of the Bettencourts, of being a collaborator, too.

In 1956 Charlotte moved to Paris to study French literature at the Sorbonne. It was an autumn of seismic political events. In late October, Israeli, British, and French troops attempted to seize control of the Suez Canal from Egypt's Nasser. And in early November, Soviet tanks rolled into Budapest to crush the Hungarian Uprising. Charlotte sided with Moscow on both issues, for by then she was a committed communist.

She left the Sorbonne in 1960 and spent the next year and a half writing reviews and political commentaries for a small literary magazine. Bored, she asked her father for enough money to move to Beirut so that she might become a foreign correspondent. Her father had grown weary of Charlotte's politics—they were barely speaking at that point—and was more than pleased to be rid of her. She arrived in Lebanon in January 1962, took an apartment near the American University, and began filing stories for several left-leaning French publications, for which she was paid almost nothing. It didn't matter; she had her family's money to support her. Still, she longed to make her mark as a real journalist. She frequently sought advice from members of the large community of foreign correspondents, including one who drank at the bar of the Hotel Normandie.

"Philby," said Gabriel.

"Kim," replied Charlotte. "He'll always be Kim to me."

She was seated at the edge of a brocade chair, her hands folded neatly atop her knees, her feet flat on the floor. Eli Lavon sat in the chair next to her, gazing absently into the middle distance like a man on a rail platform waiting for a long-delayed train. Mikhail, it seemed, was having a staring contest with a figure in one of the darkened paintings, a poor copy of an El Greco. Keller, feigning indifference, had opened the back of the ormolu clock and was tinkering with the mechanism.

"You were in love with him?" asked Gabriel, who was pacing the room slowly.

"With Kim? Very much."

"Why?"

"Because he wasn't my father, I suppose."

"Did you know he was a Soviet spy?"

"Don't be silly. Kim never would have entrusted his secret with me."

"But surely you must have suspected."

"I asked him the question once, and I never asked it again. But it was obvious he was in a great deal of pain. He used to have the most terrible nightmares after making love to me. And his drinking was . . . like nothing I had ever seen."

"When did you realize you were pregnant?"

"The beginning of November. I waited until the end of December to tell him."

"How did he react?"

"He nearly killed us both. He was driving at the time," she explained. "A woman should never tell her lover that she is pregnant when he is behind the wheel of a car. Especially when her lover is drunk."

"He was angry?"

"He pretended to be. Actually, I think he was heartbroken. Say what you like about Kim, but he adored his children. He probably thought he would never see the one I was carrying in my womb."

Probably, noted Gabriel. "Did you make any demands of him?"

"Of Kim Philby? I didn't bother. His finances were in dreadful shape. There was no possibility of any support or of marriage. I knew that if I had the baby, I would have to look after it myself."

Philby's birthday was on New Year's Day. It was his fifty-first. Charlotte had hoped to spend at least a few minutes with Kim, but he telephoned to say he couldn't come to her apartment. He had fallen the night before, twice, and had split his head open and blackened both his eyes. He used his dreadful appearance as an excuse to avoid seeing her for the next two weeks. The true reason for his absence, she said, was Nicholas Elliott's arrival in Beirut.

"When was the next time you saw him?"

"The twenty-third."

"The day he fled Beirut."

She nodded. "Kim came to see me in the late afternoon. He looked worse than ever. It was pouring rain, and he was soaking wet. He said he could stay for only a few minutes. He was supposed to meet Eleanor for dinner at the home of the first secretary from the British Embassy. I tried to make love to him, but he pushed me away and asked for a drink. Then he told me Nicholas had accused him of being a Soviet spy."

"Did he deny it?"

"No," said Charlotte pointedly. "He did not."

"How much did he tell you?"

"Much more than he should have. And then he gave me an envelope."

"What was in it?"

"Money."

"For the baby?"

She nodded slowly.

"Did he say where he'd got it?"

"No. But if I had to guess, it was from Petukhov, his KGB contact in Beirut. Kim left later that night aboard a Soviet cargo ship. The *Dolmatova*. I never saw him again."

"Never?"

"No, Monsieur Allon. Never."

When the news of Philby's defection broke, Charlotte continued, she briefly considered writing a personal exclusive. "The Kim Philby I knew and loved, that sort of drivel." Instead, she filed a couple of stories that made no reference to their personal relationship and waited for their child to be born. She delivered in a Beirut hospital, alone, in the late spring of 1963.

"You never told your family?"

"Not then."

"The French Embassy?"

"Appropriate declarations were made, and a passport was issued."

"There was a birth certificate, I assume."

"Of course."

"And what did you put down as the name of the father?"

"Philby," she answered in a mildly defiant tone. "Harold Adrian Russell."

"And the child's name?"

"Bettencourt," she replied evasively.

"And the first name?" pressed Gabriel. "The Christian name?"

Charlotte Bettencourt stared at the wooden box. "You already know the child's name, Monsieur Allon. Please don't make me commit another act of betrayal."

Gabriel didn't. Not then, not ever. "You returned to France in 1965," he prompted her.

"The winter."

"Where did you go?"

To a small village near Nantes, she said, in the Loire Valley of western France.

"Your parents must have been surprised."

"That's putting it mildly. My father sent me away and told me never to come back."

"Did you tell your parents the name of the child's father?"

"Had I done that," she said, "it would have only made the situation worse."

"Did you tell anyone?"

"No. I told no one. *Ever.*"

"What about the birth certificate?"

"I *lost* it."

"How convenient."

"Yes."

"What really happened to it?"

She glanced at the wooden box, then looked away. In the courtyard a trio of security guards stood like statuary in the gathering darkness. Eli Lavon was still waiting for his train, but Keller and Mikhail were now staring at Charlotte Bettencourt, rapt. The clock had stopped working altogether. So, too, it seemed, had Gabriel's heart.

"Where did you go next?" he asked.

Back to Paris, she answered, this time with a small child in tow. They lived in a garret room in the Latin Quarter. It was all Charlotte could afford now that she had been cut off financially by her father. Her mother used to give her a few francs whenever she came to visit, but her father did not acknowledge the child's existence. Neither, it seemed, did Kim. With each passing year, though, the child looked more like him. The very blue eyes, the unruly forelock. There was even a faint stammer, which faded by the age of eight. Charlotte forsook journalism and devoted herself to the Party and the revolution.

They had no money to speak of, but they didn't need much. They were in Paris, and the glorious city was theirs. They used to play a silly game together, counting the steps between their favorite landmarks. How many steps from the Louvre to Notre-Dame? How many steps from the Arc de Triomphe to the Place de la Concorde? From the Tour Eiffel to Les Invalides?

There were eighty-seven steps between their garret apartment and the courtyard of the building, Charlotte explained, and another thirty-eight to the door leading to the rue Saint-Jacques. Which was where, on a warm summer's day in 1974, when most Parisians had wisely fled the city, a man was waiting.

"What was the date?" asked Gabriel.

"August," Charlotte answered. "It was the day after Nixon resigned."

"That would make it the tenth."

"If you say so."

"And the man's name?"

"On that occasion, he introduced himself as Comrade Lavrov."

"And on others?"

Sasha, she answered. He called himself Sasha.

50

SEVILLE

He was thin—gulag thin, said Charlotte—and pale as candle wax. A few strands of lank unwashed hair lay plastered to his skull, which was wide at the forehead, conferring upon him the appearance of superior intelligence. The eyes were small and rimmed with red, the teeth were gray and jagged. He wore a tweed jacket, too heavy for the broiling heat, and a formerly white shirt that looked as though it had been rinsed out too many times in a kitchen basin. His beard was in need of a trimming.

"Beard?"

"He wore a small one." She moved her thumb and forefinger from her upper lip to her chin.

"Like Lenin?" asked Gabriel.

"A younger Lenin. Lenin in exile. Lenin in London."

"And what brought him to Paris?"

"He said he had a letter."

"From Philby?"

"He never uttered the name. He said the letter was from a man I had known in Beirut. A famous English journalist." She dropped the register of her voice to a masculine pitch and added a thick Russian accent. "'Would it be possible for us to speak somewhere private? The matter I wish to discuss is quite sensitive in nature.' I suggested the brasserie across the street"— her normal voice again—"but he said my apartment would be better. I explained it was modest. He said he already knew this."

"The implication being that he had been watching you for some time."

"He comes from your world, not mine."

"And the letter?"

It was typewritten, which was not like Kim, and unsigned. Even so, she knew the words were his. He apologized for having deceived her in Beirut and said he wished to renew their relationship. As part of that renewal, he wished to see his child. For obvious reasons, he wrote, the meeting could not take place in France.

"He wanted you to come to Moscow?"

"Not me. The child only."

"And you agreed?"

"Yes."

"Why?"

She gave no answer.

"Because you were still in love with him?" suggested Gabriel.

"With Kim? Not then, not any longer. But I was still in love with the *idea* of Kim."

"And what idea was that?"

"Commitment to the revolution." She paused, then added, "Sacrifice."

"You didn't mention betrayal."

Ignoring his remark, she explained that Sasha and the child left Paris that very night, on a train to Germany. They crossed into the eastern sector by car, drove to Warsaw, and then flew to Moscow, the child on a false Russian passport. Philby's apartment was near Pushkin Square, hidden away on a narrow lane near an old church, between Tverskaya Street and the Patriarch's Ponds. He lived there with Rufina, his Russian wife.

"His fourth," Charlotte Bettencourt added acidly.

"How long did—"

"Three days."

"I assume there was another visit."

"Christmas, that same year."

"Again in Moscow?"

"Ten days," she said, nodding.

"And the next visit?"

"The following summer. A month."

"A month is a very long time."

"It was hard on me, I admit."

"And after that?"

"Sasha came to Paris to see me again."

They met on a park bench, the way Philby had met Otto four decades earlier. The bench was not in Regent's Park, but in the Jardin des Tuileries. Sasha said he had been ordered by Moscow Center to embark on a historic endeavor on behalf of international peace. Kim would be his partner in this endeavor. It was Sasha's wish, and Kim's, for Charlotte to join them.

"And what was your role in this endeavor?"

"A brief marriage. And an enormous sacrifice."

"Who was the lucky groom?"

"An Englishman from a well-connected family who also believed in peace."

"By that, you mean he was a KGB agent."

"His exact affiliation with Moscow was never made clear to me. His father had known Kim at Cambridge. He was quite radical, and quite homosexual. But that didn't matter. It wasn't to be a real marriage."

"Where were you wed?"

"England."

"Church?"

"Civil."

"Did your family attend?"

"Of course not."

"And how long did this union last?"

"Two years. Ours wasn't a match made in heaven, Monsieur Allon. It was a match made at Moscow Center."

"What precipitated the divorce?"

"Adultery."

"How fitting."

"Apparently, I was caught in flagrante with one of my husband's closest friends. It was quite a scandal, actually. So was my heavy drinking, which had left me unfit to be a mother. For the good of the child, I agreed to surrender custody."

A long and painful period of estrangement followed so that the child would become thoroughly English. Charlotte stayed in

Paris for a time. Then, at Moscow Center's behest, she settled in a *pueblo blanco* in the mountains of Andalusia where no one would find her. There were letters at first, but soon the letters stopped. Sasha claimed they were slowing the transition.

Occasionally, Charlotte received vague, bland updates, such as the one that arrived in 1981 concerning admission to an elite British university. The update did not specify which university, but Charlotte knew enough of Kim's past to make a reasonable assumption. Without informing Sasha, she returned to England in 1984 and made her way to Cambridge. And there, on Jesus Lane, she spotted the child of treason, Philby's child, walking through the shadow cast by a tall redbrick wall, an unruly forelock covering one very blue eye. With her camera, Charlotte surreptitiously snapped a photo.

"It was the last time I . . ." Her voice trailed off.

"And after Cambridge?" asked Gabriel.

Charlotte received an update saying the endeavor had proven successful. She was never told which department of British intelligence it was, but she assumed it was MI6. Kim, she said, would have never settled for MI5, not after the way they pursued him so relentlessly.

"And you've had no contact in all these years?"

"Occasionally, I receive a letter, a few empty lines no doubt composed by Moscow Center. They contain no information about work or a personal life, nothing that I might use to—"

"Find the child you abandoned?" The remark wounded her. "I'm sorry, Madame Bettencourt, I don't understand how—"

"That's right, Monsieur Allon. You don't."

"Perhaps you could explain it to me."

"It was a different time. The world was different. *They* were different."

"Who?"

"The Russians. As far as we were concerned, Moscow was the center of the universe. They were going to change the world, and we were obliged to help them."

"Help the KGB? They were monsters," said Gabriel. "They still are."

Greeted by silence, Gabriel asked when she had last received a letter.

"It was about two weeks ago."

Gabriel concealed his alarm. "How was it delivered?"

"By an oaf called Karpov from the Madrid *rezidentura*. He also informed me that Moscow Center would like me to take a long holiday in Russia."

"Why now?" asked Gabriel.

"You would know better than I, Monsieur Allon."

"I'm surprised they didn't come for you a long time ago."

"It was part of my original arrangement with Kim and Sasha. I had no desire to live in the Soviet Union."

"Perhaps it wasn't such a Marxist utopia after all."

Charlotte Bettencourt suffered his rebuke in penitential silence. All around them, Seville was beginning to stir. There was music in the air, and from the bars and cafés in a nearby plaza came the chiming of glasses and cutlery. Evening breeze swirled in the courtyard. It carried the scent of oranges into the room and, quite suddenly, the sound of a young woman's laughter. Charlotte Bettencourt cocked her head expectantly, listening as the laughter faded. Then she stared at the Victorian box resting on the table.

"It was a gift from Kim," she said after a moment. "He found it in a little shop in the Christian quarter of Beirut. It's rather fitting, don't you think? Leave it to Kim to give me a box to lock away my secrets."

"His, too," said Gabriel. He lifted the lid and removed a stack of envelopes bound by a faded ribbon of Lenten violet. "He was rather prolific, wasn't he?"

"During the first weeks of our affair, I sometimes received two letters a day."

Gabriel reached into the box again. This time, he withdrew a single sheet of paper, a birth certificate from Saint George Hospital in Beirut, Lebanon's oldest, dated May 26, 1963. He pointed to the child's given name.

"Was it ever changed?" he asked.

"No," she answered. "As fortune would have it, it was sufficiently English."

"Like yours." Gabriel reached into Kim Philby's box of secrets again. This time, he withdrew a British marriage certificate dated April 1977. "A spring wedding. It must have been lovely."

"It was quite small, actually."

Gabriel pointed to the groom's family name. "I assume you both took it."

"For a time," she answered. "I became Charlotte Bettencourt again after the divorce."

"But not—"

"That would have been counterproductive," she said, cutting him off. "After all, the entire point of the marriage was to acquire a name and a pedigree that would open the doors of an elite university and eventually the Secret Intelligence Service."

Gabriel laid the marriage certificate next to the birth certificate and Philby's love letters. Then he reached into the box a final time and removed a Kodak snapshot dated October 1984. Even Gabriel could see the resemblance—to Philby, unquestionably, but to Charlotte Bettencourt as well.

"You took the photograph and then walked away?" he asked. "You didn't speak?"

"What would I have said?"

"You could have begged for forgiveness. You could have put a stop to it."

"Why would I have done a thing like that, after everything I'd sacrificed? Remember, the Cold War was at a low point. Reagan the cowboy was in the White House. The Americans were pouring nuclear missiles into Western Europe."

"And for this," said Gabriel coldly, "you were prepared to give up your daughter?"

"She wasn't mine alone, she was Kim's, too. I was only a salon militant, but not her. She was the genuine article. She had betrayal in the blood."

"So do you, Madame Bettencourt."

"Everything I did," she said, "I did as a matter of conscience."

"You obviously don't have one. And neither did Philby."

"Kim," she said. "He'll always be Kim to me."

She was staring at the photograph. Not in anguish, thought Gabriel, but with pride.

"Why?" he asked. "Why did you do it?"

"Is there an answer I could give that you would find satisfactory?"

"No."

"Then perhaps, Monsieur Allon, we should leave it to the past."

"Yes," said Gabriel. "Perhaps we should."

PART THREE

DOWN BY THE RIVER

51

SEVILLE—LONDON

There were several flights between Seville and London the next morning, but Gabriel and Christopher Keller drove to Lisbon instead, on the assumption that Moscow Center was checking the outgoing Spanish manifests. Keller paid for their tickets with a credit card that bore the name Peter Marlowe, his MI6 work name. He did not inform Vauxhall Cross of his pending return to British soil, and Gabriel did not alert his station. He had no luggage other than his Office-built attaché case. Concealed in its false compartment were three items taken from the Victorian strongbox Kim Philby had given Charlotte Bettencourt on the occasion of her twenty-fifth birthday. A birth certificate, a marriage certificate, and a snapshot taken without the subject's knowledge on Jesus Lane in Cambridge. On Gabriel's

BlackBerry were photographs of the remaining items. The silly love letters, the notebooks, the beginnings of a memoir, the many intimate photos of Philby taken inside Charlotte Bettencourt's Beirut apartment. Madame Bettencourt herself was at the house in Seville, under Office protection.

The plane touched down at Heathrow a few minutes after ten. Gabriel and Keller cleared passport control separately and reunited in the chaos of the arrivals hall. Keller's MI6 BlackBerry pinged with an incoming message a few seconds later.

"We're busted."

"Who's it from?"

"Nigel Whitcombe. He must have been watching my credit card. He wants to give us a lift into town."

"Tell him thanks, but no thanks."

Keller frowned at the taxi queue. "What harm would it do?"

"That depends on whether the Russians followed Nigel from Vauxhall Cross."

"There he is."

Keller nodded toward the Ford hatchback waiting outside the terminal doors, its headlamps flashing. Gabriel reluctantly followed him outside and climbed into the backseat. A moment later they were speeding along the M40 toward central London. Whitcombe's eyes found Gabriel's in the rearview mirror.

"The chief asked me to take you to the Stockwell safe house."

"We're not going anywhere near it. Take me to the Bayswater Road instead."

"It's not exactly the safest of safe flats."

"Neither are yours," said Gabriel beneath his breath. The clouds were low and heavy, and it was not yet properly light. "How long does the chief intend to keep me waiting?"

"He's meeting with the Joint Intelligence Committee until noon. Then he's going to Downing Street for a private lunch with the prime minister."

Gabriel swore softly.

"Shall I tell him to cancel lunch?"

"No. It's important he keep to his normal schedule."

"Sounds bad."

"It is," said Gabriel. "As bad as it gets."

It was true that the Office safe flat located on the Bayswater Road was no longer fully secure. In fact, Gabriel had used it so often that Housekeeping referred to it as his London pied-à-terre. It had been six months since his last stay. It was the night he and Keller returned to London after killing Saladin at his compound in Morocco. Gabriel had arrived at the safe flat to find Chiara waiting. They had shared a midnight supper, he had slept a few hours, and in the morning, outside the security barrier at Downing Street, he and Keller had killed an ISIS terrorist armed with a radiological dispersion device, a dirty bomb. Together they had spared Britain a calamity. Now they were delivering one to her doorstep.

Housekeeping had left a few nonperishables in the pantry and a Beretta 9mm with a walnut grip in the bedroom closet. Gabriel warmed a tin of minestrone while Keller, from the sitting room window, watched the traffic moving along the road, and the man, vaguely Russian in appearance, resting on a bench in Hyde Park. The man left the bench at half past twelve, and a woman took his place. Keller rammed the loaded magazine into the Beretta and chambered the first round. At the sound, Gabriel poked his head into the room and raised an inquisitive eyebrow.

"Maybe Nigel was right," said Keller. "Maybe we should go to one of our safe houses."

"MI6 doesn't have any. Not anymore."

"Then let's go somewhere else. This place is giving me the heebies."

"Why?"

"Her," said Keller, pointing toward the park.

Gabriel walked over to the window. "Her name is Aviva. She's one of ours."

"When did you contact your station?"

"I didn't. King Saul Boulevard must have told them I was coming to town."

"Let's hope the Russians weren't listening."

Twenty minutes later the woman left the bench, and the same man returned. "That's Nir," said Gabriel. "He's the ambassador's primary bodyguard."

Keller checked the time. It was nearly one o'clock. "How long does it take for a prime minister and his intelligence chief to have lunch?"

"That depends on the agenda."

"And if the intelligence chief were confessing to his prime minister that his service was completely compromised by the Russians?" Keller shook his head slowly. "We're going to need to rebuild MI6 from the ground up. This is going to be the scandal to end all scandals."

Gabriel was silent.

"Do you think he'll survive it?" asked Keller.

"Graham? I suppose it depends on how he handles it."

"An arrest and trial are going to be messy."

"What choice does he have?"

Keller didn't answer; he was staring at his phone. "Graham has left Downing Street. He's on his way. In fact," said Keller, looking up from the phone, "here he comes now."

Gabriel watched the approaching Jaguar limousine. "That was quick."

"He must have skipped the pudding."

The car stopped at the building's entrance. Graham Seymour climbed grimly out.

"He looks like he's going to a funeral," observed Keller.

"*Another* funeral," added Gabriel.

"Have you given any thought as to how you're going to tell him?"

"I don't have to say a word."

Gabriel opened the attaché case and from the hidden compartment removed three items. A birth certificate, a marriage certificate, and a snapshot taken without the subject's knowledge on Jesus Lane in Cambridge. It was bad, thought Gabriel. As bad as it gets.

52

BAYSWATER ROAD, LONDON

The birth certificate was issued by Saint George Hospital in Beirut on May 26, 1963. It listed BETTENCOURT, CHARLOTTE as the mother and PHILBY, HAROLD ADRIAN RUSSELL as the father. The child weighed slightly under seven pounds at birth. She was called REBECCA. She took the family name of her mother rather than her father—he was married to another woman at the time—but acquired a new surname when BETTENCOURT, CHARLOTTE married a MANNING, ROBERT in a civil service in London on November 2, 1976. A simple check of Cambridge University's admission records would confirm that a MANNING, REBECCA went up to Trinity College in the autumn of 1981. And a check of U.K. immigration records would similarly confirm that a BETTENCOURT, CHARLOTTE entered the country in 1984. During her brief stay, she snapped a photograph of MANNING, REBECCA as she walked along Jesus Lane—a photograph she gave to ALLON, GABRIEL in a house in Seville. Thus proving beyond a shadow of a doubt that MI6's Head of Station in Washington was the illegitimate child of history's greatest spy and a long-term agent of Russian penetration. In the jargon of the trade, a mole.

"Unless," said Gabriel, "you have a different explanation."

"Such as?"

"That MI6 knew about her from the beginning. That you turned her around and have been playing her back against Moscow Center. That she is the greatest double agent in history."

"If only it were true." Seymour was staring at the photograph, almost in disbelief.

"Is it her?" asked Gabriel.

"You've never met her in any professional capacity?"

"I've never had the pleasure."

"It's her," said Seymour after a moment. "A younger version, of course, but it's definitely Rebecca Manning."

It was the first time he had spoken her name.

"Did you ever—"

"Suspect she was a Russian spy? The illegitimate daughter of Kim Philby?"

Gabriel said nothing.

"One makes lists at a time like this," said Seymour, "rather like when one suspects one's wife of being unfaithful. Is it him? Or him?"

"What about *her*?" said Gabriel, nodding toward the photo.

"I was the one who made Rebecca our Head of Station in Washington. Needless to say, I had no qualms about her loyalty."

Keller was staring into the Bayswater Road, as though unaware of the two spymasters confronting one another over the laminated coffee table.

"Surely," said Gabriel, "you must have reviewed her file thoroughly before giving her the job."

"Of course."

"Nothing recorded against?"

"Her personnel file is spotless."

"What about the circumstances of her childhood? She was born in Beirut, and her mother was a French citizen who disappeared from her life when she was a child."

"But Robert Manning was from the right sort of family."

"That's why Philby chose him," interjected Gabriel.

"And her tutors at Cambridge thought very highly of her."

"Philby chose them, too. He knew how to pull the levers to get Rebecca a job at MI6. He'd done it once himself." Gabriel held up the birth certificate. "Did your vetters never notice that her mother's name appeared in your father's telegrams from Beirut?" He recited the relevant passage from his prodigious memory. "'The other woman's name is Charlotte Bettencourt. I am reliably informed Mademoiselle Bettencourt is now several months pregnant.'"

"Obviously," said Seymour, "the vetters didn't make the connection."

"A simple blood test would do it for them."

"I don't need a blood test." Seymour stared at the photograph of Rebecca Manning at Cambridge. "Hers is the same face I saw at the bar of the Normandie when I was a boy."

"Her mother remembers you, by the way."

"Does she?"

"She remembers your father, too."

Seymour tossed the photograph onto the coffee table. "Where is she now? Still in Seville?"

Gabriel nodded. "I recommend she stay there until you've taken Rebecca into custody. But I'd move quickly. The Russians are liable to notice she's no longer in Zahara."

"Arrest Rebecca Manning?" asked Seymour. "On what charge? Being the illegitimate daughter of Kim Philby?"

"She's a Russian mole, Graham. Make up some excuse to get her to London, something that won't make her suspicious, and take her into custody the minute she steps off the plane at Heathrow."

"Did Rebecca ever actually *spy* for the Russians?"

"Of course."

"I need proof," said Seymour. "Otherwise, all I have is a sad story about a young child who was brainwashed by the KGB into completing the work of her treacherous father."

"I'd read a story like that."

"Unfortunately, so will a good many other people." Seymour paused, then added, "And the reputation of the Secret Intelligence Service will be destroyed."

A silence fell between them. It was Gabriel who broke it.

"Put her under blanket surveillance, Graham. Physical, cyber, cellular. Wire her home and her office. Eventually, she'll slip up."

"Are you forgetting who her father was?"

"I was the one who figured it out."

"She's a child prodigy," said Seymour. "Philby never slipped up, and neither will she."

"I'm sure you and Christopher will think of something." Gabriel dropped the birth certificate atop the photograph. "I have a plane to catch and several pressing matters at home that require my attention."

Seymour managed a smile. "Not even a little tempted?"

"To what?"

"To finish what you started?"

"I'll wait for the movie. Besides, I have a bad feeling about how this is going to turn out." Gabriel rose slowly to his feet. "If you don't mind, I need to lock up. Housekeeping will slip a nasty letter into my file if I leave you behind."

Seymour remained seated. He was pondering his wristwatch. "There's no way you'll make the three-thirty El Al flight now. Why don't you stick around for a few minutes and tell me how you'd go about it?"

"What's that?"

"Catching Kim Philby's daughter red-handed."

"That's the easy part. All you have to do is catch a spy to catch a spy."

"How?"

"With a Ford Explorer," said Gabriel. "On the rue Saint-Denis in Montreal."

Seymour smiled. "You have my full attention. Keep talking."

53

NARKISS STREET, JERUSALEM

It was nearly midnight by the time Gabriel's motorcade turned in to Narkiss Street. An armored limousine was parked outside his building, and upstairs in his apartment a light burned softly in the kitchen. Ari Shamron was sitting at the little café table, alone. He was dressed, as usual, in a pair of pressed khaki trousers, a white oxford cloth shirt, and a leather bomber jacket with an unrepaired tear in the left shoulder. On the table before him was a packet of Turkish cigarettes, unopened, and his old Zippo lighter. His olive wood cane leaned against the opposing chair.

"Does anyone know you're here?" asked Gabriel.

"Your wife does. Your children were asleep when I arrived."

Shamron contemplated Gabriel through his ugly steel-rimmed spectacles. "Sound familiar?"

Gabriel ignored the question. "How did you know I was coming back tonight?"

"I have a highly placed source." Shamron paused, then added, "A mole."

"Only one?"

Shamron gave a half smile.

"I'm surprised you weren't waiting at Ben Gurion."

"I didn't want to be presumptuous."

"Since when?"

Shamron's smile widened, deepening the cracks and fissures in his aged face. It had been many years since his last term as chief, but he still meddled in the affairs of the Office as though it were his private fiefdom. His retirement was restless and, like Kim Philby's, largely unhappy. He passed his days repairing antique radios in the workshop of his fortress-like home in Tiberias, on the shore of the Sea of Galilee. Nights he reserved for Gabriel.

"My mole tells me you've been traveling a great deal of late," he said.

"Does he?"

"Never make assumptions about the gender of a mole." Shamron's tone was admonitory. "Women are just as capable of betrayal as men."

"I'll be sure to keep that in mind. What else does your mole tell you?"

"The mole is concerned that what started as a noble pursuit to clear your name after the disaster in Vienna has become something of an obsession. The mole believes you are neglecting your service and your family at a time when both need you desperately."

"The mole," said Gabriel, "is mistaken."

"The mole's access," countered Shamron, "is unlimited."

"Is it the prime minister?"

Shamron frowned. "Perhaps you weren't listening earlier when I said the mole is *highly* placed."

"That leaves my wife," said Gabriel. "Which would explain why you haven't dared to light one of those cigarettes. You and Chiara had a nice long talk tonight, and she read you the riot act about smoking in the house before she went to bed."

"I'm afraid your clearance doesn't allow you to know the mole's true identity."

"I see. In that case, please tell the mole the operation is almost over and that life will soon be returning to normal, whatever that means in the context of the Allon family."

Gabriel took down two wineglasses from the cabinet and opened a bottle of Bordeaux-style red wine from the Judean Hills.

"I would prefer coffee," said Shamron with a frown.

"And I would prefer to be in bed next to my wife. Instead, I will have a single drink with you and then send you happily into the night."

"I doubt it."

Shamron accepted the wine with a tremulous hand. It was blue-veined and liver-spotted and looked as though it had been borrowed from a man twice his size. It was one of the reasons why he had been chosen for the Eichmann operation, the immense size and strength of his hands. Even now, Shamron could not go out in public without being approached by aging survivors who simply wanted to touch the hands that had clamped around the neck of the monster.

"Is it true?" he asked.

"That I would prefer to be with my wife instead of you?"

"That this mole hunt of yours is almost over."

"As far as I'm concerned, it already is. My friend Graham Seymour would like me to stick around for the final act."

"I would advise you," said Shamron pointedly, "to choose another path."

Gabriel smiled. "I see you've been watching the Sergei Morosov interrogation."

"With great interest. I especially enjoyed the part about the British defector who worked with Lenin's doppelgänger to plant a mole in the heart of British intelligence." Shamron lowered his voice. "I don't suppose any of it is true."

"All of it, actually."

"Were you able to find her?"

"The other woman?"

Shamron nodded, and Gabriel nodded in response.

"Where?"

"In the files of Graham Seymour's father. He worked in Beirut in the early sixties."

"I remember," said Shamron. "It must have been interesting reading."

"Especially the parts about you."

Shamron reached for his cigarettes but stopped himself. "And the child?"

Gabriel tore a sheet of paper from the notepad on the counter and wrote out Rebecca Manning's name and position at MI6. Shamron read it gravely.

"It's the same job as—"

"Yes," said Gabriel. "The exact same job."

Shamron returned the note and pushed the Zippo lighter across the tabletop. "Perhaps you should burn that."

Gabriel went to the basin and touched the corner of the paper to the flame of the lighter.

"And the final act?" asked Shamron. "I suppose it will take place in Washington."

Gabriel dropped the charred paper into the basin but said nothing.

"And what about the Americans? Have you written them into your script? Oh, no," Shamron said hastily, answering his own question, "that wouldn't do, would it? After all, the Americans know nothing about any of this."

Gabriel opened the tap and carefully washed the ashes down the drain. Then he sat down again and slid the lighter across the table. "Go ahead, Ari. I won't tell your mole."

Shamron tore the cellophane from the packet of cigarettes. "I suppose Graham wants proof that she's actually *spying* for the Russians."

"He does have a point."

"And he needs you to run the operation for him because he can't trust anyone in his own service."

"With some justification," said Gabriel.

"Unless I'm mistaken, which is almost never the case, you probably made noises about not wanting any part of it. And then you promptly agreed."

"That sounds familiar, too."

"Actually, I can't say I blame you. Burgess, Maclean, Philby, Aldrich Ames . . . they pale in comparison to this."

"It's not why I'm doing it."

"Of course not. Heaven forbid you should ever take pleasure in any of your achievements. Why spoil your perfect record?" Shamron tapped a cigarette from the packet. "But I digress. You were about to tell me why you're risking antagonizing Israel's closest ally by running an unauthorized operation in Washington."

"Graham has promised to grant me full access to the debriefing once she's in custody."

"Has he really." Shamron slipped the cigarette between his lips and ignited it with the Zippo. "You know, Gabriel, there's only one thing worse than having a spy in your intelligence service."

"What's that?"

"Catching her." Shamron closed the Zippo with a snap. "But that's the easy part. All you have to do is seize control of her method of communication with Moscow Center and induce her into action. Your friend Sergei Morosov has told you everything you need to know. I'd be happy to show you the relevant portion of the interrogation."

"I was listening at the time."

"You'll have to think of something to tell the Americans," Shamron continued. "Something to explain the presence of your personnel. A meeting at the station should suffice. They won't believe a word of it, of course, which means you'll have to watch your step."

"I intend to."

"Where will you run the operation?"

"Chesapeake Street."

"A national embarrassment."

"But perfect for my needs."

"I wish I could be there," said Shamron wistfully, "but I'd only be underfoot. These days, that's all I am, an object around which people cautiously step, usually with their eyes averted."

"That makes two of us."

A companionable silence settled between them. Gabriel drank his wine while Shamron mechanically smoked his cigarette down to a stub, as though he feared Gabriel would not grant him permission to have another.

"I had occasion to travel to Beirut with some regularity in the early sixties," he said at last. "There was a little bar around the corner from the old British Embassy. Jack's or Joe's, I can't remember the name of it. MI6 treated it like a club. I used to pop in there to have a listen to what they were up to. And who did I see one afternoon drinking himself into a stupor?"

"Did you speak to him?"

"I was tempted," said Shamron, "but I just sat at a table nearby and tried not to stare."

"And what were you thinking?"

"As someone who loved his country and his people, I couldn't possibly understand why he did what he did. But as a professional, I admired him greatly." Shamron slowly crushed out his cigarette. "Did you ever read his book? The one he wrote in Moscow after he defected?"

"Why bother? There isn't an honest word in it."

"But some of it is fascinating. Did you know, for example, that he buried his Soviet camera and film somewhere in Maryland after learning that Burgess and Maclean had defected? It's never been found. Apparently, he never told anyone where he hid it."

"Actually," said Gabriel, "he told two people."

"Did he really? Who?"

Gabriel smiled and poured himself another glass of wine.

"I thought you said one drink."

"I did. But what's the rush?"

Shamron's lighter flared. "So where is it?"

"What?"

"The camera and the film?"

Gabriel smiled. "Why don't you ask your mole?"

54

RUE SAINT-DENIS, MONTREAL

T hree far-flung events, all seemingly unrelated, portended that the quest for the Russian mole had entered its final and climactic phase. The first occurred in the sometimes-French, sometimes-German city of Strasbourg, where French authorities handed over a set of badly burned remains to a representative of the Russian government. The remains were purported to be those of a Russian business consultant from Frankfurt. They were not. And the representative of the Russian government who took possession of them was actually an officer of the SVR. Those who witnessed the transfer described the atmosphere as notably chilly. Little about the exercise, conducted on a rain-slickened tarmac of Strasbourg Airport, suggested the matter would end there.

The second event transpired later that same morning in the *pueblo blanco* of Zahara in the south of Spain, where an elderly Frenchwoman known as *la loca* or *la roja*, a reference to the color of her politics, returned to her villa after a brief visit to Seville. Uncharacteristically, she was not alone. Two other people, a woman of perhaps thirty-five who spoke French and a bullet-shaped man who might have spoken no language at all, settled into the villa with her. Additionally, two of their associates took up residence at the hotel located one hundred and fourteen paces along the paseo. In early afternoon, the woman was seen quarreling with a shopkeeper in the Calle San Juan. She took her lunch amid the orange trees at Bar Mirador and afterward paid a call on Father Diego at the church of Santa María de la Mesa. Father Diego gave her his blessing—or perhaps it was his absolution—and then sent her on her way.

The last of the three events took place not in Western Europe but in Montreal, where at 10:15 a.m. local time, as the elderly Frenchwoman was exchanging a few cross words with the check-out girl at the El Castillo supermarket, Eli Lavon alighted from a taxi on the rue Saint-Dominique. He then walked several blocks, pausing occasionally, apparently to take his bearings, to an address on the rue Saint-Denis. It corresponded to a former town-house that had been converted, like most of its neighbors, into flats. A flight of stairs climbed from the pavement to the unit on the second floor, which Housekeeping, its budgets strained, had acquired on a sublet for a period of three months.

The door opened with a sharp crack, as though a seal had been broken, and Lavon slipped inside. Morosely, he surveyed the stained, cigarette-burned furnishings before parting the gauzy curtains and peering out. At approximately forty-five degrees to Lavon's right, on the opposite side of the street, was a patch of empty asphalt where, if the gods of intelligence were smiling upon them, a dark gray Ford Explorer would soon appear.

If the gods of intelligence were smiling upon them . . .

Lavon released the curtains. Another safe flat, another city, another watch. How long would it be this time? The great undertaking had become the great wait.

Christopher Keller arrived at midday; Mikhail Abramov, a few minutes before one. He was carrying a nylon duffel bag emblazoned with the name of a popular brand of ski equipment. Inside was a tripod-mounted camera with a telephoto night-vision lens, a long-range phased-array microphone, transmitters, two Jericho 9mm pistols, and two Office laptops with secure links to King Saul Boulevard. Keller had no operational paraphernalia other than his MI6 BlackBerry, which Gabriel had expressly forbidden him to use. Rebecca Manning had worked for MI6 during the critical transition from analogue to digital technology. She had no doubt given her first mobile phone to the Russians for analysis, and every one since. Eventually, MI6 would have to rewrite its software. For now, however, in order to maintain the illusion that all was normal, MI6's officers around the globe were chattering and texting away on phones the Russians had cracked. But not Keller. Keller alone had gone dark.

His task now was to sit in a fleabag flat in Montreal with two Israelis and keep watch on a few meters of asphalt along the rue Saint-Denis. They assumed the Russians were watching it, too—perhaps not continuously, but enough to know whether the site was secure. Thus, the three veteran operatives did more than simply wait for a dark-gray Ford Explorer to appear. They watched their new neighbors as well, along with the many pedestrians that passed beneath their window. With the aid of the microphone, they listened to snatches of conversations for any trace of operational banter or a Russian accent. Those who appeared too regularly or lingered too long were photographed, and the photos were dispatched to King Saul Boulevard for analysis. None produced positive results, which gave the three veteran operatives precious cold comfort.

The traffic they monitored as well, especially in the small hours, when it thinned to a trickle. On the fourth night, the same Honda sedan—a 2016 Civic with ordinary Canadian license plates—appeared three times between midnight and one in the morning. Twice it passed from left to right, or southeast to northwest, but the third time it came from the opposite direction, and at a much slower speed. Mikhail captured a decent image of the driver with the long-lens camera and forwarded it to Gabriel at King Saul Boulevard. Gabriel in turn bounced it to his station chief in Ottawa, who identified the man behind the wheel as an SVR hood attached to the Russian consulate in Montreal. The drop site was most definitely in play.

As is often the case, the surveillance operation unwittingly exposed the secret lives of those who, through no fault of their own, lived within close proximity of the target. There was the handsome jazz musician across the street who entertained a married woman for an hour each afternoon and then sent her happily on her way. And there was the jazz musician's shut-in of a neighbor who subsisted on a diet of microwave lasagna and Internet pornography. And the man of perhaps thirty who passed his evenings watching beheading videos on his laptop computer. Mikhail entered the man's apartment during an absence and discovered stacks of jihadist propaganda, a printout of a crude bomb design, and the black banner of ISIS hanging on the bedroom wall. He also found a Tunisian passport, a photograph of which he sent to King Saul Boulevard.

Which presented Gabriel with an operational dilemma. He was obligated to tell the Canadians—and the Americans—about the potential threat residing on the rue Saint-Denis in Montreal. Were he to do so, however, he would unleash a chain of events that would almost certainly prompt the Russians to move their dead drop. And so he reluctantly decided to keep the intelligence to himself until such time as it could be passed to his allies without collateral damage. He was confident the situation could be contained. Three of the most experienced counterterrorism operatives in the world were residing in a safe flat across the street.

Fortunately, their dual watch would not last long, because three nights later the Honda Civic returned. It passed the safe flat left to right—southeast to northwest—at 2:34 a.m., as Keller kept a solitary vigil behind the threadbare curtain. It made a second pass from the same direction at 2:47, though by then Keller had been joined by Eli Lavon and Mikhail. The third pass occurred at 3:11, right to left, which exposed the driver to the long lens of the camera. It was the same SVR hood from the Russian consulate in Montreal.

It would be another two and a half hours before they saw him again. This time, he was driving not the Honda Civic but a Ford Explorer, Canadian registration, dark gray. He parked along an empty stretch of curb, killed the headlights, and switched off the engine. Through the lens of the camera, Keller watched the Russian open and close the glove box. Then he climbed out and locked the door with a remote key and walked away—right to left, northwest to southeast, a phone to his ear. Mikhail tracked him with the long-range phased-array microphone.

"What's he saying?" asked Keller.

"If you shut up, maybe I can hear."

Keller counted slowly to five. "Well?" he asked.

Mikhail answered him in Russian.

"What does that mean?"

"It means," said Eli Lavon, "that we're all going to be leaving for Washington soon."

The Russian rounded the next corner and was gone. Mikhail fired a flash message to King Saul Boulevard, setting in motion a rapid movement of Office personnel and resources from their fail-safe points to Washington. Keller stared at one of the windows across the street, the one that was lit by the faint glow of a computer.

"There's something we should take care of before we leave."

"Might not be a good idea," said Lavon.

"Maybe," replied Keller. "Or it might be the best idea I've had in a long time."

55

MONTREAL—WASHINGTON

At eight fifteen that morning, Eva Fernandes was drinking coffee in her room at the Sheraton on the boulevard René-Lévesque, in downtown Montreal. During her last visit, she had stayed up the street at the Queen Elizabeth, which she preferred, but Sasha had ordered her to vary her routine when visiting her phantom sick relative. He had also instructed her to hold down her expenses. The room-service coffee was a minor infraction. Sasha was from another time, a time of war and famine and communist austerity. He did not tolerate his illegals living as oligarchs—unless, of course, it was called for by their cover. Eva was confident her next transmission from Moscow Center would contain a reprimand for her profligate ways.

She was showered, her suitcase was packed, her clothing for

that day was laid out neatly on the bed. The remote for the Ford Explorer was in her handbag. So, too, was the flash drive. On it was the material Eva had received from Sasha's mole during the last wireless drop, the one that had taken place on M Street in Washington, at 7:36 on a cold but sunny morning.

Eva had been inside the yoga studio at the time, preparing for her 7:45 class, and the mole had been across the street at Dean & DeLuca, surrounded by several of Eva's regular students. She recognized the mole from other wireless drops and from Brussels Midi, where she dined frequently, usually in the company of British diplomats. Eva had actually exchanged a few words with her once regarding a reservation that had been made under someone else's name. The woman was cool and assured and quite obviously intelligent. Eva suspected she was a member of MI6's large Washington station, perhaps even its Head. If the woman were ever arrested, Eva would probably be arrested, too. As an illegal, she had no diplomatic protection. She could be charged, tried, and sentenced to a long prison term. The idea of spending several years locked in a cage in a place like Kentucky or Kansas held little appeal. Eva had vowed long ago she would never allow it to come to that.

At nine o'clock she dressed and went downstairs to the lobby to check out. She left her suitcase behind with the bellman and walked a short distance along the boulevard to an entrance for the Underground City, the vast labyrinth of shopping malls, restaurants, and performing-arts venues buried beneath downtown Montreal. It was an ideal place to do a bit of "dry cleaning," especially early on a Tuesday morning when the crowds were sparse. Eva performed this task diligently, as she had been trained to do, first by her instructors at the Red Banner Institute and later by Sasha himself. Complacency, he had warned her, was an illegal's greatest enemy, the belief that he or she was invisible to the opposition. Eva was the most vital link in the chain that stretched between the mole and Moscow Center. If she made a single mistake, the mole would be lost and Sasha's endeavor would turn to dust.

With this in mind, Eva passed the next two hours wandering the arcades of La Ville Souterraine—two hours because Sasha would not permit a minute less. The only person who followed her was a man of perhaps fifty-five. He was not a professional, he was a stalker. It was one of the drawbacks of being an attractive female agent, the unwanted attention and long hungry looks from sex-starved men. Sometimes it was difficult to distinguish lust from legitimate scrutiny. Eva had backed out of four wireless encounters with the mole because she *thought* she was being followed. Sasha had not chastised her. Quite the opposite. He had saluted her vigilance.

At five minutes past eleven, confident she was not under surveillance, Eva returned to the boulevard and hailed a taxi. It took her to the church of Notre-Dame-de-la-Défense, where she spent five minutes feigning silent meditation before walking to the rue Saint-Denis. The Ford Explorer was in its usual place, parked on the street outside the townhouse at 6822. Eva unlocked the doors with her remote key and climbed behind the wheel.

The engine started without hesitation. She pulled away from the curb and then made a succession of rapid right turns designed to expose a trailing vehicle. Seeing nothing suspicious, she parked along a bleak stretch of the rue Saint-André and placed the flash drive in the glove box. Then she climbed out, locked the door, and walked away. No one followed her.

She hailed another taxi, this one on the avenue Christophe-Colomb, and asked the driver to take her to the Sheraton to collect her suitcase. The same taxi then took her to the airport. A permanent U.S. resident, she cleared the American passport check and went to the gate. Her flight began boarding on time, at one fifteen. As always, Eva had booked a seat at the front of the cabin so she could scrutinize the other passengers as they filed past. She saw only one of interest, a tall man with very fair skin and light gray eyes, like a wolf's. He was quite handsome. He was also, she suspected, a Russian. Or perhaps a former Russian, she thought, like her.

The tall man with pale skin was seated several rows behind Eva, and she did not see him again until the flight landed in Washington, when he walked behind her through the terminal. Her Kia sedan was in the short-term parking garage, where she had left it the previous afternoon. She crossed the Potomac into Washington via Key Bridge and made her way to the Palisades, arriving at Brussels Midi promptly at four. Yvette was smoking a cigarette at the bar; Ramon and Claudia were setting tables in the dining room. The phone rang as Eva was hanging up her coat.

"Brussels Midi."

"I'd like a table for two this evening, please."

Male, arrogant, English accent. Eva foresaw trouble ahead. She was tempted to hang up but didn't.

"I'm sorry, did you say that table was for two?"

"Yes," drawled the man, exasperated.

Eva decided to torture him a little more. "And what time are you interested in joining us?"

"I'm interested," he sniffed, "in seven o'clock."

"I can't do seven, I'm afraid. But I have a table free at eight."

"Is it a good one?"

"We only have good tables, sir."

"I'll take it."

"Wonderful. Name, please?"

The Bartholomews, party of two, eight o'clock, were a blot on an otherwise dull Tuesday night. They arrived twenty minutes early and, seeing several empty tables, flew into a rage. Mr. Bartholomew was balding and tweedy, and waved his arms while he ranted. His wife was a curvy, Rubenesque woman with hair the color of sandstone. The slow-burn type, thought Eva. She moved them from their assigned table—table number four—to lucky table thirteen, the one with the draft from the overhead vent. Not surprisingly, they requested a change. When Eva suggested the table next to the kitchen door, Mr. Bartholomew snapped.

"Haven't you got anything else?"

"Perhaps you'd like a table outside."

"There are none."

Eva smiled.

From there, the meal went predictably downhill. The wine was too warm, the soup too cold, the mussels were a sacrilege, the cassoulet was a crime against cuisine. The evening ended on a positive note, however, when Mr. Bartholomew's wife approached Eva to offer her apologies. "I'm afraid Simon has been under a great deal of stress at work." She spoke English with an accent Eva couldn't quite place. "I'm Vanessa," she said, offering her hand. Then, almost as a confession: "Vanessa Bartholomew."

"Eva Fernandes."

"Do you mind if I ask where you're from?"

"Brazil."

"Oh," the woman said, mildly surprised. "I never would have guessed."

"My parents were born in Europe."

"Where?"

"Germany."

"Mine, too," said the woman.

The remainder of the dinner service passed without incident. The last customers departed at ten thirty, and Eva locked the doors a few minutes after eleven. A car followed her as she drove home along MacArthur Boulevard, but by the time she reached the reservoir the car was gone. She parked about a hundred yards from her small redbrick apartment building and checked license plates as she walked to her door. As she reached for the keypad, she realized there was someone standing behind her. Turning, she saw the man who had been on her flight. The tall one with eyes like a wolf. His pale skin was luminous in the darkness. Eva took a step back in fear.

"Don't be afraid, Eva," he said quietly in Russian. "I'm not going to harm you."

Suspicious of a trap, she responded in English. "I'm sorry, but I don't speak—"

"Please," he said, cutting her off. "It's not safe for us to be talking on the street."

"Who sent you? And speak English, you idiot."

"I was sent by Sasha." His English was better than hers, with only a slight accent.

"Sasha? Why would Sasha send you?"

"Because you are in grave danger."

Eva hesitated a moment before punching the correct code into the keypad. The man with the eyes of a wolf opened the door and followed her inside.

———————

While climbing the stairs, Eva reached into her handbag for the keys to her apartment and instantly felt the man's powerful hand seize her wrist. "Are you carrying your gun?" he asked quietly, again in Russian.

Pausing, she gave the man a withering look before reminding him that, earlier that day, they had both flown commercially between Canada and the United States.

"Maybe you had it in the car," he suggested.

"It's upstairs."

He released her wrist. She drew the keys from her bag and a moment later used them to open the door to her apartment. The man closed it quickly and engaged the deadbolt and the chain. When Eva reached for the light switch, he stilled her hand. Then he went to the window and peered around the edge of the blind, into MacArthur Boulevard.

"Who are you?" she asked.

"My name is Alex."

"Alex? How deceptive! It's a miracle none of our adversaries has ever managed to penetrate your cover with a name like that."

He released the blind and turned to face her.

"You said you had a message from Sasha."

"I do have a message," he replied, "but it's not from Sasha."

It was then Eva noticed the gun in his right hand. The end of the barrel was fitted with a sound suppressor. It was not the sort of weapon an operative carried for the purposes of protection. It was a weapon of assassination—of *vysshaya mera*, the highest measure of punishment. But why had Moscow Center decided to kill her? She had done nothing wrong.

She backed slowly away from him, her legs gelatinous beneath her. "Please," she pleaded. "There must be some mistake. I've done everything Sasha asked of me."

"And that," said the man called Alex, "is why I'm here."

Perhaps it was some vendetta inside Moscow Center, she thought. Perhaps Sasha had finally fallen out of favor. "Not in the face," she begged. "I don't want my mother to—"

"I'm not here to harm you, Eva. I've come to make you a generous offer."

She stopped backpedaling. "Offer? What sort of offer?"

"One that will prevent you from spending the next several years in an American prison."

"Are you from the FBI?"

"Lucky for you," he said, "I'm not."

56

FOXHALL, WASHINGTON

S he made a move on him, and a rather good one at that. It was a Moscow Center–trained move, full of elbows and kicks and compact punches and a knee toward the groin that, had it landed, might very well have ended the contest in her favor. Mikhail was left with no choice but to retaliate. He did so expertly but judiciously, making great effort to inflict no damage on Eva Fernandes's flawless Russian face. At the conclusion of the match, he was straddling her hips, with her hands pinned to the floor. To her credit, Eva showed no fear, only anger. She made no attempt to scream. Illegals, thought Mikhail, knew better than to call out to the neighbors for help.

"Don't worry," he said as he licked blood from the corner of his mouth. "I'll be sure to tell Sasha that you put up a good fight."

Mikhail then calmly explained that the building was surrounded and that even if Eva managed to escape the apartment, which was unlikely, she would not get far. At which point, a battlefield truce was declared. From the freezer Eva extracted a bottle of vodka. It was Russian vodka, the only Russian item in the entire apartment other than her SVR covert communications equipment and her Makarov pistol. She extracted those, too, from the hidden compartment beneath the floorboards in her bedroom closet.

She laid out the equipment on the kitchen table. The gun she surrendered to Mikhail. He addressed her only in Russian. It had been more than a decade, she explained, since she had spoken her mother tongue. It had been stolen from her the minute she entered the illegals program at the Red Banner Institute. She already had a bit of Portuguese when she arrived there. Her father was a diplomat—first for the Soviet Union, later for the Russian Federation—and she had lived in Lisbon as a child.

"You realize," said Mikhail, "you have no diplomatic protection."

"It was drilled into us from the very first day of our training."

"And what did they tell you to do if you were caught?"

"Say nothing and wait."

"For what?"

"For Moscow Center to make a trade. They promised us we would never be left behind."

"I wouldn't count on that. Not when the Americans find out you've been servicing the biggest spy since the Cold War."

"Rebecca Manning."

"You know her name?"

"I figured it out a few months ago."

"What was on the flash drive you left in the glove box of that Ford Explorer?"

"You were watching?"

"From a flat across the street. We made a nice video."

She picked nervously at her nail polish. She was human after all, thought Mikhail.

"I was assured the drop site was clean."

"Did Moscow Center promise you that, too?"

Eva drained her glass of vodka and immediately refilled it. Mikhail's was untouched.

"You're not drinking?"

"Vodka," he proclaimed, "is a Russian illness."

"Sasha used to say the same thing."

They were seated at the kitchen table. Between them were the bottle of vodka and the glasses and Eva's SVR communications paraphernalia. The centerpiece was a device about the size and shape of a paperback novel. It was fashioned of polished metal and was of solid construction. On one side were three switches, an indicator light, and a couple of USB ports. There were no seams in the metal. It was designed never to be opened.

Eva downed another glass of vodka.

"Take it easy," said Mikhail. "I need you to keep your wits about you."

"What do you want to know?"

"Everything."

"Like what?"

"How does Rebecca tell you when she wants to hand over material?"

"She leaves the light on at the end of the walk."

"Where are the drop sites?"

"Currently, we have four."

"What are the fallbacks? What's the body talk?"

"Thanks to Sasha, I can tell you all of that in my sleep. And more." Eva reached for the vodka again, but Mikhail moved the glass aside. "If you know the identity of the mole," she asked, "why do you need me?"

Mikhail didn't answer.

"And if I agree to cooperate?"

"I thought we covered that ground."

"No prison?"

Mikhail shook his head. No prison.

"Where will I go?"

"Back to Russia, I suppose."

"After helping you catch Sasha's mole? They'll interrogate me for a few months in Lefortovo Prison and then—" She fashioned her hand into the shape of a gun and placed the tip of her forefinger to the nape of her neck.

"*Vysshaya mera*," said Mikhail.

She lowered her hand and reclaimed her glass of vodka. "I would prefer to remain here in America."

"I'm afraid that won't be possible."

"Why not?"

"Because we're not Americans."

"You're British?"

"Some of us."

"So I'll go to England."

"Or perhaps Israel," he suggested.

She made a sour face.

"It's really not so bad, you know."

"I hear there are a lot of Russians there."

"More every day," said Mikhail.

There was a small window next to the table. MacArthur Boulevard was quiet and damp. Christopher Keller was sitting in a parked car at the edge of the reservoir, along with a couple of security kids from the embassy. In another car was a courier from the station who was awaiting Mikhail's order to come upstairs and take possession of Eva's SVR communications gear.

She had finished her vodka and was drinking Mikhail's. "I have a class tomorrow morning."

"A class?"

She explained.

"What time?"

"Ten o'clock."

"Save a spot for me."

She smirked.

"Any scheduled deliveries from Rebecca?"

"I just serviced her. I probably won't hear from her for another week or two."

"Actually," said Mikhail, "you'll be hearing from her a lot sooner than you think."

"When?"

"Tomorrow night, I suspect."

"And after I take delivery?"

"Poof," said Mikhail.

Eva raised her glass. "To one more night at Brussels Midi. You wouldn't believe the customers I had tonight."

"Bartholomew, party of two, eight o'clock."

"How did you know?"

Mikhail picked up the polished metal device. "Maybe you should show me how this thing works."

"It's easy, actually."

Mikhail flipped one of the switches. "Like this?"

"No, you idiot. Like this."

57

FOREST HILLS, WASHINGTON

Forest Hills is a moneyed enclave of colonial, Tudor, and Federal-style homes located in far Northwest Washington between Connecticut Avenue and Rock Creek. The house on Chesapeake Street, however, bore little resemblance to its stately neighbors. A postmodern slab of gray perched atop its own leafy promontory, it looked more like a gun emplacement than a dwelling. The high brick wall and formidable iron gate only added to the air of belligerence.

The owner of this neighborhood eyesore was none other than the State of Israel, and the unlucky occupant was its ambassador to the United States. The current envoy, a man with many children, had forsaken the official residence for a home in an affluent golfing community in Maryland. Unoccupied, the house on Chesapeake Street had fallen into a state of disrepair, thus making it entirely suitable for use as a forward command post for a large operational team. From adversity, believed Gabriel, came unit cohesion.

For better or worse, the crumbling old house was laid out on a single level. There was a large open sitting room at the center, with a kitchen and dining room on one side and several bedrooms on the other. Gabriel established his office in the comfortable study. Yossi and Rimona—known at Brussels Midi as Simon and Vanessa Bartholomew—worked at a folding trestle table outside his door, along with Eli Lavon and Yaakov Rossman. Ilan the computer geek inhabited a private island at the opposite end of the room. The walls were covered with large-scale maps of Washington and the surrounding suburbs. There was even a rolling whiteboard for Gabriel's personal use. On it, in his elegant Hebrew script, he had written the words of Shamron's Eleventh Commandment. *Don't get caught . . .*

Gabriel had accepted Shamron's suggestion of a routine meeting to explain the presence of the team in Washington. He had not, however, informed the Americans about the "meeting" directly. Instead, he had made enough noise through insecure phone calls and e-mails to let them know he was coming. The NSA and Langley had picked up on his signals. In fact, Adrian Carter, the CIA's longtime deputy director for operations, sent Gabriel an e-mail a few minutes after he arrived at Dulles, wondering if he was free for a drink. Gabriel told Carter he would try to squeeze him into his busy schedule but wasn't optimistic.

Carter's sarcastic response—*Who's the lucky girl?*—nearly led Gabriel to get back on his plane.

The house on Chesapeake Street was the target of NSA surveillance whenever an ambassador was present, and Gabriel and his team assumed the NSA was eavesdropping on them now. While inside the house, they maintained a benign background chatter—in the jargon, it was known as "talking to the walls"—but all operationally sensitive information they exchanged by hand signals, in writing on the whiteboard, or in muted conversations conducted outside in the garden. One such conversation occurred shortly after 2:00 a.m., when a courier arrived at the residence bearing Eva Fernandes's SVR communications hardware, along with Mikhail's operating instructions. Gabriel surrendered the device to Ilan, who reacted as though he had just been handed a day-old copy of the *Washington Post* rather than the crown jewels of the SVR.

By four that morning, Ilan had yet to crack the device's formidable encryption firewall. Gabriel, who was watching over him with the anxiety of a parent at a recital, decided his time would be better spent catching a few hours of rest. He stretched out on the couch in the study and, lulled by the sound of tree limbs scratching against the side of the house, fell into a dreamless sleep. He woke to the sight of Ilan's pasty face floating above him. Ilan was the cyber equivalent of Mozart. First computer code at five, first hack at eight, first covert op against the Iranian nuclear program at twenty-one. He had worked with the Americans on a malware virus code-named Olympic Games. The rest of the world knew the worm as Stuxnet. Ilan didn't get outside much.

"Is there a problem?" asked Gabriel.

"No problem at all, boss."

"Then why do you look so worried?"

"I'm not."

"You didn't break the damn thing, did you?"

"Come have a look."

Gabriel swung his feet to the floor and followed Ilan to his worktable. On it was a laptop computer, an iPhone, and the SVR SRAC device.

"The Russian agent told Mikhail that the range is one hundred feet. It's actually closer to a hundred and ten. I tested it." Ilan handed Gabriel the iPhone, which was displaying a list of available networks. One was identified by twelve nonsensical characters: JDLCVHJDVODN. "That's the Moscow Center network."

"Can any device see it?"

"No way. And you can't get in without the correct password. It's twenty-seven characters and hard as rock."

"How did you crack it?"

"It would be impossible to explain."

"To a moron like me?"

"What's important," said Ilan, "is that we can add any device into the network we want." Ilan took the phone from Gabriel. "I'm going to step outside. You watch the laptop."

Gabriel did. A moment later, after Ilan had had sufficient time to slip through the iron gate at the end of the drive and make his way across the street, eight words appeared on the screen:

If she sends a message, we'll nail her.

Gabriel deleted the message and tapped a few keys. An encrypted video feed appeared on the screen—a small house, about the size of a typical English cottage, with a peculiar Tudor facade above the portico. At the end of the flagstone walkway stood an iron lamp, and next to the lamp stood a woman. Gabriel thought of the message he had received from his friend Adrian Carter of the CIA. *Who's the lucky girl?* If you only knew.

58

TENLEYTOWN, WASHINGTON

As Rebecca passed the large colonial house at the corner of Nebraska Avenue and Forty-Second Street, she thought about the day her father had revealed his plan for her. It was summer, she was staying at his little dacha outside Moscow. He and Rufina had presided over a luncheon party for a few close friends. Yuri Modin, his old KGB controller, was there, and so was Sasha. Her father had drunk a great deal of Georgian wine and vodka. Modin had tried to keep pace with him, but Sasha had abstained. "Vodka," he told Rebecca, not for the last time, "is a Russian curse."

In late afternoon they moved into the screened porch to escape the mosquitos, Rebecca and her father, Modin and Sasha. Even now, forty years later, Rebecca could recall the scene with photographic clarity. Modin was seated directly across the wooden table from her, and Sasha was to Modin's left. Rebecca was next to her father and was leaning her head against his shoulder. Like all his children—and like her mother—she adored him. It was impossible not to.

"Rebecca, my d-d-darling," he said with his endearing stutter, "there's something we need to discuss."

Until that moment, Rebecca believed her father was a journalist who lived in a strange, gray country far from her own. But on that day, in the presence of Yuri Modin and Sasha, he told her the truth. He was *that* Kim Philby, the master spy who had betrayed his country, his class, and his club. He had acted not out of greed but out of faith in an ideal, that workers should not be used as tools, that they should own the means of production, a phrase Rebecca did not yet understand. He only had one regret; he had been forced to defect before completing the task of destroying Western capitalism and the American-led NATO alliance.

"But you, my precious, you are going to finish the job for me. I can promise you only one thing, you'll never be bored."

Rebecca was never given an opportunity to refuse the life her father had chosen for her, it simply *happened*. Her mother married an Englishman named Robert Manning, the marriage ended, and her mother returned to France, leaving Rebecca behind in England. As the years passed, she had trouble recalling her mother's face, but she never forgot the silly game they had played in Paris, when they were poor as church mice. *How many steps . . .*

Each summer, Rebecca traveled clandestinely to the Soviet Union for political indoctrination and to see her father. Sasha always took extraordinary care with her movements—a ferry to Holland, a passport change in Germany, another in Prague or

Budapest, and then an Aeroflot flight to Moscow. It was her favorite time of the year. She loved Russia, even the grim Russia of the Brezhnev years, and always hated to return to Britain, which at the time was scarcely any better. Gradually, her French accent faded, and by the time she arrived at Trinity College her English was flawless. At Sasha's direction, however, she made no secret of the fact she spoke fluent French. In the end, it was one of the reasons why MI6 hired her.

After that, there were no more trips to the Soviet Union, and no contact from her father, but Sasha watched over her always, from afar. Her first overseas posting was Brussels, and it was there, in May 1988, she learned her father had died. Word of his death was flashed to all MI6 stations simultaneously. After reading the telegram, she locked herself in a closet and wept. A colleague found her, an officer who had been in her IONEC class at Fort Monckton. His name was Alistair Hughes.

"What the devil is wrong with you?" he asked.

"I'm having a bad day, that's all."

"That time of the month?"

"Sod off, Alistair."

"Did you hear the news? That bastard Philby is dead. Drinks in the canteen to celebrate."

Three years later the country to which Kim Philby had devoted his life died, too. Suddenly bereft of their traditional enemy, the intelligence services of the West went in search of new targets to justify their existence. Rebecca used these years of uncertainty to focus relentlessly on advancing her career. At Sasha's suggestion she studied Arabic, which enabled her to serve on the front lines of the global war on terrorism. Her tenure as Amman Head of Station had been a triumph and had led to her posting to

Washington. Now she was just one step away from the ultimate prize—the prize that had eluded her father. She did not consider herself a traitor. Rebecca's only country was Kim Philby, and she was faithful only to him.

Her run that morning took her to Dupont Circle and back. Returning to Warren Street, she passed her house twice without going inside. As usual, she drove herself to the embassy and embarked on what turned out to be an uncommonly dull day. For that reason alone, she agreed to have drinks with Kyle Taylor at J. Gilbert's, a CIA hangout in McLean. Taylor was the chief of the Counterterrorism Center and one of the least discreet officers in all of Langley. Rebecca rarely left a meeting with Taylor without knowing something she shouldn't.

On that evening, Taylor was even more loquacious than usual. One drink turned to two, and it was nearly eight by the time Rebecca crossed Chain Bridge and returned to Washington. She took a deliberately lengthy route back to Tenleytown and parked in front of her house. Warren Street was deserted, but as she made her way up the flagstone walk, she had the uncomfortable feeling she was being watched. Turning, she saw nothing to justify her fear, but once inside she discovered unmistakable evidence her home had been entered in her absence. It was the Crombie overcoat tossed carelessly over the back of a wing chair, and the man sitting at the end of her couch in the dark.

"Hello, Rebecca," he said calmly as he switched on a lamp. "Don't be afraid, it's only me."

59

WARREN STREET, WASHINGTON

Rebecca filled two tumblers with ice and several ounces of Johnnie Walker Black Label. To her own glass she added a dash of Evian water, but the other she left undiluted. The last thing she needed was another drink, but she welcomed the opportunity to collect herself. It was fortunate she wasn't carrying her gun; she might very well have shot the director-general of the Secret Intelligence Service. It was upstairs, the gun, in the top drawer of her bedside table, a SIG Sauer 9mm. The Americans knew about the weapon and approved of Rebecca keeping it in her home for protection. She was forbidden, however, to carry it while in public.

"I was beginning to think you'd fled the country," Graham Seymour called out from the next room.

"Kyle Taylor," explained Rebecca.

"How was he?"

"Talkative."

"Did he drone anyone today?"

Rebecca smiled in spite of herself. She knew Kyle Taylor to be a man of relentless career ambition. It was said of Kyle Taylor that he would drone his mother if he thought it would earn him a job on Langley's cherished seventh floor.

Rebecca carried the two glasses into the sitting room and handed one to Seymour. He watched her carefully over the rim as she lit an L&B. Her hand was shaking.

"Are you all right?"

"I will be eventually. How did you get in here?"

Seymour held up a spare key to Rebecca's front door. She kept a copy at the station in case of emergency.

"And your car and driver?" she asked.

"Around the corner."

Rebecca chided herself inwardly for not having taken a pass through the surrounding streets before returning home. She drew heavily on her cigarette and exhaled a lungful of smoke toward the ceiling.

"Forgive me for not telling you I was coming to town," Seymour said. "And for dropping in unannounced. But I wanted a word in private, away from the station."

"It's not secure here." Rebecca nearly choked on the absurdity of her words. No room in the world was secure, she thought, so long as she was in it.

Seymour handed her his BlackBerry. "Do me a favor and drop this in a Faraday pouch. Yours, too."

Faraday pouches blocked incoming and outgoing signals from smartphones, tablets, and laptop computers. Rebecca always kept one in her handbag. She placed Seymour's BlackBerry into the pouch, along with her own BlackBerry and personal iPhone, and stowed it in the refrigerator. Returning to the sitting room, she found Seymour lighting one of her cigarettes.

"I hope you don't mind," he said, "but I could use one."

"Sounds ominous."

"I'm afraid it is. At eleven o'clock tomorrow morning, I'm meeting with Morris Payne at Langley. I will tell Director Payne that my government has obtained definitive proof the SVR was behind Alistair's murder in Bern."

"You told me it was an accident."

"It wasn't. Which is why, at noon tomorrow, our foreign secretary will telephone the secretary of state at Foggy Bottom and deliver a similar message. What's more, the foreign secretary will tell the secretary of state that the United Kingdom intends to suspend all diplomatic ties with Russia. The prime minister will break the news to the president at one o'clock."

"He's not liable to take the news well."

"That," said Seymour, "is the least of our concerns. The expulsions will begin right away."

"How sure are we about Russia's involvement in Alistair's death?"

"I wouldn't allow the prime minister to take such a drastic step without ironclad intelligence."

"What's the source?"

"We've received critical assistance from one of our partners."

"Which one?"

"The Israelis."

"Allon?" asked Rebecca skeptically. "Please tell me we're not taking this step based on the word of Gabriel Allon."

"He's got it cold."

"From where?"

"Sorry, Rebecca, but I'm afraid—"

"Can I see the intelligence before we meet with Morris?"

"You're not coming to Langley."

"I'm H/Washington, Graham. I need to be in that meeting."

"This one is going to be chief-to-chief. I'm going to Dulles directly from Langley. I'd like you to meet me there."

"My role has been reduced to waving good-bye to your airplane?"

"Actually," said Seymour, "you're going to be *on* the plane."

Rebecca's heart banged against her breastbone. "Why?"

"Because I want you to be at my side in London when the storm breaks. It will provide you with invaluable experience in managing a crisis." Lowering his voice, Seymour added, "It will also give the mandarins of Whitehall a chance to meet the woman I want to succeed me as chief of the Secret Intelligence Service."

Rebecca felt as though she had been struck mute. Four decades of plotting and scheming, and it had worked out exactly as Sasha and her father had planned.

But you, my precious, you are going to finish the job for me . . .

"Is something wrong?" asked Seymour.

"What is one supposed to say at a moment like this?"

"It *is* what you want, isn't it, Rebecca?"

"Of course. But I'm going to have very big shoes to fill. You've been a great chief, Graham."

"Are you forgetting that ISIS laid waste to the West End of London on my watch?"

"Five was to blame, not you."

He gave her a smile of mild rebuke. "I hope you don't mind if I give you a piece of advice now and again."

"I would be a fool not to accept it."

"Don't waste time fighting old wars. The days when Five and Six could operate as adversaries are long past. You'll learn very quickly you need Thames House watching your back."

"Any other advice?"

"I know you don't share my personal fondness for Gabriel Allon, but you would be wise to keep him in your arsenal. In a few hours' time, a new cold war is going to commence. Allon knows the Russians better than anyone else in the business. He has the scars to prove it."

Rebecca went into the kitchen and retrieved Seymour's Black-Berry from the Faraday pouch. When she returned, he was wearing his overcoat and waiting by the door.

"What time do you want me to be at Dulles?" she asked as she handed him the phone.

"No later than noon. And plan to be in London for at least a week." He slipped his phone into his coat pocket and started down the flagstone walkway.

"Graham," Rebecca called out from the portico.

Seymour stopped next to the darkened iron lamp and turned.

"Thank you," she said.

He frowned, perplexed. "For what?"

"For trusting me."

"I could say the very same thing," replied Seymour, and disappeared into the night.

The car was parked on Forty-Fifth Street. Seymour slid into the backseat. Through a gap in the trees, he could just make out Rebecca's house in the distance, and the darkened lamp at the end of the walk.

"Back to the ambassador's residence, sir?"

Seymour was spending the night there. "Actually," he said, "I need to make a phone call first. Mind walking around the block a couple hundred times?"

The driver climbed out. Seymour started to dial Helen's number but stopped; it was long past midnight in London, and he didn't want to wake her. Besides, he doubted Rebecca would make him wait long. Not after what he had just told her about the plan to sever ties with Russia. She had a narrow window of opportunity to warn her masters at Moscow Center.

Seymour's BlackBerry pulsed. It was a text from Nigel Whitcombe in London, a bit of chickenfeed to make it appear to Vauxhall Cross that all was normal. Seymour typed out a response and tapped the SEND key. Then he gazed through the gap in the trees, toward Rebecca Manning's house.

The iron lamp at the end of the walk was burning brightly.

Seymour dialed a number and lifted the phone to his ear. "Do you see what I see?"

"I see it," said the voice at the other end.

"Keep an eye on her."

"Don't worry, I won't let her out of my sight."

Seymour killed the connection and stared at the light. Tomorrow, he told himself, would be a mere formality, the signing of a name to a document of treachery. Rebecca was the mole, and the mole was Rebecca. She was Philby incarnate, Philby's revenge. The truth was written on Rebecca's face. It was the one thing about her Philby hadn't been able to undo.

I'm Kim. Who are you?

I'm Graham, he thought. I was the one who gave her your old job. I'm your last victim.

60

THE PALISADES, WASHINGTON

It was 11:25 p.m. when Eva Fernandes locked the front door of Brussels Midi restaurant on MacArthur Boulevard. Her car was parked a few doors down, outside a small post office. She climbed inside and started the engine and pulled away from the curb. The man she knew as Alex—the tall one with pale skin, the one who spoke Russian like a native and who had been following her all day—was standing on the corner of Dana Place, outside a darkened Afghan steak house. He had a backpack over one shoulder. He dropped into the front seat next to Eva and with a nod instructed her to keep driving.

"How was work?" he asked.

"Better than last night."

"Any calls from Moscow Center?"

She rolled her eyes. "You have my phone."

He extracted it from the backpack. "Do you know what will happen if anything goes wrong tomorrow?"

"You'll assume I'm to blame."

"And what will be the result?"

She placed the tip of her forefinger to the back of her neck.

"That's what the SVR would do to you, not us." He held up the phone. "Does this thing ever stop pinging?"

"I'm very popular."

He scrolled through the notifications. "Who are all these people?"

"Friends, students, lovers . . ." She shrugged. "The usual."

"Any of them know you're a Russian spy?" Receiving no answer, he said, "Apparently, there's a light burning outside a house on Warren Street. Remind me what happens now."

"Not again."

"Yes, again."

"Someone from the *rezidentura* drives past the house every night at eleven. If they see the light burning, they tell Moscow Center, and Moscow Center tells me."

"How?"

She exhaled heavily in frustration. "E-mail. En clair. Very bland."

"Tomorrow is a Thursday."

"You don't say."

"An odd-numbered Thursday," Mikhail pointed out.

"Very good."

"Where will the drop take place?"

"Odd-numbered Thursdays are the Starbucks on Wisconsin Avenue." Her tone was that of a deficient student.

"Which Starbucks on Wisconsin? There are several."

"We've been over this a hundred times."

"And we're going to keep going over it until I'm convinced you're not lying."

"The Starbucks just north of Georgetown."

"What's the window for transmission?"

"Eight to eight fifteen."

"I thought you said eight fifteen to eight thirty."

"I *never* said that."

"Where are you supposed to wait?"

"In the seating area upstairs."

She followed MacArthur Boulevard along the edge of the reservoir, which was lit by a low-hanging moon. There was a space available outside her apartment building. The man she knew as Alex instructed her to park there.

"I usually park farther away so I can check to see whether the building is under surveillance."

"It *is* under surveillance." He reached across the console and killed the engine. "Get out."

He walked her to the door, the backpack over one shoulder, her phone in his pocket, and kissed the back of her neck while she punched the code into the keypad. "If you don't stop that," she whispered, "I'm going to break your instep. And then I'm going to break your nose."

"Trust me, Eva, it's only for the benefit of your neighbors."

"My neighbors think I'm a nice girl who would never bring home someone like you."

The deadbolt opened with a snap. Eva led him upstairs to her apartment. She went straight for the freezer and the bottle of vodka. The man she knew as Alex removed the SVR secure-communications device from his backpack and laid it on the kitchen table. Next to it he placed Eva's phone.

"Were your friends able to break through the firewall?" she asked.

"Rather quickly." He handed her the phone. "Are any of these from Moscow Center?"

Eva scrolled through the long chain of notifications with one hand and with the other held her drink. "This one," she said. "From Eduardo Santos. En clair. Very bland."

"Are you supposed to reply?"

"They're probably wondering why they haven't heard from me."

"Then perhaps you should send it."

She typed it out, dexterously, with her thumb.

"Let me see it."

"It's in Portuguese."

"Do I need to remind you—"

"No, you don't."

She tapped the SEND icon and sat down at the table. "What now?"

"You're going to finish your drink and get a few hours of sleep. And I'm going to sit here and stare into the street."

"Again? You did that last night."

"Finish your drink, Eva."

She did. And then she poured another. "It helps me sleep," she explained.

"Try a cup of chamomile tea."

"Vodka is better." As if to prove her point, she drank half the glass. "Your Russian is very good. I assume you didn't learn it at a language institute."

"I learned it in Moscow."

"Were your parents Party members?"

"Quite the other thing, actually. And when the door finally opened, they went to Israel as fast as they could."

"Do you have a girl there?"

"A nice one."

"Too bad. What does your girl do?"

"She's a doctor."

"Is that the truth?"

"Mostly."

"I wanted to be a doctor once." She watched a car pass in the street. "Do you know what will happen to me if anything goes wrong?"

"I know exactly what will happen."

"*Poof,*" she said, and poured another drink.

61

SVR HEADQUARTERS, YASENEVO

At that same moment, at SVR headquarters in Yasenevo, the man known only by the cipher Sasha was awake, too. Owing to the time difference, it was a few minutes after eight in the morning. But because it was Moscow, and still winter, the skies beyond the frosted windows of Sasha's private dacha had yet to brighten. He was unaware of this fact, however, for he had eyes only for the flimsy that had arrived an hour earlier from the code room of the main building.

It was a copy of an urgent cable from the Washington *rezidentura*—in point of fact, the *rezident* himself—stating that Sasha's mole intended to transmit another batch of intelligence later that morning. The *rezident* regarded this as encouraging news, which was hardly surprising; he bathed in the mole's reflected glory, and his star rose with each successful delivery. Sasha, however, did not share his enthusiasm. He was concerned about the timing; it was too soon. It was possible the mole had discovered a piece of vital intelligence that required immediate transmission, but such instances were rare.

Sasha placed the flimsy on his desk, next to the report he had received the previous evening. SVR forensic specialists had performed a preliminary analysis of the badly burned body that had been handed over by the French authorities at Strasbourg Airport. As yet, they had been unable to determine whether the corpse was Sergei Morosov's. Perhaps it was Morosov, said the scientists, perhaps not. Sasha found the timing of the road accident suspicious, to say the least. As an officer of the SVR, and the KGB before that, Sasha did not believe in accidents. Nor was he convinced that Sergei Morosov, the man whom he had entrusted with some of his most precious secrets, was really dead.

But was there a link between Sergei Morosov's "death" and the cable from Washington? And was it time to bring the mole in from the cold?

Sasha had nearly ordered her exfiltration after the traitor Gribkov approached MI6 with an offer to defect. Fortunately, the British had dithered, and Sasha was able to arrange for Gribkov's recall to Moscow for arrest, interrogation, and, eventually, *vysshaya mera*. Execution of the prisoner had occurred in the basement of Lefortovo Prison, in a room at the end of a dark corridor. It was Sasha who fired the fatal shot. He did so without an ounce of pity or squeamishness. Once upon a time, he had done his share of wet work.

With Gribkov dead and buried in an unmarked grave, Sasha had set about attempting to repair the damage. The operation unfolded precisely as Sasha planned, though he had made one miscalculation. It was the same miscalculation others had made before him.

Gabriel Allon . . .

It was possible he was jumping at shadows. It was an affliction, he thought, common to old men who stayed in the game too long. For more than thirty years—longer, even, than her father—the mole had operated undetected inside MI6. Guided by Sasha's hidden hand, she had risen steadily through the ranks to become H/Washington, a powerful position that allowed her to penetrate the CIA as well, just as her father had.

Now the brass ring was at last within her reach. Sasha's reach, too. If she were to become the director-general of the Secret Intelligence Service, she would be able to single-handedly undermine the Atlantic Alliance, leaving Russia free to pursue its ambitions in the Baltics, Eastern Europe, and the Middle East. It would be the greatest intelligence coup in history. Greater, even, than Kim Philby's.

It was for that reason Sasha chose a middle course. He wrote the message by hand and called for a courier to carry it from his dacha to the code room. At ten fifteen Moscow time—two fifteen in Washington—the courier returned with a chit confirming the message had been received.

There was nothing to do now but wait. In six hours, he would have his answer. He lifted the cover of an old file. It was a report written by Philby in March 1973, when he had worked his way back into favor at Moscow Center. It concerned a young Frenchwoman he had known in Beirut, and a child. Philby did not make clear in the report that the child was his, but the implication was clear. "I am inclined to think she might prove useful to us," he wrote, "for she has betrayal in the blood."

62

FOREST HILLS, WASHINGTON

The target of Sasha's suspicions was waiting, too. Not inside a private dacha, but in a ruined house in the northwest corner of Washington. Given the lateness of the hour, he was stretched on the couch in the study. For the previous two hours, he had reviewed his battle plan, searching for the flaws, for the weak joint that would bring the entire edifice crashing down around their ears. Having found none, save for a nagging concern regarding the true loyalty of Eva Fernandes, his thoughts had turned, as they often did at times such as these, to a birch forest one hundred and twenty-eight miles east of Moscow.

It is early morning, snow is tumbling from an ashen sky. He is standing at the edge of a burial pit, a wound in the flesh of Mother Russia. Chiara is next to him, shivering with cold and fear. Mikhail Abramov and a man called Grigori Bulganov are farther down the line. And before them, waving a gun and shouting orders over the thud of approaching helicopters, is Ivan Kharkov.

Enjoy watching your wife die, Allon . . .

Gabriel's eyes flew open with the memory of the first gunshot. That was the moment, he thought, when his personal war with the Kremlin truly began. Yes, there were opening skirmishes, preliminary rounds, but that terrible morning in Vladimirskaya Oblast was when hostilities formally commenced. That was when Gabriel understood the New Russia would go the way of the old. That was when his cold war against the Kremlin turned hot.

Since then, they had fought one another on a secret battlefield that stretched from the heart of Russia, to the Brompton Road in London, to the cliffs of Cornwall, and even the green hills of Northern Ireland. Now their war had arrived in Washington. In a few hours' time, when Rebecca Manning transmitted her re-port—a report Gabriel had all but written for her—it would be over. In this contest, however, he had already prevailed. He had unmasked the Russian mole buried deep within the British Secret Intelligence Service. She was the child of none other than Kim Philby. All Gabriel needed was the final piece of evidence, one last brushstroke, and his masterpiece would be complete.

It was this thought, the tantalizing prospect of ultimate victory over his most implacable foe, that kept Gabriel awake through-out that long final night. At half past five he rose from his couch, showered and shaved carefully, and dressed. Faded jeans, a woolen pullover, a leather jacket: the uniform of an operational chief.

He entered the sitting room. There he found three members of his fabled team—Yaakov Rossman, Yossi Gavish, and Rimona Stern—gathered tensely around a trestle table. They were not talking to the walls, only to each other, and only in the softest of voices. Each was peering into a laptop computer. On one was a static shot of a small house, about the size of a typical English cottage, with a peculiar Tudor facade above the portico. A lamp burned at the end of the flagstone walk, and another in the window of an upstairs bedroom.

It was 6:05 a.m. The mole had risen.

63

WARREN STREET, WASHINGTON

Rebecca skimmed the London papers on her iPhone while she drank her coffee and smoked the morning's first two L&Bs. Somehow, Prime Minister Lancaster's plan to suspend diplomatic ties with the Kremlin had failed to leak. Nor was there any hint of the impending crisis in the unclassified traffic on her MI6 BlackBerry. Apparently, the information was being closely held—the prime minister and his senior advisers, the foreign secretary, and Graham. And Gabriel Allon, of course. Rebecca was alarmed by Allon's involvement in the affair. For now, she was reasonably confident she had not been exposed. Graham would not have included her on the distribution list if he suspected her of treason.

Thanks to Rebecca, Moscow Center and the Kremlin would not be caught completely off guard by the news. After Graham's departure, she had composed a detailed report about the British plans and loaded it onto her iPhone, where it was hidden inside a popular instant messaging application, inaccessible to everyone except the SVR and its digital short-range agent communications system. The message contained an emergency code phrase instructing her servicing agent—the attractive illegal who operated under Brazilian cover—to hand over the material immediately to the Washington *rezidentura*. It was risky, but necessary. If the illegal agent delivered the message to Moscow Center by the usual channels, it wouldn't arrive in Moscow for several days, far too late to be of any use.

Rebecca scanned the American papers over a second coffee and at half past six went upstairs to bathe and dress. There would be no run that morning, not with both her worlds in crisis. After making her drop at Starbucks on Wisconsin Avenue, she planned to put in a brief appearance at the station. With a bit of luck, she might have a few minutes with Graham before his meeting with CIA director Morris Payne. It would give her one last chance to convince him to take her to Langley. Rebecca wanted to hear firsthand how much MI6 had learned from Gabriel Allon.

By seven o'clock, she was dressed. She dropped her phones into her handbag—her personal iPhone and her MI6 BlackBerry—and went in search of her passport. She found it in the top drawer of her bedside table, along with the SIG Sauer and a spare magazine loaded with 9mm rounds. Automatically, she grabbed all three items and placed them in her handbag. Downstairs, she switched off the lamp at the end of the walk and went out.

64

YUMA STREET, WASHINGTON

There was much Rebecca Manning didn't know that morning, including the fact her house was being watched by a miniature camera hidden in the communal garden across the street, and that during the night a limpet tracking beacon had been fitted to her car: a blue-gray Honda Civic with diplomatic plates.

The camera bore witness to her departure from her home on Warren Street, and the beacon charted her movement westward across residential Tenleytown. Yaakov Rossman relayed the information via encrypted text messages to Eli Lavon, who was slumped in the passenger seat of a rented Nissan parked on Yuma Street. Christopher Keller was behind the wheel. Between them, they had followed some of the most dangerous men in the world.

A Russian mole with a beacon fitted to her car scarcely seemed worthy of their talents.

"She just turned onto Massachusetts Avenue," said Lavon.

"Which direction?"

"Still heading west."

Keller eased away from the curb and headed in the same direction along Yuma. The street intersected with Massachusetts Avenue at roughly a forty-five-degree angle. Keller braked at the stop sign and waited for a car to pass, a Honda Civic, blue-gray, diplomatic plates, driven by MI6's Washington Head of Station.

Eli Lavon was looking down at his BlackBerry. "She's still heading west on Massachusetts."

"You don't say." Keller allowed two more cars to pass and then followed after her.

"Be careful," said Lavon. "She's good."

"Yes," answered Keller calmly. "But I'm better."

65

BRITISH EMBASSY, WASHINGTON

After returning to the British Embassy compound the previous evening, Graham Seymour had informed the head of the motor pool that he would require a car and driver for the morning. His first stop, he said, would be the Four Seasons Hotel in Georgetown for a private breakfast meeting. From there, he would proceed to CIA Headquarters in Langley, and from Langley to nearby Dulles International Airport, where his chartered aircraft was waiting. In a break with protocol, however, he had informed the head of security he would be making his appointed rounds that day without a protective detail.

The head of security objected but eventually acceded to Seymour's wishes. The car was waiting, as requested, at 7:00 a.m., outside the ambassador's residence on Observatory Circle. Once inside the vehicle, Seymour informed the driver of a slight change to his itinerary. He also informed the driver that he was not, under any circumstances, to tell the head of the motor pool or the head of security.

"In fact," warned Seymour, "if you breathe so much as a word about it, I'll have you locked in the Tower or flogged or something equally hideous."

"Where are we going instead of the Four Seasons?"

Seymour recited the address, and the driver, who was new to Washington, punched it into his navigation. They followed Observatory Circle to Massachusetts Avenue, then headed north on Reno Road through Cleveland Park. At Brandywine Street they made a right. At Linnean Avenue, a left.

"Are you sure you entered the correct address?" asked Seymour when the car came to a stop.

"Who lives there?"

"You wouldn't believe me if I told you."

Seymour climbed out and walked over to the iron gate, which opened at his approach. A flight of steep steps bore him to the front door, where a woman with sandstone-colored hair and child-bearing hips was waiting. Seymour recognized her. She was Rimona Stern, head of the Office division known as Collections.

"Don't just stand there!" she snapped. "Come inside."

Seymour followed her into the large main room, where Gabriel and two of his senior officers—Yaakov Rossman and Yossi Gavish—were gathered around a folding trestle table, staring into laptop computers. On the wall behind them was a large patch of mold. It looked vaguely like a map of Greenland.

"Is this *really* where your ambassador lives?" asked Seymour.

But Gabriel didn't answer; he was staring at the message that had just arrived on his screen. It stated that Eva Fernandes and Mikhail Abramov were leaving the apartment building on MacArthur Boulevard. Seymour removed his Crombie overcoat and reluctantly laid it over the back of a chair. From his pocket he took his MI6 BlackBerry. He checked the time. It was 7:12 a.m.

66

BURLEITH, WASHINGTON

The traffic was already a nightmare, especially along Reservoir Road, which stretched from Foxhall to the northern end of Georgetown. It was a commuter alley for the Maryland suburbs, eastbound in the morning, westbound at night, made worse by the presence of Georgetown University Medical Center and, at that hour, a blinding sunrise. Eva Fernandes, an experienced if illegal Washington driver, knew a few shortcuts. She was dressed in her usual morning attire—leggings, neon-green Nike trainers, and a form-fitting zippered jacket, also neon-green. After two consecutive nights without sleep, Mikhail looked like her troubled boyfriend, the one who preferred booze and drugs to work.

"And I thought the traffic in Moscow was bad," he said beneath his breath.

Eva made a left turn onto Thirty-Seventh Street and headed north into Burleith, a neighborhood of small terraced cottages popular with students and young professionals. And with Russian spies, thought Mikhail. Aldrich Ames used to leave a chalk mark on a mailbox on T Street when he wanted to deliver the CIA's secrets to his KGB handler. The original postbox was in a museum downtown. The one that slid past Mikhail's window was a replacement.

"Remind me what happens after you drop me off," he said.

Eva made no protestation other than a heavy sigh. They had reviewed the plan thoroughly at her kitchen table. Now, in the final minutes before the scheduled drop, they were going to review it again, whether she needed to or not.

"I drive the rest of the way to the Starbucks," she recited, as if by rote.

"And what happens if you try to make a run for it?"

"The FBI," she answered. "Prison."

"Order your latte," said Mikhail with operational calm, "and take it to the upstairs seating area. Don't make eye contact with any of the other customers. And whatever you do, don't forget to switch on the receiver. When Rebecca transmits, it will automatically forward her report to us."

Eva turned onto Whitehaven Parkway. "What happens if she gets cold feet? What happens if she doesn't transmit?"

"The same thing that happens if she does. Wait upstairs until you hear from me. Then go to your car and start the engine. I'll join you. And then . . ."

"*Poof*," she said.

Eva pulled to the curb at the corner of Thirty-Fifth Street. Mikhail opened the door and dropped a foot to the gutter. "Don't forget to turn on the receiver. And whatever you do, don't leave that café unless I tell you to."

"What happens if she doesn't transmit?" Eva asked once again.

Mikhail climbed out of the car without answering and closed the door. Instantly, the Kia lurched away from the curb and turned right onto Wisconsin Avenue. So far so good, he thought, and started walking.

67

WISCONSIN AVENUE, WASHINGTON

As a tableau for Cold War–style espionage, it lacked the usual iconography. There were no walls or checkpoints, no guard towers or searchlights, no bridge of spies. There was only a wildly popular chain coffee shop, with its ubiquitous green-and-white sign. It was located on the western side of Wisconsin Avenue, at the end of a parade of small shops—an animal hospital, a hair salon, a bespoke tailor, a cobbler, a pet groomer, and one of Washington's better French restaurants.

Only the coffee shop had its own car park. Eva hovered in the center of the lot for two long minutes until a space opened up. Inside, the line stretched from the cash register nearly to the door. It was no matter; she had arrived in plenty of time.

Ignoring the instructions of the man she knew as Alex, she scanned her surroundings carefully. There were nine people ahead of her—edgy commuters headed toward downtown office buildings, a couple of sweatshirted habitués from the neighborhood, and three children wearing the striped tie of the British International School, which was located on the opposite side of Wisconsin Avenue. Five or six more customers were waiting for their drinks at the other end of the L-shaped counter, and four more were reading copies of the *Washington Post* or *Politico* at a communal table. None looked to Eva like operatives of the FBI, the Israeli or British intelligence services, or, more important, the Washington *rezidentura* of the SVR.

There was additional seating at the back of the restaurant, past the display case of plastic-looking cakes and sandwiches. All but two of the tables were occupied. At one sat a man in his mid-twenties with an indoor pallor. He wore a Georgetown University pullover and was staring at a laptop. He looked like a typical Wi-Fi mooch, which was exactly the point. Eva believed she had just identified the Israeli computer technician who had managed to break through the unbreakable firewall of the SVR receiver.

It was 7:40 when she finally placed her order. The barista sang Al Green's "Let's Stay Together" rather well while he prepared her grande latte with an extra shot, which she sweetened liberally before making her way to the rear seating area. The kid in the Georgetown pullover was the only man who did not look up from his device to watch Eva pass in her leggings and tight-fitting jacket, thus confirming he was indeed the Israeli computer tech.

On the left side of the room was the stairway to the upper seating area. Only one person was present, a middle-aged man in chinos and a crewneck sweater who was writing furiously on a yellow legal pad. He was sitting next to the balustrade overlooking the front of the store. Eva sat down at the back, near a door that led to an unoccupied terrace. The power switch of the SVR receiver, when engaged, emitted a muted click. Even so, the man looked up and frowned before resuming his labors.

Eva removed her phone from her handbag and checked the time. It was 7:46 a.m. The window opened in fourteen minutes. Fifteen minutes after that, it would close again, and if everything went according to plan, Sasha's mole would be revealed. Eva felt no guilt over her actions, only fear—the fear of what would happen if the SVR somehow managed to seize her and take her back to Russia. A windowless room at the end of a dark corridor in Lefortovo Prison, a man with no face.

Poof . . .

She checked the time again. It was 7:49. Hurry, she thought. Please hurry.

68

WISCONSIN AVENUE, WASHINGTON

On the opposite side of Wisconsin Avenue and one hundred yards to the north was an upscale Safeway designed to appeal to Georgetown's sophisticated clientele. There was an indoor parking garage at street level and a second outdoor lot at the back of the store that Rebecca Manning preferred. She drove slowly up the ramp while staring hard into her rearview mirror. At two points during her surveillance-detection run, she had considered abandoning the drop for fear she was being tailed by the FBI. She now considered those fears to be unfounded.

Rebecca parked in the far corner of the lot and with her handbag over her shoulder walked to the store's back entrance. The baskets were near the elevator that led to the garage level. Rebecca took one from the stack and carried it through the store, from produce to prepared food, up and down the many long aisles, until she was certain no one was following her.

She dropped off the basket at the self-checkout area and headed down a long flight of steps to the store's main entrance on Wisconsin Avenue. Rush-hour traffic poured down the slope of the hill toward Georgetown. Rebecca waited for the light to change before crossing to the other side of the street. There she turned south and while passing a darkened Turkish restaurant mentally committed herself to proceeding to the drop site.

It was forty-seven paces from the door of the Turkish restaurant to the entrance of the Starbucks, which was guarded by a homeless man clothed in filthy rags. Under normal circumstances, Rebecca would have given the man money, the way her mother always gave a few centimes to the beggars on the streets of Paris, even though she had little more than they. On that morning, however, she brushed guiltily past the man and went inside.

Eight people were queued at the register. Anxious-looking lawyer-lobbyists, a couple of future MI6 officers from the British International School, a tall man with bloodless skin and colorless eyes who looked like he hadn't slept in a week. The barista was singing "A Change Is Gonna Come." Rebecca glanced at her wristwatch. It was 7:49.

Christopher Keller and Eli Lavon had not bothered to follow Rebecca Manning into Safeway's upper parking lot. Instead, they had parked on Thirty-Fourth Street, outside Hardy Middle School, a vantage point that allowed them to witness firsthand her arrival at Starbucks. Eli Lavon flashed the news to the Chesapeake Street command post—needlessly, for Gabriel and the rest of the team were watching Rebecca live through the camera of Ilan's phone.

Everyone but Graham Seymour, who had stepped into the garden to take a call from Vauxhall Cross.

It was 7:54 when Seymour came back inside. Rebecca Manning was now placing her order. Seymour provided the sound track.

"Tall dark-roast coffee. Nothing to eat, thank you."

When the young man at the counter turned away to draw Rebecca's coffee from the warmer, she inserted her credit card into the chip reader, thus confirming her presence in the establishment on the morning in question.

"Would you like a copy of your receipt?" recited Gabriel.

"Yes, please," answered Seymour on Rebecca's behalf, and a few seconds later the young man at the counter handed her a small slip of paper, along with her coffee.

Gabriel looked at the digital clock at the center of the trestle table: *7:56:14* . . . The window for transmission was nearly open.

"Seen enough?" he asked.

"No," said Seymour, staring at the screen. "Let her run."

69

WISCONSIN AVENUE, WASHINGTON

There was a space available at the communal table. It was the seat nearest the door, which provided Rebecca with unobstructed views into the street and the café's rear seating area. The man who had been ahead of her in line, the one with pale skin and eyes, had settled at the far end of the room, with his back toward Rebecca. A couple of tables away, a young man who looked like a graduate student was tapping away at a laptop, as were four other customers. The three people seated with Rebecca at the communal table were digital dinosaurs who preferred to consume their information in printed form. It was Rebecca's preference, too. Indeed, some of the happiest hours of her extraordinary childhood were spent in the library at her father's apartment in Moscow. Among his vast collection were the four thousand books he inherited from his fellow Cambridge spy Guy Burgess. Rebecca could still recall how they smelled intoxicatingly of tobacco. She smoked her first cigarettes, she reckoned, by reading Guy Burgess's books. She was craving one now. She didn't dare, of course. It was a crime worse than treason.

Rebecca pried the lid off her coffee and laid it on the table, next to her iPhone. Her MI6 BlackBerry, which was still in her handbag, was vibrating with an incoming message. In all likelihood, it was the station or the Western Hemisphere desk at Vauxhall Cross. Or perhaps, she thought, Graham had changed his mind about bringing her to Langley. He was probably leaving the ambassador's residence now. Rebecca supposed she ought to read the message to make sure it wasn't an emergency. In a minute, she thought.

Her first sip of coffee entered her empty stomach like battery acid. The barista was now singing Marvin Gaye's "What's Going On," and the man across the communal table, perhaps inspired by the lyric, was grousing to his neighbor about the American president's latest outrage on social media. Rebecca glanced toward the rear seating area and in doing so caught no one returning her gaze. She assumed the illegal was upstairs; she could see the illegal's receiver in the network settings of her iPhone. If the device was functioning properly, it would be invisible to any other phones, tablets, or computers within range.

She checked the time: 7:56 . . . Another sip of coffee, another corrosive surge in the pit of her stomach. With outward calm she flipped through the icons on the home screen of the iPhone until she arrived at the instant messaging application with the SVR protocol buried inside. Her report was there, encrypted and invisible. Even the icon that sent it was a lie. With her thumb hovering above it, she made one last sweep of the room with her eyes.

There was nothing suspicious, only the incessant shivering of her MI6 BlackBerry. Even the man across the table seemed to be wondering why she hadn't answered it.

It was now 7:57. Rebecca placed the iPhone on the tabletop and reached deliberately into her handbag. The BlackBerry was resting against the SIG Sauer 9mm. She removed the phone carefully and entered her long password. The message was from Andrew Crawford, wondering when she was going to arrive at the station.

Rebecca ignored the message and at 7:58 returned the Black-Berry to her handbag. Two minutes before the window for transmission opened, her iPhone rattled with a new incoming message. It was from a London number Rebecca didn't recognize, and one word in length.

Run . . .

70

WISCONSIN AVENUE, WASHINGTON

un . . .

Run from what? Run from whom? Run where?

Rebecca scrutinized the number on the iPhone. It meant nothing to her. The most likely source of the message was Moscow Center or the Washington *rezidentura*. Or perhaps, she thought, it was a trick of some sort. A deception. Only a spy would run.

She frowned at the screen for the sake of the cameras that were no doubt watching her and with the press of a deceptive icon consigned her original report to digital dust. It was gone, it had never existed. Then, with the press of a second false icon, the application itself vanished. She now had no evidence of treason on her phone or among her possessions, only the gun she had stuffed into her handbag before leaving her house. Suddenly, she was glad she had it.

Run . . .

How long had they known? And how *much* did they know? Did they know only that she was a spy for Moscow Center? Or did they also know she had been born and bred to be a spy, that she was Kim Philby's daughter and Sasha's life's work? She thought of Graham's unorthodox visit to her house the night before, and the alarming news that Downing Street intended to sever diplomatic ties with Moscow. It was a lie, she thought, designed to trick her into making contact with her handlers. There was no plan to break relations with Moscow, and no meeting scheduled at Langley. She suspected, however, that there was indeed a plane waiting at Dulles International Airport—a plane that would take her back to London, where she would be within the grasp of the British legal system.

Run . . .

Not yet, she thought. Not without a plan. She had to react methodically, the way her father had in 1951, when he learned that Guy Burgess and Donald Maclean had defected to the Soviet Union, leaving him dangerously exposed. He had driven his motorcar into the Maryland countryside and buried his miniature KGB camera and film. *Down by the river near Swainson Island, at the base of an enormous sycamore tree . . .* Rebecca's car, however, was of no use to her. Surely, it had been fitted with a tracking beacon. That would explain why she hadn't spotted any surveillance teams.

In order to make her escape—to *run*—Rebecca would need a different car and access to an uncompromised phone. Sasha had assured her that, in the event of an emergency, he would be able to whisk her to Moscow, the way Yuri Modin had plucked her father from Beirut. Rebecca had been given a number to call inside the Russian Embassy, and a code word that would tell the person at the other end of the line that she was in trouble. The word was "Vrej." It was the name of an old restaurant in the Armenian quarter of Beirut.

But first she had to extricate herself from the drop site. She assumed that several of the people seated around her were either British, American, or even Israeli agents. Calmly, she slipped her iPhone into her handbag and, rising, dropped her coffee cup through the circular hole in the condiment station. The doorway leading to Wisconsin Avenue was to her right. She turned to the left instead and headed toward the rear seating area of the café. No one looked at her. No one dared.

71

CHESAPEAKE STREET, WASHINGTON

Approximately three miles to the north, at the Chesapeake Street command post, Gabriel watched with rising alarm as Rebecca Manning passed through the camera feed of Ilan's phone.

"What just happened?"

"She didn't transmit her report," said Graham Seymour.

"Yes, I know. But why not?"

"Something must have spooked her."

Gabriel looked at Yaakov Rossman. "Where is she now?"

Yaakov typed the query into his laptop. Mikhail answered within seconds. Rebecca Manning was in the restroom.

"Doing what?" asked Gabriel.

"Use your imagination, boss."

"I am." Thirty additional seconds passed with no sign of her. "I have a bad feeling, Graham."

"What do you want to do about it?"

"You have all the proof you need."

"That's debatable, but I'm still listening."

"Tell her you've changed your mind about the meeting at Langley. Tell her you want her to be there after all. That should get her attention."

"And then what?"

"Instruct her to meet you at the embassy." Gabriel paused, then added, "And then take her into custody the second her foot touches British soil."

Seymour typed the message into his BlackBerry and sent it. Fifteen seconds later the device chimed with a response.

"She's on her way."

72

WISCONSIN AVENUE, WASHINGTON

Behind the locked door of the coffee shop's omnigender restroom, Rebecca reread Graham Seymour's text message. *Change in plan. I want you to accompany me to Langley. Meet me at the station soonest . . .* The benign tone could not conceal the message's true meaning. It confirmed Rebecca's worst fears. She had been exposed and led into a trap.

The door latch rattled impatiently.

"One minute, please," said Rebecca with a serenity that would have warmed her father's traitorous heart. It was his face reflected in the mirror. "With each passing year," her mother used to say, "you look more and more like him. The same eyes. The same contemptuous expression." Rebecca was never sure her mother meant it as a compliment.

She zipped the BlackBerry and iPhone into the Faraday pouch in her handbag and tore a single sheet of paper from her notebook. On it she wrote a few words in Cyrillic script. The toilet flushed thunderously. She ran water into the basin for a few seconds, then tugged a couple of paper towels from the dispenser and dropped them into the bin.

From beyond the door came the gentle hum of the busy café. Rebecca placed her left hand on the latch and her right inside her handbag, around the grip of the compact SIG Sauer. She had released the external safety switch immediately after entering the restroom. The magazine held ten 9mm Parabellum rounds, as did the backup.

She pulled open the door and stepped out with the haste of a powerful Washingtonian who was running late for work. She had expected to find someone waiting, but the foyer was empty. The kid with the Georgetown hoodie had altered the angle of his laptop. The screen was shielded from Rebecca's view.

She turned abruptly to her right and headed up the stairs. In the upper seating area she found two people, a middle-aged man scribbling on a legal pad, and Eva Fernandes, the Russian illegal. In her neon-green jacket, she was hard to miss.

Rebecca sat down in the chair opposite. Her right hand was still inside the handbag, wrapped around the grip of the SIG Sauer. With her left, she handed Eva Fernandes the note. The illegal feigned incomprehension.

"Just do it," whispered Rebecca in Russian.

The woman hesitated, then surrendered her phone. Rebecca added it to the Faraday pouch.

"Where's your car?"

"I don't have a car."

"You drive a Kia Optima. It's parked outside in the lot." Rebecca opened her handbag sufficiently to allow the illegal to see the gun. "Let's go."

73

WISCONSIN AVENUE, WASHINGTON

In violation of all Office field doctrine, written and unwritten, spoken and unspoken, Mikhail Abramov had switched seats, exchanging his rear-facing chair for one angled toward the front of the café. He wore a miniature earpiece, left side, facing the wall. It allowed him to monitor the feed from Eva's phone, which was thoroughly compromised and acting as a transmitter. At least it *had* been acting as a transmitter until 8:04, when Rebecca Manning, after leaving the restroom, unexpectedly darted up the stairs.

In the final seconds before the phone went silent, Mikhail had heard a whisper. It was possible the words were Russian, but he couldn't be sure. Nor could he say with certainty who had spoken them. Regardless of what had transpired, both women were now headed toward the door. Eva was staring straight ahead, as though walking toward an open grave. Rebecca Manning was a step behind, her right hand inside a stylish handbag.

"What do you suppose she has inside that bag?" asked Mikhail quietly, as the two Russian agents passed within range of Ilan's camera.

"Several mobile phones," answered Gabriel, "and an SVR short-range agent communication device."

"She has more than that." Mikhail watched Eva and Rebecca walk out the door and turn left toward the parking lot. "Maybe you should ask your friend whether his Washington Head of Station carries a sidearm."

Gabriel did. Then he repeated the answer to Mikhail. Rebecca Manning did not as a general rule carry a weapon in public but kept one at her house for protection, with the blessing of the State Department and the CIA.

"What kind?"

"SIG Sauer."

"A nine, I assume?"

"You assume correctly."

"Probably a compact."

"Probably," agreed Gabriel.

"That means the capacity is ten."

"Plus ten in the backup."

"I don't suppose Eli is carrying a gun."

"The last time Eli carried a gun was 1972. He nearly killed me by accident."

"What about Keller?"

"Graham wouldn't allow it."

"That leaves me."

"Stay where you are."

"Sorry, boss, there's interference on the line. I didn't catch that."

Mikhail rose and walked past Ilan's table, through the camera shot. Outside, he turned left and started across the car park. Eva was already behind the wheel of her Kia; Rebecca was opening the passenger door. Before lowering herself into the seat, she glanced at Mikhail, and their eyes met. Mikhail looked away first and kept walking.

Thirty-Fourth Street was one-way, heading south. Mikhail walked against the flow of traffic, along the back side of the Turkish restaurant, as Eva reversed out of the space and turned into the street. Rebecca Manning was staring at him through the passenger-side window, he was certain of it. He could feel her eyes boring like bullets into his back. She was daring him to turn around for one last look. He didn't.

The Nissan was parked outside the school. Mikhail dropped into the backseat behind Keller. Gabriel was shouting at him over the radio from the command post. Eli Lavon, the finest watcher in the history of the Office, was regarding him reproachfully from the front passenger seat.

"Well done, Mikhail. That was a real thing of beauty. There's no way she noticed a smooth move like that."

Lavon said all this in sarcastic Hebrew. Keller was staring down the length of Thirty-Fourth Street, toward a rapidly shrinking Kia Optima. At the intersection of Reservoir Road, the car turned right. Keller waited for a flock of schoolchildren to cross the street. Then he put his foot to the floor.

74

BURLEITH, WASHINGTON

I'm not allowed to speak to you," said Eva Fernandes. "In fact, I'm not even allowed to *look* at you."

"It seems I've invalidated those orders, haven't I?"

Rebecca instructed Eva to make another right at Thirty-Sixth Street and again at S Street. Both times, the Nissan sedan followed. It was about six car-lengths behind. The driver was making no effort to conceal his presence.

"Make another right," snapped Rebecca, and a few seconds later Eva turned onto Thirty-Fifth Street, this time without bothering to stop or even slow. The Nissan did the same. Their crude surveillance tactics suggested to Rebecca they were operating without backup and, therefore, were not from the FBI. She would find out soon enough.

There was a traffic signal at the corner of Thirty-Fifth Street and Reservoir Road, one of only a handful in residential Georgetown. The light switched from green to amber as they approached. Eva pressed her foot to the floor, and the Kia bounded through the intersection as the light changed to red. Car horns blared as the Nissan followed.

"Turn right again," said Rebecca quickly, pointing to the entrance of Winfield Lane. A private street lined with matching red-brick homes, it reminded Rebecca of Hampstead in London. The Nissan was behind them.

"Stop here!"

"But—"

"Just do as I say!"

Eva slammed hard on the brakes. Rebecca tore the SIG Sauer from her handbag and leapt out of the car. She gripped the weapon in both hands, forming a triangle with her arms, and turned her body slightly to reduce her silhouette, just as she had been trained on the firing range at Fort Monckton. The Nissan was still approaching. Rebecca placed the sight over the driver's head and squeezed the trigger until the magazine was empty.

The Nissan swerved hard to its left and slammed into the nose of a parked Lexus SUV. No one climbed out, and there was no return of fire, thus proving to Rebecca's satisfaction that the men were not from the FBI. They were British and Israeli intelligence officers who had no legal jurisdiction to make an arrest or to fire a weapon, even when fired upon on a quiet street in Georgetown. In fact, Rebecca doubted the FBI even knew the British and Israelis were operating against her. In a few minutes, she thought, looking at the wrecked car, they would.

Run . . .

Rebecca dropped into the front seat of the Kia and shouted at Eva to drive. A moment later they were racing up Thirty-Seventh Street toward the Russian Embassy. As they crossed T Street, Rebecca tossed the Faraday pouch out the window. The SVR receiver was next.

Rebecca glanced over her shoulder. No one was following them. She expelled the empty magazine and rammed the backup into place. Eva Fernandes flinched at the sound. Guided by Rebecca, she turned left onto Tunlaw Road.

"Where are we going?" she asked as they passed the back side of the Russian Embassy compound.

"I need to make a phone call."

"And then?"

Rebecca smiled. "We're going home."

At that same moment, three men were walking along Thirty-Fifth Street toward the Potomac River. In dress and aspect, they were unlike the typical denizens of Georgetown. One of the men looked to be in considerable pain, and a close inspection of his right hand would have revealed the presence of blood. The hand itself was uninjured. His wound was to his right clavicle, the result of being struck by a 9mm round.

As they crossed O Street, the injured man's legs buckled, but his two colleagues, a tall man with pale skin and a smaller man with a forgettable face, kept him upright. At once, a car materialized, and the two uninjured men helped the third into the backseat. An employee of a popular neighborhood flower shop was the only witness. She would later tell police that the expression on the pale man's face was one of the most frightening she had ever seen.

By then, units of Washington's Metropolitan Police Department were responding to reports of gunfire on normally tranquil Winfield Lane. The car carrying the three men headed rapidly across Georgetown to Connecticut Avenue. There it turned north and made its way to a ruined house on Chesapeake Street. Inside were two of the most powerful intelligence officers in the world. They had let her run. And now she was gone.

75

TENLEYTOWN, WASHINGTON

There were only a handful of public telephones remaining in Northwest Washington. Rebecca Manning, for a moment such as this, had memorized the locations of most of them. One was at the Shell station at the corner of Wisconsin Avenue and Ellicott Street. Unfortunately, she had no change. Eva, however, always kept a roll of quarters hidden in her car for parking meters. She gave two to Rebecca and watched her walk over to the phone and dial a number rapidly from memory. Eva recognized it; she had been given the same number. It rang inside the Russian Embassy and was to be used only in the event of an extreme emergency.

For Rebecca Manning, the number represented a lifeline that would pull her safely back to Moscow. For Eva, however, it was a grave threat. Rebecca would doubtless arrive to a hero's welcome. But Eva would go straight to a debriefing room where Sasha would be waiting. She was tempted to slip the Kia into drive and leave Rebecca behind. She doubted she would get far. For all Eva knew, there were three dead men in a car on a private street in Georgetown. In addition to being an agent of a foreign intelligence service, she was now potentially an accessory to murder. She had no choice but to go with Rebecca to Moscow and hope for the best.

Rebecca returned to the car and told Eva to head north on Wisconsin Avenue. Then she switched on the radio and changed the station to WTOP. *We have breaking news this hour regarding a shooting incident in Georgetown* . . . She jabbed at the power button, and the radio went silent.

"How long?" asked Eva.

"Two hours."

"Are they going to pick us up?"

Rebecca shook her head. "They want us to get off the street and wait until the bolt-hole opens up."

Eva was secretly relieved. The longer she stayed out of the SVR's hands, the better. "Where's the bolt-hole?" she asked.

"They didn't tell me."

"Why not?"

"They want to make sure it's safe before they send us there."

"How are they going to contact us?"

"They want us to call again in an hour."

Eva didn't like it. But who was she to question the wisdom of Moscow Center?

They were approaching the invisible border separating the District of Columbia from Maryland. Two large shopping centers confronted one another across the busy boulevard. Rebecca pointed toward the complex on the right. The garage entrance was next to a chain restaurant famous for the size of its portions and the length of its wait for a table. Eva headed down the ramp and snared a ticket from the machine. Then, following Rebecca's instructions, she navigated to a deserted corner and backed into a space.

And there they waited, largely in silence, the SIG Sauer on Rebecca's lap, for the next thirty minutes. They had no phones to connect them to the world above, only the car radio. The reception was fickle but sufficient. Police were searching for a Kia Optima sedan, District plates, with two women inside. They were also searching for three men who had abandoned a bullet-riddled Nissan on Winfield Lane. According to witnesses, one of the men appeared to have been wounded in the gunfire.

The signal swelled with static. Eva lowered the volume. "They're looking for two women in a Kia."

"Yes, I heard that."

"We need to separate."

"We're staying together." Then Rebecca added contritely, "I can't do this without your help."

Rebecca increased the volume on the radio and listened to a resident of Georgetown expressing shock over the shooting. Eva, however, was watching a white commercial van, Maryland plates, no markings, coming toward them through the patchy overhead lighting. The FBI, she thought, loved unmarked vans. So did the SVR.

"We're in trouble," she said.

"It's just a delivery truck," answered Rebecca.

"Do the two in front look like delivery men to you?"

"They are, actually."

The van pulled into the next space, the side cargo door slid open. Eva stared at the Russian face just beyond her window, trying desperately to hide her fear.

"I thought we were driving ourselves to the bolt-hole."

"Change in plan," said Rebecca. "The bolt-hole came to us."

76

FOREST HILLS, WASHINGTON

The wound to Christopher Keller's clavicle was through and through. In its wake, however, the 9mm Parabellum round had left shattered bone and considerable tissue damage. Fortunately, all Israeli government buildings, even abandoned ones, maintained a store of medical supplies. Mikhail, a combat veteran, flushed the wound with antiseptic and applied protective bandages. He had nothing for the pain other than a bottle of ibuprofen. Keller washed down eight tablets with a whisky from the wet bar.

With Mikhail's help, he changed into fresh clothing and hung his right arm in a sling. The flight back to London promised to be long and uncomfortable, though mercifully Keller wouldn't be flying commercial. Graham Seymour's chartered executive jet waited at Dulles. The two men were last seen at the command post at half past nine, moving slowly down the steep, treacherous steps. Gabriel personally pressed the interior button that unlocked the iron gate. And thus the great undertaking came to an ignoble end.

Its final minutes were bitter and uncharacteristically rancorous. Mikhail clashed with Gabriel, and Gabriel with his old friend and comrade-in-arms Graham Seymour. He implored Seymour to phone the Americans and instruct them to seal Washington. And when Seymour refused, Gabriel threatened to call the Americans himself. He even started to dial Adrian Carter at CIA Headquarters before Seymour snatched the phone from his grasp. "It's my scandal, not yours. And if anyone's going to tell the Americans I planted Kim Philby's daughter in their midst, it's going to be me."

But Seymour made no such admission to the Americans that morning, and Gabriel, though he was sorely tempted, did not do it for him. And in the span of a few minutes, a relationship of historic importance crumbled. For more than a decade, Gabriel and Graham had worked hand in glove against the Russians, the Iranians, and the global jihadist movement. And in the process, they had managed to undo decades of animosity between their services, even their countries. All that was ashes. But then, Eli Lavon would later remark, that had been part of Sasha's plan from the beginning, to drive a wedge between the Office and MI6 and break the bond Gabriel and Graham Seymour had forged. In that, if nothing else, Sasha had succeeded.

Yossi Gavish and Rimona Stern left next. One of the watchers plucked the camera from the communal green garden on Warren Street and then made for the train station. The other watchers soon followed, and by 9:45 a.m. only Gabriel, Mikhail, and Eli Lavon remained at the command post. A single car waited curbside. Oren, Gabriel's chief bodyguard, stood watch inside the gate, against what, no one knew.

In the haste of their departure, the team had left the interior of the house a ruin, which was how they had found it. A single laptop remained on the trestle table. Gabriel was watching the recording of Rebecca Manning inside Starbucks when his Black-Berry shivered with an incoming message. It was from Adrian Carter.

What the hell is going on?

With nothing left to lose, Gabriel typed out a reply and sent it. *You tell me.*

Carter called him ten seconds later and did just that.

It seemed a certain Donald McManus, a veteran FBI special agent attached to the Bureau's Washington headquarters, had stopped for gas at the Shell station at Wisconsin Avenue and Ellicott Street at around twenty minutes past eight. And McManus, being naturally vigilant and aware of his surroundings, had noticed a well-dressed woman using the station's grubby old public phone, which he found odd. In his experience, the only people who used pay phones these days were illegal immigrants, drug dealers, and cheating spouses. The woman didn't appear to fall into any of those categories, though McManus was struck by the fact she kept her hand inside her shoulder bag throughout the entire con-versation. After hanging up, she climbed into the passenger seat of a Kia Optima with District plates. McManus caught the num-ber as it turned onto Wisconsin and headed north. The driver was younger than the woman who had used the phone, and prettier. McManus thought she looked a bit scared.

While heading south on Wisconsin, McManus switched from CNN on the satellite service to WTOP over the airwaves, and heard one of the station's first bulletins regarding a shooting that had just occurred in Georgetown. It sounded like road rage to McManus, and he thought nothing of it. But by the time he hit downtown, the police had released a description of the suspect vehicle. Kia Optima, District plates, two women inside. He passed the tag number of the car he had seen at the gas station to the Metropolitan Police and, while he was at it, ran the number through the Bureau's database. It was registered to an Eva Fernandes, a green-carder from Brazil, which was funny because McManus made her for an Eastern European.

About this same time, a surveillance team from the Bureau's Counterintelligence Division spotted several cars leaving the back entrance of the Russian Embassy, all containing known or suspected members of the SVR *rezidentura*. It looked to the team as though the *rezident* had a crisis on his hands, an observation they shared with Headquarters. Special Agent McManus, who worked counterterrorism, caught wind of the Russian personnel movements and told the duty officer at CI about the woman he had seen using a pay phone. The duty officer passed it up the line to the deputy, and the deputy in turn passed it to the division chief himself.

And it was there, at 9:35 a.m., on the chief's immaculate desk, that all three elements—the shooting in Georgetown, the hurried exodus from the Russian Embassy, and the two women in the Kia sedan—came together with all the makings of a rolling disaster in progress. When no one was looking, McManus ran a quick check on the pay phone and found that the call the woman had placed was to a number inside the Russian Embassy. And thus the rolling disaster became a full-blown international crisis that threatened to ignite World War III. Or so it seemed to Special Agent Donald McManus, who had just happened to stop for gas at the Shell station at Wisconsin Avenue and Ellicott Street at around twenty minutes past eight.

It was at this point the chief of the FBI's Counterintelligence Division rang his counterpart at the CIA to ask whether the Agency was running an op the Bureau didn't know about. The CIA man swore he wasn't, which happened to be true, but he thought it wise to run it past Adrian Carter, who was preparing for his daily ten o'clock with Morris Payne. Carter played dumb, his default response to uncomfortable questions from colleagues, superiors, and members of congressional oversight committees. Then, from the quiet of his seventh-floor office, he shot a quick text to his old friend Gabriel Allon, who just happened to be in town. The text was full of double or even triple meaning, and Gabriel, who knew Carter was on to him, responded in kind. Which was how they ended up on the telephone together, at 9:48, on an otherwise normal Thursday morning in Washington.

"Who were the three men?" asked Carter when he had finished briefing Gabriel.

"Which three men?"

"The three men," said Carter deliberately, "who took heavy fire on Winfield Lane in Georgetown."

"How should I know?"

"They say one of them was wounded."

"I hope it wasn't serious."

"Apparently, a car picked them up on Thirty-Fifth. No one's seen them since."

"What about the two women?" probed Gabriel gently.

"No sign of them, either."

"And they were last seen heading *north* on Wisconsin Avenue? You're sure it was north?"

"Forget about the direction," snapped Carter. "Just tell me who they are."

"According to the FBI agent," replied Gabriel, "one of them is a Brazilian national named Eva Fernandes."

"And the other?"

"Couldn't say."

"Any idea why she might be calling a number inside the Russian Embassy from a pay phone?"

"Maybe you should ask one of those SVR officers who were spotted leaving the embassy in such a hurry."

"The Bureau is looking for them, too. Any help from you," said Carter, "would be held in the strictest confidence. So why don't we start from the beginning? Who were the three men?"

"What three men?"

"And the women?"

"Sorry, Adrian, but I'm afraid I can't help you."

Carter exhaled heavily. "When are you planning to leave town?"

"Tonight."

"Any chance you could make it sooner?"

"Probably not."

"Too bad," said Carter, and the call went dead.

77

CHESAPEAKE STREET, WASHINGTON

Mikhail Abramov and Eli Lavon departed the command post at five minutes past ten o'clock in the back of an Israeli Embassy van. Their plan was to fly from Dulles to Toronto, and from Toronto to Ben Gurion. Mikhail left the Barak .45 with Gabriel, who pledged to lock it in the residence's safe before leaving for the airport himself.

Alone, he adjusted the time code on the computer and once again watched the two women walking out of Starbucks, Eva leading the way, Rebecca a step behind, gripping the SIG Sauer 9mm hidden in her handbag. Gabriel now knew that she had called the Russian Embassy from a Shell station on Wisconsin Avenue before heading north toward the Maryland suburbs. And, in all likelihood, straight into the arms of an SVR exfiltration team.

The speed of the Russian response suggested the *rezidentura* had a well-oiled escape plan in place. Which meant the chances of finding Rebecca were close to zero. The SVR was a highly capable and ruthless intelligence service, the successor of the mighty KGB. Smuggling her out of the United States would not be a problem. She would appear next in Moscow, just as her father had in 1963.

Unless Gabriel could somehow stop her before she left Metropolitan Washington. He could not ask the Americans for help; he had made a promise to Graham Seymour, and if he broke it the recriminations would hang over the rest of his tenure as chief. No, he would have to find Rebecca Manning alone. Not entirely alone, he thought. He had Charlotte Bettencourt to help him.

He rewound the recording and once again watched Rebecca following Eva from the coffee shop. It was fourteen steps, he noticed. Fourteen steps from the stairwell to Wisconsin Avenue. Gabriel wondered whether Rebecca, somewhere inside, was counting them, or whether she even remembered the game she used to play with her mother in Paris. Gabriel doubted it. Surely, Philby and Sasha would have purged such counterrevolutionary impulses.

Gabriel watched Rebecca Manning walk from the screen of his computer. And then he remembered something Charlotte Bettencourt had told him that night in Seville, very late, when they were alone together because neither could sleep. "She's more like her father than she realizes," she said. "She does things exactly the same way, and she doesn't know why."

Charlotte Bettencourt had told Gabriel something else that night. Something that sounded trivial at the time. Something only two other people in the world knew. "Who's to say whether it's still there," she said as her eyes closed with exhaustion. "But perhaps, if you have a free moment, you might want to have a look."

Yes, thought Gabriel. He might indeed.

It was ten fifteen when Gabriel slipped the Barak .45 into the waistband of his jeans and headed down the steep steps. Oren unlocked the iron gate and started toward the waiting car, a rented Ford Fusion. Gabriel, however, ordered him to remain behind.

"Not again," said Oren.

"I'm afraid so."

"Thirty minutes, boss."

"And not a minute more," promised Gabriel.

"And if you're late?"

"It means I've been kidnapped by a Russian exfiltration team and taken to Moscow for trial and imprisonment." He smiled in spite of himself. "I wouldn't hold out much hope for my survival."

"You sure you don't want some company?"

Without another word, Gabriel climbed into the car. A few minutes later he was racing past the large, tan colonial house on the corner of Nebraska Avenue and Forty-Second Street. In his thoughts he saw a desperate man climbing into a very old automobile, clutching a paper sack. The man was Kim Philby. And in the sack was a miniature KGB camera, several rolls of film, and a hand trowel.

78

BETHESDA, MARYLAND

The two Russians in the van were called Petrov and Zelenko. Petrov was from the Washington *rezidentura*, but Zelenko had made a crash trip down from Manhattan the previous night after Sasha had opened the bolt-hole. Both operatives had logged extensive prior experience in English-speaking countries before being assigned to America, which was still the SVR's "main adversary" and therefore the big leagues. Petrov had worked in Australia and New Zealand; Zelenko, in Britain and Canada. Zelenko was the larger of the two men and held black belts in three different martial arts disciplines. Petrov was good with a gun. Neither man intended to allow anything to happen to their precious cargo. To deliver both a mole and an illegal safely to Moscow would make them legends. To fail was unthinkable. Indeed, they had both agreed it would be better to die in America than return empty-handed to Yasenevo.

The van was a Chevrolet Express Cargo, owned by a Northern Virginia–based contracting company, which was in turn owned by a Ukrainian-born asset of Moscow Center. The plan was to drive south on I-95 to Florence, South Carolina, where they would acquire a second clean vehicle for the rest of the trip to South Florida. Moscow Center had access to numerous safe properties in the Miami area, including the dump in Hialeah where they would spend the next six days—six days being the length of time it would take the Russian-flag container vessel *Archangel* to reach the Florida Straits. Petrov, who had served in the Russian navy before joining the SVR, would handle the trip out in a fifty-foot sport fishing boat.

They were well provisioned for the journey, and heavily armed. Petrov had two weapons in his possession—a Tokarev and a Makarov—and Rebecca Manning still had her SIG Sauer. It was lying on the floor of the cargo hold, next to a phone she had borrowed from Zelenko. She was seated with her back against the driver's side panel, her legs stretched before her, still dressed for the office in her dark pantsuit and Burberry mackintosh. Eva was similarly situated on the opposite side of the hold, but slightly to the rear. They had spoken little since leaving the parking garage. Rebecca had thanked Eva for her skill and bravery and promised to sing her praises to Sasha when they arrived in Moscow. Eva did not believe a word of it.

The shortest route to I-95 was down Wisconsin Avenue. Rebecca, however, gave Petrov, who was driving, a different route.

"It would be better if we—"

"I'm the one who decides what's best," said Rebecca, cutting him off. And Petrov did not argue further, because long ago Rebecca had been granted Russian citizenship and was a colonel in the SVR, which meant she outranked him.

He turned onto Forty-Second Street and followed it through Tenleytown. Eva noticed Rebecca's peculiar interest in the large, tan colonial house that stood on the corner of Nebraska Avenue. They passed the Department of Homeland Security and the campus of American University. Then Petrov made a left onto Chain Bridge Road, which ran along the edge of Battery Kemble Park to MacArthur Boulevard. Through the windshield, Eva glimpsed the awning of Brussels Midi restaurant as they headed west toward Maryland.

"That's where I worked," she said.

"Yes, I know," said Rebecca disdainfully. "You were a cocktail waitress."

"Hostess," Eva corrected her.

"Same thing." Rebecca picked up the gun and laid it on her thigh. "Just because we're going to spend the next two or three weeks traveling together doesn't mean we're going to be having long heart-to-heart conversations. You performed your job well, and for that I am grateful. But as far as I'm concerned, you are a cocktail waitress, and nothing more."

She was also, thought Eva, entirely expendable. She stared out the windshield, Rebecca stared at the phone. She was following their progress on the map. They were approaching the turnoff for the westbound Clara Barton Parkway, the route to the Beltway and I-95, but Rebecca instructed Petrov to continue straight. There was a small shopping center in the village of Glen Echo. She said she wanted to pick up a few things for the drive.

Petrov again started to object but stopped himself. He continued straight, past an Irish pub and the old Glen Echo amusement park, to the intersection of MacArthur Boulevard and Goldsboro

Road. There was an Exxon station, a 7-Eleven, a pharmacy, a dry cleaner, a pizza and sub shop, and a True Value hardware store. Much to the surprise of Petrov, Zelenko, and Eva Fernandes, it was the hardware store Rebecca Manning entered.

She did so at 10:27 a.m., according to a store surveillance camera, just as a Ford Fusion passed the shopping center at a high rate of speed, headed west. Inside, there was only the driver, a man of late middle age, short black hair, gray at the temples. He had a gun, an Israeli-made Barak .45, but no bodyguard. The FBI and CIA did not know his whereabouts, and neither did the intelligence service he led. In fact, at that moment, he was entirely alone.

79

CABIN JOHN, MARYLAND

J ust west of Wilson Boulevard is the historic Union Arch Bridge. Completed in 1864 and built of Massachusetts granite and sandstone from the nearby Seneca Quarry, it is part of the Washington Aqueduct, a twelve-mile pipeline that feeds water from the Great Falls to the American capital. The bridge's roadbed is wide enough only for a single lane, and there are lights at either end to regulate the flow of traffic, which meant Gabriel had to endure a wait of nearly four minutes before he was allowed to pass.

On the opposite side of the bridge was a green athletic field and a community center and a pleasant colony of clapboard cottages set amid trees displaying the first eruptions of spring leaf. Gabriel continued west, passing beneath the Capital Beltway, until once again a traffic signal halted his progress. At length, he turned left and headed down the slope of a long gentle hill to the Clara Barton Parkway.

The road was what the British referred to as a dual carriageway, two lanes in either direction, separated by parkland. Gabriel was in the eastbound lane, headed back toward Washington. It was not a mistake on his part; he was now closer to the Potomac River and the historic Chesapeake & Ohio Canal, which stretched 184 miles from Georgetown to Cumberland, Maryland. The canal had seventy-four locks, several of which lay along the Clara Barton Parkway, including Lock 10, where there was a small car park. On a typical weekend, the lot might be jammed with the cars of hikers and picnickers. But at 10:39 a.m. on a Thursday morning, when the rest of Washington was preparing for another day of political combat, it was deserted.

Gabriel climbed out of the Ford and crossed an old wooden bridge spanning the canal. A footpath, muddy with recent rains, led through a stand of maple and poplar to the bank of the river. Swainson Island lay just offshore, across a narrow channel of dark, swiftly flowing water. An overturned boat, wooden, Park Service green in color, slept beneath an enormous sycamore.

On the opposite side of the tree, away from the erosive effects of the water moving through the channel, were three large rocks, a tiny Stonehenge. Gabriel prodded one with the toe of his brogue and found it firmly embedded in the soil.

He went back to the footpath and waited. The river flowed at his feet, the parkway at his back. Fewer than five minutes elapsed before he heard an engine die in the car park, followed by the sound of three doors opening and closing in rapid succession. Peering over his shoulder, he saw four people, two women, two men, crossing the footbridge spanning the canal. One of the women was wearing a business suit; the other, brightly colored athletic wear. The larger of the two men was carrying a shovel. Better to dig a grave that way, thought Gabriel.

He turned away and watched the black water moving through the channel. In the right pocket of his leather jacket was his Office BlackBerry. It was of no use to him. Only the gun at the small of his back could save him now. It was a Barak .45-caliber. A man-stopper. But in a pinch, he thought, it would stop a woman, too.

80

CAPITAL BELTWAY, VIRGINIA

On the way to Dulles Airport, Mikhail Abramov rang King Saul Boulevard and informed the Operations Desk that he had left the chief of the Office at the Chesapeake Street command post in a dark and unpredictable mood, with only a single bodyguard for protection. The desk promptly rang the bodyguard, and the bodyguard admitted he had allowed the chief to leave the command post alone, in a rented Ford Focus. Where was he going? The bodyguard couldn't say. Was he in possession of his Office BlackBerry? As far as the bodyguard knew, he was. Did he have a gun? Again, the bodyguard wasn't sure, so the desk called Mikhail and put the question to him. Yes, said Mikhail, he did have a gun. A big one, in fact.

It did not take the Operations Desk long to locate the chief's phone moving in a southwesterly direction along Nebraska Avenue. Minutes later, the phone was headed out of town on MacArthur Boulevard. After crossing the Beltway, it made a peculiar change of course and started back toward Washington along a largely parallel road, the name of which had no resonance in Tel Aviv. It appeared to the technician the chief was lost. Or worse. He rang the phone several times. None of the calls received an answer.

It was at this point that Uzi Navot, who had largely been a distant spectator to that morning's events, intervened. He, too, rang the chief's phone and, like the technician, was ignored. He then rang Mikhail and inquired as to his whereabouts. Mikhail replied that he and Eli Lavon were approaching Dulles. They were running late for their flight to Toronto.

"I'm afraid you're going to have to make other arrangements," said Navot.

"Where is he?" asked Mikhail.

"Lock Ten. Down by the river."

81

CABIN JOHN, MARYLAND

They were speaking in Russian, quiet and clipped. Gabriel, who had no ear for Slavic languages, could only wonder what they were saying. He supposed they were debating how to proceed now that they were no longer alone. Rebecca Manning's voice was readily discernible from Eva's; her accent was a casserole of British and French. In Eva's voice, Gabriel heard only fear.

At length, he turned slowly to acknowledge the newcomers' presence. He smiled carefully, he nodded his head once. And he calculated how long it would take to get the gun into firing position. *In the time it takes a mere mortal to clap his hands . . .* That was what Ari Shamron used to say. But that was with a Beretta .22, not the lumbering Barak. And that was when Gabriel was young.

None of the four returned his greeting. Rebecca was leading the way down the footpath, faintly comic in her pantsuit and pumps and mackintosh coat, which was pulling at one side, owing to the presence of a heavy object in the pocket. A step behind her was Eva, and behind Eva were the two men. Both looked capable of violence. The one with the shovel in his hands was Gabriel's natural ally; he would have to drop it in order to draw his weapon. The smaller one would be quick, and Rebecca had already demonstrated her proficiency with a gun in Georgetown. Gabriel reckoned he had only a slight chance of surviving the next few seconds. Or perhaps they wouldn't kill him after all. Perhaps they would load him into the back of the van and take him to Moscow and put him on trial for crimes against the Tsar and his kleptomaniacal comrades in the Kremlin.

In the time it takes a mere mortal to clap his hands . . .

But that was a long time ago, when he was the prince of fire, the angel of vengeance. Better to nod and walk away and hope they didn't recognize him. Better to leave with his honor and his body intact. He had a wife at home, and children. He had a service to run and a country to protect. And he had Kim Philby's daughter coming toward him along a footpath through the trees. He had found her out and tricked her into betraying herself. And now she was walking straight into his arms. No, he thought, he would see it through to its end. He was going to leave here with Rebecca Manning and take her back to London on Graham Seymour's airplane.

In the time it takes a mere mortal to clap his hands . . .

In her high-heeled pumps, Rebecca was teetering down the path. She slipped and nearly toppled, and as she regained her footing her eyes met Gabriel's. "Not appropriately dressed," she drawled in her borrowed upper-class British accent. "Should have brought my Wellies."

She stumbled to a stop, Kim Philby's daughter, Sasha's endeavor, not ten feet from the spot where Gabriel stood. He broadened his smile and in French said, "I thought it would be you."

Her eyes narrowed in confusion. "I beg your pardon?" she said in English, but Gabriel responded in French, Rebecca's first language. The language of her mother.

"It was what your father said to Nicholas Elliott in Beirut. And it was what your mother said to me in Spain the night we found her. She sends her best, by the way. She's sorry it turned out this way."

Rebecca murmured something in Russian. Something Gabriel couldn't understand. Something that made the smaller of the two men reach for his gun. Gabriel drew first and shot the man twice in the face, the way Konstantin Kirov had been shot in Vienna. The bigger one had dropped the shovel and was struggling to wrench a gun from his hip holster. Gabriel shot him, too. Twice. Through the heart.

Fewer than three seconds had elapsed, but in that brief time Rebecca Manning had managed to draw her SIG Sauer and grab a handful of Eva's hair. They were alone now, just the three of them, down by the river, near Swainson Island, at the base of an enormous sycamore. Not entirely alone, thought Gabriel. In the car park a man was climbing out of a very old automobile, clutching a paper sack . . .

82

CABIN JOHN, MARYLAND

How do you know about this place?"

"Your mother told me that, too."

"Was she the one who betrayed me?"

"A long time ago," said Gabriel.

He was staring directly into Rebecca's wild blue eyes, down the barrel of the smoking Barak. In the quiet of the trees, the four gunshots had sounded like cannon fire, but as yet no cars had stopped along the parkway to investigate. Rebecca was still holding Eva by the hair. She had pulled her close to her body and was screwing the muzzle of the SIG Sauer into the side of her neck, just below the hinge of her jaw.

"Go ahead and kill her," said Gabriel calmly. "Another dead SVR agent matters nothing to me. And it will give me an excuse to kill you, too."

Fortunately, he spoke these words in French, a language Eva did not comprehend.

"She *used* to be an SVR agent," said Rebecca. "Now she's yours."

"If you say so."

"She was working for you when she went into the coffee shop."

"If that were true, why did she help you escape?"

"I didn't give her much of a choice, Allon."

Gabriel's smile was genuine. "You're the closest thing to royalty we have in our business, Rebecca. I'm flattered you know my name."

"Don't be."

"You have your father's eyes," said Gabriel, "but your mother's mouth."

"How did you find her?"

"It wasn't hard, actually. She was Sasha's one mistake. He should have brought her to Moscow a long time ago."

"Kim wouldn't allow it."

"Is that what you called him?"

She ignored the question. "He was remarried to Rufina," she explained. "He didn't want to make a mess of his personal life yet again by having an old flame living in the neighborhood."

"So he left her in the hills of Andalusia," said Gabriel contemptuously. "Alone in the world."

"It wasn't so bad there."

"You knew where she was?"

"Of course."

"And you never tried to see her?"

"I couldn't."

"Because Sasha wouldn't allow it? Or because it would have been too painful?"

"Painful for whom?"

"You, of course. She was your mother."

"I have nothing but scorn for her."

"Do you really?"

"She gave me away rather easily, didn't she? And she never once tried to contact me or see me."

"She did once, actually."

The blue eyes brightened, childlike. "When?"

"When you were at Trinity College. She snapped a photo of you walking along Jesus Lane. You were next to the redbrick wall."

"And she kept it?"

"It was all she had."

"You're lying!"

"I can show it to you, if you like. I have your birth certificate, too. Your *real* birth certificate. The one from Saint George Hospital in Beirut that listed the name of your real father."

"I never cared for the name Manning. I much prefer Philby."

"He did a terrible thing to you, Rebecca. He had no right to steal your life and brainwash you into fighting his old wars."

"No one brainwashed anyone. I adored Kim. Everything I did, I did for him."

"And now it's over. Drop the gun," said Gabriel, "and let me take you home."

"Moscow is my home," she declared. "Therefore, I propose a trade. I will give you back your agent, and you will grant me safe conduct to the Russian Federation."

"Sorry, Rebecca, but that's a deal I can't accept."

"In that case, I suppose your agent and I are going to die here together."

"Not if I kill you first."

She gave him a bitter, superior smile. It was Philby's smile.

"You haven't got it in you to kill a woman, Allon. Otherwise, you would have done it already."

It was true. Rebecca was several inches taller than Eva and standing behind her on the steeply sloped path. The top of her head was exposed, the shot was there for the taking. The river was flowing at his heels. Slowly, the gun extended, he moved up the path, along the edge of the trees. Rebecca pivoted with him, keeping her gun against Eva's neck.

Her eyes moved briefly to the base of the sycamore. "I'm surprised it's still alive."

"They live for two and a half centuries or so. It was probably here when the British burned the White House."

"I did my best to finish the job." Another glance toward the tree. "Do you think it's still there? The camera that stole a thousand American secrets?"

"Why did you come for it?"

"For sentimental reasons. You see, I have nothing of his. When he died, Rufina and his *real* children and grandchildren took all his possessions. But the child of the other woman . . . she got nothing at all."

"Put the gun down, Rebecca, and we'll dig it out together. And then we'll go to London."

"Can you imagine the scandal? It will make the Third Man affair seem like—" She twisted Eva's hair harder. "Perhaps it's better if the story ends here, down by the river, at the base of an enormous sycamore."

She was wavering, losing her faith. She looked suddenly very tired. And mad, thought Gabriel. She had ended up like all the rest of Philby's women.

"How many steps do you think it is?" he asked.

"What are you talking about?"

"To my car," said Gabriel. "How many steps from the water's edge to my car?"

"She told you about that, too?"

"How many steps from the Louvre to Notre-Dame?" said Gabriel. "From the Arc de Triomphe to the Place de la Concorde . . . From the Tour Eiffel to Les Invalides . . ."

She said nothing.

"Put the gun down," said Gabriel. "It's all over now."

"*You* put the gun down," said Rebecca. "And I'll do the same."

Gabriel lowered the Barak and pointed it toward the damp earth. Rebecca was still holding her SIG Sauer to the side of Eva's neck. "All the way," she said, and Gabriel, after a moment's hesitation, allowed the gun to fall from his grasp.

"You fool," Rebecca said coldly, and aimed her gun at his chest.

83

CABIN JOHN, MARYLAND

It was a Moscow Center–trained move, and a good one at that. A heel to the instep, an elbow to the solar plexus, a backhand to the nose, all in the blink of an eye. Too late, Gabriel seized hold of the gun and tried to tear it from Rebecca's hands. The shot struck Eva in the Russian way, in the nape of her neck, and she crumpled to the wet earth.

Rebecca sprayed two more rounds harmlessly into the trees as Gabriel, still clutching the SIG Sauer, drove her backward down the footpath. Together they plunged into the frigid waters of the Potomac. The gun was beneath the surface. It recoiled in Gabriel's grasp as four tiny torpedoes streaked toward Swainson Island.

By Gabriel's count, three rounds remained in the magazine. Rebecca's face was beneath the dark, rushing waters. Her eyes were open and she was screaming at him in a rage, making no effort to conserve her breath. Gabriel pushed her deeper as two more shots split the channel.

A single round remained. It escaped the gun as the last breath escaped Rebecca's lungs. As Gabriel lifted her from the water, he heard footfalls on the path. In his madness, he expected it was Philby come to save his daughter, but it was only Mikhail Abramov and Eli Lavon, come to save him.

Rebecca, choking on river water, fell to her knees at the base of the sycamore. Gabriel hurled her gun into the channel and started up the path toward the car. Only later did he realize he was counting the steps. There were one hundred and twenty-two.

PART FOUR

THE WOMAN FROM ANDALUSIA

84

CABIN JOHN, MARYLAND

A jogger made the discovery at eleven fifteen. She called 911, and the operator called the U.S. Park Police, which had jurisdiction. The officers found three bodies, two men and a young woman, all with gunshot wounds. The men were in street clothes; the woman, in brightly colored athletic wear. She had been shot once in the back of the head, in contrast to the men, who had each been shot twice. There were no vehicles in the car park, and a preliminary search of the crime scene produced no identification. It did, however, produce two Russian-made pistols—a Tokarev and a Makarov—and, curiously, a True Value shovel.

The blade looked new, and on the handle was a spotless price tag with the name of the store where it was purchased. One of the officers rang the manager and asked whether he had recently sold a shovel to two men or a woman in brightly colored athletic wear. No, said the manager, but he had sold one that very morning to a woman in a business suit and a tan overcoat.

"Cash or charge?"

"Cash."

"Can you describe her?"

"Fifty-something, very blue eyes. And an accent," the manager added.

"Russian, by any chance?"

"English."

"Do you have video?"

"What do you think?"

The officer made the drive from the crime scene to the hardware store in four minutes flat. Along the way he made contact with his shift supervisor and expressed his opinion that something significant had occurred on the banks of the river that morning—more significant, even, than the loss of three lives—and that the FBI needed to be brought into the picture immediately. His supervisor concurred and rang Bureau headquarters, which was already on war footing.

The first FBI agent to arrive at the crime scene was none other than Donald McManus. At 11:50 a.m. he confirmed that the dead woman was the same woman he had seen earlier that morning at the Shell station on Wisconsin Avenue. And at 12:10 p.m., after viewing the video from the hardware store, he confirmed that the woman who purchased the shovel was the same woman who called the Russian Embassy from the gas station's pay phone.

But who was she? McManus rushed a copy of the video back to FBI Headquarters to begin the process of trying to attach a name to the woman's face. The chief of the National Security Branch took one look at the video, however, and told McManus not to bother. The woman was MI6's Washington Head of Station.

"Rebecca Manning?" asked Donald McManus, incredulous. "Are you sure it's her?"

"I had coffee with her last week."

"Did you tell her anything classified?"

Even then, at the earliest moments of the unfolding scandal, the chief of the NSB knew better than to answer. Instead, he rang his director. And his director, in quick succession, rang the attorney general, the director of the CIA, the secretary of state, and, lastly, the White House. Protocol dictated the secretary of state contact the British ambassador, which he did at half past one.

"I believe she's on her way to Dulles Airport," the ambassador replied. "If you hurry, you just might catch her."

It would be established that the Falcon executive jet departed Dulles International Airport at twelve minutes past one o'clock. There were six passengers on board. Three were British, three were Israeli. Only one was a woman. The staff at Signature Flight Support, the airport's fixed-base operator, would recall that she appeared slightly disoriented and that her hair was damp. She was wearing a tracksuit and new running shoes, as was one of the men, a smallish Israeli with gray temples and very green eyes. Additionally, one of the passengers—his British passport identified him as Peter Marlowe—arrived with his arm in a sling. In short, agreed the staff, they looked as though they had been put through the wringer. And then some.

By the time the plane touched down in London, official Washington was in an uproar. For the next twenty-four hours, however, the storm remained classified, compartmentalized, and largely contained to the secret realm. Of the three dead bodies found near the river, the FBI said little if anything at all, only that the case appeared to be a robbery gone wrong and that the three victims had yet to be identified, which wasn't exactly true.

But behind the scenes, the investigation was advancing at a rapid clip, and with alarming results. Ballistics analysis determined that the two men had been killed by a .45-caliber weapon—fired by a gunman of considerable skill—and that the woman known as Eva Fernandes had died as the result of a single 9mm shot dispatched at close range. Analysts from the Bureau's National Security Branch dug deeply into the woman's green card application, along with her travel history and her rather dubious claim to Brazilian nationality. In short order, they concluded she was in all likelihood an illegal agent of the SVR, Russia's Foreign Intelligence Service. The two men, the FBI determined, were similarly employed, though both were holders of Russian diplomatic passports. One was called Vitaly Petrov, the other was Stanislav Zelenko. Both men held low-level diplomatic cover jobs, Petrov at the Washington embassy, Zelenko in New York.

Which made Russia's official silence all the more puzzling. The embassy in Washington made no inquiry on behalf of the two dead men and voiced no protest. Nor did the National Security Agency detect any increase in encrypted communications flowing between the embassy and Moscow Center. It was obvious the Russians were hiding something. Something more valuable than an illegal Brazilian bagwoman and a couple of muscle operatives. Something like Rebecca Manning.

Langley did not imitate Russia's posture of silence. Indeed, if Russian eavesdroppers were listening, which they certainly were, they might very well have noticed a sharp spike in secure phone calls between the seventh floor of CIA Headquarters and Vauxhall Cross. And if the Russians had been able to break the unbreakable levels of encryption, they would have doubtless been pleased by what they heard. For in the days following Rebecca Manning's escape, relations between the CIA and MI6 plunged to a depth not seen since 1963, when a certain Kim Philby flew the coop in Beirut and landed in Moscow.

Once again, the Americans pounded their fists in indignation and demanded answers. Why had Rebecca Manning contacted the Russian Embassy? Was she a Russian spy? If so, for how long? How much had she betrayed? Was she responsible for the three dead bodies found along the banks of the Potomac near Swainson Island? What was the Israeli connection? And why, pray tell, had she purchased a shovel from the True Value hardware store at the corner of MacArthur Boulevard and Goldsboro Road?

There was no hiding from what had transpired, and to Graham Seymour's credit—at least in the eyes of his few remaining supporters within the American intelligence community—he did not try. He muddied the waters, it was true, but never once did he tell the Americans an outright lie, for had he done so, the marriage might have ended on the spot. Mainly, he played for time and pleaded with Langley to keep Rebecca's name out of the press. A public scandal, he said, would do none of them any good. What's more, it would hand yet another propaganda victory to the Tsar, who had been rather on a roll of late. Better to assess the damage in private and set about repairing the relationship.

"There *is* no relationship," CIA director Morris Payne told Seymour by secure phone four days after Rebecca returned to

London. "Not until we're confident the leak has been plugged and your service is no longer taking on Russian water."

"You've had your problems in the past, and we never threatened to withhold cooperation."

"That's because you need us more than we need you."

"How tactful of you, Morris. How diplomatic."

"To hell with tact! Where the hell is she, by the way?"

"I'd rather not say over this line."

"How long has it been going on?"

"That," said Seymour with lawyerly precision, "is a matter of great interest to us."

"I'm relieved to hear that." Payne swore loudly and with great effect. "Cathy and I treated her like family, Graham. We let her into our home. And how did she repay me? She stole my secrets and stabbed me in the back. I feel like . . ."

"Like what, Morris?"

"I feel the way James Angleton must have felt when his good friend Kim Philby defected to Moscow."

And there it might have ended, with the Russians silent and the cousins feuding, were it not for a story that appeared in the *Washington Post* a week to the day after Rebecca Manning's hasty departure from America. It was the work of a reporter who had written authoritatively on national security matters in the past, and as usual her sources were carefully camouflaged. The most likely origin of the leak, though, was the FBI, which had never been comfortable with the idea of sweeping Rebecca Manning and three dead Russian agents under the rug.

The leak was selective. Even so, the story was a bombshell. It stated that the three people found dead along the banks of the Potomac were not victims of a robbery but officers of the SVR. Two had diplomatic cover, one was an illegal posing as a Brazilian.

How they were killed, and why, was not yet known, but the FBI was said to be investigating the involvement of at least two foreign intelligence services.

The story had one important consequence: Russia could remain silent no more. The Kremlin reacted with fury and accused the United States of a cold-blooded assassination, a charge the administration vigorously and repeatedly denied. The next three days witnessed a rapid cycle of leak and counterleak, until finally it spilled onto the front page of the *New York Times*. At least a part of it did. The experts on cable television universally declared it the worst case of espionage since the Kim Philby disaster. In that, if nothing else, they were entirely correct.

There were many questions still to be answered regarding Rebecca Manning's recruitment as a Russian agent. There were questions, too, regarding the role played by one Gabriel Allon, who was reportedly on board the aircraft that spirited Rebecca Manning to Britain. From London, there was only silence. From Tel Aviv, too.

85

TEL AVIV—JERUSALEM

He was spotted that same day arriving at the prime minister's office for the weekly meeting of Israel's fractious cabinet, dressed in a crisp blue suit and white shirt and looking none the worse for wear. When a reporter asked for a comment on Rebecca Manning's unmasking as a Russian spy, he smiled and said nothing at all. Inside the cabinet room, he doodled in his notebook while the ministers bickered, all the while wondering how the Israeli people managed to thrive in spite of their dreadful politicians. When his turn came to speak, he briefed the cabinet on a recent raid that elements of the Office and the IDF had conducted against Islamic militants in the Sinai Peninsula, with the tacit blessing of the new Pharaoh. He did not mention the fact the operation had occurred while he was airborne over the

Atlantic, attempting to conduct the first interrogation of Rebecca Manning. Graham Seymour had curtly put an end to it. In London, they had parted with scarcely a word of farewell.

At King Saul Boulevard, the work of protecting the country from its myriad threats went on as normal, as though nothing had happened. At the Monday-morning senior staff meeting, there were the usual shouting matches over resources and priorities, but Rebecca Manning's name was not spoken. The Office had other pressing business. The secret strikes in the Sinai were only one facet of Israel's new strategy of working closely with the Sunni regimes of the Middle East against their common enemy, the Islamic Republic of Iran. America's retreat from the region had created a vacuum that the Iranians and the Russians were rapidly filling. Israel was acting as a bulwark against the rising Iranian threat, with Gabriel and the Office serving as the tip of the spear. What's more, America's unpredictable president had declared his intention to scrap the agreement that had temporarily delayed Iran's nuclear ambitions. Gabriel fully expected the Iranians to ramp up the weapons program in response, and he was putting in place a new program of intelligence-gathering and sabotage to stop it.

He also expected the Russians to retaliate for the loss of Rebecca Manning. And so he was not surprised by the news, later that week, that Werner Schwarz had died in Vienna after falling from the window of his apartment. It was the same window Werner had used to signal Moscow Center when he wanted to meet. No suicide note was found, though the Bundespolizei did find several hundred thousand euros stashed in a private bank account. The Austrian press wondered whether the death was somehow related to the assassination of Konstantin Kirov. The Austrian interior ministry wondered the same thing.

Internally, there was an official case history to write and a protective legal defense to prepare, but Gabriel found any number of excuses to avoid the debriefers and the Office's in-house lawyers. Namely, they wanted to know precisely what had transpired on the banks of the Potomac River in Maryland. Who had killed the two Russian field hands, Petrov and Zelenko? And what about the illegal who had agreed to entrap Rebecca Manning in exchange for sanctuary in Israel? Uzi Navot tried to pry it out of Mikhail and Eli Lavon, but both answered truthfully that they had come upon the scene after the three Russians were dead. Therefore, they could not say for certain how they had ended up that way.

"And you never *asked* him what happened?"

"We tried," said Lavon.

"And Rebecca?"

"Not a peep. It was one of the worst flights of my life, and I've had some bad ones."

They were in Lavon's little hutch of an office. It was filled with shards of pottery and ancient coins and tools. In his spare time, Lavon was one of Israel's most prominent archaeologists.

"Let us assume," said Navot, "that Gabriel was the one who killed the two hoods."

"Let's," agreed Lavon.

"So how did the girl end up dead? And how did Gabriel know that Rebecca was going to be there? And why in God's name did she stop for a shovel?"

"Why are you asking me?"

"You're an archaeologist."

"All I know," said Lavon, "is that the chief of the Office is lucky to be alive. If it had been you . . ."

"They'd be carving my name on a memorial wall."

If anyone deserved to have their name on a wall, thought Lavon, it was the man who had found Rebecca Manning, but he would accept no accolades. His only reward was the odd evening at home with his wife and two young children, but even they sensed something was troubling him. Late one night Irene interrogated him at length as he sat at the edge of her bed. He lied so poorly, not even the child believed him. "Stay with me, Abba," she commanded in her peculiar mix of Italian and Hebrew when Gabriel tried to leave. Then she said, "Please never let me go."

Gabriel remained in the nursery until Irene was sleeping soundly. In the kitchen he poured himself a glass of Galilean shiraz and sat at the little café table glumly watching the news from London while Chiara prepared their supper. On the screen, Graham Seymour was slouched in the back of a limousine leaving Downing Street, where he had offered to resign over the scandal that had befallen the Secret Intelligence Service on his watch. Prime Minister Lancaster had refused to accept it—at least for the moment, according to one anonymously quoted Downing Street aide. There were calls for the obligatory parliamentary investigation and, worse yet, an independent inquiry of the sort conducted into MI6's faulty intelligence regarding weapons of mass destruction in Iraq. And what about Alistair Hughes? howled the media. Was his death in sleepy Bern somehow linked to Rebecca Manning's treachery? Was he a Russian spy, too? Was there a Third Man lurking? In short, it was exactly the sort of public spectacle Seymour had hoped to avoid.

"How long can he keep it secret?" asked Chiara.

"Which part?"

"The identity of Rebecca Manning's father."

"I suppose that depends on how many people inside MI6 know she refers to herself as Rebecca Philby."

Chiara placed a bowl of *spaghetti al pomodoro* before Gabriel.

He whitened it with grated cheese but hesitated before taking a first bite. "There's something I need to tell you," he said at last, "about what happened that morning along the banks of the river."

"I think I have a pretty good idea."

"Do you?"

"You were somewhere you ought not to have been, alone, with no backup or bodyguards. Fortunately, you had the sense to slip a gun into your pocket on your way out the safe house door."

"A big one," said Gabriel.

"Forty-fives were never your preference."

"Too loud," said Gabriel. "Too messy."

"The illegal was killed with a nine-millimeter," Chiara pointed out.

"Eva," said Gabriel. "At least that was her Brazilian name. She never told us her real name."

"I suppose Rebecca killed her."

"I suppose she did."

"Why?"

Gabriel hesitated, then said, "Because I didn't kill Rebecca first."

"You couldn't?"

No, said Gabriel, he couldn't.

"And now you're guilt-ridden because the woman you coerced into doing your bidding is dead."

Gabriel made no reply.

"But there's something else bothering you." Greeted by silence, Chiara said, "Tell me, Gabriel—exactly how close did you come to getting yourself killed last week?"

"Closer than I would have preferred."

"At least you're honest." Chiara looked at the television. The BBC had dredged up an old snapshot of Rebecca taken while she was at Trinity College. She looked remarkably like her father. "How long can they keep it a secret?" Chiara asked again.

"Who would believe such a story?"

On the television screen, the old photograph of Rebecca Manning dissolved. In its place was yet another image of Graham Seymour.

"You made one mistake, my love," said Chiara after a moment. "If you had only killed her when you had the chance, none of this would have happened."

Late that night, as Chiara slept soundly beside him, Gabriel sat with a laptop balanced on his thighs and headphones over his ears, repeatedly watching the same fifteen minutes of video. Shot by a Samsung Galaxy, it commenced at 7:49 a.m., when a woman in a business suit and a tan overcoat entered a popular Starbucks just north of Georgetown and joined the queue at the register. Eight people waited ahead of her. Through his headphones, Gabriel could hear the barista singing "A Change Is Gonna Come" quite well. Graham Seymour, he remembered, had missed the performance. He was outside at the time, in the tangled garden of the command post, taking a call from Vauxhall Cross.

It was 7:54 when the woman placed her order, a tall dark-roast coffee, nothing to eat, and 7:56 when she sat down at a communal table and took up her iPhone. She executed several commands, all with her right thumb. Then, at 7:57, she placed the iPhone on the tabletop and fished a second device, a BlackBerry KEYone, from her handbag. The password was long and hard as a rock, twelve characters, both thumbs. After entering it, she glanced at the screen. The barista was singing "What's Going On."

Mother, mother . . .

At 7:58 the woman took up her iPhone again, glanced at the screen, glanced around the interior of the café. Nervously, thought Gabriel, which was not like her. Then she tapped the screen of the iPhone several times, quickly, and placed it in the bag. Rising, she dropped her coffee through the slot in the condiment stand. The door was to her right. She headed left instead, into the back of the café.

As she approached the Samsung Galaxy, her face was a blank mask. Gabriel clicked the PAUSE icon and stared into Kim Philby's blue eyes. Had she been spooked, as Graham Seymour had suggested, or had she been warned? If so, by whom?

Sasha was the most obvious suspect. It was possible he had been monitoring the drop from afar, with teams on the street or inside the café itself. He might have seen something he didn't like, something that made him order his life's work to abort without transmitting and make a run for a prearranged bolt-hole. But if that was the case, why hadn't Rebecca walked out of the café? And why had she run into the arms of Eva Fernandes instead of an SVR exfiltration team?

Because there *was* no exfiltration team, thought Gabriel, recalling the rapid exodus, at approximately 8:20 a.m., of known SVR assets from the back of the Russian Embassy. Not yet.

He adjusted the time code on the video and clicked PLAY. It was 7:56 at the popular Starbucks just north of Georgetown. A woman in a business suit and a tan overcoat sits down at a communal table and executes several commands on an iPhone. At 7:57 she trades the iPhone for a BlackBerry, but at 7:58 it's back to the iPhone again.

Gabriel clicked PAUSE.

There it was, he thought. The slight jolt to the body, the nearly imperceptible widening of the eyes. That was when it happened, at 7:58:46, on the iPhone.

He clicked PLAY and watched Rebecca Manning thumbing several commands into the iPhone—commands that doubtless deleted her report to Moscow Center, along with the SVR's software. Gabriel reckoned she had also deleted the message that had warned her to run. Perhaps the FBI had found it, perhaps not. It was no matter; they would never share it with the likes of him. The British were cousins. Distant cousins, but cousins nonetheless.

Gabriel opened the laptop's Web browser and skimmed the headlines of the London papers. Each one was worse than the last. *If you had only killed her when you had the chance, none of this would have happened . . .* Yes, he thought, as he lay next to his sleeping wife in the darkness, that would explain everything.

86

EATON SQUARE, LONDON

Gabriel flew to London three days later on an Israeli diplomatic passport bearing a false name. A security detail from the embassy met him upon arrival at Heathrow Airport, as did a not-so-covert surveillance team from the A4 branch of MI5. He rang Graham Seymour during the drive into central London and asked for a meeting. Seymour agreed to see him at nine that evening at his home in Eaton Square. The late hour suggested dinner would not be in the offing, as did Helen Seymour's chilly greeting. "He's upstairs," she announced coolly. "I believe you know the way."

When Gabriel entered the study on the second floor, Seymour was reviewing the contents of a red-striped classified file. He made a mark in it with a green Parker fountain pen and dropped it hastily into a stainless-steel attaché case. For all Gabriel knew, Seymour had already locked up the silver and the china. He did not rise or offer his hand. Nor did he suggest retreating to his personal safe-speech chamber. Gabriel supposed it wasn't necessary. MI6 had no more secrets to lose. Rebecca Manning had given them all to the Russians.

"Help yourself," Seymour said with an indifferent glance toward the drinks trolley.

"Thank you, no," replied Gabriel, and without invitation sat down. A leaden silence ensued. He suddenly regretted making the trip to London. Their relationship, he feared, was beyond repair. He recalled with fondness the afternoon at Wormwood Cottage when they had scoured the old files for the name of Kim Philby's mistress. If Gabriel had known it would come to this, he would have whispered Philby's name into Seymour's ear and washed his hands of the whole thing.

"Happy?" asked Seymour at last.

"My children are well, and my wife seems to be reasonably fond of me at the moment." Gabriel shrugged. "So, yes, I suppose I'm as happy as I'm ever going to be."

"That's not what I meant."

"A good friend of mine is under fire for something that wasn't his fault. I'm concerned about his well-being."

"Sounds like something I read once in a sympathy card."

"Come on, Graham, let's not do this. We've been through too much together, you and I."

"And once again, you're the hero, and I'm the one who gets to clean up the mess."

"There are no heroes in a situation like this. Everyone loses."

"Except the Russians." Seymour went to the trolley and poured an inch of whisky into a glass. "Keller sends his best, by the way."

"How is he?"

"Unfortunately, the doctors say he'll live. He's walking around with a very important secret in his head."

"Something tells me your secret is safe with Christopher Keller. Who else knows?"

"No one other than the prime minister."

"A total of three people inside HMG," Gabriel pointed out.

"Four," said Seymour, "if you include Nigel Whitcombe, who has a pretty good idea."

"And then there's Rebecca."

Seymour made no reply.

"Is she talking?" asked Gabriel.

"The last person in the world I want to talk," said Seymour, "is Rebecca Manning."

"I'd like a word with her."

"You already had your chance." Seymour contemplated Gabriel over his whisky. "How did you know she was going to be there?"

"I had a feeling she would want to pick up something on her way out of the country. Something her father left there in 1951 after Guy Burgess and Donald Maclean defected."

"The camera and the film?"

Gabriel nodded.

"That would explain the shovel. But how did you know where the stuff was buried?"

"I was reliably informed."

"By Charlotte Bettencourt?"

Gabriel said nothing.

"If only you'd taken that shovel when you left . . ."

Gabriel invited Seymour to elaborate.

"We could have slipped Rebecca out of Washington without the Americans knowing," Seymour went on. "The video of her purchasing the shovel from that hardware store is what doomed her."

"How would you have explained the three dead SVR agents?"

"Very carefully."

"And Rebecca's sudden recall to London?"

"A health problem," suggested Seymour. "A new assignment."

"A cover-up."

"Your word," said Seymour. "Not mine."

Gabriel made a show of thought. "The Americans would have seen through it."

"Thanks to you, we'll never know."

Gabriel ignored the remark. "In fact, it would have been far better if Rebecca had left Washington with the Russians." He paused, then added, "Which is what you wanted all along, isn't it, Graham?"

Seymour said nothing.

"That's why you sent a text message to her iPhone two minutes before the window opened, warning her not to transmit. That's why you told her to run."

"Me?" asked Seymour. "Why would I do something like that?"

"For the same reason MI6 let Kim Philby run in 1963. Better to have the spy in Moscow than a British courtroom."

Seymour's smile was condescending. "You seem to have it all figured out. But weren't you the one who told me that my Vienna Head of Station was a Russian spy?"

"You can do better than that, Graham."

Seymour's smile dissolved.

"If I had to guess," Gabriel continued, "you sent the message

449

from the garden while you were supposedly taking that urgent call from Vauxhall Cross. Or maybe you had Nigel send it for you, so you wouldn't leave any fingerprints."

"If anyone told Rebecca to run," said Seymour, "it was Sasha."

"It wasn't Sasha, it was you."

The silence returned. So this is how it ends, thought Gabriel. He rose to his feet.

"In case you were wondering," said Seymour suddenly, "the deal has already been made."

"What deal is that?"

"The deal to send Rebecca to Moscow."

"Pathetic," murmured Gabriel.

"She's a Russian citizen and a colonel in the SVR. It's where she belongs."

"Keep telling yourself that, Graham. Even you might believe it."

Seymour made no reply.

"How much did you get for her?"

"Everyone we asked for."

"I suppose the Americans got in on the act, too." Gabriel shook his head slowly. "When will you learn, Graham? How many more elections does the Tsar have to steal? How many more political opponents does he have to assassinate on your soil? When are you going to stand up to him? Do you need his money that badly? Is it the only thing keeping this overvalued city afloat?"

"Life is very black and white for you, isn't it?"

"Only when it comes to fascists." Gabriel started toward the door.

"The deal," said Seymour, "is contingent on one thing."

Gabriel stopped and turned. "What's that?"

"Sergei Morosov. You have him, the Russians want him."

"You can't be serious."

With his expression, Seymour made clear he was.

"I wish I could help you," said Gabriel, "but Sergei Morosov is dead. Remember? Tell Rebecca I'm sorry, but she'll just have to spend the rest of her life here in Britain."

"Why don't you tell her yourself."

"What are you talking about?"

"You said you wanted a word with her."

"I do."

"As it turns out," said Seymour, "she'd like one with you, too."

87

SCOTTISH HIGHLANDS

Gabriel spent that night at the safe flat on the Bayswater Road and in the morning boarded a military transport plane at RAF Northholt, on the fringes of Greater London. His MI6 security detail gave him no inkling of their destination, but the long duration of the flight, and the lay of the land below, left the far north of Scotland as the only possibility. Rebecca Manning, it seemed, had been banished to the end of the realm.

At last, Gabriel glimpsed a stretch of golden sand and a small town by the sea and two runways carved like a sidelong X into a patchwork quilt of farmland. It was RAF Lossiemouth. A caravan of Range Rovers waited on the windblown tarmac. They drove for several miles through gentle hills covered in heather and gorse, until finally they arrived at the gate of a remote country manor. It looked like something MI6 had borrowed during the war and conveniently forgotten to return.

Behind the double fence, guards in plain clothes patrolled broad green lawns. Inside, a disagreeable man called Burns briefed Gabriel on matters related to security and the prisoner's state of mind.

"Sign this," he said, placing a document beneath Gabriel's nose.

"What is it?"

"A declaration that you will never discuss anything you have seen or heard today."

"I'm a citizen of the State of Israel."

"That doesn't matter, we'll think of something."

The chamber to which Gabriel was eventually led was not quite a dungeon, but it might well have been one once. It was reached by a long and twisting series of stone steps that smelled of damp and drains. The original stone walls had been paved over with smooth concrete. The paint was white as bone—as white, thought Gabriel, as a *pueblo blanco* in the hills of Andalusia. The overhead lights burned with the intensity of surgical lamps and hummed with current. Cameras peered down from the corners, and a couple of guards kept watch from an anteroom through a panel of shatterproof one-way glass.

A chair had been left for Gabriel against the bars of Rebecca's cell. There was a cot, neatly made up, and a small table piled with old paperback novels. There were several newspapers, too; Rebecca, it seemed, had been following the progress of her case. She wore a pair of loose-fitting corduroy trousers and a heavy Scottish sweater against the cold. She looked smaller than when Gabriel had seen her last, and very thin, as though she had embarked on a hunger strike to win her freedom. She had no makeup on her face, and her hair hung straight and limp. Gabriel was not sure she deserved all this. Philby, perhaps, but not the child of treason.

After a moment's pointed hesitation, Gabriel reluctantly accepted the hand she thrust between the bars. Her palm was coarse and dry. "Please sit," she suggested affably and Gabriel, again with hesitation, lowered himself into the chair. A guard brought him tea. It was milky and sweet. The mug was lethally heavy.

"Nothing for you?" he asked.

"I'm only allowed at mealtime." Intentionally or not, she had forsaken her English accent. She looked and sounded very French. "It seems a silly rule to me, but there you are."

"If it bothers you—"

"No, please," she insisted. "It must have been a long trip. Or perhaps not," she added. "To tell you the truth, I have no idea where I am."

To tell you the truth . . .

Gabriel wondered if she were even capable, or whether she knew the truth from a lie.

She sat down at the edge of her cot, with her knees together and her feet flat on the concrete floor. She wore fur-lined suede moccasins with no laces. There was nothing in the cell she might use to harm herself. It seemed a needless precaution to Gabriel. The Rebecca Manning he had encountered on the banks of the Potomac was not the suicidal type.

"I was afraid you wouldn't come," she said.

"Why?" asked Gabriel candidly.

"Because I would have killed you that day were it not for—"

"I admire your honesty," said Gabriel, cutting her off.

She smiled at the absurdity of his remark. "It doesn't bother you?"

"To meet with someone who once tried to kill me?"

"Yes."

"I seem to make a habit of it."

"You have many enemies in Moscow," she pointed out.

"More now than ever, I suspect."

"Perhaps I'll be able to temper the SVR's opinion of you when I take up my new post at Moscow Center."

"I won't hold my breath."

"Don't." She smiled without parting her lips. Perhaps Gabriel had been wrong about her. Perhaps she belonged in a cage. "Actually," she continued, "I doubt I'll be dealing much with the Middle East. The Great Britain desk is the most natural place for me."

"All the more reason why your government shouldn't even consider handing over a traitor like you."

"It's not *my* government, and I'm not a traitor. I'm an agent of penetration. It's not my fault the British were foolish enough to hire me and then promote me up the line to H/Washington."

Feigning boredom, Gabriel pondered his wristwatch. "Graham said there was something you wanted to discuss with me."

She frowned. "You disappoint me, Monsieur Allon. Is there really nothing you wish to ask me?"

"What would be the point? You'd only lie."

"It might be worth a try, no? Going once," she said provocatively. "Twice . . ."

"Heathcliff," said Gabriel.

She pouted. "Poor Heathcliff."

"I suppose you were the one who betrayed him."

"Not by name, of course. I never knew it. But Moscow Center used my reports to identify him."

"And the address of the safe flat?"

"That came directly from me."

"Who told you?"

"Who do you think?"

"If I had to guess," said Gabriel, "it was Alistair Hughes."

Her expression darkened.

"How did you know he was seeing a doctor in Switzerland?"

"He told me that, too. I was the only person inside Six he trusted."

"Big mistake."

"Alistair's, not mine."

"You were lovers?"

"For nine dreadful months," she said, rolling her eyes. "In Baghdad."

"I assume Alistair felt differently."

"He was quite in love with me. The fool actually wanted to leave Melinda."

"There's no accounting for taste."

She said nothing.

"Your romantic interest in him was professional in nature?"

"Of course."

"Moscow Center suggested the affair?"

"Actually, I undertook it on my own initiative."

"Why?"

She stared long and deliberately at one of the cameras, as if to remind Gabriel that their conversation was being monitored. "On the day my father died," she said, "Alistair and I were working at

Brussels Station. As you might imagine, I was quite distraught. But Alistair was . . ."

"Pleased by the news?"

"Overjoyed."

"And you never forgave him for it?"

"How could I?"

"You must have noticed the pills when you were sleeping with him."

"They were rather hard to miss. Alistair was a mess in Baghdad. He was even worse after I broke off the affair."

"But you remained friends?"

"Confidants," she suggested.

"And when you learned he was making secret trips to Switzerland without telling Vauxhall Cross?"

"I filed the information away for a rainy day."

"The rain began to fall," said Gabriel, "when VeeVee Gribkov tried to defect in New York."

"Torrentially."

"So you told Sasha about Alistair, and Sasha put in place an operation to make it appear as though your former lover was the mole."

"Problem solved."

"Not quite," said Gabriel. "Did you know they were planning to kill him?"

"This isn't beanbag, Monsieur Allon. You know that better than anyone."

The British desk at Moscow Center, thought Gabriel, would soon be in capable hands; she was more ruthless than they were. Gabriel had a thousand more questions, but suddenly all he wanted was to leave. Rebecca Manning appeared to sense his restiveness.

She crossed and uncrossed her legs and ran a palm vigorously over the rails of her corduroy trousers.

"I was wondering"—her British accent had returned—"whether I might impose on you."

"You already have."

She frowned in consternation. "Sarcasm is surely your right, but please hear me out."

With a small movement of his head, Gabriel invited her to continue.

"My mother . . ."

"Yes?"

"She's well?"

"She's been living alone in the mountains of Andalusia for almost forty years. How do you think she is?"

"How is her health?"

"A heart problem."

"A common affliction in women who knew my father."

"Men, too."

"You seem to have developed a rapport with her."

"There was little pleasant about our meeting."

"But she told you about the—"

"Yes," said Gabriel, glancing at one of the cameras. "She told me."

Rebecca was rubbing her palm over her trousers again. "I was w-w-wondering," she stammered, "whether you might have a word with her on my b-b-behalf."

"I signed a piece of paper a few minutes ago declaring, among other things, that I would not deliver any messages from you to the outside world."

"The British government has no power over you. You can do as you choose."

"I *choose* not to. Besides," added Gabriel, "you have the SVR to deliver your mail."

"My mother loathes them."

"She's entitled."

A silence descended between them. There was only the humming of the lights. It was making Gabriel cross.

"Do you think," said Rebecca at last, "that she m-m-might . . . once I'm settled in Moscow . . ."

"You'll have to ask her yourself."

"I'm asking *you*."

"Hasn't she suffered enough?"

"We've both suffered."

Because of *him*, thought Gabriel.

He rose abruptly. Rebecca also. Once again, the hand shot between the bars. Ignoring it, Gabriel tapped a knuckle against the one-way window and waited for the guards to unlock the outer door.

"You made one mistake in Washington," said Rebecca as she withdrew her hand.

"Only one?"

"You should have killed me when you had the chance."

"My wife told me the same thing."

"Her name is Chiara." Rebecca smiled coldly behind the bars of her cage. "Do give her my best."

It was a few minutes after two when the transport plane set down at RAF Northolt in suburban London. Heathrow was three miles to the south, which meant Gabriel arrived in plenty of time to catch the 4:45 British Airways Flight to Tel Aviv. Uncharacteristically, he accepted a glass of preflight champagne. He had earned it, he assured himself. Then he thought of Rebecca Manning in her cage, and Alistair Hughes in his coffin, and Konstantin Kirov on a snow-covered street in Vienna, and he returned the glass to the flight attendant untouched. As the plane thundered along the runway, rainwater pulsed along Gabriel's window like blood through a vein. Everyone loses, he thought as he watched England sinking away beneath him. Everyone except the Russians.

88

ZAHARA, SPAIN

T he exchange took place six weeks later, on the tarmac of a desolate old airfield in far eastern Poland. There were two planes present. One was an Aeroflot Sukhoi; the other, a chartered Airbus from British Airways. At the stroke of noon, twelve men, all prized assets of the British and American intelligence services, all prison thin, came filing down the steps of the Sukhoi. As they tripped happily across the tarmac toward the Airbus, they passed a single woman walking soberly in the opposite direction. There were no cameras or reporters present to record the event, only a couple of senior Polish secret policemen who made certain everyone played by the rules. The woman passed them without a word, with her eyes downcast, and took the place of the twelve men aboard the Sukhoi. The aircraft was in motion even before the cabin door had closed. At twelve fifteen it entered the airspace of friendly Belarus, bound for Moscow.

It would be another week before the public was informed of the exchange, and even then they were told very little. The twelve men, they were assured, had supplied invaluable intelligence about the New Russia and consequently were well worth the price. In America there was outrage in the usual quarters, but the reaction in London was characterized by tight-lipped resignation. Yes, it was a bitter pill to swallow, the mandarins of Whitehall agreed, but probably for the best. The only bright spot was a report in the *Telegraph* that said the exchange had gone forward despite the fact the Russians had wanted two prisoners rather than one. "At least *some*one had the backbone to stand up to them," a retired British spymaster groused that evening at the Travellers Club. "If only it had been us."

The Russians waited another month before putting their prize on public display. The venue was an hour-long documentary on a Russian television network controlled by the Kremlin. A press conference followed, presided over by the Tsar himself. She extolled his virtues, praised Russia's return to global prominence under his leadership, and railed against the British and the Americans, whose secrets she had happily plundered. Her only regret, she said, was that she had failed to become the director-general of MI6 and thus complete her mission.

"Have you enjoyed your time in Russia?" asked a member in good standing of the Kremlin's docile press corps.

"Oh, yes, it's perfectly lovely," she replied.

"And can you tell us where you're living?"

"No," answered the Tsar sternly on her behalf. "She cannot."

In a *pueblo blanco* of Zahara in the hills of Andalusia, the events in Moscow were an occasion for a brief celebration, at least by adherents of the anti-immigrant, anti-NATO far right. The Kremlin was once again the mecca toward which a certain type of European prostrated himself. In the twentieth century, it had been the guiding light of the left. Now, perversely, it was the extreme right that toed Moscow's line, the political brutes who sneered at Charlotte Bettencourt each afternoon as she made her way through the streets of the village. If only they knew the truth, she thought. *If only . . .*

Not surprisingly, she followed the case of the female British spy more carefully than most in the village. The Kremlin press conference was a spectacle, there was no other word for it—Rebecca sitting on the dais like some specimen under a bell jar, the Tsar next to her, grinning and preening at his latest triumph over the West. And just who did he think he was fooling with that starched and pressed face of his? Real fascists, thought Charlotte, did not use Botox. Rebecca looked worn-out in comparison. Charlotte was shocked by her daughter's gaunt appearance. She was shocked, too, by how much she looked like Kim. Even the stammer had returned. It was a miracle no one had noticed.

But just as quickly as Rebecca surfaced, she vanished from view. Charlotte's Israeli houseguests departed Andalusia soon after. Before leaving, however, they scoured the villa one final time for any trace of Rebecca and Kim among her keepsakes. They took the last of Charlotte's old photographs from Beirut and, despite her objections, the only copy of *The Other Woman*. It seemed her brief literary career was over before it started.

By then, it was late June, and the village was besieged by sweating, sunburned tourists. In her solitude, Charlotte retreated once more to her old routine, for it was all she had left. Forbidden to complete her memoir, she decided to write the story as a roman à clef instead. She switched the setting from Beirut to Tangier. Charlotte became Amelia, the impressionable daughter of a collaborationist French colonial administrator, and Kim she cast as Rowe, a dashing if somewhat world-weary British diplomat whom Amelia discovers to be a Russian spy. But how would it end? With an old woman sitting alone in an isolated villa waiting for a message from the daughter she had abandoned? Who would believe such a story?

She burned the manuscript in late October, using it as kindling to light the autumn's first fire, and took up Kim's mendacious autobiography. He had reduced his time in Beirut to five vague, dishonest paragraphs. *My experiences in the Middle East from 1956 to 1963 do not lend themselves readily to narrative form . . .* Perhaps hers did not, either, she thought. Then she burned Kim's book, too.

That same afternoon she walked along the paseo through a swirling *leveche* wind, counting her steps, aloud, she realized quite suddenly, which surely was a sign she was finally going mad. She took her lunch beneath the orange trees at Bar Mirador. "Did you see the news from Palestine?" asked the waiter as he brought her a glass of wine, but Charlotte was in no mood for an anti-Zionist polemic. Truth be told, she had changed her opinion of the Israelis. Kim, she decided, had been wrong about them. But then Kim had been wrong about everything.

She had purchased a day-old copy of *Le Monde* on her way to the café, but the wind made it impossible to read. Lowering the paper, she noticed a small bespectacled man sitting alone at the next table. He looked very different. Even so, Charlotte knew at once it was him, the silent friend of Rosencrantz and Guildenstern, the bellman who had accompanied her to Seville for the confession of her secret sins. But why had he returned to Zahara? And why now?

Nervously, Charlotte considered the possibilities as they each consumed a moderate lunch while assiduously avoiding one another's gaze. The little Israeli finished first and as he was leaving slid a postcard onto Charlotte's table. It happened so furtively it took her a moment to notice it, tucked carefully beneath the serving platter so the *leveche* wouldn't carry it away. On the front was the inevitable streetscape of whitewashed houses. On the back was a brief note, in French, written in beautiful script.

Calmly, Charlotte drank the last of her wine, and when the bill came she left twice the requested amount. The light in the square dazzled her eyes. It was twenty-two steps to the entrance of the church.

"I thought it would be you."

He smiled. He was standing before the votive candles, gazing upward toward the statue of the Madonna and Child. Charlotte glanced around the nave. It was empty except for a couple of quite-obvious bodyguards.

"I see you've brought along an entourage."

"No matter how hard I try," he said, "I can't seem to get rid of them."

"It's probably for the best. The Russians must be furious with you."

"They usually are."

She smiled in spite of her nerves. "Did you have anything to do with the decision to send her to Moscow?"

"Actually, I did my best to prevent it."

"You're vengeful by nature?"

"Pragmatic, I like to think."

"What does pragmatism have to do with any of this?"

"She's a dangerous woman. The West will live to regret the decision."

"It's hard for me to think of her in that way. To me, she'll always be the little girl I knew in Paris."

"She's changed a great deal."

"Has she really? I'm not so sure." She looked at him. Even in the red glow of the candles, his eyes were shockingly green. "Have you spoken to her?"

"Twice, in fact."

"Did she mention me?"

"Of course."

Charlotte felt her heart begin to flutter. *Her pills* . . . She needed one of her pills. "Why hasn't she tried to contact me?"

"She was afraid."

"Of what?"

"Of what your answer might be."

She lifted her gaze toward the statue. "If anyone has anything to fear, Monsieur Allon, it's me. I gave away my child and allowed Kim and Sasha to turn her into that creature I saw sitting next to the Tsar."

"It was a long time ago."

"For me, yes, but not for Rebecca." Charlotte crossed the nave to the altar. "Have you spent much time in Catholic churches?" she asked.

"More than you might imagine."

"Do you believe in God, Monsieur Allon?"

"Sometimes," he answered.

"I don't," said Charlotte, turning her back to him, "but I've always loved churches. I especially like the smell. The smell of incense and candles and beeswax. It smells like . . ."

"Like what, Madame Bettencourt?"

She didn't dare answer, not after what she had done. "How long will it be until I hear from her?" she asked after a moment, but when she turned she found the church deserted. Forgiveness, she thought as she went into the square. It smells like forgiveness.

AUTHOR'S NOTE

*T*he Other Woman is a work of entertainment and should be read as nothing more. The names, characters, places, and incidents portrayed in the story are the product of the author's imagination or have been used fictitiously. Any resemblance to actual persons, living or dead, businesses, companies, events, or locales is entirely coincidental.

The headquarters of Israel's secret intelligence service is no longer located on King Saul Boulevard in Tel Aviv. I have chosen to keep the headquarters of my fictitious service there, in no small part, because I like the name of the street much more than the current address. As we learned in *The Other Woman*, Gabriel Allon shares my opinion. Needless to say, he and his family do not live in a small limestone apartment house on Narkiss Street, in the historic Jerusalem neighborhood of Nachlaot.

Frequent travelers between Vienna and Bern undoubtedly noticed that I manipulated the airline and train schedules to meet the requirements of my plot. Apologies to the management of the fabled Schweizerhof Hotel for running an intelligence operation in its lobby, but I'm afraid it couldn't be helped. There is a private medical facility in the picturesque Swiss village of München-buchsee, birthplace of Paul Klee, but it is not called Privatklinik Schloss.

MI6's school for fledging spies is indeed located at Fort Monckton, adjacent to the first fairway of the Gosport & Stokes Bay Golf Club, though the service maintains other more secluded training sites as well. To the best of my knowledge, there is no safe house at the edge of Dartmoor known as Wormwood Cottage. I have no clue where MI6 stores its old files, but I rather doubt it is a warehouse in Slough, near Heathrow Airport.

Visitors to the Palisades neighborhood in Washington will search in vain for a Belgian restaurant on MacArthur Boulevard called Brussels Midi. There is a Starbucks on Wisconsin Avenue in Burleith, not far from the Russian Embassy, but there is no longer a pay telephone at the Shell station on the corner of Ellicott Street. Lock 10 of the Chesapeake & Ohio Canal is faithfully rendered. So, too, unfortunately, is the official residence of the Israeli ambassador to the United States.

Harold Adrian Russell Philby, better known as Kim, did indeed reside in the large, tan colonial house that still stands on Nebraska Avenue in Tenleytown. The brief biography of Kim Philby that appears in chapter 41 of *The Other Woman* is accurate, save for the final two sentences. Philby could not have met an MI6 officer named Arthur Seymour the day after his arrival in Beirut because Arthur Seymour, like his son, Graham, does not exist. Neither do Charlotte Bettencourt and her daughter, Rebecca Manning. Both were created entirely by me and were not inspired by anyone I encountered during my review of Kim Philby's life and work as a spy for Moscow.

It is true that Philby devoted only five paragraphs to his time in Beirut in his unreliable autobiography, *My Silent War.* He fled the city in January 1963 after admitting to his old friend Nicholas Elliott he was a Soviet spy. It is unlikely he would have told a mistress the truth about his past before boarding the *Dolmatova.* According to Yuri Modin, Philby's KGB controller, he never told any of his wives or lovers the truth about his secret work for Russian intelligence. "We never had a single problem on this score," Modin recalled in his memoir, *My Cambridge Friends.*

In Moscow, Philby married a fourth time and after several years in the wilderness happily undertook several projects for the KGB. Much of the work was analytical and instructional, but according to Modin, some of it was operational in nature, such as "identifying agents from photographs shown to him." There is no evidence to suggest he was involved in preparing an agent of penetration, a mole. But then there is no evidence to suggest he did not. In my experience, it is wise to read the memoirs of spies with a jaundiced eye.

In the summer of 2007, while researching the novel that would come to be titled *Moscow Rules*, I visited the KGB's private museum in its looming old headquarters in Lubyanka Square. And there, in a protective glass case, I saw a tiny shrine to the Cambridge Five—or the Magnificent Five, as the KGB referred to them. They were recruited, beginning with Philby, just sixteen years after the birth of the Soviet Union, a time of great paranoia in Moscow when Stalin and his henchmen sought to defend their nascent revolution, in part, by waging political warfare against their adversaries in the West. The NKVD, precursor of the KGB, referred to this program as "active measures." They ranged from disinformation campaigns in the Western media to political violence and assassinations, and their goal was to weaken and eventually destroy the capitalist West.

There are striking parallels between then and now. Russia under Vladimir Putin is both revanchist and paranoid, a dangerous combination. Economically and demographically weak, Putin uses his powerful intelligence services and cyberwarriors as a force multiplier. When Putin sows political chaos in Western Europe and seeks to disrupt and discredit an American election, he is reaching deep into the KGB's old playbook. He is engaging in "active measures."

Like the tsars and Party chairmen who came before him, Vladimir Putin readily uses murder as a tool of statecraft. Witness the case of Sergei V. Skripal, a former Russian military intelligence officer and MI6 asset who was poisoned at his home in Salisbury, England, on March 4, 2018, with a military-grade Soviet-era nerve agent known as Novichok. At the time of this writing, Skripal remained hospitalized in serious condition. His thirty-three-year-old daughter, Yulia, also sickened by the toxin, was unconscious for three weeks. Forty-eight other people reported symptoms, including a police officer who spent time in a critical-care unit.

The attack on Sergei Skripal came twelve years after Alexander Litvinenko, a critic of Putin living in London, was murdered with a cup of polonium-laced tea. In 2006 Britain's official reaction to the use of a radioactive weapon on its soil was limited to a single extradition request, which the Kremlin gleefully ignored. Following the attempted murder of Sergei Skripal, however, Prime Minister Theresa May expelled twenty-three Russian diplomats. The United States, Canada, and fourteen members of the European Union followed suit. In addition, the United States imposed economic sanctions on seven of Russia's richest men and seventeen top government officials, in part over Russia's interference in the 2016 U.S. presidential election. Vladimir Putin, regarded by many observers to be the richest man in the world, was not on the list.

Security analysts estimate that two-thirds of the "diplomats" stationed at a typical Russian embassy in Western Europe are actually intelligence officers. Therefore, it is unlikely a modest round of tit-for-tat sanctions will deter Putin from his present path. And why should it? Putin and Putinism are on the march. The strongman and the "corporate state"—by another name, fascism—are all the rage. Western-style democracy and the global institutions that created an unprecedented period of peace in Europe are suddenly out of vogue.

"Probe with bayonets," advised Lenin. "If you encounter mush, proceed; if you encounter steel, withdraw." Thus far, Putin has encountered only mush. In the 1930s, when the world witnessed a similar simultaneous rise of authoritarian and dictatorial regimes, a calamitous world war ensued, leaving more than sixty million dead. It is wishful thinking to assume the twenty-first century's flirtation with neofascism will proceed without conflict.

Look no farther than Syria, where an axis of Russia, Hezbollah, Iran's Revolutionary Guard Corps, and Shiite militias from Iraq and Afghanistan have propped up the regime of Bashar al-Assad, the Kremlin's closest friend in the Middle East. Assad has repeatedly and flagrantly used chemical weapons against his own people, presumably with Moscow's blessing, perhaps even with Moscow's help. Thus far, an estimated four hundred thousand people have perished in Syria's civil war, and there is no end to the conflict in sight. Putin is probing with bayonets. Only steel will stop him.

ACKNOWLEDGMENTS

I am grateful to my wife, Jamie Gangel, who listened patiently while I worked out the themes and plot twists of *The Other Woman* and then expertly trimmed one hundred pages from the pile of paper I euphemistically refer to as my first draft. My debt to her is immeasurable, as is my love.

My dear friend Louis Toscano, author of *Triple Cross* and *Mary Bloom*, made countless improvements to the novel, large and small, and my eagle-eyed personal copy editor, Kathy Crosby, made certain it was free of typographical and grammatical errors. Any mistakes that slipped through their formidable defenses are mine, not theirs.

I am forever indebted to David Bull, who is truly one of the world's finest art restorers, and the great Patrick Matthiesen, of the Matthiesen Gallery in London, whose wit and charm animated the Allon series from the beginning.

ACKNOWLEDGMENTS

To write a novel about a spy who plied his trade in the middle of the twentieth century required enormous research—indeed, my bookshelf resembles Charlotte Bettencourt's in Zahara. I am indebted to the memories and scholarship of Yuri Modin, Rufina Philby, Richard Beeston, Phillip Knightley, Anthony Boyle, Tom Bower, Ben Macintyre, Anthony Cave Brown, and Patrick Seale and Maureen McConville.

A special thanks to my Los Angeles superlawyer, Michael Gendler. Also, to the many friends and family members who provide much-needed laughter at critical times during the writing year, especially Nancy Dubuc and Michael Kizilbash, Andy and Betsy Lack, Jeff Zucker, Elsa Walsh and Bob Woodward, Ron Meyer, and Elena Nachmanoff.

Finally, I wish to thank my children, Lily and Nicholas, who are a constant source of love and inspiration. Recent college graduates, they have embarked on careers of their own. Perhaps not surprisingly, given what they witnessed as young children, neither has chosen to become a writer.

A NOTE ON THE TYPE

The text of this book was set in Sabon, an old-style serif typeface designed by the German-born typographer and designer Jan Tschichold (1902–1974), and released jointly by the Linotype, Monotype, and Stempel foundries in 1967. The Sabon design is closely related to the Garamond font styles of the sixteenth century; Tschichold based it upon a particular type cut by the French type designer, publisher, and punch cutter Claude Garamond. The typeface is named for Jacques Sabon, who bought up much of Claude Garamond's collection of type after his death.